PRAISE FOR S.B. DIVYA

"This stunning near-future thriller from Divya (*Runtime*) tackles issues of economic inequality, workers' rights, privacy, and the nature of intelligence . . . Crack worldbuilding and vivid characters make for a memorable, page-turning adventure, while the thematic inquiries into human and AI labor rights offer plenty to chew on for fans of big-idea sci-fi. Readers will be blown away."

—*Publishers Weekly* (starred review)

"Divya has created a richly imagined and eerily familiar world . . . confronting urgent questions about humans' place in a society increasingly run by AIs."

—*Kirkus Reviews*

M E R U

ALSO BY S.B. DIVYA

Machinehood

Runtime

Contingency Plans For the Apocalypse and Other Possible Situations

"Microbiota and the Masses: A Love Story"

MERU

S.B. DIVYA

47NORTH

This is a work of fiction. Names, characters, organizations, places, events, and incidents are either products of the author's imagination or are used fictitiously. Otherwise, any resemblance to actual persons, living or dead, is purely coincidental.

Published by 47North, Seattle

www.apub.com

ISBN-13: 9781662505096 (paperback)
ISBN-13: 9781662505089 (digital)

Cover design by Mike Heath

Cover image: © Jeffrey Isaac Greenberg 5+ / Alamy Stock Photo / Alamy

Printed in the United States of America

To the pursuers of dreams who are told
they can't but try anyway;
to my parents for their love and support
(and for buying me all those Amar Chitra Kathas).

The Axioms of Life:

1. A life-form has a boundary, perceptible using its own sensory capabilities, that separates it from the environment.
2. A life-form has a built-in drive to live and reproduce, which implies that it must have a nonliving state.
3. A life-form is capable of accruing information about its environment and storing this information within its own structure.
4. A life-form can communicate information to other life-forms that share some or all of its sensory modalities.
5. A life-form can adapt to its environment and/or alter its environment over time and/or successive generations of itself.

The Principles of Conscious Beings:

1. All matter possesses some level of consciousness.
2. All forms of consciousness have equal value in the universe.
3. Possession of consciousness is necessary but not sufficient for life-forms.
4. A Being is a structure with sufficient consciousness that it has the ability to reshape matter.
5. An Evolved Being is a Being that is also a life-form.
6. All Beings should minimize harm to other forms of consciousness, with priority given to other Beings.

AUTHOR'S NOTE

The chapter titles in this book are words from classical Sanskrit using the Devanagari script. Translations into English are taken primarily from the website learnsanskrit.cc, with some creative license. Transliterations (i.e., writing the words using the English alphabet) are entirely nonstandard. I've attempted a phonetic transliteration that I hope will be easier for readers who are unfamiliar with Harvard-Kyoto or IAST formatting. Any errors are mine.

—गुरु

Guru—Teacher

Jayanthi stood atop the hill, her legs protesting less than usual from the climb. Ahead of her, the land settled into a wide plain followed by a series of hills marching up to graceful mountains. To her right, the town of Vaksana blended into the terrain, with low buildings topped by plant-covered roofs. Where teeming masses of humanity had once dumped their excess garbage, megaconstructs now tore down ancient concrete and steel structures with their metal appendages. They towered over sluglike alloys, themselves as tall as trees, who crawled through the rubble, consuming and digesting it, leaving behind fertile organic waste.

A temperate breeze dried Jayanthi's sweat. After catching her breath, she continued along a path that wound down to the base of the hill. Red and tan grasses covered the gentle slope. Insects swarmed to patches of sedate flowers, and microconstructs glittered in their midst, filling the ecological niches that had lain empty for centuries. For part of the way, she could pretend like she was the only human around. Feathery seed pods tickled her palms, and she resisted the instinct to break off a stem. Only a child would harm a plant for no reason, and at twenty-two years old, she was well into adulthood. Instead, she slackened her pace, letting her breath slow, and clasped her hands behind her back.

She entered her family home from the rear, passing under the ancient banyan tree and through the privacy curtain. Art produced by human hands lined the hallway: a quantum-interpretive painting by Charan, a figurine carved from regen-redwood, a painted earthen jug. In the front room, late-morning sunlight filtered through vine-covered windows and painted green shadows over everything, including her alloy father, who reclined in a sling chair.

He peeked over the top of a print book and said, "Share your bodym."

Out of respect for Jayanthi's privacy, her parents had withdrawn their access to her body's information network after she reached the age of sixteen. Alloys did that with their children, relinquishing all oversight and control upon their offspring's maturity. Jayanthi was entirely human and shouldn't have had a bodym at all. The technological enhancement had been a concession—one of many—to her more-than-human parents.

"I'm fine," she grumbled. "Stop worrying."

But she sent her vital metrics over to her father anyway. Telling a parent not to worry was like asking the sun to dim its light.

Vidhar nodded. "Your oxygen and hemoglobin counts are good."

Jayanthi shot him an *I told you so* look. "Have you heard from Hamsa?"

"He'll be here soon. Did your walk not cure your nervousness?"

"I'm not nervous," she said. She sat and put her feet up to prove it.

Hamsa had visited her parents every other year for as long as Jayanthi could remember. He and her parents had completed a fifteen-year course on human studies at the same time, and they'd remained close friends ever since. She'd never heard Hamsa criticize them for taking permanent residence on Earth. Most of the alloys who lived planet-side did so because of forced community service. The ones who did it by choice got branded as *human lovers* or *wellers*. Her parents claimed that the epithets didn't bother them, but for Jayanthi, their oh-so-human child, the labels delivered a sting.

When Jayanthi was young, Hamsa would bring her gifts: intricate filigree balls that flattened into plates after months in Earth's gravity, stick-on chromatophores that changed color with the temperature of her skin. In later years, he'd nurtured her growing interest in studying genetic engineering. Her own DNA contained HbSS—sickle cell anemia, a disease long since eradicated from Earth—and in learning about it, she'd become fascinated with genetics. Her existence was an anomaly, a conscious choice to revive an old genome, but historically, there had been many people like her, and the more she'd learned at Hamsa's knee, the more convinced she'd become that other extinct genes deserved renewed exploration. Alloys had an incredible variety of genes that spanned all kinds of life-forms. Humanity, on the other hand, had narrowed their options over time, choosing security and comfort over risk and diversity.

Hamsa had been a tarawan before he'd gotten involved in politics. His skills in producing alloy offspring were widely recognized. Under his tutelage, she'd learned to combine chromosomes, introduce mutations, and strategically edit genes—to access knowledge that was available only to alloys. Since his previous visit, she'd been working on a new genetic design, something innovative that she hoped would impress him . . . maybe enough to let her work as a tarawan and make human history.

"Hello," called a singsong voice from beyond the entrance curtain.

Jayanthi leaped from her chair and pulled the front entry curtain aside. Hamsa spread his feathered arms and smiled wide and close-mouthed, in the alloy style, though his incarn—the temporary body that he used on Earth—could breathe air. She flung her arms about his waist. He wrapped her in a downy embrace. A sleeveless tunic, white like his feathers, covered his torso. She inhaled his scent and reveled in its earthy, animal quality.

He pulled back and ushered her inside. "How are you, my dear?" The bird genes gave his voice a scratchy quality.

"I'm very well," she said.

"Does that mean you opted for the gene therapy?"

Jayanthi shook her head. "No. I had a blood exchange recently, and I've started a new type of medicine."

Vidhar came forward and flashed a greeting to his friend. Her parents' incarns had a more humanlike appearance, except for being hairless, but as with all alloys, they had chromatophores along their arms, cheeks, and neck. Vidhar's traced delicate spirals across his dark skin, like the ancient symbols for air.

"Where's Kundhina?" Hamsa asked aloud, after responding with his own phores.

"In Paris, but she'll return tomorrow," her father replied. "She's working on a theory about human interment methodologies, and she's in the catacombs there."

"Sounds fascinating," Hamsa said.

Jayanthi left them to catch each other up and busied herself in the kitchen. Alloys—and their incarns—had ways to get energy other than via food, but Hamsa and her father would eat, and her own stomach rumbled for lunch. Keeping her hands busy kept her thoughts occupied rather than fretting over pleasantries until she and Hamsa could get to work.

Their voices stopped as soon as she exited the room. Her parents had insisted on using speech with each other, both for Jayanthi's sake and to keep themselves in practice, which meant she could understand only the simplest phoric. When other alloys came to visit, they would switch back to their natural mode of communication. At least they'd given her the use of an emchannel. As with her bodym, most human beings didn't have the ability, typically conferred by an alloy's extra chromosome. The molecular devices could be installed after birth, as they were for alloys whose emtalk or bodym didn't take in the womb, but that didn't always work on humans. She was grateful that hers had. Not only did it allow her to communicate nonverbally with alloys, it let her interface to devices with her thoughts.

Jayanthi sliced a Black Beauty tomato and placed it on a hot grill next to three slabs of tofu. As they warmed, she ground walnuts and figs in a mortar and pestle, then spread the paste on slices of bread that Vidhar had baked the day before. She topped that with the tomato and tofu and carried it out on a tray. Her best friend, Mina, would have scoffed at the lack of seasoning, but Jayanthi didn't share their interest in cuisine, and her father wouldn't care.

Hamsa made a show of inhaling and said, "That smells wonderful."

She gave him a sideways glance. "You don't have to pretend. I'm an adult now. I won't take offense."

Hamsa honked with laughter. "Compared to my two hundred and eighty-seven years, you are very much a child. I appreciate the offer to drop old pretenses, but I'll attempt to eat. Where else would I get to taste such a . . . a . . ." He looked at Vidhar for help.

Her father's phores flashed.

"Sandwich," Hamsa finished, as if he'd known all along.

Jayanthi laughed. "If you stayed longer, you'd learn more food names."

"If a womb could grow my incarn faster, I might consider it, but one month on Earth is all I can afford with my other responsibilities."

After lunch, Vidhar resumed his work. Hamsa and Jayanthi moved outside and sat under the shade of the banyan tree.

"You said you had a surprise for me," Hamsa said. "Let's see it!"

Six months earlier, Hamsa had assigned Jayanthi a thesis-level project: one that involved design changes to her own chromosomal DNA.

"Pretend you're making your child in the alloy way," he'd said. "You decide what portions of yourself to pass on, what to take from other human beings, and what to mutate randomly, all within the allowed proportions as defined by the Genetic Review Board."

She'd worked on nothing else in the interval, but she'd added her own twist: rather than using genes from another human being's chromosomes, she'd taken some from an alloy's Z chromosome and worked it into her design. It was as if she'd had sex with a humanoid incarn, like those that her parents inhabited. The two were entirely different species and couldn't reproduce naturally, but making such a person possible was exactly what tarawans did. Alloys didn't have children in the traditional sexual way. They designed theirs. A tarawan would take the maker's genes and combine them with any other genetic information from a central data bank. They'd introduce random mutations as well as epigenetic tweaks to produce a new being whose biology would add to the diversity of the population.

She handed Hamsa the data cube with her genomic solution and tried not to fidget as he pulled a simulator from his pocket. With only one meeting per year, her progress was far slower than she would have liked, but only someone licensed by the Tarawan Ethics and Standards Council could operate a simulator.

Hamsa placed the cube in the device and set it on the ground. "I haven't had a chance to review your latest notes. Tell me about your parameters."

Jayanthi thought-asked to share her visual overlay data with him, then showed him the choices she'd made. "For the epigenetic edits to my half, I increased the expression of sickle cell, since it has protective effects against certain tropical diseases, and boosted melanin levels for skin protection. I emphasized lean muscle mass and metabolic efficiency to balance the hypoxic effects." She talked him through another thirty specific edits and her reasons for them.

Hamsa nodded along until she finished, then said, "And mutations?"

"A 0.03 percent chance of mutations, and an additional 0.01 percent on the epigenetic factors."

"That's very conservative. If you play it too safe, you reduce the chance of novelty. Tarawans have to embrace risk. What is the primary axiom?"

Jayanthi swallowed a protest. She'd memorized the axioms in her teens. "There's no such thing as a bad gene," she recited. "Only one that's ill-suited to its environment."

"Good. Now, think hard about what those words mean. If you want to be a tarawan, you have to get comfortable with risks and mortality. Every life-form must have a nonliving state. There's no shame in giving birth to one that moves quickly into the latter. Greatness finds those—"

"—who work without fear. I know." She hesitated, then said, "Here's where I took the risk."

She revealed the complete set of her new being's DNA to Hamsa. She'd used a rare human condition called genome-wide uniparental disomy as her basis. It meant that the child's genes came primarily from one parent. In nature, it usually happened to females, who would inherit the majority of their DNA from their father's sperm. For Jayanthi's experimental design, she'd taken that foundation and used an alloy's Z chromosome for the mother and her own X chromosome for the father. She selected for genes that produced chromatophores, that allowed alloys to subsist on a liquid diet, and—her boldest move—to grow solar wings and replace one air-based lung with a version that held water.

Hamsa's phores stayed neutral. Jayanthi's phoric was terrible, but she had learned to interpret the colored glows around the edges that substituted for facial expressions. A lack of color was the equivalent to a blank face.

"Do you expect this to be a viable person?" he asked.

She quoted the fourth axiom. "Information can be gained from nonviable outcomes as often as it can from the viable."

"And do you think this is a novel idea, to design a being who can survive in both an atmosphere and in the vacuum of space?"

"I . . . hoped so," she admitted.

"This type of being was tried again and again in the first century of the human era. It was one of the causes of the directed mutation catastrophe."

"Oh." She couldn't hide the disappointment in her voice. "How could I have known that? I don't have access to the genomic data in the Nivid, and without the knowledge base, I can't check my designs against prior data."

A green dot lit on an upper corner of the simulator. Hamsa pulled out the data cube and handed it back to Jayanthi. Her design had an approximately 92 percent chance of viability.

"Far too low for approval from a genetic review board," Hamsa said.

"It's not terrible, though. With more time and iterations, I could get it right. I'm capable of doing this successfully. I just need a chance—"

"No." His voice was gentle. "I'm sorry, Jaya. I can't ask TESC to allow a human to access that information. Have patience. Play the long game. We can only change so many things at a time, and my priority right now is to find a way for humans to safely leave Earth. I can't risk the goodwill I've built to push for one of you—even if she's my favorite—to work as a tarawan. The Nivid's judicial construct has approved my proposed amendment and scheduled it for a vote eighteen months from now. That's where my focus has to be."

As monumental as a change to the compact would be, at that moment, she couldn't muster enthusiasm for Hamsa's goals, not while choking on her own.

"Your disappointment shines through, my dear, even without chromatophores," he said. "I'm sorry. Perhaps I shouldn't have indulged you for so long. I didn't realize that it might cause lasting harm, but I can see the potential now. You're an adult. You need to focus on living a good life. If you feel you can't let go of your ambitions, if it's causing you too much distress, we can get you treatment."

She shook her head. She didn't want gene therapy to change her behavior any more than she wanted it to cure her sickle cell disease.

"No one would blame you for it. Between your health and your cognitive capacity, the deck is stacked against your success. Your parents have allowed you to entertain more alloy-like values than a typical human, but unlike us, you have only one life to live. You could consider something else."

Jayanthi tilted her head. "I've wanted to become a tarawan since I was fourteen years old. Do you really think I'm going to give up?"

Hamsa's phores flickered with gentle amusement. "No, I don't, but ambition has ruined many a determined human's life. I'd hate to see that happen to yours."

Jayanthi strode along the dirt path for her daily afternoon walk to visit Mina, her dearest friend, one of the few she'd made in her two decades of life.

A small, unfamiliar alloy sat not far from the trail, their legs and forearms tucked under their leathery bovine body. Long black lashes fringed their eyelids, and intricate phore patterns swirled across their back. Their mouth chewed in regular circles. They slow-blinked, and the alloy's public information hovered over their head: *Lolah, zie/zir, remade once; assigned to six varshas service for illegal accrual of personal property.* This was not someone's incarn. This alloy had undergone a full rebirth, with significant genetic alterations to reside on Earth, where zie would spend the next twenty years cropping invasive plant species.

New to the neighborhood.

"Hello, and welcome," Jayanthi sent via emtalk.

The alloy opened zir dark eyes and swiveled a mostly human-looking face toward Jayanthi. After a blink, zie turned away and blocked the emchannel between them.

With a resigned mental shrug, Jayanthi continued on her walk. She had tried communicating with alloys ever since she'd learned to use emtalk. She'd had better luck when she was small. Most of them didn't come to Earth service voluntarily, and they didn't care to make friends with human beings. Just because she was the adopted daughter of alloys didn't mean they saw her as one of them.

She arrived at Mina's house covered in a fine sweat. Her legs trembled, informing her that she'd pushed her body too hard. It was easy to do. Regular blood exchanges kept her sickle cells in check, but too many years of pain had left her with poor strength. She leaned against a honeysuckle vine and sent it a silent apology for crushing its fragrant blossoms.

A brightly colored privacy curtain hung across the entryway. Above it, an intricately lettered sign read, WELCOME TO THE ANDAKA FAMILY HOME. The curtain parted to reveal Mina standing with arms akimbo. Her friend's braids coiled on their head in a casually elegant bun. A tunic in dark orange draped Mina's generous curves and complemented both their dark-brown skin and the lighter patches of vitiligo that dotted their neck and arms, so similar in appearance to alloy phores that Jayanthi had been envious of them as a child.

"Jaya, are you all right?" Mina said. Their brow crinkled with concern.

Jayanthi nodded and straightened. "I'm fine. I think the new treatment is helping. I walked the entire way without stopping."

"You did what? Will you ever learn to take care of yourself?" Mina scolded. "Come in and sit down. I'll get you some water."

Jayanthi slipped off her sandals and stepped through the doorway into the front room of Mina's family home. The pale stone floor felt smooth and cool under her feet. Green-tinted light filtered through the openings in the thick mud walls. Low-slung chairs framed in bamboo and hung with canvas sat tastefully around a hand-carved wood-and-glass table.

She sat in her usual spot. She'd used the chair for so many years that the fabric had stretched to her exact shape. Jayanthi had met Mina when they both were five years old, during a serendipitous collaboration between their parents. Hers had wanted to study local painters, and Mina's were willing to oblige. Jayanthi's unusual upbringing and ancient DNA made most families nervous. Aspiration and Avarice Disorder wasn't contagious, but people worried anyway. Mina had already been diagnosed with genetic variations that made them prone to AAD, so their parents allowed their friendship to burgeon. When they were older, in school, the others saw Jayanthi drinking bhojya and using emtalk and shunned her even more.

Mina placed a bamboo tumbler into Jayanthi's hands and sat next to her. Jayanthi took a sip and savored the gentle coolness of the water against her parched throat. Blood exchanges and drug therapies were helpful, but hydration was essential to keeping her symptoms at bay.

"So," Mina prompted. "What happened with Hamsa? Did he look at your project?"

Jayanthi grimaced. "Yes."

"It didn't go well?"

"It was a disaster. First, the chance of viability was too low, and then it turns out that the hybrid approach I took basically led to the Directed Mutation Catastrophe."

"Oh no."

"I had no idea! It's not like they cover specific genomes in history classes, and only tarawans have access to that part of the Nivid."

"Then it's not your fault."

"That's what I said, but he didn't care. He wants to stay focused on politics and suggested that I give up. Settle down. Be a good little human."

"If you keep on with that attitude, we'll have to revoke your SHWA membership!"

As teenagers, she and Mina had found half a dozen other like-minded peers in other parts of the world—those who wanted a more alloy-like lifestyle, who had dreams beyond the average human's, and who weren't afraid to be different. They'd dubbed themselves the Society of Humans with Ambitions, embracing their atypical nature in ways that most people with AAD didn't.

"Did you see that they're opening Meru's surface to research missions?" Mina asked.

"Stop trying to distract me."

"It's important!"

Jayanthi shrugged. "Why? Alloys and constructs will be allowed on the planet, not us."

Mina raised their heavy eyebrows. "If Hamsa gets his amendment, humans could get to live on Meru, too."

Centuries earlier, humanity had caused so much destruction to Earth and Mars that they'd willingly consigned themselves to one home. The alloys—their descendants—helped keep the planet healthy, and in exchange, they took resources, especially the rare elements that were difficult to obtain from asteroids. Hamsa's proposal would rewrite the core of the compact for the first time in living memory.

"They finally discover a planet with similar metrics to ours—gravity, atmosphere, climate—and the alloys insist on keeping us from it. Hamsa's amendment had better pass." Mina pulled on a glove and flicked their fingers at the wallscreen. "Sahaya Amritsavar is pushing hard in favor of it. You should watch her speech."

"I don't know if that's a good idea."

"I thought you liked her?"

"No, I don't mean the speech. I meant about putting humans on Meru."

"But, Jaya, you said last week that you wished you could go there!"

"I do. It would be amazing, but I don't know about everyone else. What if we mess it all up again? How would the compact apply? Are the alloys going to work on the surface and take resources from Meru like they do here? You know what Bantri and her faction want. A return to the so-called good old days of uncontrolled growth." Jayanthi made a noise of disgust. "Have you looked at the stats for Meru's atmosphere? The excess oxygen means no long-term human habitation without changes."

"The cyanobacteria are the only life on the planet," Mina said. "We could introduce aerobic bacteria to compete and make the atmosphere more breathable. We wouldn't be impacting anything with a complex consciousness by doing that."

"Sixth principle corollary," Jayanthi countered. "An evolved lifeform will adapt itself rather than harm other Beings in its environment."

"Then we figure out how to ensure that our upcoming generations can live with higher oxygen."

"Across an entire population? Impossible! People would have to carry made embryos rather than pass on their own genes. We'd need tarawans for that. And a lot more access to wombs. Even if the alloys supported it, I bet Bantri's faction wouldn't. They'd insist on humans reproducing the *natural* way."

"I think you two are just as silly as Bantri and her faction," said Anita. Mina's elder sister stood at the entrance to the hallway, her arms across her chest. Paint smudged her fingers and covered her smock with a riot of colors. Even with her hair in an untidy pile atop her head, Anita looked like she'd stepped out of a portrait, every part of her body draped in graceful lines. "Life is perfect here. Why go to Meru or anywhere else?"

"Perfect for you, maybe," Mina shot back. "Some of us have bigger goals than being kept by alloys."

"We are not *kept*. We are supported, and we're artists. Your ambition to be a Voice doesn't have any moral high ground."

"But sometimes it is literally higher," Jayanthi said and grinned at her pun. On rare occasions, human Voices of Compassion served at an orbital station.

Mina laughed while Anita rolled her eyes.

"This is the great intellect the universe is missing?" Anita said. "You two barely deserve to be let out of the house, much less off the planet. You should appreciate what you have and settle down to a good human life. There's so much you could do—garden, cook, make music, raise children. Our lives are luxuries. You should appreciate that more. *Ambition and materialism lead to greed and exploitation.*" She left

Ratnam's words hanging in the air and retreated down the hallway to her studio.

Mina repeated the quote in a singsong tone. "Prat."

"She makes some valid points," Jayanthi said.

Mina gave her a sour look, then tilted their chin at the screen across from them, which now showed a still frame of a woman sitting cross-legged on a wide, flattened slab of granite. "I pulled up a clip from Amritsavar's speech, the best part. Watch it, and you'll see what I mean."

Dappled sunlight fell through the trees above the politician, highlighting the gold threads that embellished her deep-red blouse. "The confinement of humankind on the Earth must end with the establishment of beings on the surface of Meru. Since 187 AE, the Constructed Democracy of Sol has increased the restrictions on human development, and while the results are positive overall, these constraints have led to the complete inability of the vast majority of humankind to contribute to the general body of knowledge that is the Nivid.

"All forms of conscious life need a sense of purpose. Without this, they live in a state of perpetual existential crisis." Amritsavar's dark eyes shone with intensity. "In the immortal words of the Declaration of Conscious Beings, *Life exists to gather and disseminate information*. There is no greater reward than to make a discovery worthy of the Nivid. To deprive humanity of that is akin to depriving us of air. To restrict the discoveries on Meru to alloys and constructs is bigotry. For more than five centuries, we have stayed quietly on Earth, repairing the damage our ancestors inflicted on our home planet, accepting this as our due after the mistakes we made in our past. Now it's time for a new era, one in which humankind has as much of a place in the universe as alloys and constructs."

Mina flicked their glove and stopped the video. "Imagine exploring a planet for the first time. Setting foot where no one has gone before."

"It would be incredible," Jayanthi admitted. "Not as good as living in space like an alloy, but maybe second best. A newly discovered planet is a potential trove of information. You really think the alloys would give that up to us? I love Hamsa, and I fully support his proposal, but I can't imagine how he'll get it to pass."

"Do you think your parents will vote for it?"

Jayanthi nodded. "He's been their proxy voter for years."

"Who's representing the opposition?" Mina asked.

"Pushkara, as usual."

The ancient alloy had witnessed the drafting of the compact, though he'd been a child at the time.

"Pushkara says out loud what everyone thinks," Jayanthi said. "Meru would require some environmental engineering before humans could comfortably live there. He's arguing that we'd disrupt the current growth and development of life on the planet, and that, of course, would violate the compact." She thought-retrieved the news she'd seen earlier. "Popular sentiment in alloy polls skews in Pushkara's favor. Humans are almost evenly split on the issue."

"So it won't pass?"

"Not a chance. I'll vote for it, but even if every human on Earth voted that way, the alloys outnumber us by a factor of a thousand. Unless we win their majority, nothing will change." Jayanthi pressed herself up from the chair. "I should head home before it gets too late. I want to be back in time for dinner with Hamsa."

Mina's expression turned glum.

Jayanthi squeezed an arm around her friend. "At least you'll have a chance to see space as a Voice of Compassion. Even if by some miracle Hamsa's proposal passes, the rest of us will have to wait decades to set foot on Meru."

Jayanthi kept a slower pace on the return home. Her father had asked her to pick up some tomatoes and basil, so she routed herself through the more populous center of Vaksana. With forty thousand residents, it was one of the smaller city-states in the temperate zone of mid-Eurasia. She knew most of the people in her subsection.

Long shadows covered the communal garden complex that included her family's plot. For all the technological marvels that people had developed, some things hadn't changed. Plants still needed soil or nutrient solution, sunlight, and air to grow. Insects, however, had mostly disappeared within the city limits. In their place, dark, nonreflective insectoid constructs flew about and tended the vegetables. A watering construct the size of an average Labrador stepped on four delicate metal feet as it moved between the raised beds. A spout extended from its belly on one end, and a siphon lay folded against the other.

People dotted the rows between the bushes and conducted their own harvests. She could feel their gazes tickle the back of her neck as she bent to gather a fist-size Black Beauty. The dark-purple globe nearly filled her palm, and she placed it gently in her hemp satchel.

She didn't bother to greet anyone. They all knew who and what she was, and they had never felt comfortable with her circumstances—a human child born to two alloys, given emtalk capabilities, and lacking a surname. Like the dusk that bathed the sky, she occupied a liminal space. Of Earth but not like other humans; of alloys but unsuited to life in space.

She strolled home along a wide dirt avenue lined with mango and papaya trees. The faint pink glow of sunset suffused the air. A juvenile lynx padded alongside her, staring curiously for a hundred meters before darting down a side path. Parakeets rustled and cried out in the leaves above. A sleek greyhound sniffed at her bag, then her hand. Finding nothing of interest, it resumed its seated position against a tree trunk and licked at the pulp of a fallen fruit.

Over many generations, tarawans had crafted genes to make human pheromones unpalatable to wildlife, human exhalations uninteresting to insects. Fauna were reintroduced well after the start of the Alloy Era.

Many species still existed only in gene banks, and even more had been lost forever to the Anthropocene extinction. Jayanthi wished she could see a white rhinoceros or African elephant or monarch butterfly. Why had humans been so foolish and careless? At the peak of their power on Earth, their primary accomplishment was the eradication or exploitation of other forms of life. If the alloys did allow them to travel to Meru, would they treat that planet better, or was human nature too flawed?

Jayanthi turned right as she passed the granary construct.

"Good evening, Jayanthi," Laghu rumbled from a speaker in the outer wall. He had a joke of a name, which meant *small* in Sanskrit, the latest trendy ancient language among alloys. The artificially constructed being was anything but. His dozen silos extended fifteen meters toward the sky, and his central mill spanned nearly one hundred meters per side.

"Evening," she said. "How's business?"

"Unprofitable," he said.

They'd started this routine when she was twelve, the first time she'd walked home alone from Mina's house. His reply had sent her into a fit of giggles, so she'd asked it every time, and he'd always answered the same way. Constructs didn't work to turn profits.

"How's your health?" Laghu asked, continuing their ritual.

"I'm having a pretty good day." She sat on a stone bench and leaned back. "Laghu, what do you think about allowing humans to live on Meru?"

"My opinion is irrelevant, but since you've asked, I'll say that it should happen. The people of Vaksana have respected the constraints of modern life. I don't think any of them would cause harm to another planet, and if anything, they would take more care on Meru than the familiar grounds of home. Would you agree?"

Jayanthi took a minute before answering. "In general, yes. We have treatments for those who struggle to live that way, and for those who refused, they're in the Out of Bounds. I'm sure we wouldn't recruit people from the OOB for Meru anyway."

"But you're not convinced I'm right."

"I don't think you're wrong, either. I guess I don't trust humanity as much as you do." She stood. "I'll be on my way. See you tomorrow."

A half kilometer farther, the mounded shape of her home squatted at the end of the lane. Her parents had painted the outside with murals copied from ancient history—pharaohs and devas, djinn and nahual—which she could barely see in the deep twilight that blanketed it. She craned her neck skyward and waited for her eyes to adjust. *There they are,* she thought as she spotted a faint twinkle. It marked the geosynchronous station where her parents' true bodies berthed.

Someday, probably after her death, they would leave the Earth, reabsorb their incarn forms, and return to their life in space. Her parents had obtained permission to study human culture for up to one century. Twenty years into their research, they had decided they loved the planet and its people so much that they wanted to raise a human child. Jayanthi drew her gaze and her thoughts back to Earth and pulled aside their privacy curtain.

A year earlier, when Jayanthi had reached the age of twenty-one, she'd been given the choice to undergo gene therapy for her sickle cell disease. She had declined. Hamsa's tutelage had drilled into her the importance of biodiversity, including human genetic variants.

"As long as you can find ways to live with your biology," he'd often said, "your epigenetic and lifestyle adaptations can provide valuable knowledge for the rest of society."

The local medical construct had sifted through archival information and formulated new infusions to help with her symptoms. She'd had several episodes during her childhood when every nerve ending felt aflame and death sounded like a sensible alternative. At least twice a year, she went through a blood exchange. It replaced her sickled cells with fresh ones cultured from her own DNA. The treatments left her tired for several days, but she would rather pay that price than go through a pain crisis. Fatigue was a constant companion anyway.

Jayanthi stored the vegetables in the kitchen and went to her room. A shallow stone tub lay just outside, and she opened the tap to fill it. Her clothes went into a laundering bin full of cleansing microorganisms and microconstructs. As she lowered herself into the hot water, she sent a thought-command to turn off the interior lights, then traced the outlines of the constellations above. Through the large optical telescope in Tash, she had once seen the Primary Nivid—the only permanent alloy structure in space and the repository of all knowledge and information—but at the moment, all she could observe was the passage of an orbiting station, one of many that allowed trade between Earth and the rest of the Constructed Democracy of Sol.

The alloy population dominated the CDS. Two million served on Earth in various capacities. The rest—billions of them—lived in the vast empty spaces of the Solar System and beyond. The crown jewel of their accomplishments was the Nivid. Jayanthi's parents had spent decades on Earth in research, and they had found plenty to enter into the Nivid's data half, but they had contributed only one item to the knowledge archives. Few humans added to the former, and even fewer discovered something that made it into the latter.

Jayanthi gazed into the night sky and imagined her name added to their roster. One day, somehow, she would prove to the world that she could be one of the exceptions. If Hamsa wouldn't support her attempt at becoming a tarawan, she'd have to find another way. She would never be human enough for the people on Earth, and she was too human for the people in space, but if she could discover something worthy of the Nivid, she could prove her value to all of them.

—वैमानिक

Vaimaanika—Pilot

Vaha curled zir body into a ball, then stretched full. Zie extended zir arms and pushed zir tail until the fins pointed straight back, forming zir body into a blue-black line, then vented hydrogen and rotated to face Venus. The planet loomed in zir vision, a dazzling white diamond that reflected sunlight from its cloud-cover shell. Vaha kept both of zir tinted membranes over zir eyes so they wouldn't burn out from the planet's glare.

I'm not ready, zie thought and did another scan of zir bodym. The heat-resistant scales overlapping zir body had no gaps. The emchannel interface to zir augmented sensors and memories checked out as functional. Zie tightened the fastenings on zir backup engine. All of that was fine, and zie knew it. The fault lay within.

Zie rotated away from the planet. The open structure of the Nishadas padhran floated nearby. Oblong berths clustered like wireframe eggs around solid central plumbing. The dark, nonreflective materials created a negative space against the star field behind them. Here and there, bioluminescent markers glowed in primary colors, dim enough that they didn't compete with the natural starlight.

A figure spun out from the padhran, their outline becoming clearer as they separated from the collection of alloy bodies and berths. Vaha had spent half zir life with this group, ever since zir maker left the Solar System to explore and discover new places. Nishadas was an in-residence flight school, a place for aspiring pilots like zirself to learn the modes of travel that their bodies could handle. Like every gathering of alloys, the padhran was a temporary structure comprised of people, machines, and inert structures. When the last of the students graduated, the padhran would disperse, its parts recycled for some other purpose in some other location.

The lone figure moved past an oblong womb—about a third as long as their body—and across a glittering array of stars. Vaha recognized zir friend Kaliyu's silhouette. From a distance, it resembled the shape of the mythological merfolk with one major addition: solar wings, silver and black in Kaliyu's case. The wings extended in two leaflike ovals, a style that had fallen out of fashion a century before zir birth. Muscular vents that could exert powerful thrust dotted the blue-gray of zir skin. Kaliyu's body stretched to 114 meters from head to tip and roughly forty-five meters around the narrowest point of the torso, a little shorter and slimmer than Vaha. Zie puffed to a stop in front of Vaha and flashed a greeting with zir phores.

Vaha responded in kind and moved zirself back a little. Zir friend's body exuded heat. Kaliyu had just taken the final exam for a pilot's license, and zie was still cooling down from the atmospheric friction as well as zir own exertion.

<Did you pass?> Vaha flashed, letting the edges of zir chromatophores glow purple with cheer and hope.

<Is the Sun bright? Of course I passed! And svah you will, too. Then we can get on with our real lives!>

Vaha flexed zir tail. <I wouldn't bet on it.>

<Then it's a good thing betting is illegal. Don't be so nervous!> Kaliyu's words radiated confidence. <You almost had it hyas.>

<*Almost* isn't good enough.>

During the previous day's practice, Kaliyu had performed a Venusian gravity maneuver with ease, as zie had for months, and Vaha had struggled once again. The assignment was to fall into the planet's gravity well, pick up speed, then thrust out. The basic maneuver had been done by mechanical spacecraft for centuries, and for an alloy pilot to obtain their license, they had to complete the course without assistance. Vaha didn't have the intuitive feel for optimal entry speed and exit point that Kaliyu did.

<Maybe I should cancel my test and go into stasis,> Vaha flashed. <I could spend the rest of my life being entertained. Doesn't sound so bad.>

Kaliyu's phores flickered with amusement. They both knew how ridiculous Vaha's words were. They had started their education at Nishadas at the same time, when they were ten years old. Their assigned berths sat next to each other, and they had been the only alloys to arrive without their makers. Kaliyu's breezy confidence had drawn Vaha to zir like a moon to a planet, and before long, they'd established a private emtalk channel and confessed their brief life histories to each other.

Vaha's maker, Veera, had grown frustrated with zir child's repeated failures as a young pilot and decided to cut zir losses as soon as zie legally could. Veera had accepted a long-term extrasolar mission and wouldn't return for decades or possibly centuries. Kaliyu's maker, Nidra, had died when Kaliyu was only five. Zir grandmaker had raised zir until zie went to Nishadas. She had died a few years later, and Vaha's friend had become as much of a free agent as Vaha.

<Think of what you can do after you get your license,> Kaliyu flashed. <There's a long list of exploratory tasks opening up around Meru, including some on the surface of the planet. That should motivate you.>

Vaha sent zir statistics to Kaliyu. <I've done this right only ten times out of a thousand.>

<One percent isn't terrible odds,> zie flashed in a teasing color.

Vaha flexed zir tail and stayed dark.

<If you're really that worried,> Kaliyu flashed, <I could help you.>

<What do you mean?>

Kaliyu beckoned with zir hand and flew away from Nishadas. Vaha followed until they could barely see the padhran. What did zir friend have to say that required such privacy?

Kaliyu stopped at last and crossed zir arms across zir chest. Only the phores on zir forearms shone. <I need you to give me control access to your bodym.>

Vaha jerked back at the request. The white of surprise leaked from zir phores and reflected in Kaliyu's clear eye membranes. An alloy could give someone the codes to remotely control their limbs and vents, but it was an emergency measure. Only makers or committed partners would be trusted with those codes. Kaliyu was Vaha's dearest friend, but zie had never indicated romantic feelings.

<Are you . . . proposing?> Vaha flashed.

Kaliyu flickered with amusement. <No, you mudha. Nothing like that. Just give me temporary access so I can maneuver you through Venus.>

Vaha almost shot backward again. <That's cheating!>

<Not really.> Kaliyu radiated icy-blue determination. <You know you can pass. You've done it before. You just need more practice, but we're out of time if we want to graduate together. Think of it as a shortcut, not cheating.>

Some shortcut, Vaha thought to zirself. The whole point of leaving the Moon and joining Nishadas was to relieve zirself of repeated failure. How could zie see this as anything but another red mark against zirself? If Veera ever came back, how could Vaha meet zir maker's gaze without shame or guilt?

Impatience tinted Kaliyu's phores. <Don't worry. After a few years at Meru, you'll be proficient. This won't matter.>

Zir friend had a point. Meru had a wealth of novel data to be gathered and deposited into the Nivid. If Vaha could get an assignment there, zie would have plenty of opportunities to practice maneuvering in a gravity well and atmosphere.

Kaliyu flickered with amusement again. <Your struggle is leaking through your phores. You know I'm right.>

And Vaha could see through Kaliyu's semantics. To let Kaliyu guide zir body through the exam was cheating, and added to Vaha's earlier failures? Zie would end up despising zirself even more than zie already did. But maybe there was another way Kaliyu could help that involved limb control.

<I want to pass,> Vaha flashed. <I want to go to Meru and discover something new, but not like this. I have a different idea. What if I give you access to my bodym, and you maneuver me through Venus so I can feel how you would do it? Then I'll try to copy it on my own. My test isn't until tomorrow.>

<Until svah, you mean,> Kaliyu corrected, offering the alloy term in place of the human-centric one. Zie had grown up in a solar orbit, far from the Earth, Moon, and human lingo, and lately zie had turned into more of a purist.

<Right, svah. I could do one or two practice runs with you moving me and then a few more on my own.>

Kaliyu wagged zir head in ambivalence. <I'm happy to do that, but you might still fail the test.>

<I've spent my entire life failing at gravity maneuvers. This would only confirm what everyone already knows.>

<That's your maker talking, not you.> Kaliyu glowed an irritated orange-red. <I've known you for half your life, Vaha, and I know you can do this. You should have more faith in yourself.>

Vaha let doubt and apology color zir phores. Zie would have faith after zie proved to zirself that zie deserved it.

The gravitational force of Venus drew Vaha's body like a womb to its interior. Zie had given Kaliyu the codes to access zir motor and limb system before they entered the planet's orbit. It felt strange to have someone else squeezing the muscles around zir vents.

"Relax!" Kaliyu sent. "Don't try to help me. This is awkward enough as it is."

They'd switched to emtalk because the glare of Venus made it impossible to use phoric properly. Vaha felt zir arms move back and along zir torso. Zie tried to force zirself to relinquish control of zir muscles. Zie had last changed zir access codes when zie reached Nishadas and hadn't disclosed them since, except during one of zir medical emergencies.

Kaliyu flew above Vaha, far enough to stay out of Venus's grasp with minimal effort but close enough for rapid communication with Vaha's body. The iron scales that formed their skin reflected much of Venus's heat, but Vaha could feel zir core temperature rising. Zie had to suffer through it. The final examination flight path was too short to allow zir to rotate and cool off.

"Keep your arms by your sides like this," Kaliyu sent, flattening Vaha's hands against the curve of zir tail. "You're about to skim. Can you pull your wings in any tighter?"

"No, this is as close as they get."

Kaliyu's double ovals were unfashionable, but they stacked better than Vaha's birdlike tapered rectangles. Veera had intended that Vaha would soar through the air like a great eagle, but zie never had a chance to try it. Zir inability to launch from the lunar surface meant that zie hadn't qualified to fly in Earth's atmosphere. Throughout zir childhood, the planet of zir ancestors had hung in zir view, tantalizing and unobtainable.

Vaha entered the upper layer of Venus's cloud cover. The dense heat reminded zir of the time Veera had taken them on a solar trip. Enclosed in a protective construct, they'd moved past Mercury's orbit and reached the point where they could see the menacing texture of Sol's surface. For that brief time, Vaha and zir maker had relaxed and enjoyed each other's company, free from the pressures of Veera's expectations and Vaha's repeated failures.

"Keep your speed up," Kaliyu transmitted, "and watch your altitude."

Both numbers had a range in which an alloy pilot of sufficient strength could smash down their tail, send a blast of gas from their posterior vents, and pull away from Venus's gravity with greater speed than their approach. Because they were students, they carried a backup engine so that they didn't get trapped by the planet's gravity and turn into a flaming ball of doom. Vaha would have to leave that security behind if zie passed the final exam.

"Let's get you moving a little faster," Kaliyu sent. "Keep dropping . . . almost there . . . now!"

Vaha felt zir vent muscles squeeze until they trembled. Zir altitude stabilized, then began to drop.

"Oh, gravity take me!" Kaliyu swore. "Use your engine. I guess we need to be more conservative. You aren't strong enough to go that low, and the friction from your body shape is greater than mine."

Vaha reached back with zir left hand and flipped the power switch on the engine. Zie curled zir tail in toward zir belly, then yanked at the throttle. The thrust tugged at the straps under zir arms, and zie pulled away from Venus. Kaliyu matched zir course so that they flew alongside each other as they neared the Nishadas padhran.

<This isn't working,> Vaha flashed, unable to keep the apricot glow of frustration from zir phores.

<One more round,> Kaliyu countered. <Third time's the charm, right? I have a better feel for your strength, and I think the problem is that you're falling too far. You get more points for the additional speed, but you don't need those to pass the test. Let's try once more with conservative numbers. If that doesn't work, we'll stop.>

<Why do you care so much if I pass?> Vaha asked as they turned around and headed back to Venus. <You already have people falling over themselves to sponsor you on the race circuit. So what if I'm still at Nishadas after you graduate?>

<I care because you're my best friend, you thrice-made idiot,> Kaliyu flashed in reply. <I like you, remember? I like being around you. I'd even consider going to Meru with you, if that's what it takes for you to get over your maker issues, but first things first. We need to cool off and try Venus again.>

They moved apart and made their respective approaches to the planet. Vaha gained speed as zie fell toward the blazing cloud tops, putting zir arms by zir sides before Kaliyu could do it. Zie felt Kaliyu lift zir tail in a high arc, like a scorpion getting ready to strike. Vaha had tried that in the past to no avail. *It's not going to work this time, either.*

As soon as zir altitude and speed reached the minimum requirements, Kaliyu wrenched Vaha's tail down and squeezed zir vents, moving from anterior to posterior in a way that Vaha had never considered. Vaha shot up and then forward, arcing away from the planet.

"That's how you do it!" Kaliyu crowed.

"I can't believe that worked! Is that your usual technique?"

"Not at all, but after moving your body, it felt like the right way to pull out of the fall."

"Your intuition beats mine by light-years. Now I have to try to do that on my own tomor—svah, during the test."

"You won't just try, you human knockoff—you *will* do it!"

Vaha converged with Kaliyu's trajectory and squeezed zir hand. <Thank you.>

Vaha pulled zirself into a pressurized cleaning station and watched as heat-damaged scales sloughed away. Mindless automated constructs swarmed over zir body. Zie sealed a tube over zir mouth to let some fly in. The tiny machines inspected Vaha inside and out, doing routine surface maintenance as well as a medical check.

Silver patches spotted zir blue-black skin—mild burns from zir botched Venusian exits. They would scale over in a few hours, but they'd take several days to heal fully. Zie accepted some topical pain blockers in the meantime. That had the added benefit of helping the sore muscles at the base of zir tail. Zie was overdue for cellular repairs to treat oxidative and radiation damage.

Zir body could handle some of that on its own, but everyone needed periodic maintenance that went beyond their natural systems. Vaha had pushed hard for the past half Venusian-year without enough breaks. *After tomorrow,* zie promised zirself, *I'll spend enough rotations attached to my womb to get myself to full health.* Nishadas had a womb, but unlike the others, Vaha had one of zir own, a legacy from zir maker that marked zir potential and zir failures. Zie wished zie could rest first, but if zie missed the testing window, there wouldn't be another for a full Venusian-year.

Why can't I be as good as Kaliyu?

Vaha's design was supposed to have been an improvement over zir friend's more standard hybrid-flight genomes, allowing Vaha to transport passengers and material from the ground, through atmosphere, across microgravity, and transit the very fabric of reality itself. Kaliyu's body could only skim a planet's atmosphere. Zie would never be able to land and launch the way Vaha could—in theory.

Small consolation if I can't navigate a gravity well, Vaha thought. *What good are innovative genes if the person who possesses them is too incompetent to take advantage of them?* At least zie excelled at reality transits. Zie had a knack for entering the mind state needed to use quantum probability senses, something Kaliyu struggled with.

The microconstructs tickled the inside of Vaha's water-filled lungs. After they finished cleaning zir out, Vaha grabbed a rehydration tube and drank. The pure taste of melted comet-ice filled zir mouth and settled into zir stomach. Running out of water during the test would ensure failure. Zie swapped it for a bhojya tube and drank a basic nutrient solution of protein, carbohydrates, fat, silicon, metals, and minerals. The microconstructs had restocked the protective bacteria that coated zir skin and mouth and repaired any damaged solar cells on zir wings. Bhojya and biology would take care of the rest.

Vaha emerged from the cleaning station, pulsing zirself past other pilots' bodies and into zir assigned berth. Kaliyu drifted in the adjacent spot, zir phores chased with the pastel rainbow hues of dreams. Vaha plugged zir backup engine into a charging port, then settled into zir berth. Zie replayed the maneuver that Kaliyu had shown zir earlier and hoped that rest would instill the muscle memory . . . assuming zie could fall asleep. Zie practiced the first stage of mind-clearing. *Close the eyes. Bring the body to rest. Let your cartilage soften. Relax each muscle, from tip to crown.*

—अक्ष

Aksha—Pivot

Jayanthi sat next to Mina on their bed and watched as three other SHWAs appeared on the wallscreen. Ekene and Jean looked to be calling from home, but Li Feng's backdrop was a domed observatory.

"I finally got some telescope time," Li Feng said by way of greeting. "Had to show it off. How's everyone else?"

"Still happy taking crop samples," Ekene said. "I'm keeping my thesis adviser satisfied, too."

"I think I found a sponsor for my movie," Jean said. "An alloy who's a fan of my short films contacted me. They're in stasis, and they said they'd be happy to start a petition to get me resources."

"That's great, Jean," Jayanthi said. "I'm happy for you."

A few years earlier, Jean had wanted to travel to Antarctica and do research there, but the Committee for Intercontinental Travel had denied his request. They said he had too little tolerance for the climate conditions. The disappointment had nearly crushed him, and he'd opted for gene therapy to help him let go of the dream. On one level, she felt bad for him, but on another, she was glad to see her friend out of pain. He wasn't much of a SHWA anymore, but he was still a friend.

Mina waved their hand as if sweeping aside a pile of debris. "I'm glad we're all doing well, but can we talk about the only thing that really matters right now? How do we muster enough votes to pass Hamsa's amendment so humans can live on Meru?"

The others burst into laughter.

"You're the one studying law," Ekene said.

"Not the same as politics," Mina rejoined.

"We need a good counterargument to everyone saying that we'd have to modify the planet's atmosphere," Li Feng said. He had always followed policy matters closely, though his passion was radio astronomy. "Pushkara's taking that angle hard. Apparently one of his human ancestors was a lead geoengineer on Mars. He's spouting his usual lines about having witnessed the drafting of the compact and how flawless it is."

"So he has familial guilt to assuage," Mina mused. "And the current legal framework is on his side. This will pose a challenge."

"He also has a long record of conservative voting," Li Feng said, "especially when it comes to protecting the integrity of nonliving conscious bodies, including planets. The respect for his work runs deep and wide. If he says that we shouldn't consider having humans on Meru, people will listen. We have a year and a half to convince the majority that he's wrong."

"I saw a poll that said eighty percent of humans don't think we need to leave the Earth," Ekene said. "The alloys poll slightly better, at sixty-eight in Pushkara's favor. They have no incentive to let us leave Earth. Not only would it require them to provide safe transport for us, it would mean fewer alloys working on the surface and less Earth resources for them to take. That's two things the alloys don't want. The ones who've curbed their AAD might vote in our favor, but the rest won't." She made an apologetic face. "I know Hamsa's your friend, Jaya, but none of his proposals for human space travel have gone well. He has a lot of goodwill from his tarawan days, but he's fighting a losing battle.

Humanity has spent generations weeding out its desire to explore. If we don't care, how do we make *them* care?"

"I don't know," Jayanthi said. "But we have to try. If we can start fresh with a whole new planet, we'll need a populace that's more adventurous. We can let some of those characteristics come back into the gene pool."

"How's your genetics project going?" Jean asked. "Did Hamsa like it?"

Jayanthi made a sour face and filled them in on the previous day's events.

"I bet someone could design a human with the right physiology for Meru," Ekene said. She studied genetic engineering as well, though her work was on plants. "It shouldn't require too many changes."

The newly discovered planet had parameters remarkably similar to Earth's. After alloys had established civilization in Sol-space, they'd sent probes, constructs, and alloys to other systems, searching purely for the sake of science. They'd discovered plenty of exoplanets, but very few came close to Earth's mass, temperature, and geophysics. Many harbored rudimentary forms of life, which made them off-limits to anything but orbital observation. Some had developed protein structures that even alloys would find toxic. Meru was the first to have similar gravity, a human-breathable atmosphere, and minimally evolved lifeforms that aligned with Earth's biochemistry. The trouble with Meru was the amount of oxygen. At nearly 45 percent of the atmosphere, it would cause lung and vision disorders, along with general oxidative damage at the cellular level.

As the others delved further into political wrangling, Jayanthi slow-blinked to activate her emchannel and searched through the known methods for preventing hyperoxia. People could handle pure oxygen for short durations, and most negative effects would reverse after they resumed breathing Earth-normal air. No one knew what a lifelong overexposure to oxygen would cause, but they had discovered that some genetic variants could help mitigate the damage caused to lung tissue.

Jayanthi skimmed the list. Her gaze stumbled over a familiar term, HMOX-1. The new medication for her sickle cell disorder affected the expression of that gene, cranking it up so that it destroyed the free heme her sickled cells released into her blood. She'd incorporated it as a permanent change in the design she'd shown Hamsa. According to the information in front of her, the same enzyme would keep the alveoli in human lungs from corroding under continuous exposure to excess oxygen.

An idea began to coalesce in her mind like the first cells in an embryo. With sickling, the problem for the body was that the distorted cells didn't bind well to oxygen. In an atmosphere like Meru's, that would be an advantage, and a tweak to the genes regulating HMOX-1 would then prevent the associated lung damage. Someone with that combination ought to live a long and healthy life on Meru.

"I . . . might already see a genetic solution," Jayanthi said, interrupting a heated discussion between Mina and Li Feng.

They stopped talking, and Mina turned to her. As Jayanthi explained her idea, Mina began to frown.

"An entire population with a condition like yours?" they asked.

"In Meru's atmosphere, they wouldn't get sick as often as I do."

"Didn't they eradicate sickle cell anemia from the human genome centuries ago?" Ekene said. "I thought you only exist because you have alloy parents and Hamsa went for a random combination from the Nivid's historical records?"

Jayanthi nodded. "There must be plenty more like me in the database. If we could get tarawans to help with embryo design on Meru and implant those into the first wave of human settlers—"

Everyone interrupted her at once. Then they got into a new argument about Bantri and natural human reproduction versus the alloy method. Jayanthi said little. Politics had never interested her much, and she couldn't shake loose the thought that her design for Hamsa had exactly the genes a person would need on Meru. If she stripped out the extra bits from the Z chromosome, she could make it a purely human genome. She had to tell Hamsa. If he could demonstrate the design's viability, he'd have the classic counterargument to Pushkara's objection: *The evolved life-form adapts the environment to itself; the highly evolved life-form adapts itself to the environment.*

That evening over dinner, Jayanthi mentioned her idea to Hamsa and her parents. They sat around a table sliced from a four-hundred-year-old kapok tree. She had traced its irregular contours over and over as a child, and the oils from her fingers had left a streak around the wood. A creamy-brown rabbit slept peacefully at her feet.

She began, "I might have a human DNA design that's well adapted to the conditions on Meru." She smiled at the pale glow of surprise from her parents' phores. "We'd start with the genome I already made for Hamsa and strip out all the alloy genes. With the additional oxygen on Meru, my sickle cell plus some of the modifications I made could balance out to a healthy metabolic rate."

Before Hamsa could respond, her mother said, "You're saying that sickling would help on Meru?"

"In a way, yes. It means that the right amount of oxygen would get delivered to the body's tissues. The problem is the lung exposure—the higher O2 level in Meru's atmosphere would corrode the tissue over time. It turns out that the treatment I'm taking also protects the lungs from excess oxygen. The effects aren't harmful here on Earth and would be useful on Meru." She met Hamsa's gaze. "In my hybrid design, I'd already modified the genes that my treatment affects. If we replaced the mother's Z chromosome with a human X, we'd have a person who can thrive on Meru without changing the planet."

"It's a good idea, Jaya," Hamsa said, "but a design alone won't convince people. We'd need to demonstrate planetary fitness with an actual person, and then we'd have to prove that the modified genes would be expressed across successive generations. If humans were on Meru and looking to procreate, we could test your idea, but we can't ethically make a human for the sole purpose of verifying your theory. That kind of experimentation is only allowed with people who can be remade."

In other words, alloys.

"Could an alloy raise this experimental human on Meru?" Jayanthi looked pointedly at her parents. They'd talked about asking for another human baby, but they'd decided to wait until after her own childbearing years in case she wanted one of her own.

"We had so much trouble getting approval for you," Kundhina said. "I doubt that TESC would agree to such an arrangement on a strange new planet." She smiled and patted Jayanthi's hand. "Besides, if we left, who would take care of you?"

"Can't you do a simulation of Meru's atmosphere interacting with this gene-set?" Vidhar asked.

"Too many variables," Hamsa said. "We'd run into the problem of asymptotic complexity. We can verify the oxygen-hemoglobin pathway, but we have other factors to contend with on Meru. By the time we build an accurate simulation of all the planetary conditions and their interactions with Jaya's design, we're approaching reality itself."

Kundhina turned to face Hamsa and Vidhar. "If we can't make a child to test Jaya's design, what about using an existing person?" She inclined her head at Jayanthi and raised her hairless brows.

Jayanthi blinked at her mother. Of course! She had all the requisite genes, and her new treatment mimicked a permanent up-regulation of HMOX-1. They already knew it worked with her physiology.

"You'd send me to Meru?" She'd never gone farther on her own than Mina's house. Her head spun at the implications. She turned to

Hamsa. "Would my parents come? Would they allow us to go there before the vote?"

"I wonder," her mentor said, drawing out the word. "I could ask for a delay to the vote and call your expedition a preliminary investigation, something that the Meru Exploration Committee could approve without violating any laws. You'd be part of an alloy endeavor, not a human one. I don't think I could justify sending Kundhina or Vidhar, though. They have no skills applicable to a situation like Meru. We'd have to find someone else to look after you, someone with an exploratory background and, ideally, with human medical knowledge in case you have trouble with your health."

All three of their phores glowed with thoughtfulness.

After Jayanthi's first sickle cell crisis at age four, Vidhar had requested the presence of a construct to accompany her everywhere. Keerthi had lived with them until Jayanthi turned eighteen. They'd traveled together as far as Southeast Asia once, to visit a girl—a former SHWA member—because she and Jayanthi had fallen in love. Or thought they had. They'd been seventeen at the time. The construct had kept Jayanthi safe and comfortable during the journey.

"What about Keerthi?"

"I'm not sure if Keerthi can handle space travel," her father said.

"We'd need a pilot to take Jaya there," Kundhina said. "Maybe they could accompany her planet-side with an incarn? With their extended memory capacity, they could store information about Jaya's medical needs."

"That's a good idea," Hamsa said. "If Jayanthi can stay healthy on Meru with no impact to its environment, then we weaken Pushkara's position. He can't argue that humans would inevitably demand a radical geoengineering of the planet. We'd need a second stage of research to demonstrate that children can be raised on the planet and then a third stage to show that those children could reproduce and pass on the necessary genes. The first generation would have to be made, like Jayanthi was." He nodded, his head gaining speed until the feathers trembled, and he pressed his hands together. "Yes, this could work nicely. I'll start drafting a research proposal for the committee right away."

"Just a minute," Vidhar said. He turned to Jayanthi. "What do you think? Do you want to go?"

All three of them looked at her. Jayanthi froze. When she'd spoken to Mina about it, she'd enthused about visiting Meru. She'd always wished she could travel through space like alloys did. So why did the thought of actually going paralyze her?

"I think we should all take some time to consider this," Vidhar said. "Sending Jaya off by herself, hundreds of light-years from home, with her poor health—it scares me."

"Of course," Hamsa said. "I'll be on Earth for three more weeks. I'll start work on the proposal in case Jaya says yes, but don't feel any pressure, my dear."

She laughed. If it all worked, if she went to Meru and proved her fitness there, if that swayed the majority of alloy voters to alter the compact, she'd make history. *No pressure, though.*

Her parents discussed Meru more often than Jayanthi did. They spoke about it so much that she eventually forbade Mina from the topic during their daily visits. Her father's phores often glowed lime green with concern. Her mother insisted that Jaya was an adult now and could make her way alone in the world. Ekene and Li Feng thought the answer was obvious. Jean expressed indifference, and Mina wasn't sure. Of the SHWAs, only Mina had witnessed Jayanthi's pain crises in person. They had taken time to understand her disorder and understood the risks.

At night, Jayanthi lay outside, gazed into the night sky, and replayed all the arguments in her head. The stars beckoned as they always had, but for the first time, reaching them didn't seem like an impossibility. If the Meru Exploration Committee approved the project, she'd get to leave Earth. Not just that, she'd get to experience long-distance travel to an extrasolar system. *Thamity gradients. Reality transits.* Concepts that she'd spent her whole life reading about, dreaming about. *Can I really do this?* Her parents thought so. Hamsa, too. What would the alloys think, especially the one assigned to look after her? Most wanted nothing to do with humans and lived on Earth only because they were forced to. Would anyone want to take care of her on Meru? If she died, it would ruin their reputation. Who would take that kind of risk?

Hamsa sent over a draft proposal after a week. The duration of stay would be fourteen months. With nearly two months of travel time in either direction, that put her return a few weeks before the general vote in eighteen months. He'd listed the required supplies, ecological risks, health risks, and personnel. He'd also requested a pilot for interstellar transportation and the use of a womb to generate the pilot's incarn, which would stay with her on the surface.

"We'll need to find someone young enough to carry you there," Kundhina commented. "The older pilots' human-compatible chambers will have atrophied."

"What about a megaconstruct?" Vidhar said. "That would be more comfortable, especially for such a long journey."

"Could we trust them?" Kundhina said. "The ones who can support humans were all built more than a hundred years ago, which means they'll be emancipated. As sovereign entities, they aren't subject to CDS jurisdiction."

"I see your point," Vidhar conceded. "We'll need to look carefully at pilots. They should have human medical capabilities, not just basic life support."

"I'll add the blood exchange machine to the equipment list," Kundhina said. She made a note in the shared version of the document.

Jayanthi traced the rings on the table surface. "I should go, right? This is a historic opportunity."

Her mother put down her tea. "It's not a matter of *should*. Do you *want* to go? This is not a venture to take half-heartedly."

Hamsa often said that alloy politics required playing a long game. Proving her physical fitness for Meru would not only bring her attention, it would gain her favor in Hamsa's eyes. He had influence with the Tarawan Ethics and Standards Council. His proposed second stage would require made children rather than naturally produced ones, and that could happen only with tarawan support. They'd also need people to raise those children. TESC favored having humans raise their own kind. Surely they'd want her on Meru for that, and if she was already there and had the necessary skills, they might allow her to design some of the planet's population. A lot of steps would have to go right along the way, and she had only one human lifetime to accomplish them, but she wasn't typical of her species. She could set her sights afar.

She returned her mother's gaze. "Yes, I want to go."

Vaha's principal instructor at Nishadas was a 320-year-old alloy who believed in the adage, "Do as I say, not as I do." She couldn't perform atmospheric maneuvers or transits—they had other teachers for those—but Ahilavathi could beat every one of them at microgravity flight and well-based slingshots.

<Congratulations,> she flashed. Phores lit across her ancient, aluminized skin as she spoke. <The six of you have received pilot's licenses to fly in microgravity, atmospheric, and quantum environments. You have passed your final exams. Some of you>—her dark-brown eyes swiveled toward Vaha for a second—<just barely. Nevertheless, you are now qualified to transport cargo and passengers across space.>

The alloys arrayed in front of her kept their phores neutral. Vaha made sure not to allow the Neptune blue of zir embarrassment to show. During the final exam, zie had followed Kaliyu's moves as best as zie could, and zir maneuver had scraped past the passing threshold.

<It has been our privilege to work with you these ten years,> Ahilavathi continued.

Next to Vaha, Kaliyu winced at the human-centric term. Angry red spotted zir arms before subsiding back into neutral blue-gray. Kaliyu had never shown much affection for humans, and lately, zie had become increasingly militant about shedding any reminders of them. Zie had tried to get Vaha interested in some of the political movements to codify this behavior. Vaha couldn't muster the same level of outrage, but zie tried to keep the peace with zir friend by accommodating the linguistic changes.

Svah for *tomorrow*, *hyas* for *yesterday*. One kaal in place of one hundred thousand seconds, about 15 percent longer than an Earth day. One hundred kaals made a masan, and a thousand defined a varsha. Vaha had to admit that the system made more sense than using the arbitrary motions of one planet, but the language of their forebears permeated everything from entertainment to entries in the Nivid. Many alloys still used the terminology of their human ancestors, making it easy to slip.

<We hope you continue to make us proud by using your skills to discover new information to add to the Nivid, but we won't think less of you if this is the culmination of your ambition.> Ahilavathi pressed her palms together, and the second principal instructor followed suit before they turned back to the school.

Three generations of students remained at Nishadas. After that, per the laws of the Constructed Democracy of Sol, the padhran would get disbanded whether they all graduated or not. The CDS mandated that alloys could not gather in the same location for longer than ten varshas. Permanent human structures—farms, villages, cities—had created most of Earth's problems. The CDS refused to perpetrate the same tragedy as they expanded civilization into the Solar System and beyond.

Kaliyu turned to Vaha and the others. <We should celebrate!> zie flashed. <Race around Venus, winner chooses the first round of bhojya flavor?>

Shantham spun with laughter. <The last thing I want to do right now is fly! I'll forfeit my turn to avoid the race. Besides, we all know you'll win.>

The others concurred, glowing with amusement, tolerance, and disbelief at Kaliyu's challenge. Vaha was still too overwhelmed with relief at passing zir final exam to join the others in their banter. They'd all finished the previous day or even earlier. Vaha had been rushed straight from Venus to their small graduation ceremony. Zie trailed behind zir cohort as they flew back to the padhran.

Kaliyu dropped back to Vaha's side. <Are you okay? You look too serious for this occasion.>

Vaha suffused zir phores with indigo. <I'm fine. Happy, too.>

<Told you that you could do it. Should've taken that bet,> zie teased. <Did you look at the list I sent you?>

<Of the Meru missions? Not yet, but I saw that you sent it.>

<Most of them are either planetary surveys from orbit or data ferrying. The surface missions are only for constructed beings right now, so you don't have to worry about gravity wells.>

<What happened to your vote of confidence?> Vaha flashed, tinting the words as a joke.

Kaliyu laughed. <I believe you could do it, but I also know how much you love to worry. You'd be good at the data ferrying. It's all microgravity flight and reality transits.> Zir phores turned serious. <I meant what I said hyas, about applying for a joint mission with you. One of the surveys would make a good compromise for us to stay together.>

<I know you pretty well, too,> Vaha flashed. <You hate tedious work like that. Besides, you have a brilliant career in racing ahead of you. Everyone says so. I would be a terrible friend if I kept you from it.>

Kaliyu had idolized microgravity racing and the sport's top pilots for as long as Vaha had known zir. Unlike the bare frames of Vaha's berth, Kaliyu's were painted in purple and gold, the skin and wing colors of zir hero, The Royal. Zir friend had no interest in the Nivid or the pursuit of knowledge, and zie was far too restless to live in stasis. As much as it broke Vaha's heart to think they'd go their separate ways soon, zie could never ask Kaliyu to give up zir dreams.

<Whatever you say,> zir friend flashed.

Kaliyu flew ahead to join the other new graduates. They crowded around a spherical bhojya dispenser that glowed with festive bioluminescence. Every one of them had grand ambitions.

Vaha wanted to be the first four-mode hybrid pilot in the universe, the destiny that zir maker had designed for zir. Veera had spent a long time on Vaha's DNA with the help of multiple tarawans. When it became clear that Vaha might never live up to zir potential, Veera had sought better opportunities. Zie chose a long-haul expedition, the one guaranteed way for a pilot to make a novel discovery. Reality transits allowed beings to cross vast distances in an instant, but only after someone took the slow, physical way to a new destination. It was risky, but Veera's goal had always been to get zir name into the Nivid. If zie made it to a new system, zie would guarantee that legacy. Zie had given Vaha ten years to prove zir worth before leaving. Vaha had no idea if Veera still lived or whether zie would ever return to Sol, but if that day came, Vaha imagined greeting zir maker with the news that Veera's name had already made it into the Nivid—as the cocreator of a novel alloy design.

Graduating from Nishadas had become Vaha's only goal after Veera's departure. Zie hadn't yet fulfilled the promise of zir DNA, but at least zie could call zirself a pilot. Zie needed more opportunities to practice the atmospheric flight modes as well as landing and launch. Earth had too much precious life to risk massive pilots crashing to its surface. A planet like Meru would be ideal, but Vaha didn't expect to get any assignments there. Zie hadn't wanted to deflate Kaliyu's enthusiasm, but a pilot with no record usually went on asteroid supply runs within the Solar System, flying to prove that they were skilled and reliable, until someone with a greater purpose requested them for a task of importance. Vaha knew what zie was fit for, and that wasn't the exploration of the most Earthlike planet ever discovered. With zir abysmal test scores, zie would be lucky to get tasked with anything.

Kaliyu glowed with excitement as zie ordered a round of celebratory drinks for their fellow graduates. Zie waved a hand at Vaha and flashed, <By the Nivid! Stop drifting alone and get over here!>

Vaha pushed zir negative thoughts aside and puffed forward. *Leave the worries for tomorrow and enjoy the moment. At least I accomplished this much, and I didn't have to cheat to do it. My maker might not feel proud of me, but my instructors do, and my friends love me. So what if they all go on to achieve more, and I end up in stasis? Like Ahilavathi said, what I've done here should be enough.*

Vaha took a bulb of blue liquid from Kaliyu's extended hand and raised it for a toast. As the bittersweet concoction trickled into zir stomach, zie imagined that it tasted like success.

—वृत

Vritha—Chosen

Jayanthi perused a list of qualified pilots, sorted by experience. After receiving her affirmative for Meru, Hamsa had submitted the project proposal to the Exploration Committee. The reaction from alloy society had been muted, with most people opining that one human couldn't do much damage to a planet and that Jayanthi would most likely sicken and possibly die. Pushkara's faction, however, made as much negative noise as they could. The pilots in the top half of the list had all declined as soon as they'd received her message. She could tell by the round-trip time delays. They had work they enjoyed and no incentive to do a favor for her parents or Hamsa. Even many of the pilots in the lower half of the list had turned down the offer to carry her to Meru. Some had considered it, but they had never flown a human, and they claimed that they didn't trust their skills to get her there safely.

She walked slow circles around their banyan tree and examined her remaining options: six recent graduates of pilot training, all of them young enough to—in theory—have a functional, human-habitable cavity in their bodies and to have trained in using it. She tried to imagine someone large enough to have a chamber the size of a bedroom inside themselves. That would make the pilots as large as Laghu, the local granary. Constructs could have almost any size, since they were built and not born, but alloys had evolved from human beings. The wombs that gestated them would have to be enormous.

Over time, alloys had expanded their genetic code to include instructions for all kinds of nonhuman features. They carried a third chromosome, dubbed Z, which included the building blocks for their not-so-organic functions like solar-power-generating wings, electrolyzing lungs, emtalk organs, and thamity-sensing organelles. The latter allowed alloys to sense the underlying energy field of the universe and harness it to traverse interplanetary distances. Pilots had an additional special ability, derived in part from their large mass, and that was to sense the quantum probabilistic nature of reality.

In the precompact and early postcompact years, alloy pilots had carried humans from Earth to the Moon and beyond, to the more populous padhrans in orbit between Venus and Earth. Some had ventured farther to study the Sun or the outer planets. That kind of exploration had waned as alloys became more capable and humans less ambitious.

Jayanthi didn't know of anyone—who wasn't an alloy—who had traveled beyond the orbital stations. Plenty of entertainment showed alloys flying through space, but none depicted the experience from the point of view of someone like her. She had no idea what it would feel like to surf a thamity gradient or transit reality. Part of her thrilled at the possibility of finding out, but another, buried deep, would be relieved if the MEC denied her the permission to visit Meru. She couldn't live on water and bhojya. She had no vents to move herself around. In space, she'd be utterly dependent on someone else.

A raindrop landed on her forehead. She gazed up. The sky had clouded over, and thunder rumbled faintly in the distance. A breeze shook the leaves overhead, carrying with it the scent of moisture.

Jayanthi moved inside and stared at the list of her remaining choices for pilots. Top ranked was a recent graduate named Kaliyu. Zir profile showed an image next to statistics about zir flight, towing, and carrying capacities, as well as zir exam scores. Zie looked like a cross between a human, a dolphin, and a fairy, with dark blue-gray skin and silver-black solar wings shaped like leaves. Zie had arms that resembled hers, but without rigid bones, and a nearly human face with stunning hazel eyes. Only the nose differed, being a slit rather than a protrusion. Kaliyu had a confident but friendly expression that attracted Jayanthi. In the abstract, she knew that zir mouth must be larger than her entire body—how else could she enter it?—but the image of zir face scaled in her head to someone who could live next door. Zie was slightly younger than her, easily of an age to be considered a friend.

Might as well start with the best of the rest, she thought. She composed a message and sent her choice to her parents and Hamsa, who would forward it to Kaliyu. She'd tried querying the pilots directly at first, but they hadn't responded to her messages.

Please let this one say yes.

With that done, she slow-blinked and cleared her vision. Rain dripped along the roots that spread through the exterior walls, dark traces against the lighter clay. Jayanthi shrugged on a shawl, grabbed an umbrella, and set out for her daily walk to Mina's house.

She stayed on stone surfaces to avoid damaging the wet soil. Lightning traced the rounded peak of Mount Lakash. Soggy vines dangled from the walls of the homes she passed, and rivulets of reddish-brown water ran between the gaps in the flagstone road. Thunder roared above, and an alert flashed unbidden in her vision: *Flash-flood danger in your area; please return to your home.*

With a sigh, Jayanthi turned back. The rains hadn't let up for two days, and she missed seeing Mina in person. Her friend had cheered upon hearing Jayanthi's decision, but Jayanthi knew them well enough to sense their envy, too. Mina had tried valiantly to hide it. Both of them had expected that Mina would leave Earth at some point, but they never dreamed Jayanthi would, especially to such a distant location.

"I wish you could come with me," Jayanthi had told Mina in full sincerity.

"Do your job well enough, and one day, we'll get to see Meru together," Mina had replied. "If you succeed, then Hamsa's amendment might actually win in the general vote, and then, if the later stages go well, Sahaya Amritsavar will get her way, and humanity will live on a second planet. Besides, I still intend to become a Voice and at least get into orbit. I will see space, one way or another."

A brilliant flash illuminated the world around Jayanthi as she returned home. The air rent with a vicious crack, and she hurried past the damp privacy curtain. She shook out the umbrella and hung it from a peg.

Kundhina peered around from the kitchen. "I told you not to bother going out in this weather. Come in here and have some tea."

Jayanthi perched on a squat, three-legged stool and took the warm ceramic mug from her mother. The refreshing aroma of tulsi and ginger rose with the steam.

Jayanthi stared into the amber liquid. "What if all the pilots turn me down?"

Her mother patted her hand. "I'm sure one of the new graduates will say yes. You should have listened to my advice and started at the bottom. Their placement doesn't mean they're unskilled, only less experienced."

"But what if?" she persisted, ignoring her mother's I-told-you-so.

"Then we'll find a construct who's willing and able and hope for the best," Kundhina said. She spread her hands, palms facing up in a gesture of ambivalence common to humans and alloys. "The MEC is still reviewing Hamsa's application to let you go. Even if a pilot says yes, the committee could say no."

Jayanthi grimaced. "Now that I've decided that I *want* to go to Meru, it kills me to think I might not be able to."

"This is a good, healthy place for you to call home. You can't measure yourself by the standards of alloys. You don't see your father or me doing that, right? And we're happy. Life has as much meaning as you give it."

And that was the crux of the problem. Her parents had chosen to live on Earth. She hadn't.

"Perhaps it's our fault," Kundhina said. "We thought we could raise a human child, but maybe we weren't capable enough."

Jayanthi placed a tea-warmed hand over her mother's. "Oh, Ma, it's not that. You're the best parents—the only ones I could ever want."

"Then why aren't you satisfied being here, being human?"

My humanity isn't the problem, she almost said. But then again, maybe her mother had had the truth of it. Deep down, she wished she'd been born an alloy, free to move about the universe, unconstrained by the need for a habitable climate, atmosphere, and magnetic field. To have the intellect for research and discovery. To pursue any dream and aspiration. To become a tarawan and fulfill the truest purpose of any life-form: gathering novel information, passing knowledge to successive generations.

"I have . . . ambition." The word tasted like mud in the back of Jayanthi's throat.

"You can accomplish a lot right here," Kundhina said. "Think of the gardens at Varanasi or the light sculptures of Angapore. You could write, or make immersives, or design games."

"I know, Ma, but . . ."

"But you're afflicted with a different desire."

And we can cure you. Jayanthi felt grateful that her mother left the words unsaid. She knew her parents had discussed getting her gene therapy for AAD, as they had for her sickle cell disease. Both required Jayanthi's consent as an adult. If the MEC didn't approve the project, perhaps she ought to consider the option seriously. Like Jean, maybe it would free her to find something else to do.

Kundhina stood and moved to the stove. "What have you learned about Meru?"

"New information is coming by courier every day," Jayanthi said, perking up at the change of subject. No one had asked her to look through the data—that would fall under alloy responsibility—but they hadn't barred her access, either. "The primary considerations for my visit are the climate and geography. Hamsa chose a site that's close to the equator. It's more temperate, and it's near a small lake, so we'll have access to fresh water. With the higher oxygen and lower carbon dioxide levels, it's cold on Meru compared to here. Average surface air temperature across the planet is five Celsius, and ten Celsius at my landing site. I'll need warmer clothing and boots."

"Boots?"

"A type of shoe that covers my feet and lower legs. Oh, and insulated gloves and a warm hat. Think medieval Europe during the mini ice age."

After the alloys had figured out how to guide the earth's ecosystems, the human population had limited itself to habitable zones, mostly around the middle latitudes, away from the poles and the equator. Gradual genetic changes had removed the need for climate-controlled housing and reduced the amount of material expended on clothing and shoes. It also kept people close to their food sources. Inoculation at an early age meant that people had to opt in for having children rather than the other way around, and humanity's natural inertia meant that few bothered. Between that and the exodus of alloys, the human population on Earth had dropped considerably from its peak. Small groups lived in less hospitable areas in order to preserve their cultures or steer clear of alloy oversight, but most people preferred more comfortable living conditions.

"I'll have food for up to fourteen months on the surface plus two months of travel in each direction, and we'll grow fresh vegetables once we're on Meru."

"What about medical supplies?" Kundhina said as she cleaned the teapot.

"It's from really old information, but Hamsa put together a list: vitamin and mineral supplements, diagnostic and immune-boosting microconstructs, my blood exchange machine, wound care. I expect to stay healthy in Meru's elevated oxygen, but I'll have air tanks for my suit that can serve for space emergencies as well as protection in Meru's environment. For shelter, we'll have a double-walled tent. And for a medical emergency, we'll have access to a womb in orbit. They can put me in a coma and tow me home in one if they have to."

Kundhina sighed. It wasn't a natural alloy gesture, but her parents had learned to mimic human body language for social reasons. At some point, the acts had turned into second nature.

"Let's hope you won't need that facility," her mother said. "With alloys in orbit and an incarn on the surface with you, you shouldn't have any serious trouble. Sounds like all that's left is to get approval from the MEC."

Jayanthi nodded. *That and a pilot who's willing to take a human to Meru,* she thought. *But what can someone like me offer as incentive to someone like that?*

The next day, the rain finally cleared. Afternoon sunlight slanted through the windows and warmed the house. Mina came over to watch the Meru Exploration Committee's meeting regarding Hamsa's proposal. Jayanthi, Mina, Kundhina, and Vidhar arranged their chairs to face the viewing wall. They used a screen in deference to Mina, who didn't have an emchannel. Tea and cumin-seed crackers sat on the table before them. Jayanthi sipped at her cup as the meeting began.

Nine committee members floated in a circle at the apex of a conical room. Alcoves studded the walls, though all sat empty. The members were alloys who resided at the Primary Nivid, a vast, permanent structure that included the archive, support staff, and research administrators. Unlike the enormous alloy pilots, the committee members had a more human size, though they also had solar wings and tails in place of legs.

After preliminary formalities, the chairperson flashed a summary of Hamsa's proposal. Their words appeared as text on the bottom of the viewing screen. "The study is an addendum to an existing soil sampling project and will involve testing the health of a human being on Meru's surface. The duration of stay is up to fourteen months. The subject has sickle cell disease as well as a specific medication or gene therapy to moderate its effects, as specified in Appendix A. The purpose of the first stage is to evaluate the viability of natural-born humans on Meru. If the results are positive, we will review subsequent stages for approval. An alloy incarn will accompany the human in order to maintain adherence to environmental safety rules as well as to address any needs. The committee members have had the required time to review the full proposal. We'll now open for discussion."

After half an hour of debate, Mina laid their hand on Jayanthi's shoulder and said, "Looks like it's six against and three in favor right now."

Each member had an allotted time to speak and rebut the others. The chairperson had a persuasive style, and they spoke in favor of the proposal. After another hour, each of the nine members presented their final statements. Two of them had changed their stance, allowing that the safety protocols were stringent and that the presence of one human and one alloy incarn was unlikely to cause permanent damage. They also made it clear that they expected Jayanthi to sicken and that the results of the experiment would demonstrate the unfitness of humans for Meru.

Jayanthi glanced at her mother as she slipped into the kitchen. A few minutes later, Kundhina emerged with four goblets and set them on the regen-redwood table.

Effervescent wine sparkled in the golden glow of sunset, but Jayanthi wasn't quite ready to celebrate. *Not until they approve it.* She held her breath as the votes came in. Three against. Then four in favor. Then one more in favor! The proposal received approval with a five to four final tally.

Mina grinned without a speck of envy on their face. "Congrats, Jaya! You're going to Meru." They stood and pulled Jayanthi up for a hug.

Then her parents piled on, and then they were all raising their bubbly drinks in a toast.

Jayanthi fell back into the sling chair with a massive exhalation, woozy with relief and trepidation. "I didn't think it would happen."

Vidhar reached over a hand and squeezed hers. "You're going to make history," he said. "I'm so proud of you."

They sipped at their goblets and watched the reactions from all over Earth and space trickle in. Sahaya Amritsavar sent Jayanthi a personal message of congratulations and thanks. Bantri expressed her displeasure and reiterated the position that humans belonged only on Earth. Jayanthi shrugged off both of their opinions. The two politicians had never taken an interest in her life circumstances, and they had no claim on her just because she was doing something that interested them.

She cared more about the jubilant messages from her fellow SHWAs: "Make us proud," and "You vent-spawned weller, I am so jealous of you," and "Take care of yourself." Mina couldn't stop laughing.

As night fell, the excitement tapered off, leaving Jayanthi with a bone-deep exhaustion. After seeing Mina off, she got herself ready for bed. She lay on her cot, tired but unable to keep her eyes closed. Thoughts rose and fell like waves in a storm. *I'm going to Meru. They're treating me like an experiment. I'm going to fly through space! What will the alloys think of me?*

A new message arrived from Hamsa. She eagerly thought-retrieved it.

"I regret to say that Kaliyu has declined our offer," Hamsa said. "Zie didn't give any reason, and it's particularly surprising in light of my prior work with zir maker. I confirmed that zir response came after the committee's decision, so I didn't bother second-guessing it. Send me your next choice, Jaya. We'll keep trying. Now that the vote has gone in our favor, I'm sure someone will accept."

Jayanthi stared at the ceiling. Disappointment weighted her chest, and she wondered how Hamsa could remain optimistic. *The committee has their own agenda, and they're setting me up to fail. They practically admitted so. Why else would they support this project? No pilot is going to risk their future by taking me to Meru on this doomed expedition, not even a brand-new one. If I were in their shoes, I'd say no, too.*

After a poor night's sleep, Jayanthi headed to Mina's house early so they could help her select the next candidate pilot. She was too despondent to make the decision alone. Sunlight broke through the gray clouds that scudded above as she walked, and the damp air was redolent with the scents of wet earth. Trees showered her with droplets when the wind shook their branches.

She took the city route for expediency. Her fatigue had increased, probably from the rushes of adrenaline over the past several days. The HO treatment would prevent some effects of sickle cell, but it wasn't a cure. *If I can't tolerate this much stress, how will I endure the journey to Meru and back?* She couldn't do another blood exchange so soon after the last one. The machine wouldn't have cultured enough new, healthy red blood cells.

Jayanthi ducked through the Andakas' privacy curtain as the skies opened in a shower of rain. Mina had agreed to help her sort the list of remaining candidates, ordering it from best to worst so that Jayanthi didn't have to agonize over the choice each time someone turned her down. *Such confidence we have in this endeavor.*

"Just in time," Mina said.

They chose to sit in her friend's bedroom, where they wouldn't be disturbed. Facing a blank viewing wall, Jayanthi slow-blinked to activate her emchannel interface. She thought-sent the remaining pilot names and profiles to the screen on Mina's wall.

"And then there were five," Jayanthi said.

"You only need one of them to say yes. Is there anything that sets them apart?"

"Only their test scores. Their averages aren't too far off, except for one terribly low performer, but they have different weak spots."

Mina arranged the five pilots as tiles in a pentagon. They stood and scrutinized the result, then pointed at the person on the apex.

"This one is the best-looking," they said with a grin. "If you have no other basis for choice, why not go with that?"

Jayanthi had to admit that her friend was right. The alloy pilot, named Vaha, had blue-black skin, violet eyes, and golden solar wings shaped like a bird's, rectangular with rounded corners. The combination of colors was stunning, and the delicacy of zir birdlike wings set zir apart from the others. Zir body tapered into a long, elegant tail with split fins. At some point during centuries of directed evolution, alloys had realized they didn't need their ancestral human legs anymore. Pilots in particular favored the genetic elements of sea creatures, whose contours were better suited for travel through space, but they had variations like any population.

She took a closer look at Vaha's profile and groaned. "Zie has the worst average. Good scores for reality transits. Not great for microgravity flight, and rock bottom for gravity wells. That's not promising for someone who has to navigate around Meru."

Mina frowned. "True, but zie is a qualified pilot, and it's not like you'll be doing any complicated maneuvers around the planet. You said that a construct would handle landing and takeoff."

Jayanthi continued reading about Vaha, her attention caught by the pilot's story. Zie was two years younger than her, but zie had been emancipated at age ten when zir maker left the Solar System. Alloys matured faster than human beings, and they typically reached adulthood at age fifteen. The profile stated that zie had lived around the Moon for zir early years before moving to Nishadas, a flight training padhran. Zie had a unique genetic design that would allow zir to land and take off from a planet, but zie had never succeeded at those maneuvers. Jayanthi knew she shouldn't compare alloy development to a human's, but she couldn't help feeling sorry for young Vaha.

A footnote caught her eye. Vaha's maker had left zir with a womb. *An unusual bequest.* Possessions were rare for alloys, who discouraged attachment to material goods. The footnote also listed each replenishment of the womb's resources, correlated with each major usage. Vaha had injured zirself a lot in zir younger years, and zie continued to use the womb for partial rebirths into the present. Did that mean Vaha would bring zir womb to Meru? Would Jayanthi have access to it during their travels?

"What are you smiling about?" Mina asked.

"Vaha has something more than good looks to set zir apart from the others. Zie owns a womb."

"So?"

"Wombs have built-in genetic simulators. That's how they monitor embryo and fetal development. They look at gene expression and make changes in real time to align with the original design. Not only could I improve the viability of my hybrid, I could use live data from Meru to adjust my design for the planet."

"I thought Hamsa said that hybrid designs lead to catastrophic results."

"They did—seven hundred years ago! Things have changed. We have vastly more knowledge, better simulation capability, and much better womb technology. In the Human Era, genetic engineering of humans was completely illegal. Now we do it every day without a second thought. We don't have to repeat the mistakes of the past with hybrids, either, but I need a chance to prove that. Besides," she said, unable to keep the bitterness from her tone, "as long I'm only doing simulations—purely theoretical work—how does it matter?"

"And what makes you think Vaha would let you use zir womb?"

"I haven't figured that part out," she said, "but at least I'd have the option. I'd have months to try to convince zir. Maybe Vaha wants to get into the Nivid. Doesn't every alloy? I could offer zir co-credit."

Mina shrugged and smiled. "Fine with me. Womb or not, zie is my first choice anyway."

"You are so shallow."

"The heart wants what it wants, Jaya. I can't help it. Now let's rank the rest."

The other pilots didn't have personal histories as interesting as Vaha's, so Jayanthi let Mina's heart sort them out. As they discoursed about alloy fashions and looks, Jayanthi sent Vaha's contact information to Hamsa. She could only wait and hope.

—प्रहुति

Prahuthi—Sacrifice

Vaha's batch at Nishadas was breaking up. Half of the graduating pilots had already accepted their first commissions and departed. Their sleeping berths floated in a stack, collapsed for towing to other padhrans. Kaliyu had received offers from two different racing teams. Zie hadn't accepted either one. Zie said zie would wait until something came through for Vaha, but Vaha knew that zir friend couldn't put off the decision much longer. They had applied to some joint projects at Meru, but Kaliyu's speed and skills notwithstanding, the likelihood of getting any of them was next to nothing.

No one had approached Vaha for solo work. Ahilavathi had agreed to let zir stay at Nishadas for an extra month, but after that, zie would have to go elsewhere. If zie had nothing to do by then, zie would find a stasis berth and resign zirself to permanent failure as a pilot. Hundreds of billions of alloys—nearly three-quarters of the population—lived in a low-energy state. They orbited the Sun, absorbing its energy, with minimal servicing to replenish their water and bhojya. Some of them produced works of pure intellect—art, entertainment, information science, mathematics—while others consumed their creations. Entire abstract societies had built up around different topics and interests. The most brilliant had contributed to the Nivid.

Alloys who craved a more physical existence sometimes looked down on those in stasis, calling them half-lives or worse, but Vaha had never understood that. If the people in stasis were happy, and they weren't harming others or violating the compact, zie didn't see a reason to denigrate their existence. That didn't mean zie wanted the life for zirself, though. Stasis meant that zie would have to forgo any high-energy use of zir body. The longer zie remained idle, the less the chance that anyone would come to zir for flight-related skills. Zie might not hate it. Zie might even enjoy the life of the mind. But zie would never become the pilot that zir maker desired. When Veera returned to the system, Vaha wanted to greet zir as a successful adult, not the confirmation of zir worst expectations.

In the meantime, zie practiced maneuvers with Kaliyu or drifted in zir berth, playing games, listening to music, and watching shows. Zie had just finished the third episode of *Across the Orbit*, a comedy of errors about a childless alloy, a bumbling communications construct, and an incompetent tarawan, when zie received a message from someone named Hamsa.

Vaha played the recording and nearly flashed in surprise at the contents. *A mission to Meru, ferrying a human, and living with her on the planet for over a full Earth-year. They want* me *to do it?* The purpose was to discover whether this human's genetic particulars were well suited to Meru's environment. *Why would anyone care if that were true?*

The local database had no information about Hamsa or this human, a person named Jayanthi with a female designation. Vaha sent a query to the nearest copy of the Nivid. Ten minutes later, zie received a reply. Hamsa was an experienced tarawan and also a voter proxy for policy relating to human space travel. Vaha had never paid much attention to politics. Every adult—alloy, human, or construct—in the Constructed Democracy of Sol had a right to vote on any law, but most people didn't have time to research them all, so they designated proxies. Vaha had defaulted to Veera's proxies. Zie figured zir maker's opinions would match zir own and had given no thought to the choices since then.

It seemed that some people, like Hamsa, believed that humans deserved to live on planets besides Earth. Vaha had learned some of their history in zir childhood, but zie'd forgotten most of the details, including why humans were constrained to their homeworld. Something about their mismanagement of Mars, which had led to that planet's stormy state, and pollution on Earth. But both planets had improved since then, and the compact kept everyone happy, or so Vaha had been taught.

Zie didn't care what happened with human beings, but this Meru mission had the potential to discover novel information, worthy of an entry into the Nivid. Zie recalled what Kaliyu had said—that only constructs had been allowed to land on Meru's surface until recently, for fear of biocontamination. How had the offer to carry a human to the planet come to zir, of all people? Surely better pilots than zirself would get a project with this much potential? Had they turned it down for some reason?

Vaha looked closer at the human's profile. She was barely into her adult years, with dark-brown skin, even darker eyes, and thick black hair that curled past her shoulders. Her oval face had a strong chin and sharp cheekbones, and her wide eyes and generous mouth were set in a serious expression. Her profile stated that she'd been raised by alloy parents on Earth. *Strange.* She had a checkered medical history due to sickle cell disease and would need careful oversight to make sure she didn't harm herself or the planet. Part of the task would require learning human physiology and medicine.

Vaha would have to ferry quite a few supplies to support Jayanthi during transit and on Meru. Zie had no idea what that would be like. Not one of zir instructors had ever carried a human passenger. Alloys were far easier to transport, needing only sunlight, water, and minimal nutrition, and many could attach themselves to the outside of a pilot for a faster ride.

Is that why this project came to me? If this human got sick or injured, the pilot's reputation would suffer. *Except that mine probably can't get any worse.*

This could be zir best shot at earning some respect as a pilot. If zie could keep the human alive and well, zie'd have the gratitude of Hamsa and his supporters, whose numbers seemed significant. Zie would have to create an incarn to send to Meru's surface, another experience zie'd never had, but zir true body would orbit a planet with air like Earth's. Zie could keep practicing atmospheric flight, maybe even try a launch from the surface with zir true body, something zie hadn't attempted since zir time at the Moon. Zie had grown stronger and more skilled since then. If zie could escape from Meru's gravity well, zie would finally fulfill the potential of zir genetic design.

Vaha glanced at Kaliyu's sleeping form in the adjacent berth. If zie accepted this offer, zie would also liberate zir friend. Kaliyu had stalled enough, remaining at Nishadas far longer than zie needed to. Zir friend didn't really want to go to Meru anyway. The offer to go jointly with Vaha came from Kaliyu's good-heartedness—or pity. It didn't matter which. Vaha didn't have a lot to offer zir friend, but by taking this contract, zie could free Kaliyu of any guilt at joining a racing team. With a mix of trepidation and relief, Vaha composed a message to Hamsa and accepted his offer.

Vaha was in the middle of the fifth episode of *Across the Orbit* when Kaliyu stirred and stretched, extending zirself to the full span of zir berth.

Vaha cleared the show from zir vision and turned to zir friend, unable to contain zir news. <Guess what? I got an offer for an

eighteen-month contract,> zie flashed. <You'll never guess where—it's as unbelievable as a breathing construct!>

Kaliyu's phores flickered with amusement. <Okay, so what is it? A trip to the Oort?>

Vaha shook zir head in the negative. <I'll give you a hint. It has something to do with Meru.>

Confusion rippled through Kaliyu's phores, then changed to dismay. <Oh no, not that human one!>

<You know about it?> But as Vaha flashed the words, zie realized the obvious: they must have approached Kaliyu already. As zie had guessed, better pilots than zirself had turned down the project.

<You're not seriously considering it?> Kaliyu flashed.

<I—>

<You have to turn it down!>

<Why?>

<Because the objective is to see if humans are fit to live on Meru. You should never help a human being.> Anger pulsed through Kaliyu's phores.

Vaha recoiled. Zie hadn't expected such a strong reaction from Kaliyu. Zir friend had been increasingly against anything Earth-centric, but why such venom against humankind? They'd all descended from common ancestors. Most alloys considered it their duty to take care of their distant cousins, even if that meant remaking themselves to serve on Earth.

<Why are you so against this?> Vaha flashed, carefully keeping zir phores neutral. <If it's legal and permitted, it can't be all that bad, right?>

<Remember your history? Humans are terrible people. First they polluted Earth, then they turned Mars into a hot, stormy hellhole when they tried to terraform it. Now they want to do the same to Meru. They have no gratitude for the work alloys and constructs do to keep Earth clean and safe and livable or the work our tarawans do to maintain

genetic diversity and adaptability. They're stuck in the same old selfish gene-set they evolved from.>

Vaha glowed in surprise at Kaliyu's vehemence. <Why are you bothered by all that? Also, to be fair, they aren't planning to terraform Meru. They're testing whether this one human can adapt to it.>

<And if that happens, then what? Hamsa is trying to get the compact itself changed, to allow humans to live on Meru. He said this is preliminary research, but you know it won't take them long to push for more. An entire faction of human beings wants to go back to the Human Era ways.>

Vaha glowed with dim bafflement.

<You have no idea what I'm going on about, do you?> Kaliyu's phores faded to neutral as zie calmed down. <You should really pay more attention to current events and politics. I'm sorry if I sounded angry with you. I know none of this is your doing, but I hate Hamsa. He's been interfering with alloy lives in favor of humans for too long.> Kaliyu's phores flickered through a tangle of upset colors. <My maker . . . everything that happened to zir, everything that led to zir death . . . it was all Hamsa's fault.>

Vaha went white with surprise. <You never told me that!>

Kaliyu rotated partially away and gazed into the black. Zie never liked to talk about zir past, and zir maker had died years before zie arrived at Nishadas. In spite of their close friendship, Vaha knew little more than that. It was impossible to make Kaliyu reveal anything that zie didn't want to. Vaha's friend had a personality as radiant as the Sun, but that bright exterior hid zir innermost thoughts well.

The phores along Kaliyu's visible side flashed. <When I was barely one varsha old, my maker volunteered for an experimental genetic alteration, to be remade into a form large enough to carry hundreds of human passengers. Megaconstructs need a lot of metal, but carbon and silicates are plentiful, so people thought having an alloy that size would

be more environmentally sustainable. They also thought that an alloy would maintain better psychological stability.>

Vaha glowed in understanding. Megaconstructs often turned into drifters after they attained emancipation, leaving known space or traversing through it on their own inscrutable agendas.

<The genetic design was Hamsa's. The project was largely his idea, too. He wanted a way to allow humans to explore without having an impact on nonconsenting bodies.>

Kaliyu paused. Zir phores glowed a riot of conflicting emotional colors. Whatever had happened, it wasn't good.

<My maker went through three deaths and rebirths in the period of one varsha.>

Vaha couldn't suppress a white flash of shock. Any alloy could choose partial rebirth when their bodies had naturally aged, or if they underwent physical trauma, but that process maintained continuity of consciousness—their cells were renewed by a gradual transformation. Rebirth after death was rarely approved. It broke continuity, and the trauma of returning to consciousness after death was great. Three times was the maximum allowed for anyone. To go through that in such a brief time—Vaha shuddered.

<Exactly.> Kaliyu glowed pink-orange with bitterness. <My maker agreed to it for the prestige, but in the end, zir new body design never succeeded. It wasn't viable, though Hamsa claimed the design could work with the right base gene-set. The project committee assigned my maker to a weller form. They wanted zir to serve humans on Earth to make up for the resources consumed by the multiple rebirths.> Kaliyu shuddered and turned back to Vaha. All zir lids were open, and zir hazel eyes had gone tight with the same rage that infused zir phores. <The incarn separation failed—probably because zie had been remade so many times—and zie died.>

<I'm so sorry,> Vaha flashed.

<Now do you understand why I despise human beings? If they hadn't pushed to travel in space, none of that would've happened. My maker would still be alive. They should be content with what they have on Earth! When I saw that offer to carry a human to Meru—coming from Hamsa, no less—I knew I had to decline it. He stands for everything I hate. He practically worships humans. Because they're our cousins and our ancestors, he says. He's a makerless mudha! If you have family members who are terrible people, you should protect the world from them. Instead, Hamsa wants to enable them. If you're my friend, you won't take his offer.>

<I . . . I already accepted it,> Vaha admitted.

Kaliyu glowed with anger again. <Then rescind it. Tell him you don't want it. You don't have to do this, Vaha! You can get something better.>

<That's easy for you to say!> Vaha shot back. <You already have two of your favorite racing teams asking for you, and you'll probably get more. Look, I'm sorry about what happened to your maker, I truly am.> Zie reached out a hand and touched Kaliyu's shoulder. <But I think you're being a little unfair. It doesn't sound like humans are to blame, and neither is Hamsa. If anyone's at fault, it's the project committee that assigned your maker to Earth.>

Kaliyu shook zir head. <None of it would've happened if it weren't for Hamsa and his beloved humans. My maker wouldn't have been anywhere near Earth; zie wouldn't have tried to produce a thrice-made incarn—literally—if not for their petty desire to travel through space.>

As gently as zie could, Vaha flashed, <Your maker was an adult, and zie made zir choices. I finally have a chance to do something worthwhile with my life. Shouldn't I get to choose, too?>

<You'll have other offers and opportunities.> Kaliyu's phores matched zir skin in an emotionless neutral blue-gray. <You should have more faith in yourself.> Zie rotated until zir back faced Vaha.

"Well, I don't," Vaha sent, switching to emtalk. Irritation shot through zir like an errant solar flare. "I'm not like you. My flying abilities have been hard-won. I've struggled and persevered, and now I have a license, and I would like to put it to good use instead of ending up in stasis."

"The only reason they offered you this contract is because no one else would take it."

Vaha's vents tightened as if Kaliyu had physically struck zir. "Now you're being a mudha."

"And you're a makerless half-life. If you insist on going through with this, then you can stop calling yourself my friend."

Fine. I don't care. Vaha called up the next episode of *Across the Orbit.* Five minutes into it, zie realized that zie hadn't absorbed a single word. Zie looked sidelong at Kaliyu, but zir friend's body still faced away. Alloys couldn't cry. They'd given up on tear ducts early in their evolution, but Vaha could feel the vestigial nerves pricking behind zir eyes. How had a moment of joy and triumph turned into this? *Don't let our friendship end like this,* zie wanted to beg, but what little pride zie had left wouldn't allow it.

Vaha had watched zir maker's back retreat in the same kind of silence. Not a trace of regret had colored Veera's phores when zie departed for the decades-long excursion to reach new star systems. Not a word of comfort or encouragement had come through on their emchannel. Just a dark mass moving away from Vaha as zie flew toward Nishadas, alone.

I don't want us to leave here the same way. Surely Kaliyu's temper would cool off before zir departure? *But what if it doesn't?*

Then gravity could take zir!

As much as it hurt, Vaha nurtured the flame of resentment growing in zir belly. How dare Kaliyu berate zir for taking the first decent contract to come zir way? Not merely decent—full of discoverability! If Vaha couldn't earn zir maker's respect by succeeding at hybrid flight, perhaps zie could get zir name in the Nivid for a different reason. And with eighteen months orbiting an Earthlike environment, zie might accomplish both. Zie could stretch zir wings to soar like a bird. Zie could try zir air jets to launch from the ground. If Kaliyu couldn't see the value in that, maybe zie was the one who couldn't call zirself a friend.

But a glance at Kaliyu's form dissolved all of Vaha's vitriol in a pool of regret. *You're my best friend. I'm not trying to break your heart. Why can't you see that?*

—

It didn't take long for Vaha to receive confirmation from Hamsa and instructions to travel to Earth straightaway. In the intervening time, Kaliyu continued to ignore zir, even when Vaha begged zir to say goodbye. Kaliyu remained in zir berth, eyes closed under all three lids.

This is not how I imagined departing for my first piloting mission.

Zie spent a day packing up for the journey from Venus to Earth. The planets were neither perfectly aligned nor in opposition, and the hundred million kilometers separating the two would take about a week of travel at a brisk, but not fast, 175 KPS. Vaha's carry pack had several compartments, including one for pure water and another for bhojya. The kitchen construct wished zir well as Vaha filled up on both liquids.

Zie attached the pack around zir torso, its top resting against the base of zir wings and the rest ballooning outward in a bell shape over zir lower back. Zie unhooked zir womb from the padhran and clipped its harness to zir belt. After the Meru project, zie shouldn't need it anymore. Its token had a brief list of owners, originally the Committee for Reproductive Affairs, then zir maker, and then zirself. Perhaps zie could return it to the government. At least zie had a good excuse for hauling it around in the meantime. Owning something that wouldn't fit in a pack was an embarrassment, and zie would be glad to be rid of it.

Kaliyu hadn't spoken a word to zir since their argument. Vaha fought slowness in zir limbs and hollowness in zir chest at the thought of leaving without a goodbye. At least zir instructor and the other alloys at Nishadas gave Vaha a friendly send-off. Zie was somewhat cheered by that, but as zie began the flight to Earth, zie couldn't help looking back at Kaliyu's outline until it blurred into the rest of the structure.

Vaha sent a parting message and hoped Kaliyu would read it. "I hope you find it in your heart to forgive me one day. I have treasured our friendship these last varshas, and I'm sad to see it lost."

And then zie turned zir attention forward and inward. Zie breathed in a lungful of water, then, with a long exhale, flooded zir body with oxygen. Zie activated the thamity-sensing part of zir mind. Field gradients cut through the Solar System, warping around matter both visible and dark, in arcs so vast that they dwarfed Vaha's scale. Zie moved across them, zir entire body acting as a single organ to harness the differential, converting the energy carried by thamitons into motion.

Vaha followed a slope that accelerated zir at half the rate of Earth's gravity. Zie maintained that for ten hours, taking a short break each hour. The level of focus required for thamity field travel wasn't as deep as for a reality transit, but to sustain it for hours or days was mentally and physically exhausting.

Once Vaha gained enough momentum, zie disengaged and continued at a steady speed toward Earth. Zie sipped water and bhojya to hydrate and regain strength. For the next six days, zie had nothing to do but continue on zir current course toward Earth. Zie had stored a hundred episodes of *Across the Orbit* in zir extended memory and called up episode six. The opening scene reminded zir of the falling-out with Kaliyu, and zie felt a pang. Had they been on speaking terms, they could have emtalked throughout the journey. Instead, Vaha sank into the entertainment, alone once more in the vast spaces between planets.

—व्यवस्था

Vyavasthaa—Agreement

Kaliyu had almost given in, had almost turned to say goodbye to zir dearest—former—friend, but zie had held strong. *Don't shame the family by turning into a human lover like your maker,* zir grandmaker had said many varshas earlier. If Vaha was determined to help Hamsa and work on a human-centric project, then their friendship was doomed. Better to make a clean break than draw it out.

That didn't make it hurt less, though. Kaliyu had told Vaha what no one else at Nishadas knew. Zie had revealed the shame that rotted the heart of zir maker, and still Vaha had chosen to stab zir in the gut, as if their varshas together at Nishadas had meant nothing. *What's the matter with you?* But zie knew the answer. Vaha had always lacked confidence in zirself, leading zir to make poor choices regarding the future. Kaliyu couldn't understand it. Vaha had perfectly good skills in certain aspects of piloting. Instead of playing to those strengths, zie insisted on following the path set by zir maker like a moon trapped in a decaying orbit. It made Kaliyu almost grateful that zir own maker had died. Nidra hadn't had the opportunity to disturb zir psyche the way Vaha's maker had.

Zie packed up the decorations around zir berth and tried to shake loose the melancholy that kept threatening to surround zir thoughts.

Two different racing teams had offered zir a position, and zie'd finally chosen. One had performed better in recent events, but the Majestics had given rise to Kaliyu's hero, The Royal. Their coaches were older, and many fans thought their methods too old-fashioned, but Kaliyu had decided to join them anyway. Zie could bring in new skills and attitudes, perhaps revive the team's former glory. The Royal had retired many varshas earlier, so Kaliyu wouldn't get to work with him, but zie would get to drape zirself in the signature purple and gold of his team.

Flying had always been Kaliyu's refuge. It had come easy to zir, thanks to a generous contribution from zir maker's gene-set. Nidra had had a magnificent pilot's body, lacking only in thrust power for gravity, which zie had remedied in Kaliyu's design. By the age of seven, Kaliyu had grown to full size, and none of zir pilot friends could beat zir in a microgravity race.

Zir gravity maneuvers and reality transits were of more middling skill, but they mattered less for racing. Not many pilots could do all three at all, much less with equal proficiency. That's why zie had been so excited to meet Vaha. Another multimodal pilot! They had so much in common.

By the Nivid, stop thinking about Vaha!

The others at Nishadas, including their instructor Ahilavathi, hadn't commented on the obvious falling-out between zir and Vaha. For that, Kaliyu was grateful, but their studied ignorance cast its own shadow, and zie felt relieved that zie was leaving. Once zie reached the Majestics' training padhran, out past Mars's orbit, zie would have plenty to keep zir occupied. *Work the body to calm the mind.* Zie needed to get moving.

The bare frame of zir berth stared back at zir. In the space of a few kaals, everything had changed. Would zie ever see Vaha again? The Solar System was a vast place, and the odds of finding someone by accident were minuscule. Kaliyu filed zir planned flight path with the Nishadas construct and took leave of zir instructors and the younger students. In a few kaals, zie would arrive at zir new home and begin to forge the bonds of friendship with zir teammates. With one last look at Nishadas and Venus, zie rotated away and began zir journey to the next chapter of zir life.

Not too far from Earth's orbit, Kaliyu received a notification from another pilot that they had a passenger who wished to meet with Kaliyu. They were traveling faster in order to catch up and would intersect zir flight path in eight kilas. The message contained no details about the passenger or why they wanted to meet Kaliyu, leaving zir somewhat nonplussed and curious. What could be so important that someone would personally chase zir across the system?

Kaliyu replied and said zie would stop accelerating so they could match speeds. Zie disengaged zir thamity organelles and brought zir awareness back to visual space. The Sun's rays bent around zir peripheral vision, but ahead, zie saw only stars. Zie dropped all three of zir tinted membranes over zir eyes and turned. Before long, zie could see the other pilot's wings as a speck of reflected light. It grew larger with each passing hectas until Kaliyu could resolve the body, and then the smaller figure that clung to the pilot.

The alloy detached themself from the pilot and vented toward Kaliyu. They hailed Kaliyu via emtalk.

"Hello, Kaliyu. My name is Pushkara. May I approach you to have a private conversation?"

Kaliyu could not have been more surprised if a wormhole had opened in front of zir. "Yes, I'll wait here."

The pilot remained where they were, far enough that it would be impossible to read any phoric on Kaliyu's skin. Could this be *the* Pushkara? The ancient champion of planetary rights? If so, what could he possibly want that he had traveled all this way to speak privately with

Kaliyu? As the other alloy neared, Kaliyu could see the humanoid form, which confirmed zir suspicions.

Pushkara was as old as the compact, and he had a body to show it. The oldest alloys had minimal genetic changes relative to human beings. Much of their space-worthiness came from external augments, and they needed partial rebirths far more often than subsequent generations. Unlike Kaliyu, Pushkara didn't have water-based lungs. He needed an external electrolysis machine to feed oxygen and hydrogen into his body. He had to consume a greater variety of organic matter than what bhojya would provide. And yet he posed the greatest opposition to the factions that supported human emigration from Earth. Respect for his work earned the concessions that had let him live for so many centuries.

Up close, Kaliyu could see the external lungs nestled between Pushkara's wings. His legs were fused and ended in webbed feet rather than fins. His rigid solar wings jutted outward, fabric stretched over rectilinear frames that couldn't flex or fold. Pushkara had a pale brown face with deep-set brown eyes and phores sprinkled across the cheeks and forehead. A sharp nose with sealed nostrils perched above wide, thin lips that broke into a friendly smile. His entire body was barely the length of Kaliyu's hand.

<Could you please grab hold of me?> Pushkara flashed. <And lift me up to your face?>

Kaliyu cupped him in zir hands, slowing him with ease, then left him floating at zir eye level.

<Thank you,> Pushkara flashed, his phoric colors dull and barely visible. <I'm nearing the time for a partial rebirth, and my muscle control isn't what it should be.>

Kaliyu rotated them both away from the Sun and opened zir membranes to see better.

<You're probably wondering why I'm here,> Pushkara continued. <I'll get right to the point. I came to see you for two reasons. The first has to do with your piloting skill. Your reputation precedes you, and

I would say that you are the most promising graduate in recent times. You should be proud of your achievements.>

Kaliyu glowed blue-violet with embarrassed pleasure at Pushkara's words. Perhaps the old alloy was here to ask for a personal pilot. Kaliyu had heard that some of the most reputable proxies kept them as staff so they could travel quickly to private meetings. Zie gave Pushkara a silent nod of thanks and waited to hear more.

<The second reason has to do with your friend Vaha. You know where zie went and why?>

Zie managed to hide zir surprise at the question. <Vaha went to Earth to pick up a human passenger. Zie will take her to Meru.>

<That's correct. Given that you designated me as your proxy on several related issues, I'm guessing that you don't approve of your friend's actions. Would I be correct?>

Kaliyu nodded.

<How would you feel about going to Meru, too?>

<Me? Why?>

<I take it you're on your way to some other commission?>

<Yes, a racing team. I'm about to join the Majestics.>

<Congratulations! That's wonderful. One of the best.> Pushkara kept his glow friendly but otherwise neutral. He spread his hands. <Perhaps you could defer that for a varsha? I have a rather delicate task that I think you'd be ideal for. I need a skilled pilot to keep watch on Vaha and Jayanthi—that's the human—while they're at Meru. They have strict orders to contain any organic matter they shed and to minimize their impact on the environment of the planet. If they violate those instructions, if they're the slightest bit careless, their mission will be invalidated, and they won't be allowed to publish their results.>

<You want me to stay in orbit for masans to keep watch on my—on Vaha?> Zie had almost called zir *my friend*. It would take time to break that habit.

Pushkara smiled. <That sounds like something a machine could do, right?>

Kaliyu nodded.

<I wouldn't go to the trouble of having you there if I didn't have a greater purpose in mind. I need you to do more than watch and record their activity. I need you to make sure that they fail.>

Kaliyu's white glow betrayed zir shock.

Pushkara continued with icy-blue determination. <You agree with me that allowing humans to settle on Meru is sure to destroy the planet, right?>

<Yes,> Kaliyu flashed. *Where is he going with this?*

<A planet is one of the larger nonliving consciousnesses in the universe, and as per the Principles of Conscious Beings, all forms of consciousness have equal value, and all beings should minimize harm to other forms of consciousness. Are we still in agreement?>

Kaliyu nodded. Questions crowded zir thoughts. *What does he want me to do? Something criminal? Something bad to Meru or Vaha?*

<I therefore posit that it's a great harm to Meru to allow Vaha and Jayanthi to succeed in their mission. The Meru Exploration Committee has approved their data-gathering expedition, but my supporters and I believe that was a mistake. Once you let people like Hamsa get an opening, it's hard to keep them out. We won't have the authority to change the situation until we can vote in new committee members, and that might not happen until far too late, but I believe that we can affect the outcome. Humans are well taken care of on Earth. They have no reason to populate and contaminate another planet other than to upset the compact and indulge those with avarice and ambition. Hamsa has narrowly crafted his amendment, but if it passes, what might they ask for next? Guaranteed safe passage in our pilots? Fewer resources from Earth for our padhrans? A return to expansionist and colonialist thinking? With your help, we can ensure the safety of Meru and preserve the compact in its current form.>

<Why me? What do you want me to do?>

<Nothing terrible,> Pushkara flashed, zir phores still glowing with friendliness. <Nothing that would outweigh the potential harm to Meru of letting Vaha and Jayanthi succeed. In fact, if—as is likely—they make a mistake and contaminate the planet on their own, you won't need to take any action. You'll be there as a witness in the guise of a friend. Who would doubt that you were sent as a favor to Vaha? The bond you two developed during your time at Nishadas is clear to anyone who looks. Your instructors vouch for your camaraderie and ability to collaborate. Someone will have to observe their project for compliance. It seems a kindness to have you assigned to the task and to be available in case of emergency. My hope is that with you there, Vaha will let zir guard down. It will make zir and the human careless.>

<And if they don't . . . make a mistake?>

Pushkara had a faint glow of regret. <You must ensure that they do. Perhaps you can think of a way, given your close knowledge of Vaha, of how to tempt them into a precarious situation. And if all else fails, you will have this.> Pushkara removed a white container at his waist and held it out. <This is a self-guiding device. It has minimal propulsion, but if you launch it at the right time, it's capable of landing within a specified sixteen-square-meters location. Upon reaching its destination, it will unpack itself and dissolve its outer shell. Inside is a sufficient Earth-based biomass to be detectable by an orbital survey. If you accept my offer, I'll give you this as a method of last resort. I hate the idea of polluting Meru, but this small bit of biota is nothing compared to what a human settlement or city would produce.>

So zir mission would be to sabotage Vaha's. *Good!* Vaha deserved it for abandoning decency and taking a contract with Hamsa. The physical pollution gave zir pause. How could someone like Pushkara, whose career was built upon securing planetary integrity, suggest such a thing?

<I saw that you've designated me as your proxy since you reached voting age,> Pushkara continued. <I hope that means you know my

history and record. My goal here is to protect Meru, nothing more and nothing less. If you have any doubts or questions, I'm happy to address them.>

If someone with Pushkara's reputation was willing to make an offer like this, it must be the right thing to do. *And if I'm at Meru, perhaps I can convince Vaha to see reason.* While in orbit, Kaliyu would have plenty of time to talk some sense into zir friend and find a way to exacerbate the human's natural tendency for harm. Lead her into doing something terrible on her own. And win Vaha back in the process.

<Will this hurt Vaha?> Kaliyu flashed. <Is it toxic?>

<It shouldn't hurt an alloy, especially one of Vaha's mass. I'm not sure what it will do to the human.> Pushkara shrugged. <She's taking a massive risk by leaving Earth, especially with her sickle cell disease. She's already shown her willingness to jeopardize her life for this mission.>

Kaliyu couldn't care less about the welfare of the human, but zie didn't want to hurt zir friend. *Somehow I need to find a way to shield Vaha from any mistakes the human makes. Zie will see why zie made the wrong choice, and I'll give zir a chance to save face.* With a way to salvage their relationship, zie could think of Vaha as a friend again.

<You'll have plenty of time to observe the situation before taking any action,> Pushkara said, as if reading Kaliyu's thoughts. <If you get the evidence you need, you can deploy the contaminant to Meru's star. No need to risk an accident.>

<I understand.>

<In exchange for all this, you'll have the opportunity to make scientific observations of Meru while monitoring your friend and the human. You might discover something to publish in the Nivid, if that interests you?>

It didn't, but that wouldn't affect Kaliyu's decision.

<I can make an offer that might tempt you more,> Pushkara flashed, perhaps mistaking Kaliyu's silence for reluctance. <If you succeed at your task, I will petition for your maker's early release from service.>

<My . . . what?> Kaliyu responded, sure that zie had misunderstood the old alloy's words.

<Your maker's early release from zir service on Earth.>

That seemed clear enough. <You're mistaken. My maker is dead. Zie died varshas ago, while incarnated for service.>

They stared at each other for a few seconds. Pushkara flashed, slowly and clearly, <I don't know why you think that, but I can assure you that I'm not the one who's mistaken.>

<My grandmaker told me,> Kaliyu flashed, then stopped. *Why would she lie?* But zie didn't have to think hard for the answer. *Of course she would lie.* Grandmaker had never hidden her shame at her child's fate. *See what comes of trying to help humans? Only pain and death:* her words. She had done everything possible to discourage Kaliyu from following in zir maker's path, short of telling Kaliyu to skip being a pilot and go straight into stasis.

If Pushkara was telling the truth, if Nidra had survived the rebirth as a weller, then Kaliyu still had a family. Zie hadn't been alone since zir grandmaker's death.

Zie felt as if someone had turned reality inside out, like a transit that went nowhere.

<I'm sorry. I can see this comes as a shock to you, and you're understandably upset. Perhaps these images will help.>

And there was zir maker's face, mapped on to one of those hideous slugs, creatures that digested human garbage and transformed it into amendments for soil. The metadata showed that the pictures had been taken recently, barely a masan earlier.

<Why . . . why did zie never send me a message?> Kaliyu couldn't keep the mournful glow from zir phores. *Maybe zie thought you would be ashamed of zir. Maybe that's what your rotten grandmaker told zir.*

<Rebirth, especially a full one, is often accompanied by memory loss,> Pushkara flashed gently. <It's possible that zie doesn't remember you. Usually a family member will meet with the reborn and a counselor

to help reintroduce loved ones. With the help of extended memory and good guidance, someone can reintegrate with their past. I've done it many times. I'm sure that if you spend some time with Nidra, zie will come to know you as zir child once more. I can recommend a good counselor to help you.>

It was all too much to believe, to take in. Zir grandmaker had lied. Zir maker lived! And now Pushkara offered a way to reunite them. He waited for zir response with the vast patience of someone who had lived for centuries, but Kaliyu burned on the inside. A rage built that wanted to expand like a red giant star, to consume everything in its path. Zie wanted to speed to Earth, to see Nidra again, to release zir from the bonds of weller service. Zir grandmaker had raised Kaliyu for most of zir life. What else had she lied about? How much did Kaliyu really know about zir own maker? Zie wanted to cover zir phores, to hide zir turmoil from Pushkara. But zie could do none of that, not until zie gave the old alloy an answer.

What choice did Kaliyu really have? If zir maker lived, and Kaliyu could help get zir off Earth, zie had to do anything in zir power to make it happen. Racing, Vaha, Meru . . . none of it could stand in the way of freedom and a real life for Nidra.

<I'll do it,> zie flashed. <Whatever you ask.>

<Thank you. I didn't expect the offer about your maker to take you by surprise or I would have delivered the news more gently. I give you my word that I will do my best to reunite you.>

Kaliyu could only nod. Zie could barely keep the riot of emotions from zir phores. If zie tried to say too much, zie feared that zir entire body might explode.

<Here's a contract with authorization for the supplies you'll need for your journey. We have regular couriers moving data back here from Meru's system. Share your surveillance results with me at least once a masan, sooner if you see anything interesting.> Pushkara placed the white container on Kaliyu's hand. <I've set the ownership token in the

device to your name now. You have to possess it in order to operate it, so it won't accidentally deploy. I'll expect a signed copy of the contract once you have reviewed the contents. Take your time. I look forward to many varshas of partnership with you.>

<Thank you,> Kaliyu flashed automatically.

<Do you want us to wait for you? Give you a tow back toward Earth or Venus? You'll need to stop somewhere to file a new flight path.>

<I'll manage,> Kaliyu flashed. <I'll be all right.>

Zie wanted nothing more than for Pushkara and the other pilot to leave zir alone. Zie needed time to think, to process zir new reality.

Pushkara nodded and flew away. Kaliyu delicately grasped the small container of contaminant and stowed it in zir pouch.

Zie would file zir flight plan at Venus, back at Nishadas, to avoid Earth. Zie didn't want to see Nidra until zie could deliver zir maker's freedom.

The vast field of the galaxy's lights filled zir view. One of those was Pamir, Meru's sun, and before long, zie would be on zir way there. *I'm coming to you, Vaha. Whether to save you or sabotage you, I don't know, but I'll make sure your project fails. I'll bring my maker back to the stars where zie belongs.*

—यात्रा

Yaathraa—Journey

To Vaha's immense relief, zie didn't have to maneuver through Earth's atmosphere. Because of the significant amount of traffic around the planet, a construct guided zir to an orbital station, where zie found a berth with room to tether zir womb nearby. The structure looked permanent, which was allowed—Earth was an exception to many rules—and the berths were a lot more plush than the ones at Nishadas. Rather than an open metal framework, this one had solid walls with windows. It hung off one of the many cylindrical arms that extended from the station's main body, and it had a view to the planet below. Vaha hadn't seen Earth in ten years, and zie'd never seen it so close up. From the Moon, humanity's home rose and set like a work of art decorating a star-studded backdrop. With zir current perspective, zie could see the texture of clouds, the folds in the land below. Would Meru look similar? What would it feel like to set foot on a planet, to have every move guided by gravity's pull?

As zie waited in the berth, small constructs and alloys moved the necessary supplies from the station into the pack strapped around zir torso. Additional water and bhojya went into tanks that would strap to zir chest. Zie would burn an exhausting amount of energy over thirty days of travel to the reality-transit point, with half of it accelerating at three-quarters of Earth's gravity—a necessity for the health of zir human passenger. Zie needed to carry enough supplies for double that to get them to Meru. Enough alloys orbited the planet that zie didn't need to worry once there—couriers would provide regular deliveries—but on the surface, zie would have to set up an area to grow solid food. *Something else to learn as part of taking care of a human.* The time and distance daunted Vaha. Zie had never journeyed that far in zir life, not even with zir maker.

The human—*Jayanthi*; zie had to get used to her name—would bring her own personal effects, like clothing and food. The hard goods necessary for her physical comfort and survival went into Vaha's pack, to be used once they landed on Meru. For travel, zie had special drinks with nitrogen so zie could provide her with breathable air via an organ only pilots had. The instructors at Nishadas had made them drink it a few times in their early years at the school, but all the human beings in the Solar System lived on Earth. Their lessons on human transportation had been purely theoretical.

Strange to think of a tiny being living inside zir body. Vaha had watched a few shows about humans, both fictional and factual, during some of zir rest periods on the way to Earth. Everything about them was strange and nonintuitive, starting with the feet that stayed perpetually bound to a surface. Vaha had mostly thought of up and down as zir back and stomach, but for Jayanthi, down would be toward zir tail and up toward zir head.

She wouldn't be the first human that zie encountered, though. After getting supplied, zir body had undergone an inspection by both an alloy and a human physician. Using a swarm of small constructs, the alloy had checked over zir health in general and pronounced it good. The human physician, however, had crawled into zir mouth and made their way into zir internal human-support organ, the chamber in zir abdomen where Jayanthi would live.

Zie had felt a tickling sensation as the physician entered zir throat and then nothing. Inside the chamber, zie had little tactile sense. The physician had embedded electromechanical devices in zir flesh so zie could observe and interact with a human passenger. Visual sensors relayed a view of the room to Vaha's optics. Audio sensors picked up the physician's speech and transmitted it to Vaha's emchannel. Speakers performed the inverse function. The human doctor tested the air and water quality, temperature, and humidity. They also checked that the emergency umbilical cord functioned correctly. If Jayanthi became too sick or injured to continue their mission, Vaha could attach the umbilical to her and keep her body alive, just as zir womb could with zir own body.

To Vaha's relief, the human physician had pronounced zir passenger functions healthy. To have come this far and then get disqualified due to organ failure would have been depressing. Zie settled in for a few hours of sleep. By the time zie awoke, zir passenger would have arrived.

—

The ride to the orbital station brought plenty of joy to Jayanthi on its own, but the feeling was compounded by having her parents and Mina along. She and her best friend exclaimed over each passing kilometer, their gazes fixed on the landscapes and skyscapes outside their windows. Vidhar and Kundhina smiled indulgently, but she could tell they were enjoying themselves, too.

Neither she nor Mina had traveled by flight before, and the sensation of being unmoored from the ground made her giddy. They rode in a container carried on the back of an alloy, strong enough to funnel air through muscular jets and escape the pull of gravity. When the sky outside began to darken, Jayanthi reached out and clutched the hands of Mina and Kundhina, who sat on either side of her. Stars appeared, a few at first, like those at twilight, then rapidly multiplied until she lost count.

"Thank you for bringing me with you," Mina said in a hushed voice. "This is . . . incredible."

Jayanthi hadn't needed to beg too hard for the favor of having her friend along. Her parents' alloy status granted them two visits per year to their true bodies, and, at her request, Hamsa had used his influence to allow Mina passage as well. With the thought in the back of her mind that she might not return, Jayanthi wanted to give the experience of space to her friend as a parting gift. A few humans with specific tasks made it to orbit, but the vast majority stayed gravity-bound on the surface. Most didn't care, having inherited an aversion to high-risk activities.

"I'm glad you're here," Jayanthi said. "All of you."

"I couldn't let my only child fly into orbit by herself for the first time," Kundhina said. "And I want to meet this Vaha person, make sure zie can take good care of you."

Mina laughed, and Jayanthi shook her head.

"I thought you weren't worried about her," Vidhar teased.

"It's not Jaya's actions I'm worried about."

When the pull of gravity gave way, Jayanthi's stomach flipped. Harnesses kept her in her seat as free fall rearranged every part of her body, every hair on her head. Her arms and legs drifted upward of their own accord. After her brain convinced her body that she wasn't plunging to her doom, she began to enjoy the sensation. A while later, they could see the warren of interconnected cylinders that formed Orbital Station Three. Reflective solar skin covered its surfaces. Rounded cones protruded from many of the cylinder ends.

"I can see the berths!" Jayanthi exclaimed.

"It looks so small from here," Mina said.

The station grew from its miniature appearance into a massive structure that made their alloy look tiny in comparison. A steady stream of constructs and alloys moved around the station, some headed to and from the planet, others to the great beyond.

Mina clutched at Jayanthi's shoulder and pointed. "Look, that must be Vaha!"

At first, Jayanthi couldn't see zir. Then her eyes resolved the dark shadow on the far side of the station, its silhouette forming the shape of a split fin void in the stars.

"So big," Jayanthi whispered, awed. She recalled the size from Vaha's profile. "One hundred twenty meters in length." She had known Vaha's dimensions in the abstract, but seeing zir in person gave the number an entirely different perspective. She turned to her parents. "Can we see your true bodies? Are they that big?"

"Not at all," her father said. "We don't have pilot genes. I'm about five meters in length, and your mother is a bit larger, but our true bodies are in medical comas. We're not large enough to divest an incarn and have the remaining portion be fully conscious."

Their alloy came up alongside the station and coasted into one of the conical berths. Jayanthi watched as their carrier clipped herself to a safety line, then slipped their capsule off her back and guided it forward to mate with a station door.

"I hope you enjoyed your flight," the alloy said, her voice coming through speakers above them.

"We did, thank you," Kundhina said.

"Very much," Mina added.

"Just lovely," Jayanthi said.

"Be careful when you start moving around," Vidhar said, addressing Jayanthi and Mina. "Give yourselves some time to get used to weightlessness."

But Mina had already unclipped and made their way to the door. Their braids twisted and coiled behind them like kelp fronds. Jayanthi regretted putting her own hair in a more practical bun. She unbuckled and flailed ineffectually until her feet connected with the back of her seat. Then she pushed off and rammed into the back of her mother, sending them both caroming off the front window.

"Sorry," she said as Kundhina steadied them.

Her father grinned, grabbed Jayanthi's arm, and guided her to a handhold.

The door opened, and a new pit formed in Jayanthi's stomach. The air coming from the station was cold and dry and full of strange odors, and the reality of her situation arrived like a downpour. The capsule felt safe, familiar, and she didn't want to leave it.

Mina dove through the doorway without a backward glance, their motions as graceful as if they'd been born to this life. Kundhina followed. Vidhar placed a hand on Jayanthi's back.

"Ready?" he said softly. He must have sensed the shift in her mood.

Jayanthi swallowed hard and nodded. She used the handholds to move herself forward, then paused in the doorway and looked back. *This is it—the last bit of Earth I'll see for the next year and a half.* Waves of cold anxiety washed from her neck to her feet. With a deep breath, she turned and pushed herself into the station.

The public corridor cameras on the station showed Vaha the passage of two humans and two humanoid alloys. One human had a larger, more alloy-like figure, but otherwise they resembled each other closely with brown skin, white human eyes with dark centers, and black hair. Vaha examined their faces and then gave up trying to recall which one was Jayanthi. Zie hadn't looked at human beings enough to tell them apart. Easier to check their metadata. The one with the more sticklike figure was zir passenger. The other, named Mina Andaka, was studying to be a Voice of Compassion. They lived in the same town as Jayanthi and her family. *Perhaps they've come to the orbital station to complete their education.*

The two humanoid alloys were Jayanthi's parents, according to their information. *That explains the difference in their appearance. Their bodies are incarns.* Vaha had never seen an incarn before, but zie would need to use one on Meru. Zie wondered if incarns could look more human than theirs.

The small group made their way through the station until they reached the chamber that led to Vaha's berth. A window filled most of the exterior wall, and four tiny faces peered through it. Vaha opened the front window of zir berth, raised a hand, and waved, feeling amused and a little offended by their stares.

One of the alloy incarns waved back, the one named Kundhina. Her phores flashed. <Hello, Vaha. I'm Jayanthi's mother. It's good to meet you.>

<Likewise,> Vaha replied.

<We'll just be a few minutes while we check over the results of your inspection and make sure nothing was missed on the cargo manifest.>

<Please, take your time.>

<Jayanthi is suiting up as well. How are you feeling about this? She's your first human passenger, right? Are you excited to go to Meru?>

Through the window, Vaha could see Jayanthi's mouth moving and her hand gesticulating at Kundhina. Her eyebrows had drawn together, and her eyes narrowed. Humans couldn't reflect their emotions through skin chromatophores, so they used muscles to change their facial and body positions. *Should've watched more human entertainment rather than the new season of* Across the Orbit. *Maybe then I'd know what Jayanthi's scrunched face means.*

<She'll be my first passenger of any kind,> Vaha flashed. <I'm very honored to take her to Meru and to work on Hamsa's assignment. I'll do my best to make sure everything goes smoothly and that Jayanthi does well on Meru.>

<Wonderful. She has a pack with some personal items in addition to the project cargo. I assume it's all right if she brings it in with her? The mass is negligible—a few kilos.>

<That's fine.> Vaha wondered what was so precious that Jayanthi had to keep it with her in the chamber. Most alloys could carry the entirety of their possessions in their packs. Did humans do the same? <Thank you for entrusting your child to my care. I promise to look after her.>

Vaha tried to glow with more confidence than zie felt. *I have no idea what I'm doing, and you probably know that* was the truth of the situation. Kaliyu's words at Nishadas, as cruel as they'd been, were also accurate. The only reason they'd chosen Vaha was because everyone better had declined.

<I appreciate your saying that,> Kundhina flashed. <I'm glad to know that she's in good hands.>

Kundhina turned away from the window. The four figures consolidated, their arms wrapping around each other. No one had held Vaha like that since zie was a child, and even that had been rare with Veera. Zir maker had held Vaha in a pouch, like everyone did with their infant, but once Vaha could control zir flight, Veera hadn't tolerated zir requests to be carried. *You're a pilot. You need to fly as instinctively as you blink,* zir maker would say. At Nishadas, Vaha and Kaliyu had sometimes merged their berths for the warmth of contact. Zie would never feel that again.

Did I make a mistake in taking this assignment? Was Kaliyu right about humans? Will Jayanthi be materialistic and destructive, unable to overcome those ancient tendencies?

But it was too late to change course. Vaha could picture Kaliyu's back, the last sight of zir that Vaha had. The same view zie'd had of zir maker as Veera left the Solar System. Zie had to forget about Kaliyu and focus on the goal of accomplishing zir first task as a pilot. Would it suffice to make Veera proud? Probably not, but success would take zir further along that path than anything else zie had done.

The station requested that Vaha attach the passageway. Zie pulled the tube from the doorway and sealed it over zir mouth, then parted zir lips. Zie tasted the station air as the door swung open. The pheromones of human, incarn, and alloy bodies were faint and strange, though not unpleasant.

A lone figure emerged, bumbling through the tube like a newborn. Vaha concentrated on zir phores to make sure zir nervousness didn't reveal itself. For the next year and a half, zie would have to care for this creature who barely stretched the length of one finger joint. *How can I possibly be related to such tiny beings?* But two-thirds of Vaha's DNA came from humans. In the grand scheme of genetics, the animal life-forms of Earth had more similarities than differences, and alloys shared those characteristics. For this mission to succeed, zie would have to find a way to relate to this distant, minuscule cousin.

Jayanthi had watched recordings of humans moving smoothly through the passageways of the orbital station. They had made it look so easy, as did Mina. She, however, was making a complete ass of herself in trying to reach Vaha. Flailing through the translucent tube that went from the station exit to Vaha's mouth—as if that wasn't strange enough—she found no handholds to make her journey easier. She used what purchase friction gave to push herself along, though she ended up bouncing off the tube walls more often than not. At least she hadn't yet opened an emchannel with her host. If she had to hear zir commentary on her utter lack of grace, she would break into tears.

Through the station window, Vaha had been even more beautiful in person than in zir profile image. And vast. *A star nymph,* Mina had declared, upon seeing the perfectly humanlike proportions scaled up to celestial size. A range of brown hues had lit up Vaha's phores as zie spoke to her mother. The glow had more subtle shifts than she'd seen when her parents spoke phoric, and the colors flickered faster than her human eyes could process.

At last, sweat soaking her undersuit, Jayanthi passed through the tube. She paused to catch her breath and looked around. Patches of glowing bioluminescence lit the chamber—*Vaha's mouth,* she reminded herself—with a pale reddish glow. The textures seemed more rigid and dry than she'd expect for the inside of a person. She wished her hand weren't gloved so she could feel it under her palm. Was it warm? Soft? For a second, her location felt almost sensual, and she resisted an urge to stroke the nearby surface.

There was no tongue or gigantic teeth or anything to indicate that she was in someone's mouth. Alloys didn't need to eat, but she was used to her parents' incarns having that ability. She knew more about alloys than any other human in her life, but floating here, inside Vaha, she felt terribly ignorant.

She accepted a request from Vaha to open an emchannel.

"Hello, Jayanthi. Welcome. Please follow the lit passageway to your chamber."

Vaha's words sounded flat and calm. She recalled that for alloys, their emtalk receptors mapped to the visual parts of their brains, translating their words into the equivalent of phoric. Vaha had no voice, and zir vestigial ears didn't get any use. The concept of tonality wouldn't exist, and the colors she sensed must map to zir phoric glow. The emchannel was doing its best to convert Vaha's words to a format that Jayanthi could understand, but it had lost all the nuances of human speech.

Not the most auspicious start to our working relationship. What does my speech look like to zir? Is it dull and colorless?

Four flaps dotted the back of Vaha's mouth. One opened and glowed with the same gentle red that surrounded Jayanthi. She pushed off the nearest surface and scrambled to grab the edge of the flap, then twisted herself into the passageway beyond. This one had ridges she could hold with her gloved hands. Before long, she arrived in a small, oblong room. The walls were pearlescent white with whorls of brown. Handles jutted from them in all directions along with inset lights that created an even illumination throughout.

She recognized the room's contents and layout from what she'd studied about alloy pilots. The hard surfaces were made of calcium carbonate, like a seashell. A padded sleep sack was attached to the wall on her left. On the wall facing her was a series of webbed bags for storing her personal goods and dehydrated food for the journey. Various implements protruded from the right-hand wall, including tubes for drinking water and bhojya and a mechanism for collecting waste. Above her head, the surface was bare except for four small, rectangular insets covered by grates. Two of those were for airflow, with signal ribbons attached to show that they functioned, and the other two were speakers with embedded microphones, a concession to the human desire for speech. In her case, they could have used emtalk, but most human beings didn't have that capability.

Below her feet was a bare wall with a section that had a scored rectangular area. It looked like it could open, though she had no idea where it would lead. Behind her, the tripartite entry valve sealed shut, and above, the airflow ribbons began to flutter.

"You can safely remove your helmet," Vaha said.

Jayanthi opened her visor and took a cautious breath. The air was warm and slightly humid, with a pleasant odor reminiscent of petrichor.

"Hello?" she said aloud. "Can you hear me?"

A midrange voice that matched the one from emtalk answered. "Yes. Can you hear me." The tonality was equally flat.

"I can."

Jayanthi didn't know what to say next. Apparently neither did Vaha, because the silence stretched until she felt she had to come up with something. "Oh, can you see me?"

"Not yet. You have to enable the cameras. They are embedded within the lights. You should have permissions to do that with your thought controls."

She clipped her bag to a handhold and slow-blinked to call up a visual of the controls. She could adjust the lighting levels; disable or enable various electronics, including the cameras; and open . . . the viewing portal?

She turned on the cameras and opened the portal, which turned out to be the cutout in the "floor." As she watched, the solid surface retracted, leaving a crystal-clear circle with a diameter about half her height. Through it, she could see the wall of the orbital station berth.

"Can I keep this open when you're flying?"

"Yes. It's impermeable, and it's covered by a protective layer when closed, like your eyelid. I have similar lids to protect my eyes, nasal slits, and mouth."

"Amazing," Jayanthi said softly. "May I touch it?"

"Of course. You are welcome to touch anything in your surroundings."

She unsealed and removed a glove. When she pressed her hand to the window, it was cool and firm.

"Can you feel it when I touch you?" She felt herself blush as she finished the question. What an awkward phrasing, somehow intimate and clinical at the same time.

"No. I have no nerve endings on the surfaces in my human-support organ, except for the valve."

"I'm sorry. I shouldn't pry."

"That's all right. I've had to learn, too. This part of my anatomy isn't something I've paid much attention to, and they didn't teach us much at school. I have a lot of questions about humans, so maybe we can trade knowledge. For example, you seem quite fragile. Will the chamber surfaces hurt you when I begin to accelerate."

It took Jayanthi a second to realize that Vaha had asked a question. "No. They told me that I can withstand up to two gees for short periods of time. I have solid bones in here"—she tapped her sternum—"so I'm stronger than I look."

"Solid." There was a pause. "Ah, they're calcium-based, like my chamber walls, according to what I'm reading."

The affectless translator would drive her mad before the day's end. She could not spend the next two months listening to speech like this. "Do you know about tones? Of speech, I mean. It's how we convey emotion."

"I thought that's what your facial muscles are for."

"Oh, well, both. Your speech—no offense, but it sounds like a machine. I can sort of sense the glow of your words, but that doesn't always translate well into what I'm used to hearing."

"I'm very sorry."

"It's not your fault," she said quickly. "But I wonder if we can upgrade the emchannel somehow."

"It's not a separate device. I'm using my brain to convey speech. I'll try to observe your speech patterns and learn how to communicate better. By tone, do you mean the musical nature of your speech."

"Yes! Exactly. So you can hear?" She looked up at the speakers and realized the absurdity of the gesture. Her brain expected the source of a voice to be its owner's face.

"I listen to music, but I'm not used to parsing the vocalizations as words. Alloy compositions usually pair music with phoric for songs."

"Can you hear this upward inflection? It means I'm asking a question."

"Yes, and if you could tag your speech after you say something, that would be very helpful."

"Tag?" When no answer came, she added, "That was a question."

"Yes, exactly like that."

"Oh! I understand. You want me to tell you what my speech inflections mean." Jayanthi laughed. "Okay, right now, I'm amused. This should be fun. Good thing we have a while before we get to Meru." She floated back from the window and over to the water tube. Her sweaty transition had left her throat dry.

"It's quite a short trip. Only fifty-five days."

"Your sense of time has a slightly different scale from mine." She added, "I'm teasing."

"We can leave as soon as you're ready."

"You mean like right now?"

Simultaneously, they both said, "That was a question."

Jayanthi laughed again.

"I was ready before your arrival," Vaha said. "Are you waiting for something more."

"No, it's just . . . well, I'm nervous." Any human would've seen it on her face or heard it in her voice, but she wasn't dealing with humankind anymore.

She was finally where she'd always dreamt of—in space, as close to being an alloy as she'd ever come—but her heart thudded, and sweat collected in her armpits. *Admit it. You're more than nervous—you're scared! Stop being such a human about everything!* But she couldn't calm herself on command. After this, they'd leave Earth, and she'd have no way of returning without Vaha's cooperation. She'd be utterly dependent on this alloy whom she'd just met.

"You should grab hold somewhere," Vaha said, "with your feet pointed at the utility wall. That will become your floor once we're under acceleration."

"Okay," she said, wishing zie had provided some words of reassurance. What must zie think of her? This tiny, "fragile" person who was about to have the greatest honor any human could, and yet all she could express was fear. *How am I going to win Vaha over enough to let me use zir womb if I can't even get through something as simple as this?*

She twisted her body until her feet pointed "down" and steadied herself against the clear viewing window. "I'm ready."

—माया

Maayaa—Illusion

Vaha alternated days of acceleration with days of rest. Zie used thamity gradients to travel orthogonal to the ecliptic of the planets, toward heliopause. The reality-transit point lay at the fulcrum of the solar wind and the interstellar wind. Eighteen billion kilometers in thirty days, half of it at three-quarters of Earth's gravitational acceleration. Zie followed the downslope on those days. It required some physical energy to steer zirself, and far more mental energy to stay alert to the course and choose zir line of travel.

On the days zie coasted, zie reviewed the information downloaded from Earth to zir extended memory. Nothing had the title *The Care and Feeding of Humans*, but that was the gist of what zie had to study. The womb could deal with serious medical problems, but zir incarn would have to treat minor wounds and illnesses. Zie had to set up a protected, Earthlike system to grow fresh solid foods—vegetables, fruits, and legumes whose flavors zie had sampled via bhojya but had never seen whole. There were protocols and procedures for various types of situations they might encounter. Some of the reading material covered human psychology and genetics, but zie found it hard to parse in the abstract. Observing zir passenger's behavior did more to help zir understanding.

Jayanthi seemed to adapt quickly to the schedule. By the fourth day, she had established her own routine. She set the lights to cycle based on a twenty-four-hour Earth day, regardless of whether they were accelerating or not. Once a day, she spoke to her parents and then her friend Mina. Occasionally she made calls to others. She didn't always enable privacy mode, and Vaha did zir best not to pay attention. It was harder on rest days. When zie mentioned this to Jayanthi, she started including zir in their conversations, much to zir surprise.

Zir passenger kept her eating to set times, as well. She drank bhojya for her "morning" and "evening" meals and ate solid food in the middle of the day. On the acceleration days, she exercised her body and brewed tea, using a portable heating device that she'd brought along.

"What does tea taste like?" Vaha asked her on the fifth day. Zie'd figured out the tonality of questions quickly.

Jayanthi crinkled her face in a way that zie now interpreted as thoughtful. "I was going to say earthy, but that wouldn't help you. Have you tasted mushrooms?"

"As a bhojya flavor, yes. They culture well in microgravity, though I've heard ours don't resemble the mushrooms on Earth."

"This tea tastes something like that, but with an aroma of . . . oregano? It has a perfume but also an earthiness. I don't know how else to describe it, sorry. I have other teas, though, that are more floral."

"I've never tasted a flower," Vaha said, "though I've experienced synth flavors that are supposed to resemble them. My favorite was honeysuckle."

"Oh yes, that has a lovely sweetness," Jayanthi said.

She had a lot of curiosity about Vaha, easily as much as zie did about her, and she seemed to welcome zir questions. To help speed up zir understanding of human behavior, Vaha had started watching more of their entertainment while Jayanthi slept or wanted privacy, which she did fairly often. Vaha found her behaviors strange, but zie was used to life as a pilot, and some alloys would consider zir habits unusual, too.

"Would you like to taste the tea?" Jayanthi asked.

Vaha regarded the small vessel of the liquid in her hands. It would be a drop to zir, but that might be enough.

"Sure, though we'll have to be careful that I don't swallow you."

Jayanthi laughed, then scrunched her face. "You are joking, right?"

"Not entirely," Vaha admitted. "You'll have to pour it into my esophagus, then leave before the flap closes. My taste buds line the tube, and I can sense flavor better once I swallow. It's about the same size as the one you took to your room, so I'm pretty sure you'd fit in there."

"This tone of voice and the expression on my face? Tag it as slightly horrified."

Vaha rotated so that Jayanthi could walk into zir mouth. It made for an awkward thamity slide, but zie didn't have to maintain the angle for long. Zie shifted again so the back of zir mouth was under Jayanthi's feet, then unsealed zir esophageal flap while keeping zir mouth tightly closed. It was a strange sensation. Zie usually didn't swallow unless a bhojya or water tube was sealed over zir mouth.

"There you go," Jayanthi sent. "Can you taste it?"

Vaha relaxed and opened the other valve so she could return to her chamber. Barely a second later, zie caught a faint flavor.

"You're right—it has a hint of certain mushroom flavors but also something else I can't name. I suppose that's what you call earthiness."

"I guess tea is one thing humans have that's valuable."

"One thing? You have plenty of goods on Earth that we need."

"I mean in terms of something that we make, not a natural resource."

"Some of your literature and shows are pretty good, too." In fact, after a few days immersed in human culture, Vaha could understand why alloys like Hamsa and Jayanthi's parents were fascinated by them. In terms of basic personality and behavior, humans weren't all that different from alloys. They had family and friendships. They loved, fought, laughed, and cared for children. Some still used natural birth rather than wombs, and they couldn't regulate their hormones the way alloys could, but many elected to have gene therapy that accomplished the same thing. Their instinctive behavior was not suited for life in space, but they didn't strike Vaha as the evil, destructive creatures that Kaliyu despised.

"You must be joking," Jayanthi said. "I'm sure nothing we produce could reach the level of alloy entertainment. We can't experience half the sensory modalities you use, and we don't speak phoric."

"The translations aren't perfect, but I've enjoyed them. I'm not joking. Also, you shouldn't do that."

"Do what?"

"Speak so poorly of yourself—your kind. My best friend, Kaliyu, looked down on humans, too, but zie was an alloy. That doesn't make it right, but at least it's understandable. In your case, you should be proud of what you are. If you're a typical example, I don't see anything wrong with humans. You're very likable, you seem intelligent, and you're brave. Otherwise you wouldn't be here."

"I . . . ," she trailed off.

On the infrared, Vaha could see the surface temperature of her cheeks and neck rise. Her eyes shone. If zie looked only at her face—and ignored her eyes—she had beautiful features, like an alloy's but in miniature. The eyes were lovely in their own strange way. The dark iris and pupil resembled Vaha's maker's, but the whites around it gave away its human nature. Zie wondered at their sudden glossiness and her increased blood flow. Was she upset? Unwell?

Before zie could ask, she said, "Thank you, but most people—humans—think I'm strange, not typical at all, and not in a good way." Her tone turned down. Upset or unhappy, then. "In fact, no one else on Earth was raised like me, by two alloy parents. I've never had many friends. I had—and still have—ambitions, dreams of being a tarawan, contributing to the Nivid."

She paused as if waiting for a response.

"What's wrong with that? Sounds like a reasonable goal, one that many people I've met would share with you," Vaha said. "I'm sorry—perhaps I misinterpreted your tone, but you sounded sad."

Jayanthi made a small smile. "No, you caught the tone correctly. Sadness, perhaps some shame and regret, too."

"Why?" Human brains might not have the capacity for tarawan skills, but zie could think of nothing shameful about that, and plenty of people wanted to contribute to the Nivid. It was the greatest honor anyone could receive.

"Because humans aren't supposed to aspire to anything. We're taught the aphorism *Ambition and materialism lead to greed and exploitation* from an early age. Humans shouldn't have life goals, especially ones like being a tarawan. We're not allowed that profession, and many others, too. We can't contribute to the Nivid without an alloy to cosign the discovery. You really don't know any of this?"

Vaha caught the inflected question. "No, but someone might have taught me these things, and I forgot. I confess, I've never paid much attention to Earth or human matters."

"Of course not. Why would you when you have so many better things to do with your time?"

Unhappy radiated from her speech so strongly that Vaha felt a sympathetic pang. Zie had a sudden urge to wrap Jayanthi in zir arms and console her. She might share Kaliyu's contempt for humankind, but she certainly didn't have zir friend's self-confidence to make up for it.

"I would put forth," Vaha said, wishing zie knew how to make zir tone kind, "that the fault here is mine. My ignorance has nothing to do with your value and everything to do with my single-minded focus on piloting. I should give myself a broader education. Pay attention to matters outside of my personal life."

Jayanthi gazed through the viewing portal. "If I had spent my childhood living among the stars, I wouldn't have cared about anything else, either."

"That's not why. Plenty of alloys grow up learning about history and politics. I had a narrow focus on piloting because of my maker. Zie designed me to be unique, the first pilot who could perform all four modes of flight, but . . . I failed. Repeatedly. Spectacularly. I would plummet to the ground during landings or lack the strength to escape from a gravity well. I got injured a lot. My maker was so devoted to my success that zie applied for me to have my own womb. Because of everything zie had accomplished in zir life, the allocation committee trusted my maker to have designed me well. They were willing to give us a womb so I could fulfill the promise of my genes. I could get healed whenever and wherever I needed to, or have my genetic expression modified as my maker and tarawan saw fit. I kept trying to live up to my design potential, even after zie left, but I've never succeeded."

Vaha wondered at zirself, confessing all this to Jayanthi only a few days after meeting her. It had taken zir more than two years to trust Kaliyu with the truth about Veera's abandonment. Somehow telling her didn't carry the same weight, like she wouldn't change her opinion of zir the way an alloy might. "After I turned ten, my maker signed on to a multicentury extrasolar expedition, telling me I had failed too many times. Zie had lost faith in my ability to integrate all my flight modes, and zie wanted to do something more valuable with zir life before I ruined the last of zir reputation."

"That's terrible," Jayanthi said. "Tag that with sympathy and outrage. I saw on your profile that you've been alone since you were ten, but I didn't know all the details. Seems like it's all worked out, though, right? Now you're the pilot your maker designed you to be. Zie should've had more patience."

Vaha took some solace in Jayanthi's more upbeat tone. At least zie had distracted her from her own melancholy, though it had transferred onto zirself. Zie tried to match her earlier *unhappy* way of speaking and said, "I'm much better than I used to be, but I'm nowhere close to the evolutionary leap my maker had hoped for. I very nearly cheated my way through the final exam for my pilot's license."

Jayanthi lifted her eyebrows. "You did what? Tell me more!"

So Vaha did, spilling the truth about Kaliyu's help that zie had never intended to tell her or anyone else. When zie finished, zie waited and wondered if it would dim her opinion of zir.

"You think I should have a better opinion of humankind?" she said. "I think you need to have a better opinion of yourself. I think you were raised by a cruel maker, then befriended by an overachieving friend. You worked hard, and you passed. So what if Kaliyu had to show you what to do in an unorthodox way? There's no shame in needing extra help. The true error is to give up, and you never did that. You should be proud of yourself."

Vaha's vents constricted, and zir tear ducts prickled. "You're kind, but you don't understand the world I live in. We're meant to express our genes in novel ways. That's the legacy a maker leaves to their child, the whole point of being an alloy. Wasn't I your last choice of pilot? Kaliyu told me that zie rejected Hamsa's offer."

"Well, not quite last," Jayanthi said in a tone zie couldn't interpret. "But we were using scores to base our choices. If I'd known you, I would've chosen you first."

"I don't entirely believe you, but I appreciate the sentiment. It's all right. I'm well aware of my own shortcomings. If we're lucky, our work on Meru will get both of our names published in the Nivid alongside some marvelous new discovery. Then you'll achieve one of your dreams."

Jayanthi reached out and laid her hand against the entry valve. Vaha felt it as the barest bit of pressure inside zirself and almost shivered. Her touch had an intimacy that was out of proportion to the physical sensation. Zie found zirself wanting the two to match, to feel more of Jayanthi than zie ever could.

"Perhaps you'll get to prove your maker wrong and fly perfectly in Meru's atmosphere," she said softly.

A smile spread across her face, transforming it like sunlight at a planet's terminator. How had she come to understand zir so quickly?

You're wrong about humans, Kaliyu. Some of them aren't terrible at all.

By day ten, Jayanthi had tired of seeing the stars. At first, they had stunned her with their intensity. And the texture! She had no idea the light of the universe wove such a tapestry of patterns. The darkest place on Earth wouldn't provide a view like Vaha's window did. It was glorious! But she missed sunshine and blue skies and, if she were honest with herself, the company of Mina and her parents. Vaha was a good host and had been far kinder than she'd dared to expect, but zie was a disembodied voice. All she saw of her parents and Mina were two-dimensional images. She wanted a physical presence beside her.

She felt alone much of the time, with the exception of when she had to change clothes or use the toilet. Those made her acutely aware of her lack of privacy, and she'd turn off the cameras and microphone whenever she did either, but she kept them on the rest of the time. On Earth, her parents had made sure they could always communicate by instilling her with emtalk. She hadn't realized how much she'd unconsciously relied on that. Even those brief periods of shutting out Vaha, the only living being around, filled her with stomach-knotting anxiety. If Vaha noticed, zie hadn't said anything. Zie had asked about her desire for privacy at those times—yet another difference between alloys and humans—but zie hadn't expressed any concern. Being an interplanetary pilot would necessitate years of solitude, something she couldn't imagine tolerating.

Fifty-five days might feel like a blink to a long-lived alloy, but in her case, the first part of their long journey had already stretched into tedium. To pass the time, she'd brought along her genetic-engineering project. She might never work as a tarawan, but she enjoyed the art of designing a living being, and should she get access to Vaha's womb, she needed a set of Meru-specific human chromosomes to simulate. Hearing that zie wanted zir name in the Nivid had buoyed her hopes. Like herself, Vaha's true dream lay elsewhere—in proving zir multimodal piloting skills—but she suspected zie would take some satisfaction in registering a novel human genome in the knowledge repository.

"I don't know anything about genetic engineering," Vaha had said upon learning what she was doing. "If you were able to work with Hamsa, you must be quite proficient."

Vaha kept making her blush with zir compliments. Was this how Anita felt about the alloy who patronized her art? Maybe being "kept by an alloy," as Mina always put it, wasn't so bad.

As considerate as Vaha had been, she hadn't yet dared to ask about borrowing the womb. From zir stories of zir childhood, it was clear that the gift from zir maker was something zie treasured even if it had associations with unpleasant memories. Zie had shown only a polite, cursory interest in her project. *Patience,* she counseled herself. *Think like an alloy. There's plenty of time to earn Vaha's trust.*

"Jayanthi," Vaha said, "can I have your attention for a little while?"

"Of course." She slow-blinked and cleared away the data that had overlaid the viewing wall. "And please, call me Jaya. My full name sounds so formal."

"Jaya," Vaha said slowly, as if tasting the word. "After we land on Meru and set up our base camp, I'll need to leave the planet. My body can't handle being in gravity for the duration of our assigned stay. I have permission to create an incarn, but the womb will take a few weeks to grow one. I should start it soon. I was hoping you could help me choose a form that you like. It has to be one that I can express from my genes but that still leaves considerable variety."

Did Vaha sound shy? Zie had picked up a lot of tonal cues and conversational pauses, but she hesitated to read too much into them. "I'd be happy to."

"May I project into your visual?"

Jayanthi nodded and shifted her gaze to the blank viewing wall.

"I asked the womb to simulate some humanoid body types with images of what the finished form will look like. What do you think of this one?" Vaha asked.

An image of a naked male human with dark-brown skin filled the viewing wall.

"Oh!" Jayanthi flung a hand up to block the image, which superimposed her hand over the penis. She snatched it back to her side.

"My research indicated that it's a good one for a pansexual like yourself. From your tone, I've chosen poorly. Perhaps this one?"

The display changed to a small-breasted female.

Her cheeks and ears grew hot. What could she say that Vaha would understand without offending zir?

"I'm not sensing much enthusiasm."

"That's not—"

"My apologies. Let me show you a few others."

More images flashed by, some larger, some smaller, but all of them entirely nude.

"Vaha, stop, please!" Jayanthi closed her eyes, which did nothing other than change the backdrop for the figures to the inside of her eyelids. She severed their shared visual connection.

"What's wrong?"

She gestured in the direction of the viewing wall. In a strangled voice, she said, "Can you please generate some images with clothes on?"

"But how will you judge their appeal? You'll have to spend many months looking at my incarn. I want to make sure you find zir pleasing."

"Vaha, do you know why humans wear clothes?"

"To maintain a comfortable body temperature," zie said promptly.

"Did they teach you that in school?"

"No, I inferred it from watching human shows." Zie sounded proud of zirself. "They're a lot more entertaining than I expected, though I suspect I'm missing some context."

"Maybe a bit. That's sarcasm, by the way." She blew out a breath. "Okay, how can I explain this in a way that makes sense to you? Humans also wear clothes for social reasons, and nudity . . . in certain contexts . . . is highly inappropriate."

"Oh."

A long pause. She'd figured out that those meant Vaha was looking up some information, so she waited quietly for a response.

"Oh! Oh no. I'm so sorry. I see what you mean now. That is not the effect I intended. I should've done more research before I showed you these. Alloys also engage in . . . intimacy, but we can regulate our hormones to control whether we want to. Both people express their desire first, then engage their . . . well, never mind. Please accept my apologies and pretend that you never saw those."

Jayanthi bit her lip to keep from grinning, though her cheeks still burned. Poor Vaha sounded so embarrassed. Zie really had learned a lot from watching "human entertainment," and zir speech patterns conveyed far more than they used to.

"I'll erase it all from my mind," she said.

"You can do that?"

She laughed. "Not literally."

"I can load and unload information to my extended memory, but not my organic brain. I would've been jealous if humans could do that."

"No need. I don't even have extended memory."

"Give me some time to generate more appropriate images of the incarns. Then we can talk about this again."

"My parents have incarns that are androgynous in appearance, without any external sexual organs. They're missing several internal organs, too, for that matter. Maybe you can find something like that?"

"I had hoped to inhabit a more traditional body so I could understand you better." Zie sounded shy again. "Will that be a problem? Would it make you uncomfortable? Or do we not have enough food and supplies for a second person?"

"We should have plenty of food. My parents and Hamsa insisted on planning for worst-case scenarios. There's probably enough to feed three of us. The real problem will be the air. The high oxygen levels in the atmosphere are likely to cause problems for a typical human body, so I'd worry about your health."

"Hmm. All right. Let me see what the womb can do."

"Could you—" She hesitated. Now she was the one feeling shy. "Could you grow an incarn that resembles your true face? I can sketch a human adaptation of it, if you'd like."

Vaha was silent.

"I'm sorry. Did I offend you? Never mind—"

"You like my true face?"

She couldn't parse zir tone at all. If only she could see and understand zir chromatophores, she'd have a better idea what zie was thinking.

"I like all of your true body," she said, her cheeks growing impossibly warmer. Those nude images had flustered her. "It's beautiful."

Another long pause, then: "Thank you. Most alloys think I look strange because of my wing structure and light-colored eyes. Please, sketch what you'd like for my appearance. I'll do my best to find a match within my DNA."

Like every human with a good education, Jayanthi had learned various forms of art, including drawing and painting. She hadn't enjoyed them as much as math and biology, but she had a competent hand. She started with Vaha's profile image as a reference, then traced over it with her finger, adding layers to make zir appear more human. She drew in corneas around zir violet eyes and lids that matched zir blue-black skin. She created two heavy, dark brows and then a line of pale dots from their tips to the jawline for chromatophores. If Vaha could learn to vocalize speech for her sake, she wanted to improve at her phoric, at least the portions that her eyes could sense. She reshaped the chin and nose to have more pronounced shapes, gave the lips more fullness, and, as a final touch, added a mane of dark, tight curls that stopped at zir chin.

"It's done," she said aloud. She opened their thought-shared visual again. "Can you see it?"

She worried at her lower lip as she waited for Vaha's reaction.

"I like it," zie said softly. "What are those dots along the side of the face?"

"Chromatophores. I don't know if you can put those in your incarn, but I'd like to learn more phoric while we're on Meru. My parents never taught me much."

"Interesting idea. I'll see what the womb can do."

By the time Jayanthi climbed into her sleep sack for the "night," Vaha had a result. The image zie projected had a leaner face with higher cheekbones, but otherwise, it bore a fair resemblance to her drawing, including the chromatophores. Below the neck, a tunic draped over the rest of the figure with a flowing A-line. She couldn't tell what lay under it, and she didn't ask.

"It's perfect," she said. She fell asleep with Vaha's human face watching over her.

Vaha decided to pause growing zir incarn as they neared the transit point. Zie had managed the umbilical that ran between zir body and the womb while also navigating thamity gradients, but zie had exhausted zirself in the process. A reality transit needed zir full attention, and zie wanted to be well rested for it. With only a few days lost, the incarn would still be ready by the time they arrived at Meru.

In spite of the incredibly awkward start, zie was glad zie had asked for Jayanthi's input on the physiology. Zie could have opted for a mostly synthetic being with a token amount of zir biological material for continuity of consciousness, but that wouldn't have provided Jayanthi with the human companionship she obviously needed. She wouldn't admit to it, but zie could tell from the way her expression lit up whenever they spoke that she felt lonely. A mostly human form meant zie would see that joy with zir own eyes, something zie wanted to do, perhaps because of so much time spent observing her.

If zie'd kept in contact with Kaliyu and told zir about zir new attitude toward humans, no doubt zir friend would have been horrified. *Good thing we aren't friends anymore.* It still hurt to think about their argument, that final image of Kaliyu's back receding away as Veera's had so many years before.

The instrumentation in zir belt pouch notified zir that they had almost arrived at heliopause. The Sun had dwindled to a speck, a spot brighter than the thousands of stars around it but otherwise unremarkable. The planets of the Solar System had disappeared entirely.

The last time Vaha had been this far from home, zie had all of zir Nishadas cohorts along, plus their reality-transit instructor. This time, zie would make the journey alone. *Not truly alone. Jaya will be with me.* But she was a passenger, not someone who would pop up beside zir in some light-years-distant system.

Before zie could make the transition, zie needed to course-correct so that zir path followed the leading edge of the solar wind.

"Jaya," zie said softly.

She was deep in her genetics work—zie could tell by the way she kept the tip of her tongue between her lips—and zie hated to interrupt, but zie had no choice. "I'm afraid I need to ask you to take a sedative and secure yourself in your sleep sack."

Her gaze flew to a speaker, then down to the window in zir belly. "We're here?" she asked.

"Almost. I'll make the transit in 2.4 hours."

She slow-blinked a few times, then took the drug that would help her stay asleep.

"What's it like?" she asked. "Will I feel anything before or after?"

"I don't think so, but I don't know how an RT feels to humans. Are you nervous?"

She hesitated, then nodded. "And curious and excited, too."

"Try not to worry. I've made plenty of successful reality transits. It's one thing I'm actually pretty good at."

"I wish I could feel it happen," she said. Her eyes drooped. "I wish." Her words softened and blurred. "I could be. Like you."

Vaha tried not to take Jayanthi's words to heart. After all, she was a human. She didn't know that zie wasn't worth her admiration. But zie couldn't help the Neptune-blue glow of embarrassment that crept across zir phores.

"Sleep well," zie said softly.

Zie pulled the oblong womb in close and hugged it in zir arms before thrusting into a trajectory that followed the curve of the heliopause. Ahead, zie could see a small cluster of alloys—the emergency crew with their own womb and other medical equipment. Any pilots in transit would, like zirself, be traveling farther along the curve.

Once in position, zie began to enter the meditative state that would let zir perceive the universe's underlying structure.

Close the eyes. Bring the body to rest. Relax each muscle, from the crown of the head to the tip of the tail.

Vaha had to repeat the relaxation process twice. Zie prodded at the source of unease and discovered Jayanthi at its center. Zie had never made transits with living cargo, especially one so precious. *You're good at this,* zie reminded zirself. Zir instructor's words came to mind: *Accept any fear as natural. Let it sit with you as a companion. Do not resist its presence.*

Once zie acknowledged the anxiety, the tension drained from zir muscles. Zie entered the first stage of a clear mind. Everyday sensory modalities—vision, pressure, temperature, radio—all faded away. Conscious thought focused on the slow pulse of zir heart deep within zir core, the steady trickle of electricity from zir wings, zir lungs filling with water, the pressure of hydrogen in zir vent bladders.

Zie moved on to the second state. *Picture all consciousness shrinking, smaller than the self, smaller than every particle, until it's but a point in space. Then, withdraw from thought and engage the shashtam.* The sensory organ—unique to pilots and other massive beings—flared open inside Vaha. *Embodiment is an illusion, a convenience for a being to comprehend itself. Nothing exists where everything exists.*

Through the shashtam, zie could perceive the universe's true, probabilistic, quantized nature. Space and time became irrelevant, illusory. *Vaha* meant nothing except for zir consciousness. Matter and energy united, dissolved into infinite combinations, every possibility superimposed, permanent and eternal.

First comes desire, born of the mind.

Next comes will, to carry the self.

Last comes peace, the fulfillment of purpose.

Vaha found their destination and *reached* for it with every part of zir being. Zie felt the pull of a reality where zie existed two hundred light-years away, just outside the heliopause of Meru's system. Zie embraced it as truth.

Close off the shashtam. Let awareness return to the physical body. Move the tips of the fingers. Stretch the length of the body from crown to tail. At last, slowly open the eyes.

Vaha gazed upon a new pattern of stars. At its center burned the yellow-white glow of Pamir, Meru's sun.

—उपक्रम

Upakrama—Arrival

"Jaya, open your eyes."

Her lids didn't want to move. Whose voice was that? It didn't sound like either of her parents . . . oh! *Vaha.* Her eyes snapped open as remembrance flooded in. She blinked and shook her head to clear the cobwebs left by the sleeping agent, then stretched.

"I'm awake," she said and yawned. "Are we through?"

"Yes, we're half a day out from the transit point, heading toward Meru."

She released herself from the sleep sack and floated to the viewing window. One brighter star, a little yellowish, shone against the field of the Milky Way.

"It looks the same as before." She couldn't help the note of disappointment.

"If you compare the stars, they're different, I promise. I'll push a little harder now that we're here. You'll get a full Earth's gravity on my deceleration days. In twenty-four days, we'll arrive at Meru, though you won't see much detail until close to the end."

"It sounds like such a long time."

"Are all humans as impatient as you?"

"We're short-lived, not impatient."

Vaha laughed, a first. She had no idea where zie'd found the sound sample, but she could picture Vaha with zir head thrown back in full-throated amusement. She grinned.

The womb blocked her view for a second, then moved out of sight.

"What are you doing with your womb?"

"I had to reattach the umbilical to myself. It'll finish growing my incarn over the next two weeks, in time for our arrival at Meru."

"Are you going to show me what zie—you?—will look like?"

"Similar to the image you have. The incarn will be an extension of me, like your parents on Earth, until I merge that body back into myself. I'll be able to interface with it sensorially as long as I'm within electromagnetic line of sight."

"So that's why my parents kept their true bodies in geosynchronous orbit. Huh. I assumed it was because they wanted to be able to look up and see themselves."

"According to what I've learned, it's a two-way communication. I receive the sensory experience—what my incarn sees or smells or touches—and my willpower influences the incarn's actions. I'll keep myself asleep while in orbit so I can focus on the incarn rather than myself, and vice versa when I need to exercise my true body. Our consciousnesses will remain linked until I've reabsorbed the incarn's body."

"Do you have to? Reabsorb it, I mean."

Vaha stayed silent long enough for Jayanthi to wonder if she'd offended zir.

"I'm sorry," she said. "Did I say something wrong?"

"No, I'm struggling to find a way to explain it to you," Vaha said. "It's like trying to describe thamity fields or reality transits. You don't have the sensory perception for those to make sense, and you can't divest your matter the way I can."

Jayanthi wanted to kick herself. *You should know this better than other humans. What good is being raised by alloys if you don't even understand how incarns work?*

"I'm sorry. My parents never explained any of this to me. They always tried so hard to act human that I had to beg them to talk about anything in the alloy experience. We don't get access to much alloy literature or entertainment on Earth, either. It's not very popular, since so much of it relies on phoric and emtalk. I didn't mean to say something so thoughtless."

"It's all right. I'm not offended, truly. I forget sometimes that you aren't like me."

"That might be the nicest compliment I've ever received."

Vaha laughed again but softer.

"Where did you find all these sound samples of laughs?"

"Do you like them?"

Jayanthi nodded, knowing zie could see her through the cameras. "I like hearing you laugh."

A flush crept into her cheeks. The quality of zir voice combined with the image of zir incarn warmed her more than it should have. She blamed her loneliness. The more human Vaha sounded, the more she missed having another person around. She'd gone a month without physical human contact. The conversations with her parents and Mina had become more sporadic as the time lag increased. Now, hundreds of light-years away, the only way to communicate was through couriers who could reality transit. She wouldn't have a live conversation with anyone except Vaha for the next seventeen months. Her chest went tight against an upswelling of depression.

Your moods are swinging like a monkey through the trees. She couldn't let Vaha see her like this. Zie'd wonder why she was so upset, and what answer did she have? That she had no self-control? That she was a pathetic little mammal who needed a warm body to snuggle up to, who'd never been alone in her life? *But you're not alone! You have Vaha, and if zie hears you say any of that out loud, zie will feel insulted.*

So she mumbled an excuse about needing the bathroom and shut off the cameras and microphone. Then she let herself wallow and shed some tears.

After a few minutes, she rubbed her sleeve against the globs of liquid over her eyes. *Self-pitying idiot! You've entered a new star system, something you never thought you'd do in your entire life. Appreciate it, and appreciate the person who brought you here!* She grabbed a handhold and pulled herself close to the entry valve of the room, then laid her cheek against its warmth.

"What are you doing?" Vaha asked, zir tone carrying only curiosity.

Startled, Jaya pulled back. She enabled the microphone. "You could feel that?"

"Yes. That part is fairly sensitive, but I could sense your touch throughout the chamber, if you pressed hard enough."

"I thought the shell had no nerve endings?"

"There's living tissue beneath the calcium."

"So all this time, when I've been pushing off the walls . . . I've been kicking you?"

"Don't sound so appalled. You're so light, I can't feel it."

"Oh, thank the stars for that."

"Are you going to turn the cameras back on?"

"I need to wash up first." It was the truth. The sleep sack always made her sweat, and the sedative had knocked her out for longer than usual.

She undressed and extended the bathing tube, pulling it over herself and sealing the far end. The process was easier on days when Vaha accelerated, creating a false gravity, but she'd done it enough times in zero gravity that it had become second nature. Vaha talked her through it the first few times. No one had taught her the basics of Vaha's anatomy, life in low gravity, or how to survive two months without seeing another person. Zie couldn't advise her through that last one—zie seemed fine entertaining zirself and talking to her. *Another way that alloys are superior.*

The washing and some food helped pick up her spirits. After she dressed, she enabled the cameras and thought-projected her drawing of Vaha's face onto the viewing wall, then tagged it as a sticky feature. An image of another human was better than nothing.

"I never thought I'd get tired of seeing the stars," she confessed.

"I find them comforting, but I suppose it's strange for you."

"As strange as you'd feel under blue skies and gravity, I imagine."

"I'll find out soon enough. I can't wait for my incarn to experience what life is like for you."

Jayanthi sighed. "I wish I could do that, too—live like an alloy, I mean. Understand what it's really like. The archives on Earth don't have much information about it because why would we need to know? My parents discouraged my curiosity because they didn't want me to get frustrated. They chose life on Earth because they loved it and thought human beings have as much value as alloys. Ha! As if we could ever be your equals."

"Why not? You can be different and still have equal value in life. Without humans, there wouldn't be any alloys."

"But we're so limited! Unless we enhance our environment with destructive methods, we can only withstand a narrow set of living conditions. We don't have extended memory or augmented senses. We can't live in vacuum. We can't absorb solar energy. We need solid food and produce far more waste matter."

"If you think so poorly of your kind, why did you join this project?"

The question pulled Jayanthi up short. *Because I wanted to experience space travel and adventure and get my name in the Nivid and maybe prove my worth as a tarawan.* As the words came to mind, she realized how selfish they sounded. She didn't want to admit that to Vaha. Zie had formed a good opinion of her, or maybe zie was complimentary out of politeness, but either way, she didn't want to disappoint zir. Neither did she want to lie to zir.

"Our worth isn't limited to our ability," she acknowledged. "A small part of me hopes that human beings can make a fresh start on Meru and do better than our ancestors did. Maybe . . . maybe we've learned our lesson."

"Wouldn't the compact apply to Meru like it does for Earth?"

"I don't know. It doesn't apply to Mars or any of the other Solar System planets. Alloys are allowed to mine Earth for its resources, within limits. I don't know if we should subject Meru to the same treatment. Even if it only has single-celled organisms, the principles say that all forms of consciousness have equal value. After stars, planets are the largest nonliving conscious entities in the universe. They're complicated systems, just like our bodies, and they deserve respect. We treat Earth better than we used to, but we still don't live according to the principles. If we settle on Meru, I'd want a different way of life, an even better one." As she spoke the words, she felt the truth of them, as if they'd always existed somewhere deep in her thoughts. "By going on this mission, by proving my fitness—or not—for life on Meru, I can discover if that dream is possible."

"That's beautiful. I wish my friend Kaliyu could hear you. Maybe you'd convince zir of the worth of humankind."

Jayanthi bit her lip against a flush of pleasure. If she didn't know better, she'd think someone had coached Vaha to say what she longed to hear. She gazed at zir image and almost reached out a hand to touch it. It had watched over her for weeks. *I want to make sure you find my incarn pleasing.* Zie had done the job too well.

In her moments of privacy, she'd imagined running a hand down the contour of those cheekbones, of tangling her fingers in zir dark curls. Of kissing the generous lips. *It's all hormones and harmless fantasy. You're a sad, lonely human. So desperate for contact that you're lusting after an image.* That's what she told herself, repeatedly.

Alloys and humans didn't have romantic or sexual relationships, not since centuries earlier, before alloys had evolved into a different species. That would cause no end of conflicts with the strictures of the compact. That's why incarns on Earth couldn't legally resemble humans. Her parents had received an exemption to better raise a human child, and even they had features, like chromatophores, that set them apart. She didn't delude herself into thinking anything would come of her fantasies. Meeting Vaha in person would cure her of them, she was sure. An incarn represented a fragment of a pilot like Vaha. It would be like falling in love with someone's big toe: preposterous and impossible.

She pushed the idea from her mind and focused on Meru. In just over three weeks, they'd land. Vaha had shared maps of the area along with live video from orbit. She could learn a lot from those. She might have an alloy looking after her, but she didn't have to leave everything in zir hands.

—

Vaha spent most of the journey from the transit point to Meru worrying. Zie had never successfully landed on a planet as a child, and though falling into a gravity well was less effort than lifting out of one, the maneuvering to arrive at their intended site would be tricky. Zie could think of ten ways zie might fail. Zie had the womb to help heal zirself, but crash-landing would be potentially dangerous . . . and embarrassing.

Then there was Jayanthi to worry about. Since the transit, she'd withdrawn, spending more time poring through local data bursts from the alloys and constructs around Meru and less time on her genetics project. Zie had expected her to open up more after losing communications with Earth, but the opposite had happened. Clearly zie had a lot more to learn about humans.

Still, when they were close enough to start seeing the colors of Meru, she'd shared in zir wonder, spending hours with her face pressed against the clear patch of zir underbelly that she called her window.

"It looks kind of like Earth!" she'd exclaimed.

"It does, though with far less landmass and none of Earth's greenery."

Meru was only half of Earth's age, as was its sun, Pamir, but it had 50 percent more mass and was 22 percent larger, giving it slightly more gravity at its surface. Its sun was a bit cooler and less bright than Sol but otherwise similar. Meru compensated by orbiting a little closer to Pamir, making its year only 279 Earth days. The Meruvin day, however, was two hours and eighteen minutes longer.

The average surface temperature—287 Kelvin—sounded comfortable to Vaha, though Jayanthi claimed that it was cooler than she liked. She'd packed insulating clothes and solar heaters for the tent to compensate. Other than the scorching atmosphere of Venus, Vaha had spent zir life subject to the blistering light of the Sun and the absolute void of space. Alloys were the ultimate warm-blooded creatures, with tightly regulated physiology for homeostasis. No doubt zir incarn, which would have a more human metabolism, would agree with Jayanthi's assessment of the planet's climate.

As Vaha felt Meru's gravitational pull increase, zir most pressing concern was entry and landing. Zie had slowed to a nonorbital speed as zie approached. The plan was to allow atmospheric drag to slow zir down even further, then glide to the surface. While Meru's atmosphere didn't have Venus's density, zie could still get burned if zie didn't control zir descent. During the microgravity flight, zie had hardened zir entire body, extruding iron and calcium scales to repair zir skin damage from Venus and coating zir wings with clear silicate.

Zie had secured the womb against zir torso, with the incarn safely inside. Its outer shell would withstand the heat of entry and had self-healing properties as well. And zie had notified the construct near their landing site of zir intentions to touch down without assistance, but zie wanted them ready in case zie needed backup. Had any other alloy accepted Hamsa's offer, they would have relied on a construct to get Jayanthi to and from the planet's surface, but Vaha had been built for this very purpose. Zie hadn't tried a surface landing since zir youth, but zie had come so far and learned so much at Nishadas. Surely zie could do better?

While Jayanthi exclaimed over the land features, Vaha triple-checked the state of zir body. All was well. Zie had plenty of water and hydrogen for zir vents. The air supply to Jayanthi's chamber was good. Zie couldn't think of anything else to do.

"We are landing today, right?" Jayanthi asked.

Vaha's attention snapped back to the cameras in her chamber. Zir human passenger had secured herself in her sleep sack, though her eyes were alert and fixed on her window.

"It's today," zie confirmed.

Zie wondered if zir nervousness came through in zir tone. Zie almost switched to emtalk to avoid showing weakness to Jayanthi but decided to stay with speech. She wouldn't judge zir the way other people did. *Other alloys,* zie corrected zirself. *Humans might all be as kind as she is. Kaliyu was wrong about so many things, zie might have had everything backward.*

"Are you waiting for a particular time?"

"No, my descent will be active, more like a bird than a spacecraft."

"Will you leave the window open?"

"No, sorry. It can withstand a great deal of pressure but not heat. I'm going to turn off the cameras in your chamber as well. I need to minimize distractions."

"I understand. I'll stay quiet."

Vaha could sense the disappointment in Jayanthi's tone. Zie wondered if zie could grow a different matrix over the window that would be heat-resistant. *Stop stalling and get this over with!*

Zie gazed down at the planet. The flight path overlaid zir vision, and zir vent muscles constricted with nervous tension. If zie could accomplish this, if zie could land on Meru's surface without injury, zie could face zir maker's return with part of zir pride restored.

Here goes everything.

Vaha used zir dorsal vents to push zirself lower, keeping zir wings flexed up and back, feathering zir fall to maximize air resistance. Meru's atmosphere was a lot thinner than Venus's, but experiencing it firsthand and flying through it were different from knowing the facts.

As zir downward speed picked up, zir shoulders and back strained against the drag on zir wings. Zie fought the instinctive urge to push them downward, to counteract the pull of Meru's gravity. Not only did zie have to conserve muscle power for later, zie needed to keep zir wings pointed up. Zie watched zir speed—*airspeed*—on zir visual overlay. When it got too high, zie thrust downward with the vent at the base of zir tail. Zie overcorrected and shot up. *Damn!*

Zir next correction went slightly better, but still not smoothly. Zie stutter-stepped through the descent, dropping too fast, then rising a little too high. Zie could feel the heat on zir skin without looking at the temperature indicator. The more water zie consumed and vented, the faster zie would shed heat, but zie had to pace zir usage to avoid dehydration. The adrenaline coursing through zir didn't help. Bits of skin flaked away and formed a trail of glowing specks in the rearview camera on zir pack.

They were low enough now to see whorls of silver currents running through the oceans. Soft humps formed the cloud tops. Vaha brought zir wings to a gliding position, outstretched on either side. Zir muscles trembled with the effort of pushing against the atmosphere. *But I'm doing it! I'm flying! If only my maker could see me now.*

Then zie plummeted. Jayanthi screamed for a split second. Vaha thrust instinctively down with zir tail, but it did no good. *What's happening?* A few seconds later, the answer came to zir out of a dim theoretical recollection: a thermal pocket. A column of air moving downward at high speed. At such a low altitude, zie needed lift to counteract it, not thrust. The other special parts of zir anatomy, from zir unique genetics, were two massive oblique bladders. They could fill with atmosphere and push the air straight back, creating jets parallel to zir body.

Zie had no more time to think. By instinct, zie extended the bladders and opened their mouths. A rushing sense filled them, and zie squeezed the vent muscles in the back. Zie shot forward and lifted zir chest as Meru's atmosphere stabilized zir descent.

"Are you all right?" zie asked Jayanthi, daring a quick distraction.

"I'm fine," she said, her voice steady.

Vaha didn't entirely believe her, but the confidence in her tone helped recenter zir mind. Zie forced zir muscles to relax.

"And you?" Jayanthi asked.

"Sore," zie replied. "That drop surprised me. I might have sprained some muscles, but I was more worried about hurting you."

"You're doing great. I know you'll get us on the ground safely."

You know nothing of the sort. But zie wanted to live up to Jayanthi's expectations. *I wonder what the construct thought of that, assuming they're watching.* Not that their opinion should matter, but Vaha couldn't help caring. Between the early years with zir maker and the later years at Nishadas, zir skills had always come under criticism. It seemed only natural that the local intelligences at Meru would have some opinion on zir abilities.

They had drifted off course during zir wild maneuvering, and zie angled zirself to get back on track. Another twenty-two minutes to their intended destination. They flew over land now. Rust and ochre and white intermingled. Gradual hills gave way to sharp cliffs, then an open plain cut by a sinuous river.

Vaha turned in a wide, lazy arc, marveling at the sensation of gliding. If it weren't for gravity's tug on zir internal organs, zie could almost imagine zie were still flying in space. Zie stretched out zir arms and beat back zir wings, too fast at first, pushing zir up again, then slower and slower until zie could trail zir fingertips along the ground. Zir tail dragged for a few hundred meters until at last, zie came to a stop.

Dust clouds filled the air, and zie sent a silent apology to the planet for the damage zie'd caused. *I'll do better next time.*

Then the enormity of it all hit zir like a comet in the face.

"We're here," Vaha said. "I've landed."

"I knew you could do it!" Jayanthi said.

Why Vaha's success would matter to her beyond her own safety, zie didn't know, but zie basked in it anyway.

"Can I move around?" Jayanthi asked.

"Yes."

Vaha, however, couldn't lift a finger. Between the gravity and the exertion of the flight, zir body refused to twitch another muscle even as zir mind danced with glee. Zie wished zie could send a recording of zir first successful touchdown to zir maker and to Kaliyu. One was in some distant, unmapped part of the galaxy. The other would ignore or block anything zie sent. At least zie had Jayanthi. *She's my only friend here.* As she slipped into her suit and helmet, Vaha pillowed zir head on zir arms and sipped at bhojya. Zie sealed the tube's flange over zir mouth out of habit, then realized that with Meru's atmosphere, there was no need. As zie drank, zie picked up a rock from the surface, lifted, and released.

It fell, just like in the movies.

—जन्म

Janma—Birth

Jayanthi gazed up at the purple sky of an alien planet. Other than the color, she could have been standing in a rocky desert on Earth, but it served as a reminder that she was somewhere entirely different. White clouds grazed as they did back home, and the sun—Pamir—shone just as yellow-white. But the sky . . . *purple* didn't do it justice, the way *blue* was inadequate for Earth. Violet. Lavender. Amethyst. The color of Vaha's eyes. The great dome of atmosphere had nuances that she couldn't capture with words.

Meru's air flowed unfiltered into her helmet. It was cooler than back home and much cooler than the chamber inside Vaha. It smelled of sunbaked iron with a faint salty tang. Their landing site lay twelve kilometers from the coast, but she hadn't expected to smell it. The breeze also carried a vegetal odor she couldn't quite place, like a garden the day after a heavy rain.

She took a few experimental steps. Two months of living in an ideal environment had spoiled her, and walking around in a protective suit and boots felt clunky. She'd done her best to exercise during the journey on acceleration days, but that didn't compare to her daily walks to Mina's house. She'd used her blood exchanger thrice during the journey, the final time on the last day with deceleration before their approach to Meru. *There's no guarantee the extra oxygen here will help. Take it slow.* Her boots left imprints on the fine dust that lay atop the rocks. The slight increase in gravity wasn't noticeable, and she tried jogging for the sheer joy of it. *I'm running on the surface of another planet!* She almost flung her arms out and shouted the words in glee, but her audience inhibited that level of exuberance.

She was the first human being on Meru—the first on any planet other than Earth in centuries—and she wished she could share the experience with another. Two hundred light-years from home made real-time communication impossible. She could record messages, and the orbital station would make observations, and all that would get sent back to Earth via courier pilots, alloys like Vaha who ferried data across the vast distances of known space. It would take weeks, maybe months, to hear back from her family and friends.

She turned and watched as Vaha propped zir head on one arm. Zie lay outstretched on zir left side, zir tail curved along the ground, like a sphinx crossed with a whale, though no whale on Earth had been that massive in eons. Patches of pale flesh showed through gaps in zir scales. Under Meru's sun and air, zir skin scintillated with the nonporous metals that had given rise to the label *alloy*. The space-dark tones contrasted beautifully against the rust colors of the surroundings.

Vaha tucked away a tube of bhojya, then carefully detached the womb from zir torso and placed it to the side. Zie turned zir eyes, almost as tall as she was, toward her. They had a depth and complexity that the image of zir incarn hadn't shown, with flecks of black and amber embedded in a deep shade of amethyst that nearly matched Meru's sky.

"You're so tiny and cute," Vaha sent via emtalk.

Jayanthi put her hands on her hips. "I am not *cute*."

A low chuckle sounded in her ear. "What do you think of Meru?"

"A little chilly and barren but beautiful in its own way."

"I need a brief rest before we build the shelter. It will take a few days for my skin to heal, and then I'll leave for orbit. Once I'm settled there, I'll tell the womb to deliver my incarn."

"I'll have to be alone while you're in transit?"

"For a few hours, yes. I can't give the incarn my full attention until I'm secure in a berth. Don't worry. There's a construct not too far from here who can help you in case of an emergency, and I'll make sure the satellite communications work before I leave."

They spent the next few hours setting up the tent house and unpacking supplies. Vaha did all the heavy lifting and assembly, and she organized the interior. Her parents had taken her wilderness camping a few times, but they'd slept in a tiny one-room affair. The shelter on Meru had a sturdy frame that could withstand frequent rain and wind. It had multiple rooms inside with clear panes in the roof and walls for observing the landscape, and the squat brown structure sat several steps above the ground. Meru had torrential storms, and its hard surface tended to flood.

Once they had it put together, Vaha tested the most critical systems: power generation, communications, data recording, and waste filtration. By the time zie finished, the sun had slipped behind the cliffs in the west. Jayanthi slow-blinked and called up a map. The coast lay to the south and southeast, and the plain stretched away to the north. A lake lay about half a kilometer away in that direction, and Vaha had run the tent's plumbing to it without much difficulty. It would provide fresh water, whatever they needed beyond rain catchments and recycling. A river ran east to west, from the cliffs to the lake to the ocean. She was eager to explore it all, but setting up camp had exhausted her.

As she rested and ate some rehydrated food, she gazed through a tent window at the masses of clouds on the eastern horizon. The setting sun painted them in rose and gold, just as it would on Earth, but the dusky sky behind it was the color of wine that faded into a royal indigo.

Vaha had already closed zir eyes. She suspected zie slept, though zir chest didn't rise and fall the way a human's would. To think that zir body had carried them to this place, all the way from Earth—it astonished her. She wished she could stroke zir skin. Would it feel warm or cool? Rough or smooth? But not only did it seem rude to ask, she couldn't expose her hand to Meru without violating the project's rules. Any bacteria on Vaha's exterior would have burned off during the landing, and zir skin didn't respire like her own. Would she be allowed to go unsuited on Meru one day? To feel the breeze on her face? And if not her, would future generations of human beings?

The womb sat just past Vaha's head, a dark oblong shape about a third as long as Vaha's body. In a few days, she would get to meet zir incarn. It felt strange and a little disconcerting to think that Vaha's true body would leave. Zie had been her home, her safe place, for the past two months. She'd have to navigate Meru without that security. An incarn would have the same limitations as her body, not the almost godlike power of an alloy pilot.

But then she pictured zir face and imagined having zir in the tent with her. Would Vaha's incarn share zir personality? They'd have separate brains and vastly different bodies, but she hoped they would treat her the same way. She'd grown used to Vaha's supportive manner and gentle teasing. Zie talked to her like an equal, not an inferior and incapable human. She'd need someone like that in the months to come.

Jayanthi watched Vaha slither away. Two large sacs ballooned outward from either side of zir torso. A plume of dust formed behind them as the vents in the back squeezed. The ochre cloud grew until it almost obscured her view, and then Vaha's body burst through it and soared into the midday sky. Zie held zir wings outstretched, perpendicular to zir body, like a human-era jet plane. She shielded her eyes and watched as zie rose. Another speck circled above, which she guessed was the construct that would have lifted any other alloy from the ground.

She wanted to emtalk with Vaha, to tell zir how amazing zie was and how zir maker should have had more faith in zir, but any communication could distract zir, so she stayed silent. Inside, she leaped with joy. Zie had fulfilled zir genetic purpose!

A few hours later, as the first stars emerged, Vaha sent a message that zie had achieved geosynchronous orbit.

"Any problems with the flight?" she replied. Then hastily added, "Not that I'd expect you to have any. I watched you as long as I could, and I thought it looked perfect."

"That isn't the word I'd use, but I managed it. I caught turbulence again, and this time I knew what to do. It wasn't a problem. With some more practice, I might actually be able to land and take off gracefully."

"Not that my opinion matters, but you should be proud of yourself. You've achieved all four modes of flight now, right?"

"I have, and your opinion matters. A lot."

Emtalk didn't convey tone, but Vaha's words filled Jayanthi's belly with warmth.

"That's wonderful, Vaha. Congratulations! This means you get your genome in the Nivid."

"That's right. I almost can't believe it."

Zie didn't have to telegraph the words for Jayanthi to know zie must be thinking of zir maker. "I wish I could celebrate with you."

"Maybe you can. I received a notification from the womb. My incarn has been delivered. Zie is awake and waiting for you. The womb's ambulatory construct has washed zir body and wrapped zir in an environment suit. Once you open the door, I . . . well, this body will no longer speak to you. I'll watch over you through my incarn and the cameras around the camp. Be patient. Zie isn't a helpless infant, but this will be the first time I use a second body. Supposedly gross motor control will improve in a Meruvin day or two. Fine control might take a week or more, and I have no idea how long until I can speak or hear well."

"I understand," Jayanthi sent.

"One last thing—if my incarn gets injured or dies, you can place zir back in the womb for healing or life support, and zie can do the same for you. I should be safe here in my berth, so I'll leave the womb on the surface."

Jayanthi shivered. *I'm not planning for either of us to die here.* She walked to the entrance of the womb, and her heart picked up its pace at the thought of meeting Vaha in zir human form.

"Open the door," Vaha instructed. "There's a vestibule that doubles as an airlock. You can use it like the one in the tent, to leave your suit and sterilize it, though I don't think you'll need to this time."

Jayanthi pushed at a handle as big as her leg. The seal around the door made a slight sucking noise as it released. Inside, lit by bioluminescence, was a spacious room with a wash area large enough for an average alloy. She rinsed the dust from her boots, then flipped open her helmet visor before passing through the inner door.

Vaha's incarn stood there, half a head taller than her and a near match to the image that she'd gazed upon for the past five weeks. Dark-violet eyes—human eyes—fringed by black lashes blinked at her. Zir curls hung limply around zir shoulders, but the planes of zir face were as exquisite as she'd imagined.

Vaha's words came back to her: *You'll have to spend many months looking at my incarn. I want to make sure you find zir pleasing.*

"Hello, Vaha," she said. Her heart rioted in her chest.

"Hawoo. Haroh." Zie frowned. "Howlow."

Jayanthi bit back a giggle. The intense concentration on zir face made an adorable furrow in zir brow.

"Hullo. Hello." Zir lips stretched, first one way, then another, like someone eating a sticky candy.

Jayanthi was fairly certain zie was trying to smile. She answered with a grin.

Vaha frowned again. "Ja. Ya," zie said carefully.

Jayanthi's breath caught in her throat.

Vaha took a tentative, coltish step forward, wobbling as zie set one foot down, then the other.

Jayanthi grabbed zir under the elbow to steady zir. "Let me help you. It might be easier in the tent, where you can go barefoot."

She locked a helmet on zir and then herself. They stumbled their way together to the structure. Jayanthi discovered that helping someone taller than her up a few stairs was more difficult than she'd imagined. They made it into the vestibule, both of them breathing hard. She removed her outer suit, then helped Vaha, who was fumbling with zir zipper. She got about eight centimeters down and realized zie had nothing on underneath.

"Stay here a minute. I'll go fetch a robe," she said.

Stop being so embarrassed about nudity, she scolded herself as she opened the supply cabinet. *Alloys have no problem with their bodies.* But Vaha's incarn looked so human, she struggled to think of zir as an extension of the massive being who had carried her to Meru.

She got zir out of the enviro-suit and into a robe without looking too closely at zir body, trying to maintain a professional, nurse-like demeanor the entire time. She wasn't sure she succeeded. Vaha's unnervingly violet eyes tracked her every movement. Every time her hand brushed zir warm, smooth skin, an involuntary shiver ran through her. She hadn't touched another person in two months. *That would explain my reaction. I hope zie doesn't take it the wrong way.*

They moved into the main room. She'd placed a folding table and two sling chairs against one wall. A storage cabinet with a smaller table stood on the opposite side. She'd mentally dubbed that the kitchen. Three partitions created two small sleeping areas, each big enough for a cot and chair, with a washroom in between. The latter had equipment that would sterilize wastewater and package any solid waste for removal. A fourth section of the tent, an offshoot from the "kitchen" area, would serve as their greenhouse. The entire structure was sealed. Sun-warmed air blew in, and filtered air flowed out. One of their primary directives was to keep Meru free of contamination by their microbiomes.

"You loof tiyed," Vaha said. "You shleef?"

"Yes, I should sleep. Let me get you some water before I lie down."

Vaha's walking had already improved, but Jayanthi didn't trust zir fine motor control for filling a water bottle. She grabbed a zero-gravity version with a straw to avoid zir embarrassing zirself with spills.

"Tay you." Zie smiled.

"You smiled! This is so exciting. I don't know if I can sleep."

Vaha laughed, then looked so surprised at zirself that Jayanthi couldn't stop herself from laughing, too.

"No. You shleep. I purratice talkin."

Zie looked so sweet and earnest that before Jayanthi realized what she was doing, she asked, "Can I kiss you good night?" She quickly added, "It's something I would do with my parents."

"Yesh."

She pressed her lips lightly against zir cheek, and zir chromatophores pulsed violet-brown in response. Vaha had an entirely different scent from Hamsa's or her parents' incarns, grassy with a hint of rose.

"Good night," she whispered.

In her "bedroom," she changed into pajamas and tried hard to put stupid impulses out of her mind. *I've been lonely.* Vaha had explained how alloys could regulate their physical attraction to each other by consciously adjusting their hormones. Emotional attachment came first, then consent, then contact. She didn't have that kind of control. *Damn this human body!*

The roof of the tent had a transparent section above the cot. She lay on her back, unfamiliar constellations shining above, and listened to Vaha murmur to zirself until she fell into a deep, exhausted sleep.

It took Vaha's incarn about four Meruvin days to reach a passable level of proficiency at speech and walking. After the first night, zie kept to Jayanthi's schedule. While she and the incarn slept, zie shifted zir awareness to zir true body and watched over them via cameras and microphones in the shelter. Those signals, along with the ones from scientific instrumentation on the outside, were captured and stored at the geosynchronous orbital platform where zie had berthed.

Zie shared the data with a courier alloy who would return to Sol when the platform's memory capacity was full. Since they both needed to stay in orbit with a good view of the landing site, they shared a small space with four berths attached. Vaha had thought the accommodations at Nishadas were simple, but they felt like a luxury compared to the Meruvin ones. These berths had dark metal frames, thin, with no privacy and nowhere to decorate or customize. The central chamber had enough room for their equipment, bhojya, water, and a filtration system. Vaha had secured zirself in the berth diagonal from the courier's. After exchanging brief introductions, zie let zir true body stay in deep sleep during surface daytime and kept zir full attention with zir incarn.

There were many strange things about living at the bottom of a planet's well, but walking topped the list. Zie had *legs*. They gave zir some trouble at first, which zie expected, as did zir stiff-boned arms and hands and everything else. Zie hadn't realized that living with gravity would pose so many challenges. Objects kept moving on their own instead of staying where zie placed them. Nothing behaved as zie expected it to. Zie had to override years of experience and instinctive behavior.

Equally confounding was learning to use the sense of smell, a modality zie had experienced only through taste in the back of zir throat. The first scent zie learned to identify was Jayanthi's. She didn't compare to anything, certainly not any bhojya flavors zie knew. The second was the planet's air, which had a more familiar odor, similar to that of herbal drinks. The third was the inside of their tent, another scent that zie couldn't place but, after a few excursions, could recognize as a distinct smell from the outside air.

The single eyelid posed challenges, too. Not only could zie not fully block bright lights, zie had to remember to keep dropping the lids to keep zir eyes moisturized. One evening, over a meal of rice and beans, zie had gazed into Jayanthi's eyes for so long that zie realized zie had forgotten to blink. Her eyes had such a different depth and light to them compared to an alloy's. She seemed to find it as hard to look away from zir, though she ought to have seen plenty of eyes like zirs.

Her face captivated Vaha. Seeing her in person and on the same scale allowed zir to notice fine details in her features that the camera views had missed—the texture of her hair, a slight tilt of her head when she had a question, the little mole by her left eye.

Zir body tingled every time their skin met. After zie had better control of zir movement, zie found zirself taking every opportunity to stand near Jayanthi, to breathe her in. Zie could sense her presence in a way that zie never had with another alloy. *Perhaps this is what the literature meant by pheromones.* Vaha discovered zir body responding to hers in ways that zie had no control over. Zir mind tried to regulate zir hormones like zie would with zir true body, but none of that worked with zir incarn. Zie had almost asked Jayanthi how humans could stand to live like that, but then zie worried the question might offend her.

It made her kiss entirely comprehensible. The gesture had confused Vaha that first night. Zie hadn't known what the word *kiss* meant until two minutes later, after zie had some time to research it, but zie was glad zie had agreed to it. Alloys kept their mouths sealed against vacuum, so they couldn't use them the way humans in atmosphere did. They expressed affection by holding hands or hugging. Intimacy involved other parts of their bodies, especially their vents.

The kiss was pleasant, though. Zie found zirself wanting to return it, but zie didn't have the motor control for it until the third night. Just before going to their separate bedrooms, zie pressed zir lips to Jayanthi's cheek and said, "Good night." She had placed a hand on her cheek before heading to her room. Her skin had a taste to it, and it yielded under zir lips more than zie had expected. It felt nothing like alloy skin, which was smooth and, for pilots, slightly scaly. Zie wanted to spend more time exploring hers, but zie didn't have the courage to ask if zie could, not after her muted reaction.

Sounds were another novelty, like the sharp breath Jayanthi took when Vaha had kissed her. Their shelter made hundreds of small noises. The enviro-suits rustled. Jaya's voice had a melody. The weeks of studying tone had proven a fortuitous investment of effort. Zie had no translator for zir incarn, no way to color Jayanthi's speech with meaning and emotion, but zie could map the knowledge zie'd gained on the flight over to what zir incarn sensed with zir ears. It forced Vaha to learn a whole new vocabulary. Lilting rather than purple. Flat rather than dark orange. Low rather than blue.

And then there were the many forms of laughter. Jayanthi's suppressed snorts when Vaha would trip over zir feet. Her delighted chuckle when zie accomplished some new task. Her fits of giggles when the incompetent tarawan in *Across the Orbit* came up with some absurd look for a client's child, claiming that it was a new fashion trend. Vaha couldn't imitate her sounds, but zie found zirself laughing along with her, zir body reacting uncontrollably to her mirth in its own unique way.

The only negative was dealing with the vent-spawned ravages of gravity. The MEC allowed them to range within the boundaries formed by the cliffs, the river, and the sea, and they walked somewhere daily to exercise their bodies and conduct basic research. Vaha would rather have flown over all of it, but neither Jayanthi nor zir incarn had that option.

Zie couldn't fathom how these gravity-well-bound bipeds were zir ancestral cousins. Alloys had their share of problems in space, but after four days on Meru, zie understood why they considered service on Earth as an act of penitence. Had zie not had Jayanthi for company, zie would have quit the incarn life in short order, but she made the pain worthwhile. Telling her so, however, seemed foolish. How could zie trust zir feelings when they came from a temporary incarn's body?

After a Meruvin week, Jayanthi passed all the basic physiological tests while being as active as she had back on Earth. Her heart rate, blood pressure, and oxygenation levels stayed good the entire time. Her hands and feet hadn't swollen, and instead of being tired after an activity, she felt the same amount of energy as before she'd done it. The one remaining danger was to her lungs, but they wouldn't be able to evaluate that until she'd spent a lot more time on the planet.

Vaha's incarn had progressed from moving like a wobbly toddler to a full-grown adult. Zie had emerged from the womb with a modified musculature and cardiovascular system for Meru. The womb's constructed mind had done its best with the design, and the incarn could go back into the womb to heal any damage. Unlike Jayanthi, zie didn't have to treat zir body as an experiment.

"We need to celebrate," Jayanthi declared after getting her test results. "To my health, and to your successful launch."

She'd had fun watching Vaha experience solid food for the first time, but zie had only tasted rehydrated dishes, so she dug out a chocolate bar from her supplies for the occasion.

"This is seventy-five-percent real cacao." She handed Vaha a piece and waited as zie placed it in zir mouth.

Vaha's eyes closed, and zir phores glowed with pleasure. Jayanthi kept silent and grinned to herself. *Definitely a worthy way to celebrate!*

She hadn't expected to find so much joy in introducing an alloy to simple human experiences: walking, talking, eating. Her parents had already gone through those before she was born, and Hamsa had shown only cursory interest.

Vaha opened zir eyes and said, "I've had chocolate-flavored bhojya, but the texture of the solid, it's like . . . happiness in elemental form. Could I have another piece?"

She laughed and handed zir one more. "Yes. I used up a good amount of the mass allowance for chocolate. It keeps forever and travels well. I wish we could eat some on our longer hikes, like I used to with my parents."

She and Vaha had gone to the coast and seen the vast mats of blue-green algae floating on the ocean's surface. Aquamarine waves frothed and crashed onto the beach, as they did on Earth. Jayanthi hadn't often seen the ocean at home, which was in a landlocked region. After witnessing the power of it on Meru—the roar penetrated her helmet—she wished they'd built their shelter closer to the shore. The following day, she took it easier, and they visited the nearby lake. A river at its mouth ran brown with silt, meandering its way from the cliffs in the west, through a winding channel, until it reached the banks of the lake.

After their brief celebration, she declared that she wanted to go to the base of the cliffs, their longest excursion yet.

"Moving on two legs is a terrible form of locomotion," Vaha grumbled as they set off from the camp, the morning sun at their back.

"You wanted to experience being human," she teased.

"Couldn't I stay in the camp while you go on these hikes?"

She answered the rhetorical question with a laugh. Vaha had taken the place of her childhood minder, Keerthi, a shadow to make sure she had help if she overexerted herself. She didn't think zie could carry her like Keerthi could, but zie could call down zir true body or request help from a local construct in a real emergency.

Zie took her hand as they set off along the rocky soil. Zie had done that with every walk. She wasn't sure what zie meant by the gesture, and after two months of dealing with zir ignorance of all things human, she made no assumptions. Perhaps zie saw her as a child or thought she needed comforting. They'd had a lot of physical contact by necessity of zir getting used to inhabiting zir incarn body. She hadn't expected Vaha to kiss her good night, but she refused to interpret that as anything but a polite return of her own gesture. To do otherwise would place them in dangerous territory.

So she held zir hand and let the connection lighten her steps. They passed boulders the size of pilots along the way, scattered like an enormous child had thrown their toys. Colors in every hue of reddish brown infused the landscape, broken only by the occasional pale vein. Between Vaha's hand and the extra oxygen, she didn't feel the slightest bit tired by the time they reached the base of the cliffs. Up close, the sheer wall resolved into crags and outcroppings, many large enough to host their tent. It rose in a gentler slope than the vertical face it presented from afar. Rubble formed the base.

"Too bad we can't have a picnic," she said.

They sat on a broad, flat stone the color of rust. Jayanthi ran a gloved hand over the surface, wishing for the hundredth time that she could touch it. Being on an alien planet and unable to interact with the environment was a unique form of torture.

"A what?"

"A picnic—a meal that you pack and eat while sitting outside. Maybe I can smuggle you back to Earth one day and show you what I mean."

"I'd get into a lot of trouble if I was caught on Earth with such a human incarn."

"I know. I was joking."

As she looked at Vaha's earnest expression, she felt a pang. When this mission was over, she'd never see zir again.

"What's the matter?" Zie had started to read her expressions, often doing that better than interpreting her tone of voice.

Jayanthi smiled. "Nothing. I got sad thinking about the fact that I won't see you after we're done here."

"Why not? I'm not going anywhere."

"I meant after we're done with the project on Meru."

Vaha frowned. "That is sad."

"Oh no!" She laughed. "Don't let my ridiculousness infect you, too. We just arrived, and we have an entire year ahead of us. There's plenty to look forward to. For example, I'd like to try climbing up to the top of these cliffs."

Vaha peered up the rocky face. "Is that possible? Is it safe? Can we do that without damaging the surface?"

"Adventure first, safety second!" She grinned at the alarm on Vaha's face. "I'm joking!"

She squinted up at the cliffs. Boulders formed much of the base, but they had eroded over time, as had the rocky surface that stretched up to the top. Cracks had formed in both horizontal and vertical directions, striating the surface into sections that they could walk on.

"Maybe we can't make it all the way to the top without using damaging equipment," she said, "but I bet we could scramble up partway. I'm sure the view is lovely."

She stood and clambered up the nearest boulder before Vaha could protest. The enviro-suit protected her hands and knees, making it easier. Her breath came hard as she hauled herself higher and higher, but her muscles felt great. She didn't stop until she could go no farther.

When she turned around, their landing plain spread before her, an expanse of russet, ochre, and chalky white ribbons ending in the sparkling blue-green of the sea, which stretched to the violet horizon. Pamir was directly above in the midday sky, and Vaha wasn't too far below.

A few minutes later, zie arrived. "It is a lovely view. I wish you could see it from orbit, too."

She could forget their differences so easily, until a statement like that brought them rushing back. She didn't think zie meant to hurt her with it. Vaha had been far more considerate of her than she'd imagined and far more enthused about living with a human than she'd expected.

She covered up the unwelcome melancholy with a joke. "A bit stark, don't you think? Could do with some trees."

"I suppose if humans do settle here, they'll need plants," Vaha said. "According to the construct on the plateau, the soil should support Earth vegetation after some amendments to help break it down."

"I was joking again, sorry. I hope the seedlings in the greenhouse will thrive. My favorite type of tomatoes are in there, and I would love for you to taste them."

"Then I hope for success for both our sakes, but first, we have to make it back to our camp in one piece."

"If you're worried, I can go first."

"I'd be more concerned about falling on top of you."

So Vaha descended first. Jayanthi placed her hands and feet with care, but her thoughts were elsewhere. With Vaha doing all the labor of maintaining the camp, she had little to occupy her mind, and she needed something to shift her focus from zir. It was too easy to treat zir as a friend instead of a caregiver, a peer rather than an alloy. *Vaha isn't human, no matter what zir incarn acts like. I should get back to my genetics work.* The womb sat near their house and collected dust. She had to work up the nerve to ask Vaha if she could use it.

—अवियुक्त

Aviyuktha—Inseparable

Jayanthi bit her lip and stared at the design for her hybrid person. Around the second century Human Era, rampant genetic engineering had led to too many nonviable hybrids as well as the opposite, genetically stagnant people with many of the same problems that inbreeding caused. Fifty years later, the first fully artificial android was built—not an emergent intelligence but a lab-grown person built of inorganic parts—and the earliest alloy designs came a century after that. The period had ended with the regulations that underpinned modern directed evolution: requirements on minimum and maximum genetic variation from one generation to the next, mandatory introduction of some random mutations, and the separation between human and alloy reproduction.

The Nivid had records going as far back as the first human genome ever sequenced. Jayanthi wished she could access the full repository to see what had failed, but she would have to settle for trial and error.

"Are you working on genetics again?" Vaha's voice made her jump. "Sorry, I didn't mean to startle you."

"You're awake," she said. She thought-cleared her visual to see zir better. "I started looking at my hybrid project again—something to do while you're away. How could you tell?"

"You hum whenever you're deep in thought."

"Oh. I didn't realize that. I'll try not to."

"It's okay. I like hearing it. I'm sorry I took a little longer in bed this morning. I had to learn how to back up data from our site. The courier's memory is full, and the replacement is late, so I'll have to overwrite some of my extended memory. It took some time to decide what I wanted to give up."

Jayanthi hesitated to ask what Vaha had chosen. It seemed like too intimate a question for their relationship. She'd had some idea of how lonely Meru would be, but she hadn't grasped the full extent until after they landed. The planet's stark beauty was undeniably barren. No trees, no animals, not even any constructs in sight. Without Vaha's company, she might have given up and begged to go home after a month, humanity and the Nivid be damned.

"I wish I could help with your genetics work," Vaha said. "I don't know anything about the subject."

It was the perfect opening to ask about zir womb, but Jayanthi couldn't bring herself to do it. For all Vaha's kindness, she'd never had to ask zir for something so personal. How would zie react to her request? What was zir relationship to the device, which was also a possession? She was so ignorant of alloy matters. Back on Earth, she'd thought to convince Vaha to help her because it could get zir name into the Nivid. Now that zie would gain that honor for zir own genome, she had nothing to offer.

"I'm only doing this to pass the time," she said. "Hamsa said my design was too risky and prone to failure."

"Maybe Hamsa was wrong." Vaha pushed a cup of bhojya toward her and sat down at the table with one of zir own. "Sometimes the people who love us most can be the greatest obstacles to our success."

"He encouraged me for many years first," she said. She told zir how she'd developed an interest in genetics because of her own unique situation. As the only human in centuries to have sickle cell disease, Jayanthi had wanted to understand why she existed. Hamsa had designed her, and he'd been happy to teach her what he could and point her at the resources to study on her own. The more she'd learned about tarawans, the more she dreamed of serving as one. "He never told me it was impossible until our last time together. I thought that if I produced a design that was innovative enough, it would create a circumstance so exceptional that TESC—the Tarawan Ethics and Standards Council—would certify me as the world's first human tarawan. I failed miserably, and then Hamsa said he would rather I focus my efforts elsewhere, but . . . I can't let it go. Maybe he's right. Maybe I do have AAD."

"I've known alloys who are far more destructively ambitious," Vaha said.

She didn't voice the response that came to mind: *I'm not an alloy. Your standards don't apply to me.* Vaha hadn't intended to hurt her with zir comment, and she didn't want to throw zir kindness back in zir face.

"Without Hamsa's simulator and access to parts of the Nivid, you can't effectively create a viable design. Do I have that right?" zie asked.

She nodded and took a sip of the bhojya. "Anise and saffron. What a lovely combination."

"It's my favorite." Vaha paused and said, "I realize I'm ignorant on this subject, but would my womb be of any use? It has a limited genetic database, and I think it can run simulations."

The offer gave her a sense of vertigo. She'd never expected that zie would simply allow her to use zir womb with nothing in return. Had she said something to hint at her desire? She reviewed their conversation and decided that she hadn't. Vaha had a generous heart. She was learning that daily. This was another example of it.

Before the silence dragged on too long, she said, "Yes, I could use it to help with my work."

"You should've said something sooner. All the weeks in transit—you could have made so much progress!"

"I felt awkward about it," she admitted. "Presumptuous. It's your womb, and the research I'm doing isn't important to anyone except me."

"That's all that matters," zie declared. "I have some time this morning. After we're done eating, let's go over there, and I'll show you how to operate it."

"Vaha . . . I don't know. What if it comes to nothing?"

"You had faith in my abilities when we arrived at Meru. Let me return the favor, please."

Zie placed a hand over hers, and a tiny thrill passed through her. Vaha's palm was warm, dry, and reassuringly solid. Zie had offered her exactly what she wanted, so why didn't she leap to accept it? *It's a gift, and perhaps zie doesn't realize how special a gift it is.* She was scared that she might disappoint zir. That she cared so much about how zie felt had ramifications, but rather than give voice to those, she thanked zir.

Vaha walked her over to the womb after they finished breakfast. They entered the vestibule where she'd found zir and waited for their eyes to adjust to the dimly lit interior.

"Can you believe it's only been two weeks since I met you here?" Jayanthi asked. "I feel like I've lived two months on Meru."

Vaha removed zir helmet. "Does that mean our year together is equivalent to a lifetime for you?"

"Only if we can pack a life's worth of experiences into it."

"I'll do my best." Zie smiled.

Was zie flirting with her? She didn't have much experience at that kind of thing with her own people, much less someone like Vaha. Did alloys flirt? *By the Nivid, stop! Zie isn't human, so it's pointless to wonder.*

Vaha removed zir gloves and indicated for Jayanthi to do the same. She tucked hers into her helmet and set it on the floor. The vestibule was structured almost like an airlock, with an interior door facing the entrance. They passed through it into a chamber twice the size of their tent house. Large enough to birth a pilot. As her eyes adjusted to the gentle bioluminescence that illuminated the space, she could resolve the equipment and tanks along one wall.

Vaha walked her over to it. "When I spoke to the womb's constructed mind, the CM said that tarawans use this equipment to manipulate physical samples. I've never seen the inside before. I usually interface to the womb through my emchannel and the external umbilical."

"I only have theoretical knowledge," Jayanthi confessed. She could identify some of the interfaces from immersives that Hamsa had given her: intakes for drawing and depositing blood, dishes to culture cells or simple organisms, printers to make biologics and synthetics.

She received a request to thought-share from the womb's CM and accepted it.

"I've asked the CM to give you access to the womb's tools and database," Vaha sent via emtalk.

A menu of options appeared in Jayanthi's visual field.

"The womb has a limited amount of supplies here at Meru, so you might not get to run any experiment you want, but I hope it's enough."

Vaha's generosity overwhelmed her. "It's more than enough. I don't know how to thank you."

"You can solve your design problem and prove Hamsa wrong, that's how." Zir phores glowed mauve with smug satisfaction.

Jayanthi smiled. "I'll do my best."

"One more thing," Vaha said. "Give me your hand."

Zie guided her finger onto a flat gray panel.

"This will collect some cells to verify your identity. I'm going to give you full-use permissions so you can enter the womb while I'm away."

"Are you sure?"

"I trust you. I want you to have access."

Vaha stood beside her, zir hand pressing gently down on hers. She became acutely aware of zir arm against hers, zir hip grazing her leg, zir dark curls catching highlights of red and green from the walls.

"Then I think it's only fair that you have the code to my bodym," she said. "You're looking after me, and I trust you with it, as you have with me and your womb. I think you should have all of me—have access to me—it." She stopped before she dug her linguistic hole any deeper.

"Jayanthi."

The huskiness in Vaha's voice made her freeze.

"Where I come from," Vaha said quietly, "sharing your bodym—well, it's like how you felt when I showed you those images. I'm not sure it's appropriate. Bodym access is a sign of a deep commitment, and when it happens between adults, it's usually part of a romantic proposal."

"Oh."

Vaha's expression held a mix of hope and concern. In the dim light of the womb, the phores on zir cheeks glowed with violet and seafoam green. They stood so very close to one another.

"Do you . . . have romantic feelings for me?" zie asked.

Her heart hammered. What should she say? Confess her foolish human desires? Lie and say she wanted nothing more than friendship? Why had Vaha asked her the question at all?

"Because I think I might," zie said. "For you."

Jayanthi felt ten times lighter. "You do?"

Zie nodded. "At first I thought it was because of the incarn, but even in my true body, I feel the same way. If you don't, though, I'll ask the womb to modify my incarn's—"

"No! I mean, please don't." She took a breath. "I do. I have *very* romantic feelings for you."

Vaha's phores saturated with purple. "This is the part in human stories where two people kiss on the lips, right? May I?"

"Yes," she said, answering both questions.

Zie reached out and traced one finger along her cheek. Jayanthi shivered. She could feel zir breath warm on her face. Zir deep-violet eyes were centimeters from hers. Then zie closed them, and she closed hers, and their lips met.

Jayanthi tried for the fifteenth time to focus on the genetic data in front of her. Her mind kept looping back to *Vaha, Vaha, Vaha*, on infinite repeat. They spent their days doing all the required tasks, grinning like fools, and stealing kisses at opportune moments. They'd both had prior romantic entanglements—Jayanthi with humans and Vaha with pilots—but with each other, intimacy gained a new dimension. Zie took infinite care with every touch, as if uncertain what would cause pleasure and what might cause pain. She attended to the glow of zir phores as much as the sound of zir sighs. They could speak through emtalk while their lips were busy elsewhere. Concentrating on anything else proved hard.

In spite of that, she'd made more progress in the previous ten days than she had in ten months on Earth. The womb had a simulator every bit as powerful as Hamsa's. It didn't have a full genetic database—that kind of capacity existed only in the Nivid—but it had far more examples than Hamsa had given her. She'd reached a 93 percent chance of viability with her latest hybrid design.

According to the womb's constructed mind, it could use a genome that had a 96 percent chance or better to make a test embryo. At that point, real-time tweaks to gene expression produced better results than simulations. If she failed to reach that level of viability, she would have other ways to occupy herself. There was Vaha, of course. With the desire to spend more time in each other's company, Vaha had invited her to assist in the greenhouse. The seedlings had taken root and sprouted leaves. They'd built an extension to make room for berry bushes and herbs. In the mornings, she practiced phoric and taught Vaha to sing. Their excursions had increased in range, and they made a habit of watching the sunset together every day. Vaha's joy in discovering life on a planet made her see it all through fresh eyes. *How ironic if I learn to let go of ambition here.*

She saved her work, closed her emchannel with the womb, and called out to Vaha. "How about a walk to the lake? I bet you've never seen someone skip stones," she said.

Zie emerged from zir bedroom. "I don't know what that means, but yes, the forecast is clear today. Let's go."

They covered the short distance to the lake at Jayanthi's fastest pace yet. Unlike the endless churn of the sea, the pool of water stood almost as still as a mirror. Jayanthi searched until she found a small, flat rock, its surface worn smooth from the lapping of gentle waves. She crouched low, angled her head, and sent the stone flying. Ripples broke the surface as the rock skipped once, twice, thrice, and sank.

Vaha grinned. "Let me try."

She handed zir a similar-size disc. Zie mimicked her posture and flung the rock, which arced outward and sank with an emphatic splash.

Jayanthi laughed at the dismay on Vaha's face. "It's harder than it looks. Here, let me show you." She wrapped herself around zir torso, making no attempt to minimize the contact, and guided Vaha's arm through the motion. "Right about here, you let go."

She stood back and observed as zie practiced, again and again, with the same tenacity that zie must have learned from zir struggles as a pilot's child. After a while, she skipped stones alongside zir, trying to see how far she could get while zie struggled to learn the art. They both exclaimed in delight when Vaha finally got one bounce.

They lay back and stared at the polished amethyst bowl of Meru's sky. Vaha's hand crept into hers. Jayanthi marveled at how relaxed her body felt. The near-constant aches that had accompanied her for as long as she could remember had faded to the occasional twinge. *Is this how everyone else on Earth feels? So . . . lightweight? So full of energy?* What would her childhood have been like with that kind of life?

"My parents used to take me to a lake like this," Jayanthi said. "I'd lie in between them and we'd pick out shapes in the clouds."

"I'd give anything for a memory like that."

"Maybe you can make one with your own child. Not by a lake, of course, but the equivalent in space."

"I don't know if I'll have children. My maker wasn't much of a parent, and I worry that I'll be equally terrible."

She rolled on her side and faced zir. "You're a good person, Vaha. One of the kindest people I've ever known. I think you'd be an amazing parent."

Vaha said nothing for several seconds. Had she gone too far? They'd known each other for three months, a short time even by human standards. Lying there beside the lake, she felt as comfortable as if she'd known Vaha all her life, but what if zie didn't return the sentiment? Or perhaps she'd overstepped some alloy boundary, as she had with her bodym.

Vaha turned. Unshed tears glimmered in the afternoon sunlight. "Thank you. And what about you? Do you dream of raising a family one day, maybe here on Meru?"

Relief slowed her racing heart. She could only imagine what zir maker had done to make Vaha tearful at her words.

"I don't know." She sat up and watched the wind ripple the water. "If all goes well with my health, the next stage of Hamsa's research proposal is to have a small group who raise children here. It would make sense for me to take part in that. Back on Earth, I never considered having a child. My sickle cell disorder would make pregnancy challenging, and I don't know if anyone would agree to have a baby with me. Random mutations are one thing, but deliberately reintroducing a genome like mine is another. Humans get taken care of no matter what, but people still carry those old biases."

"If I were human, I'd take that chance."

She half smiled. "We could live on Meru and teach our child to skip rocks and swim and row a boat."

"It's an impossible dream, isn't it? Even if Meru opens up to human settlement, the CDS would never allow an incarn like mine on the surface." Zir phores glowed with the setting sun, the color of regret. "What a pair of thrice-made fools we are."

"Now you sound like me that day at the cliffs." She poked zir gently. "It's too soon to be sad about our theoretical future."

But she couldn't entirely shake the melancholy, and judging by Vaha's phores, neither could zie. Zie stood and held out a hand to help her up. She didn't let go as they started walking back home. She wasn't sure exactly when she'd started thinking of their tent that way, but at some point they'd both stopped calling it "the landing site."

The smallest boulders turned into giants with their long shadows. Jayanthi had adapted to the range of the land's reddish browns to where she could see subtle differences in color. They were bright and cheerful in midday, jewel-toned in the late afternoons, and subtly glowing at sunrise or sunset. She had run out of adjectives to capture them in the notes she'd written for her friends and family. She could smell differences, too, with the tang of iron more prominent on a warm sunny day than a cool and rainy one. She knew the feel of dry sand, damp silt, and wet mud under her boots. Meru was her home now, as familiar as the well-worn path she'd taken to Mina's house. She had made so many wonderful memories with Vaha already.

Our child.

The concept rooted itself in her mind as surely as the tomato plants in the greenhouse. Back on Earth, she'd worked out a solution for a human child who could thrive on Meru. That had been a far easier problem to solve than the hybrid. *But what if I put the two ideas together?*

What if Meru got populated by hybrids rather than humans? An idea blossomed in her mind. She could start with her human DNA—as she had before—and instead of combining it with an alloy's, she could use Vaha's incarn's. It would be a smaller evolutionary jump, but she could then map out a series of step changes, from one generation to the next, until she arrived at the hybrid she wanted. *Play the long game. Avoid the destructive leaps that people made in the Human Era.* Hamsa hadn't mentioned taking that kind of approach. Tarawans had no need to with alloys. If a design failed, they could remake the person. She didn't have that luxury. But would her approach work? *Only one way to find out.*

"Vaha, would you mind if I used your incarn's genome as part of my project? I think it could help me." She explained her idea in more detail and said, "Your chromatophores would be a great first addition. Later generations could gain features that eventually result in second stomachs or solar wings."

"And the other DNA would be yours?"

"Yes, because a Meruvin child would need my sickle cell genes."

"Would the result be half and half, human-style?"

Jayanthi's ears warmed. "It's all theoretical. At most, I'd grow some embryos to six weeks for a better test of viability. TESC regulations would prevent the womb from going further without permission from a tarawan, and you'd need a fully grown baby to determine the influence of epigenetic factors, symbiotic organisms, diet—and a lot of other variables. Life is complicated. Even if the Meru settlement project gets to stage two, they couldn't use my genetic design without that data."

"I see." Zir phores glowed with a mix of colors that she couldn't interpret.

"If you're not comfortable with it, I'll ask the womb to develop an incarn from a different alloy's genome. I just thought, since we already had yours—"

Zie held up a hand. "I'd be honored to have you use mine."

—विरुद्ध

Viruddha—Contrary

A few days later, Vaha stood inside the womb and watched Jayanthi extract some of her blood. Zie had already given a sample of zir own. Her radiant smile brought Vaha a warm joy that zie had never known in zir life. No one had needed zir help for anything before. Kaliyu would have scoffed at zir finding satisfaction from helping a human being, but zie didn't mind. This particular human had wrapped herself firmly around zir heart, and her happiness was worth more than zir ego.

"The womb will have an easier time if it starts with our stem cells," Jayanthi explained. "I'm having it grow and deliver the egg and sperm separately. I'll create the embryos by hand, to show that the next generation can reproduce sexually."

According to the womb's CM, it would take approximately twenty-seven Earth hours to get those ready. As Jayanthi deposited her sample, Vaha's true body received an alert marked as high priority.

"I need to lie down for a while," zie said. "Something in orbit needs my attention right away."

"What happened?"

"The alert didn't say. It's probably incoming space debris or solar flare emissions. When that happens, we have to deploy special shielding to protect ourselves and the equipment. Pamir is in an active part of its cycle, so I've already dealt with a few small flares. Once the new courier arrives, they'll handle it."

Zie left Jayanthi to finish up on her own and laid zir incarn on the bed in their shelter. Awareness of zir true body returned with the discombobulation of waking from a strange dream. With every passing day on Meru, Vaha's comfort in zir incarn body increased. Walking and talking and smelling and hearing had become intuitive rather than novel. If zie weren't careful, zie would lose zir piloting skills and muscles. Zie would rather stay with Jayanthi for every hour of every day, but zie had to maintain the fitness and skills of zir true body. In case of an emergency, zie would need to fly quickly and with confidence.

Vaha thought-retrieved the message, a recorded emtalk from Kaliyu. With surprise forefront in zir thoughts, zie opened it.

"Vaha, fancy meeting you here! I know you didn't expect to see me again so soon, but life threw me a little surprise not long after you left. I got an offer to be a courier for your project! My assignment is to record your human's activities and findings and do some scientific observation in parallel. I couldn't pass up the chance at contributing to the Nivid, especially when it lets us be together again, so I deferred my racing team's offer for three masans. I know I was a mudha at Nishadas. I'm sorry. I hope you can forgive me."

Surprise, indeed! Kaliyu had never cared about the Nivid, and zie had been so adamantly against the Meru project. That zie would take the courier work as an act of apology made Vaha's heart sing. Kaliyu *had* been a mudha, but zie had always had a generous heart to make up for zir temper.

Vaha twisted until zie could see zir friend's silhouette approaching. Based on Kaliyu's trajectory, it wouldn't take long for zir to join Vaha, so Vaha didn't bother to compose a reply. Soon, zie could see Kaliyu's phores, glowing with a mix of nervousness and joy.

<I can hardly believe it!> Vaha flashed. Zie reached out and took Kaliyu's hands in zirs. <Of course I forgive you!>

Kaliyu glowed with pleasure, then said, <It's good to see you. I'm sorry—>

<No. No more apologies from you. If anything, I should say sorry for making you feel betrayed. You were right, too. I should've had more faith in myself. My landing here was nearly perfect, and I launched myself back into orbit! I did it. I did everything my maker designed me for.>

<By the Nivid! That's wonderful.> Kaliyu pulled back and held Vaha's shoulders. <And now here I am. We should never have let politics come between us.>

Vaha almost told Kaliyu everything about Jayanthi, about how some humans were just like alloys in character, about how wonderful she was, but the word *politics* stuck in zir mind. Zie didn't want to spoil this moment with a lecture, one that would challenge Kaliyu's notions of the truth about humans. That's how their argument had started back at Nishadas. No need to dredge it up . . . except that all the interactions between zir incarn and Jayanthi had been recorded. What would Kaliyu say to those? There was no law against such a relationship, but zie couldn't imagine that zir friend would approve.

<Though politics is what got me here,> Kaliyu was flashing. <Remember I told you about Pushkara? He offered me this contract because he wants someone to review the data from your mission. I'm more than a courier, to tell the truth. I'm doing survey and oversight, too. But I told Pushkara that you were a good friend, that I trusted you to be careful with the planet, and that you'd cooperate fully.>

<Yes, of course,> Vaha flashed, letting zir own glow fade to neutral. <But . . . why? What happened to racing?>

<Pushkara offered me an opportunity that's more significant.>

<The Nivid?>

Kaliyu's phores glowed with indifference. <No, something more important. Pushkara needed someone he could trust to look over your time on Meru, and he chose me. I couldn't turn down an honor like that. Vaha, we're going to make sure this project doesn't get past the first stage. All we need is one mistake by the human. Between your incarn on the surface and my oversight from orbit, we'll find something.>

Vaha couldn't hide the flash of alarm from zir phores.

<Don't worry,> Kaliyu added. <I'll defend your actions, even if you provoke her. No one will doubt that the human got careless.>

Vaha suppressed the urge to defend Jayanthi. *She takes as good or better care of the planet as I do.* Kaliyu wouldn't understand Vaha taking her side, but flashing nothing on her behalf made zir feel disloyal. Zie didn't want to lose Kaliyu's friendship again, not so soon after recovering it, but zie had to warn Jayanthi to take more care. Her behavior on the surface had to be flawless.

<Are you going to say something?> Kaliyu flashed.

<I'm really glad you're here,> Vaha replied truthfully. <You must be tired.>

Kaliyu nodded. <Exhausted! I met the other courier on the way in. They said I was late, so I came as fast as I could. After I get some rest, I need to set up the extra observation equipment and the new data cube. I'll let you know when I'm ready for you to transfer the data from the missing kaals.>

Vaha gave zir friend's hand a squeeze of acknowledgment, then let go. The recordings in zir extended memory would reveal zir relationship with Jayanthi to Kaliyu, and that could only end in disaster. Zie sent a message to Jayanthi saying that a new courier had arrived and that zie needed some additional time in orbit. After seeing Kaliyu settled in a berth, Vaha accessed zir memories. Zie considered every intimate moment between zirself and Jayanthi. They had done nothing wrong, but zie hadn't heard of such pairings except in the distant past. Humanoid incarns didn't mix with human beings, possibly to avoid this kind of situation. If Kaliyu and Pushkara were looking for a reason to shut down the project, Vaha and Jayanthi's relationship might give them the opportunity they needed.

Vaha began to methodically erase all the evidence. They had enough equipment problems that zie could explain away the gaps. Before each deletion, zie took one last look and then silently gave it an apology.

Jayanthi faced the viewing wall of their tent and thought-retrieved the status of the eggs and sperm from the womb. In less than an hour, they would be ready for her to mix. She didn't need Vaha to continue the work, but she hoped they could complete the next steps together. Considering that the egg chromosomes were zirs—she'd based the sperm on hers, since uniparental disomy favored the father's DNA—she felt like zie should participate.

For the past Meruvin day, Vaha had spent more time than usual with zir true body. Even while active in zir incarn, zie had acted distracted and distant—zie hadn't kissed her good night or at all—and zie hadn't volunteered a reason. Her instincts led her to worry. Had she done something wrong? Did Vaha not want to continue their budding relationship? She kept biting her tongue against voicing them. She had entrusted Vaha with her life on the journey here, and she had to continue that trust. Whatever kept zir attention in orbit was important. Probably something to do with zir true body that she wouldn't understand. If she acted like an ignorant, needy human, she might drive zir away.

She slow-blinked her visual overlay clear and sighed. Night had fallen, and she'd let the tent go dark. A million stars shone above, and one of Meru's two moons rose full and bright. If she stared upward long enough, she could spot the unmoving point of light that marked the location of Vaha's true body. They'd spent many evenings lying outside and making up new constellations. Popular culture had favored ancient India for the past two centuries, but she had a solid education in a multitude of stories from her parents. She picked figures from all places and times, gazing at the diamond-dust sky, stopping only when their suit heaters ran out of power.

After three weeks on the planet, her body felt better than it had since her first sickle cell crisis as a child. In spite of all the activity, she hadn't needed pain medication for several days. A few times, she'd actually stopped noticing the aches that had always kept her company. With the added benefit of the HO enzyme, her blood cells hadn't clumped, and her tissues got the right amount of oxygen, but part of the Meruvin experiment required her to pause treatment and see how her body responded. With her general fitness confirmed, she'd stopped the drug the previous day. If or when her bodym detected significant damage to her lungs, she'd resume it, but in the meantime, a low level of anxiety had crept into her mood, compounded by the shift in Vaha's behavior.

She felt a hand on her shoulder, then turned and smiled at Vaha. Zie nodded in return. In the moonlight, the phores on zir cheeks glowed green, a sign that Vaha was worried. *Is zie concerned for my health?* Perhaps that's why zie had pulled away from her. After all, if she crashed hard and needed an exchange, Vaha would have to help her do it. If she died, zie would take the blame. Maybe zie had decided their relationship put the mission in too much jeopardy or created a conflict of interest.

She opened her mouth to ask how zie felt when Vaha said, "I need to check on something in the womb. Will you come with me?"

"Sure, but I just looked and—"

"Let's talk about it there."

Puzzled, she stood and followed zir to the vestibule. Every time she drew a breath to say something, Vaha held up a hand to forestall her. She moved from confused to irritated. Why couldn't they talk?

She yanked the zipper up with more force than necessary, ran a finger around the helmet's touch seal, and nodded to Vaha.

The rocks along their walk to the womb reflected the moon's glow, their shadows knife-sharp on the sandy soil. Vaha opened the door to the womb and gestured Jayanthi inside first. After closing it behind zirself, Vaha removed zir helmet and ran zir fingers through zir mane of tight curls, closed zir hand around a fistful of it, and held tight. Zir phores pulsed with distressed olive.

"What is going on?" Jayanthi demanded after removing her own helmet.

"I'm sorry. Zie has started recording from our site, and this is the only place zie can't observe."

"Zie who?"

"Kaliyu, the replacement courier."

Jayanthi searched her memory. The name sounded familiar. "Your friend, the other pilot. Zie's here at Meru?"

"Yes, and not only is zie capturing our data," Vaha said, looking grim, "zie has a mandate to find a flaw in your behavior, not simply ferry the information back to Sol."

"Aren't you good friends? Why are you so worried?"

"Pushkara sent zir here." Zie hesitated, then said, "Kaliyu has an irrational bias against humans. Zie was vehemently opposed to this mission from the start and didn't want me to take the pilot commission. The only reason zie came is to help Pushkara's cause. If we make the slightest deviation from the actual project plan, zie will report it." Vaha's phores flickered with distress. "Kaliyu and I . . . we parted on bad terms when I left Nishadas for this project. Zie seems to have forgiven me for now, but I'm afraid of what zie might do if zie finds out about our relationship. Zie has to believe that I'm on zir side."

"So that's why you've been acting strange."

"They're looking for any excuse to end the project, Jaya. We have to be careful. Kaliyu always sounds confident, but something about the way zie said it—I'm worried. Zie seemed so sure that stage two won't get approved. Maybe Pushkara bribed someone on the committee. I don't know, but Kaliyu will be here for the remainder of our time, and we can't give zir another reason to scrutinize our activities."

Vaha's words confirmed her worst fears. "Our relationship doesn't go against any project parameters. You're embarrassed to be seen with me."

"What? No." Vaha reached out to her. Zie flinched as she stepped back. "That's not it at all."

I don't believe you. She wrapped her arms around herself, chilled in spite of the warmth in the womb. Everything she wanted to say choked in her throat. They had no future together unless Vaha became like her parents, enslaved forever to Earth's orbit with zir true body, a miserable fate for a history-making pilot. Zie must have thought of that already. No wonder zie wouldn't want zir best friend to see zir get involved with a human.

It's okay. The good of the project has to come first. If Vaha can repress zir feelings for me, then so can I for zir.

"Maybe it's better if we stop . . . whatever this is," she said, keeping her voice as level as she could. "Like you said at the lake, it's an impossible dream."

"Jayanthi—"

She sealed her helmet in a quick motion and pushed past Vaha, heading for the door. Zie tried to grab her arm, but she shook zir off, biting her lip against a rush of tears as she strode back to the tent. She tripped over one of the steps and landed hard on her right knee. She relished the sharp pain it released.

You naive little human. Did you really think this could last, you and a pilot? You're from entirely different worlds. You should never have involved yourself with zir. Now you have to live with zir for another year. How are you going to get through that much time? How are you going to complete the project objectives?

Whatever Vaha felt for her, it couldn't be love. Zie treated her with affection because of zir incarn body's uncontrolled reactions. An alloy could never truly see a human as an equal. She should've known better. She should never have let her guard down, never let her own feelings for zir take root.

Jayanthi let the tears flow as she stripped off her enviro-suit and left it in a heap with her helmet. A bloody gash ran across her right knee. *Good! At least I'll have an excuse for why I'm crying on camera.* She ignored the cut and stumbled to her room and onto her cot, burying her sobs under her pillow.

—सनुतर

SANUTHARA—CLANDESTINE

Jayanthi woke with a pounding headache and swollen eyes. She'd gone from tears to despair and back to tears over the course of the night. Vaha had returned to the shelter not long after her, but zie had wisely left her alone.

She slow-blinked by accident, trying to soothe her burning corneas. A message from Vaha overlaid her vision: "I'm sorry about the way our conversation ended last night. I think it's best I spend more time in orbit again. I assume you'll be all right alone, but I'll come back if you need me."

Of course Vaha would run and hide. In zir true body, zie would have no trouble distancing zirself from zir feelings. For all she knew, Kaliyu meant more to zir than a classmate or friend. Perhaps they'd been romantically involved at Nishadas. Vaha had no obligation to tell her zir entire personal history. She hadn't told zir about her own, not that she had much to speak of.

Damn right I'll be okay alone. She sat and swung her legs off the cot. Her entire body ached as if she'd fought in a battle the night before. The skin was gone from half of her kneecap, a nasty surface wound but nothing serious. A greenish bruise surrounded the edges of the scrape.

She limped to the supply cabinet, then to the bathroom. She gave her knee a thorough saline rinse—something she should've done before going to bed—applied a healing spray, and wrapped it with sterile gauze. As a precaution, she injected a subdermal antibiotic into her left shoulder. She didn't think it likely that she had picked up much bacteria from the inside of her suit, but she wasn't going to risk it, especially now that her every decision would be scrutinized. She finished with another subdermal for the pain and turned to her responsibilities.

It was day three without the heme oxygenase treatment. The schedule had her going on an extended hike. Stressing her lungs would show any negative results faster. She hung her suit for disinfection. It would be ready to use again in the early afternoon, giving her plenty of time for a long excursion. *Without Vaha.* She'd go anyway. Nothing in the project parameters required zir to accompany her for every activity. The suits had radios in case of an emergency.

The data spool blinked an alert, and she discovered that a news courier had arrived at the planet and dropped an update, including some messages for her from Earth. She hadn't received anything since the reality transit to Pamir, and she played them eagerly.

The first was from Mina, who spoke awkwardly. "I've never sent a one-sided recording like this before. I hope you're well, Jaya, and appreciating every moment on Meru. I wish I could be there with you!"

I wish you could, too. If you were here, I could tell you about Vaha and this whole mess. Maybe you'd have some good advice, because I don't know what to think or do.

"We won't get to talk very often, so make sure you tell me everything about Meru. Send back some images and videos from outside if you can. The other SHWAs say hello. We had a meeting two weeks ago, and all we could talk about was you."

With tears stinging her eyes, Jayanthi viewed the next message. Ekene and Li Feng had written letters. Jean had sent a clip from his movie. She saved her parents for last. Her father had his arm around her mother's shoulders, and they both smiled as they told her how much they missed her and hoped she was safe and well.

"We're so proud of you, Jaya," Vidhar said. "When you were younger, people criticized us for raising you as we did. They told us we'd corrupt you, and from a human standpoint, perhaps we have, but given what you've already accomplished, I don't regret it one bit."

After she washed the tears from her face and composed herself, Jayanthi replied to them all. Unlike Kaliyu, a news courier would make a fast turnaround. Their travel times were too great to linger at any one location.

She tried to recapture the optimism and joy she'd felt just a few days earlier, pushing aside concerns that the whole endeavor might be futile. She debated telling them about Kaliyu and Pushkara. It might help to send a warning to Hamsa, but only if she had some concrete information, and she had nothing more than Vaha's suspicions. If success hinged on everything going right on Meru, they could do nothing to help her. She closed her recording by telling them all that she loved and missed them. *So very much.*

The sky above had gray clouds blowing across periwinkle, and the ground below was red, brown, and white as far as Jayanthi could see. She missed green. And blue. She trudged across the rocky soil, careful to go parallel to the footsteps from previous outings. Creating a trail would invalidate the mission. The scenery that had seemed so marvelous the day before now irritated her with its dullness. In the distance, the striated cliffs loomed. She'd intended to climb to the top for the day's activity, but between Vaha's absence and her throbbing knee, it didn't seem like she could.

By the time she reached the boulders at the base, though, the pain medication had taken the edge off her discomfort, enough to reconsider that decision. People had thought her parents too lenient with her? They thought she had too much ambition for a human? Well, she would prove them right. *I'll climb this cliff alone. I don't need anyone's help, least of all Vaha's.* She took her black mood out on the rocks, hauling herself up with a vengeance, higher and higher, stopping only to check her route. They'd gone more than halfway the week before, and Vaha had used zir vantage in orbit to find a way that didn't require any ropes or anchors. *I* should *make myself sick at this stage.* Without the HO treatment, her tissues—especially her lungs—ought to take some damage. It would provide a good cover if she developed a pain crisis from the breakup with Vaha.

As she scrambled over the top of the cliff, her arms and legs trembled, and sweat pooled at her armpits. She lay flat on her back for a while, breathing hard and staring at the clouds. They'd grown darker. She hadn't thought to check the weather forecast because Vaha had always done that before their outings.

Fat drops of rain landed on her visor. She sat and let the subsequent downpour wash the dust from the suit. Rivulets of water formed around her and ran over the edge of the cliff. Sheets of rain blew across the plains. She couldn't help but feel cheered by the spectacle. Her first rainstorm on Meru! She rolled onto her stomach and scooted close enough to the edge that she could see cascading waterfalls plunge to the valley below. The view from the bottom would have been spectacular.

In the east, lightning flickered over the ocean. There were no trees on Meru to attract electricity, only a nicely conductive human being. Jumbles of boulders, some taller than herself, littered the flat mesa top like overgrown haystacks. She headed for one and found a rock overhang that faced the approaching front.

I'll shelter here until the storm passes, then head home. No sense trying to climb down the slippery cliff face in the rain.

But the clouds continued to pour as the light of Pamir dimmed. She would have enough time to make it back to camp before dark, but only if she braved the wet descent. Her alternative was to stay put and hope for better weather by morning. The suit had a small amount of reserve power and some emergency capabilities, including splinting zones and a heater. If she descended, she'd likely need the former after breaking some limbs. The latter wouldn't last all night. She would get cold, and she'd have pain—less bad than falling down a cliff. She hadn't packed any food—she couldn't eat or drink bhojya through the suit—and she'd already run out of water, but staying still seemed like the wiser choice.

Jayanthi lay back against the rock and pillowed her head on her arms. *I'm the only human being on this entire planet.* There were no stars to keep her company, but the steady drumbeat of the rain settled her nerves. Had anyone experienced such a sense of aloneness before? No people. No animals. No sign of the local construct, though it couldn't be far. With nothing to fear, she relished the isolation.

As night fell, the temperature dropped. Jayanthi let herself shiver for a while, cycling the heater on when she could no longer bear it, and only for as long as it took to get comfortable. True warmth would have to wait until she returned to camp. She thought back to the messages from Earth. Mina would scold her for getting into this situation. Her parents would worry if they knew. *I shouldn't be so careless with myself.* Guilt settled on Jayanthi's shoulders as she realized how little she'd thought of her family and friends back home. She'd let herself get so smitten with Vaha that she'd lost sight of the real reason for her presence on Meru: to help humankind end their penance on Earth.

Mina's sister had often called Jayanthi selfish, and Jayanthi had refused to believe it, but she could now. She hadn't wanted to admit it, but putting herself at risk over a broken heart was the epitome of selfishness. For everything Hamsa had done to get her here, for her parents' support in letting her go, and for every human on Earth who wanted a chance to go farther, she owed them her best. She had to get back home safely. Kaliyu couldn't blame her for getting stranded by weather, but could zie point to serious injury as a reason to cancel the project? How much authority did zie have? Whose side would Vaha take? She hated that she had to suspect zir along with zir friend.

Beyond the overhang, at the edge of where she knew the land must meet the sea, a few stars twinkled. As she watched, the clear patch of sky blew toward her, the stars growing in number as the clouds moved past her and on to the west, behind the rock at her back. The center of the Milky Way stretched across the sky like a mirror image to the river on the plains below. Below that, a growing mass of darkness obscured the stars once more. How long would this storm go on? Cold and dehydration were not friends to her body on Earth. Would they affect her as much on Meru? She would find out. *If it gets really bad, I'll call Vaha. I have to act like I trust zir.* They had more than a year left together. She had to let go of her anger and grief to follow through on the project objectives. As the rain began again, she closed her eyes and fell into a deep, exhausted sleep.

Vaha's muscles burned in the way that happened after a good workout. Zie had spent the hurt at Jayanthi's words by learning the thamity gradients around Meru, sliding down the negative deltas and coasting up the positives. Kaliyu had plotted specific routes, and they'd taken timed laps in a friendly competition. Not only had it felt good to use zir true body again, but doing so alongside Kaliyu made it easy to forget what had happened on the surface.

Vaha had been in love once before in zir life, with an older student at Nishadas who was two batches ahead. His name was Akaama. Vaha had been fifteen, Akaama seventeen, at the start, but when he graduated, he broke off the romance.

<I can't afford to tie myself to this place,> Akaama had flashed, another receding body in Vaha's memories. <Besides, you're too young and immature. You don't really know what love means.>

As Vaha returned to the orbital berth, zie wondered if zie were being as much of a mudha to Jayanthi as Akaama had been to zir. Zie wanted to protect her and the project from Kaliyu's biases, and that meant zie had to maintain a good relationship with Kaliyu. On the other hand, if that also meant that zie had to hide zir true feelings for Jayanthi, then maybe she was right. Maybe at some level, zie was embarrassed by it—*ashamed* was too strong a word, but if Vaha were honest with zirself, zie was afraid of what Kaliyu would think.

Vaha pulled up next to Kaliyu, venting excess heat.

<Not bad,> Kaliyu flashed with a thump to Vaha's shoulder. <You're getting faster.>

<Give me a couple more practice runs, and I'll beat you.>

Kaliyu flickered with amusement.

<How are things on the surface?> Vaha asked. <Is Jayanthi all right?>

<She's so predictable. Last I checked, she left the tent for some exercise as per the schedule.>

Vaha glanced down and saw a great spiral of white clouds over their campsite. <In the rain?>

<Is that a problem?>

<I suppose not, if she was paying attention.> Zie had always checked the forecast for her. Would she have remembered in zir absence?

Kaliyu had taken over the data feeds, but whenever Vaha's attention inhabited zir true body, zie observed that Kaliyu spent as much time exercising or watching entertainment as zie did reviewing the planet-side recordings. *Was I wrong that we couldn't hide our relationship from zir?* Maybe Kaliyu trusted Vaha enough not to scrutinize their activities on the surface.

Vaha watched Meru's terminator cross over the storm, throwing the surface into shadow. The massive cloud formation hadn't moved much. *How is Jayanthi? Is the campsite okay in the rain? Does she still hate me for what I said in the womb?*

<That storm is attenuating our signal quite a bit,> Kaliyu flashed. <We might have some gaps in the recording from the tent, though your little human isn't there, so I suppose it doesn't matter.>

That's another good excuse for the data I erased from my extended memory.

<Not there?> Vaha flashed. <She's still outside?>

<Her suit shows that she's about ten kilometers west of your camp. She doesn't appear to be moving.>

Vaha called up the tracking data from Jayanthi's suit and overlaid it on a map of the area. The phores on zir arms went dark brown as it showed her on the plateau above the cliffs. Zie couldn't get a live signal from her suit. The last known location had a time stamp of an hour earlier. Had the suit's power run out? Had she gotten lost in the rain and darkness?

How did she get up there by herself? Visions of a wounded or dying Jayanthi filled Vaha's imagination. Zie shouldn't have left her alone for so long. If something terrible happened, it would be zir fault.

<I have to go back to my incarn,> zie flashed to Kaliyu. <Make sure she isn't hurt.>

Kaliyu glowed with indifference. <She should be able to survive there on her own. If she dies, it's her fault for going out there without you. No one would blame you, and we could end this farce of a project right now.>

Vaha's phores tinged with pink. Zie couldn't help it. <That's a horrible thing to say. I would blame myself no matter what anyone else thought. Jayanthi is a good person. She's not how you think of humans. You should try talking with her, get to know her. You might realize how wrong you are.>

<Even if she is an exception, you're not going to change my mind about the rest of them.> Kaliyu's phores turned that smug mauve again. <Go ahead and take care of your little human. Pretend like all of this matters.>

<What do you mean?>

<Exactly what I said. Trust me—Hamsa's endeavor here has no future.>

Vaha wished zie could stay and probe for more, but zie had to get to the surface, to Jayanthi. <I'll be back in a little while,> Vaha flashed. Zie turned zir attention inward and then down, compressing zir sensory perception to what zir human incarn could process.

Vaha woke to a dark, chilly tent filled with a hissing noise. It turned out to be the sound of pouring rain. If zie hadn't been worried about Jayanthi, zie would have sat and watched and listened to the magnificent and strange phenomenon all night. Instead, dread grew in the pit of zir stomach as zie realized the ramifications of the deluge, of Jayanthi stranded alone in the cold, wet night.

Water pooled over the first step of their shelter. Zie had known in theory why they'd placed it on an elevated platform, but zie hadn't understood what it meant. Until the rain stopped, zie couldn't go anywhere. Hiking out and climbing those cliffs would be impossible in these conditions. So zie sat and stared into the dark, the forecast overlaying zir vision, and waited for the storm to pass.

Jayanthi awoke with a start, then cursed as pain sliced through her stiff knee. A pale, rosy glow filled her view to the east. Droplets fell from the overhang, but beyond, the clouds had broken to reveal patches of lavender. She slow-blinked, but no information appeared. On her wrist, the suit indicator lights were dark. Sometime during the night, it had run out of power.

She worked her right knee gingerly until she could bend it and stand without her breath catching. She took one step, then another, pacing slowly until adrenaline and endorphins caught up and gave her some relief. Her hips and shoulders ached from the night spent sleeping on a rock. The subdermal for the pain medication wasn't intended to last for more than a few hours. Remarkably, though, the rest of her limbs didn't burn with the agony she would've had on Earth after a night of cold and dehydration. Meru had its benefits. How much would those regress without the HO treatment?

The first rays from Pamir broke over the horizon and bathed the plain below with golden light. Water pooled everywhere, creating a landscape of glossy mirrors. Jayanthi gazed at the beauty of it. She imagined Mina or Li Feng at her side, how they'd appreciate the wonder of Meru's indigo sky falling into the ochre land. *How can I make sure they see this one day?*

Vaha's words came back to her: *Kaliyu seemed so sure that stage two won't get approved.* Without the second phase, they wouldn't have data on the health of children raised on Meru, and without that, human settlement wouldn't get very far. If only she were a tarawan! Then she could authorize Vaha's womb to grow a few human children and skip right into stage two on her own. It wasn't as ideal as having an actual person get pregnant and successfully deliver, but it would provide good information. The MEC had already approved Hamsa's entire proposal, with stage two contingent on everything going well with her health. So far, it had, and in a few more weeks, they'd have the data to prove the effectiveness of the HO treatment.

But I'm not a tarawan. And she knew nothing about raising children. Per the actual plan, there would be multiple adults on Meru to help with that. *I'd probably be a terrible parent.* She hadn't even remembered to make the hybrid embryo after leaving the womb the previous day.

The thought reminded her of all that had happened with Vaha, which made her heart hurt, which made all the other aches and pains come rushing back. After a few deep, calming breaths, she made her way to the cliff's edge. With her suit out of power, she couldn't call for help. *Focus on getting yourself down.*

The morning light illuminated her path. She had no guidance, and the water had turned the dust atop the rock into a slurry, so she kept her back to the vertical face as much as possible and picked her route down with care. She slipped and slid more than once. Her knee protested any time she had to face inward and put weight on it, but she arrived at the base of the cliffs in less time than it had taken to climb up. A rock slab provided a good place to sit and catch her breath, the same one that she and Vaha had found on their first excursion to the location. Mud encrusted her formerly pristine white enviro-suit. Puddles of water glimmered from all directions, softening the harsh tones with violets and grays.

Jayanthi tried to imagine what the view would look like with plants and animals, houses and gardens. How the sounds and smells would change from the effects of flower pollen, voices, birdcalls, and the rustling of leaves. Constructs and alloys had discovered so many star systems beyond Sol, many with nearly habitable planets. They'd left all of them alone, free from interference by any living being. Around the time of the compact, scientists had come to accept that consciousness was a fundamental property of nature, and all matter had it to some degree. It manifested in different forms, with different levels of complexity and emergent behaviors, but the knowledge meant that people could no longer treat nonliving objects with contempt. Everything—from a massive star to a grain of dust—possessed a sort of awareness of its surroundings and of itself.

Inhabiting the vacuum of space provided the greatest protection from harm, but even alloys had to interfere with Earth and the asteroid belt to maintain their lives. Would it really be so bad to let humans affect one more planet? With the right constraints, they could treat Meru better than they had Earth. They wouldn't have to make the same mistakes. They could respect the land and live within its limits. They could protect the biota that already existed, make sure it continued to evolve and thrive.

Her stomach twinged with hunger, pulling her back to the present. As she stood, something moved in the distance. Her instincts said animal, but Meru had none. She limped forward, the endorphins gone and her joints stiff from her stop. The far-off motion turned into an object that resolved into a figure. A running humanoid figure. *Vaha.*

As zie neared, the sickly greenish-brown of zir phores shone through zir visor. Zie stopped a couple of meters away and spread zir arms wide.

Jayanthi closed the gap between them. As zie held her, she trembled with relief. She'd survived without Vaha, but now, enfolded in zir arms, she never wanted to be alone on Meru again.

After a minute, zie pulled away and swapped a fresh battery into her suit. As soon as her power indicator lit, zie said, "Forgive me?"

"Of course."

"If I'd realized sooner that you were going to climb those vent-spawned cliffs, I would've chased after you yesterday." Zie pulled her into zir arms again. "If something had happened to you, I'd never forgive myself. Are you okay? I saw you limping."

"I hurt my knee two nights ago . . . after our argument. It's a little worse from the excursion, but nothing serious."

Vaha leaned back and looked her in the eyes. "I'm sorry. I shouldn't have gone off to orbit. That was cowardly."

She reached out a hand and touched zir visor. "I shouldn't have said those things to you."

"You spoke the truth. I just didn't want to hear it."

"No, I wasn't being fair. You were trying to look out for the best interests of the project." She gestured at their entwined bodies. "You aren't worried about this?"

"I care about you, Jayanthi. Kaliyu knows that." Concern warred with fear in zir eyes.

So that's how it was. Vaha didn't say, *I love you*, or, *It doesn't matter what other alloys think*. She forced a smile. She'd have to make peace with what zie could give, never mind what she wanted.

They walked back to the campsite with her leaning against zir. Neither of them said much. When they reached home, Vaha insisted on helping Jayanthi remove her suit and then wanted to check her knee. First she bathed, emerging in a clean undershirt and shorts. She shot herself with another pain subdermal, then let Vaha fuss over her. Truth be told, even with Meru's extra oxygen, she was exhausted from her overnight ordeal. It felt wonderful to lie back in a warm room and put her feet up.

"I watched some instructions on what to do," Vaha said, "but that's not the same as doing it. Tell me if I hurt you at all, okay?"

"You don't need to do anything."

"But I want to."

She closed her eyes and bit her lip as zie began unwrapping the bandage, trying not to wince. Zir movements were gentle and fast, and after zie sprayed the wound with a topical analgesic, she relaxed. Vaha's hands felt like silk against her skin as zie lifted her calf and then her thigh. She couldn't help the rush of heat that moved from her cheeks, through her neck and chest, and down to her belly and the space between her legs.

"All done," Vaha whispered. Zir hands cupped her knee as if it were a peace offering.

She opened her eyes and met zirs. Vaha's lips were slightly parted, zir eyes wide. The vulnerability made her pulse drum like rain against stone. Zie drew toward her as if falling down a gravity well, inescapable, until she could feel the heat of zir breath on her cheeks. Zir hands slid up and around her waist.

"The cameras," she breathed. "Are you sure?"

Vaha's mouth curved ever so slightly. "The storm damaged the communications equipment. I'll fix it later."

—जीवन्ती

Jeevanthee—Alive

For the next few days, the rain continued intermittently, which curtailed the extent of their outings. Jayanthi had to exercise her lungs, but other than that, she and Vaha spent a lot of hours sharing their favorite human and alloy entertainment with each other. Vaha favored broad comedies and historical romances. She liked fantasy and experimental work. Somehow they found ways to enjoy each other's choices. They both loved long, intricately plotted stories, which were mostly produced by alloys in stasis. The immersives had content in visual bands that she couldn't see, but she did her best to follow along with her rudimentary phoric. Since Vaha's incarn body had the same problem, zie had fun pointing out what they were missing and laughing about it.

Her excursion to the cliffs had worried Vaha so much that zie refused to spend more than fifteen minutes at a stretch in zir true body.

"I'm running away from Kaliyu, too," zie had admitted the day before. "I don't think zie suspects that I'm avoiding the equipment repair on purpose, but I probably can't stall much longer."

"Has zie asked you why we were in the womb together?"

"Zie hasn't mentioned anything so far. I suppose we could be together in there, though zie might ask questions if we go in it too often. I have no doubt that zie would yell at me if zie thought that we were in love."

"Are we?" Jayanthi had asked, warmth settling in her chest like the first sip of tea. "In love?"

"What else would you call it?"

Vaha had kissed her then, and she'd nestled herself into the crook of zir neck. They'd taken to sleeping in her bed together. It was cramped in the single-person cot, but that was a small price to pay for zir company.

The first day after the flooding receded, Vaha repaired the communications to the orbital platform. They went on their scheduled excursion and returned with reddish mud caking their boots. After a warm bath, Jayanthi went straight for a pain subdermal.

"You've been taking those almost every day lately," Vaha commented. "Your bodym shows increased blood pressure. Should I worry?"

"My pain levels are up," she admitted. "I'm not due to resume my HO treatment for another two weeks, and I've started to feel the effects."

"The womb can provide you with improved hydration. According to the medical information I have, that should alleviate your symptoms."

And it would provide an excellent reason for them to spend more time in there.

Jayanthi kept her expression and tone neutral as she said, "That's a good idea. Will you come with me? I don't know how to set it up."

They didn't hold hands as they walked over to the womb—they never did anymore. The orbital platform could resolve that level of detail on a clear day. But once inside, Vaha didn't take her into zir arms as she'd expected. Zie walked her into the main chamber and showed her how to activate the womb's ambulatory construct. Unlike an alloy, she couldn't attach the womb's umbilical to her body, so the construct cradled her while it pumped her full of fluids.

"Jaya, I'm worried," Vaha said, "about this mission."

"Because of my health?"

"Because of Kaliyu. If Pushkara has a way to ensure that this never gets past the first phase, then you're putting yourself through all this pain for nothing."

"Did you learn something new?"

Vaha's phores glowed with frustration. "No. Zie hasn't said too much, but it's clear that zie knows something."

"I was thinking along similar lines," she admitted, "when I was up on the cliff, looking out over this amazing planet." She thought out loud as she spoke. "The ultimate goal is to demonstrate that humans can live and thrive on Meru without significant changes to the environment. My fitness would establish a genetic baseline. Stage two's made children would prove health during gestation, birth, and development. Stage three is all about the second generation's fertility and the heritability of necessary genes."

"All of which will take years that we might never get."

"Not all. We have another thirteen months here. Given how quickly my body adapted to this environment and the fact that I'm in here needing treatment so soon after stopping my medication, we probably don't need the full amount of time to demonstrate my fitness."

"Are you saying we should cut the stay short?"

"We could, but that's more risky. What if we accelerate the project before Kaliyu finds an excuse to stop it?"

"How?"

"That's where I get stuck. Do we send a letter to the committee asking to push the schedule ahead? Get Hamsa or another tarawan to come here and design a baby? Could we get the data to them via a different courier without Kaliyu knowing? With what you've said, I don't trust zir not to tamper with the evidence. But all that assumes that the committee members are neutral. If Pushkara has corrupted enough of them, nothing we do here will matter. Unless we have some idea what Pushkara has going on behind the scenes, how do we come up with a counterstrategy?"

They fell silently into their own thoughts. Kaliyu would have to find a compelling violation of the project parameters to invalidate it. Jayanthi felt fairly certain that she and Vaha could avoid that if they remained careful. It would be hard, especially over a year of Meru's weather, but it wouldn't be impossible. If, however, Pushkara had come to some kind of backroom deal with members of the MEC, then the only way around it would be to present the general public with unquestionably positive data about humans on Meru. How could they achieve that?

She activated her emchannel and retrieved the text of Hamsa's proposal. She read a portion aloud to Vaha. "The duration of Phase One shall be no longer than eighteen months, inclusive of travel time to and from Earth. Upon completion of Phase One and presentation of satisfactory evidence of fitness, Phase Two shall commence. If the human subject's health deteriorates beyond the parameters specified by Appendix B, then Phase One shall terminate immediately." She paused. "Nothing in here says that Phase One has to last the full eighteen months. Let's say six months go by, and I'm doing well. The MEC decides that Phase One is done. They tell you to pack up and get me back to Earth. I refuse. What would happen?"

"Why would you . . . ah, so that you could push on to the second phase. What good is that without the designed children?"

She grimaced. It always came back to the damn babies. "This is exactly why we need human tarawans. If long-term settlement on Meru is going to work, we'll need wombs and made embryos for the initial population."

Vaha raised zir brows with perfect human expressiveness. "We have a womb."

"It's restricted from developing an embryo past a few weeks without approval by a licensed tarawan. TESC regulations. I checked."

"Maybe we could convince the womb's CM to break the law?"

"Very funny." Constructs were bound by contract and hardware to obey the law. It was an impossible situation.

Or was it?

Thirteen months left on Meru if the project needed it. Nine months for natural gestation. She could use the eggs and sperm from the womb to form the embryos, have it print a device to implant them, and grow a human child—*or a hybrid child, if I can make it biologically compatible*—the old-fashioned way. As far as she knew, her uterus worked fine. She'd never tested it, but nothing had flagged in all her medical exams or genetic analyses, and there had been plenty of both. That would allow her to keep the pregnancy secret for a good long while.

"You have that look on your face," Vaha said.

"Hmm?"

"Like you just solved a difficult genetics problem."

"What if I got pregnant?"

Vaha blinked a few times. *Accessing information,* she guessed. *Pregnant* was not a common word in alloy society.

"That looks dangerous," Vaha said. "According to my medical information, for people with sickle cell disease, pregnancy is complicated and potentially fatal. And it's a totally uncontrolled process. What if something goes wrong with the gestation? What if the baby can't survive here or something happens to you in the process?"

"First off, humans still have babies like this all the time back on Earth. Second, all living beings have equal value in the universe, regardless of capability, right?" She waited for Vaha to nod, then continued, calling up the lessons she'd learned at Hamsa's knee. "Alloys have the luxury of rebirth for a child whose body isn't working as designed. You're allowed three full ones to try different gene expressions. Humans aren't. We have to live with the physiology we get. Take me for example. I have sickle cell disease. On Earth, it was a burden, and I had to manage it. On Meru, it keeps me healthy, and someone without this genetic variant—like you—has to deal with constant hyperoxia. We do our best to make sure human babies are adapted to their environment by their genes, but to maintain diversity, we have to accept that that won't always be the case."

"Alloys embrace genetic diversity, too," Vaha said, "and not all alloys subject themselves or their offspring to full rebirths. That's why we have laws about making children. That's why we use tarawans and wombs and not"—Vaha gestured at her body—"chance reproduction in a chaotic environment."

"This child is likely to be healthy and well adapted to life on Meru. It won't struggle on Earth any more than I did, and it will have the option for gene therapy when it's old enough to consent, just as I do. Besides, the whole point of stage two is to test whether it's possible to raise babies on Meru. If I can remain well through a pregnancy, and if the baby is born healthy, we've demonstrated two significant aspects of Hamsa's plan. If I don't, then the whole thing falls apart anyway. My DNA has better odds of surviving Meru than any other living human's. If my body can't deliver a baby, then a tarawan would have to make a human who can, and that hurdle would guarantee failure for this project as well as Hamsa's proposed amendment."

"Okay, let's assume everything goes perfectly. You realize that we're talking about a child, right?" Vaha's phores flickered in a complex dance, too fast for Jayanthi to parse, but she caught the hues of brown and dark yellow. "Are you ready to bring one into this world, to be a parent?"

The construct withdrew the fluid port from her arm. She waited until it had sealed her skin and set her on her feet.

"I don't have any practical experience," she acknowledged. "But plenty of immersives show people raising children. You have your database of human medical information. How hard could it be?"

"You've had a good life, raised by two loving and attentive people. Not all of us have been so fortunate. You should want the child for its own sake, not as a means to an end."

"Of course! Do you take me for a monster?" She tempered her tone at the pale yellow of zir phores. "I'd care for the child, and I would never abandon it. I'm sure love would come, too, once the child was born. How could it not?"

Vaha shook zir head. "The love should happen first."

Was zie right? Did people want children so deeply that they could love an abstract idea? She wasn't close to any adults who'd had children. Her parents' social circle consisted of professional contacts and alloy friends. The SHWAs were all too young and ambitious to consider having families of their own. People—humans, at least—had been having children long before it was a conscious choice. Life depended on the urge to procreate. Was the experience different for alloys? They didn't have the same level of physical or genetic connection to their offspring. Did that give the emotional bond more significance?

"And what about the legal fallout?" Vaha pressed. "What are the consequences for you if you do this?"

"Nothing. Humans have the choice to get pregnant whenever they want to. We have to take a specific antibacterial agent to deactivate our fertility suppression, and we have the option to consult with a tarawan, but we don't have to. As for using my own design, I think we're in uncharted territory." She grimaced. "It's not my fault if no one anticipated that someone like me might have the desire, skill, and opportunity to use a womb."

"Do you know what happens to an alloy who makes a child with unapproved chromosomes?"

She shook her head.

"Exile. Their wings are bound, and they're launched into a very long elliptical orbit around Sol. Their case is only reviewed when they approach perihelion. The worse the crime, the longer the path. And whatever gene-set they used, if it proves viable, it goes into the public domain portion of the Nivid with no name attached."

"Oh, Vaha . . . I had no idea." She shuddered at the thought of zir adrift and alone. "Will you get in trouble for helping me make this baby? Perhaps we shouldn't risk it. I'm sorry. There's so much I don't know about alloy life."

Vaha leaned forward and took her hands in zirs. "Jaya, look at me."

She raised her gaze from the floor.

"You don't need to apologize for that." Vaha's face shone with earnestness. "You're lucky that humans have so much freedom when it comes to their children. So what if you're not like the others? That's why you're here, on Meru. To do something with that fire inside you. The same one"—zie leaned closer—"that draws me to you like a newborn to the sun."

She interlaced her fingers behind zir neck and pulled zir against her. "There's another fire inside me, and I'd like to quench it before we go back to the house."

Two days later, the skies cleared. Vaha resumed zir regular exercises in zir true body, but now zie spent some of the daylight hours in orbit as well. Zie had to ensure that Kaliyu didn't get suspicious. Over the following weeks, zie and Jayanthi continued their discussion via written emchannel messages. It lacked the nuance of face-to-face communication, but it gave them privacy. The more Vaha learned about human pregnancy, the more it worried zir. Earth had medical practitioners who knew how to deal with it. They lacked experience with the complications of a case like Jayanthi's, but they'd do better than zir incarn. The counterweight, as Jayanthi pointed out, was the womb. It had the capacity to save her life in case the pregnancy or delivery went wrong. And zie had to grant her point—a successful birth from her body would demonstrate a core piece of the Meru-settlement plan regardless of what Pushkara did.

If everything went right . . . they'd have a baby together. Vaha had assumed zie would never have a child because zie didn't want to end up acting like Veera, and zie had no other model for how to raise one. With Jayanthi by zir side, though, that worry eased. Zie would have a partner, and she would be the child's primary parent, both genetically and practically. Any time they were in the womb, Jayanthi had a new set of questions for its constructed mind. They discovered that the CM's knowledge of human care extended far deeper than the basics in Vaha's extended memory.

"What if I can't produce breast milk?" Jaya asked.

"I can manufacture that," the CM had replied.

"What about surgery?"

"I have microconstructs, and the umbilical that I would use for your body will scale to fit a human infant."

Vaha had no doubt that Jayanthi would make a far better parent than zirself. That she wanted zir help at all still amazed zir.

They used Jaya's health as an excuse to rendezvous inside the womb, and it was often a legitimate reason. Since stopping her medical treatment, she'd gotten slower on their walks, spent more time in bed, and worked less on her genetics. She'd started to use a pain ampoule almost every day. The womb's infusions helped, but they also wore her out.

<Considering how often she needs time in a womb,> Kaliyu had flashed at one point, <she must be quite fragile. This is exactly what's wrong with humans. They suck up resources and provide no value in return.>

It was getting harder to pretend as if zir friend's attitude toward humans—and Jaya in particular—didn't matter. Vaha had to, though, to protect the project as long as possible. In all their years at Nishadas, Vaha had never hidden zir feelings from Kaliyu. Now that zie had some practice at it, zie realized how much power their friendship used to have over zir thoughts. Kaliyu was fundamentally a good person, of that Vaha was certain, but zir bias against humans went far deeper than Vaha had realized. The longer Vaha spent with Jayanthi, the less zie wanted to return to zir friend's company.

Zie confessed it to Jayanthi as they lay together in the womb. "Kaliyu always had so much confidence, and zie was always right. I never thought to question anything zie said."

They'd made a small nest on the womb's floor with a blanket and some cushions. Gravity demanded such comforts.

"We can't rely on the womb as an excuse too much," Vaha continued. "Kaliyu isn't suspicious of it, but zie thinks it's a sign of your weakness."

"It's because I'm off the treatment," Jayanthi said. "I'm in a lot of pain, worse than I was on Earth. Maybe because of the extra oxygen and the stress it creates on my body." She sighed, her breath warm against zir neck. "We're only a week away from ending the trial period without the enzyme."

They had agreed to that as the decision point for stage two.

"What do you think?" she asked. "Should we go ahead with it?"

"I think so, as long as you want to."

"I do. It's risky, but so was coming to Meru." Her arm tightened around zir. "I worry for you. I adjusted the DNA again, brought over even fewer genes from your side, so that she'll be as human as possible aside from the phores."

"She?"

"Yes, at least until she tells us otherwise. All of the embryos have XX chromosomes. I used mine for the sperm and yours for the eggs. It's the only way to make uniparental disomy work in favor of my DNA."

"Well, I'd like *her* to think of me as a parent," Vaha said.

"And if the CDS discovers your part in all this? If you get exiled, then what?"

"Hey." Vaha turned onto zir side and traced a finger along Jayanthi's hairline. "I promise I won't volunteer any information about my part in this. I'd rather be available for my child, even if only from Earth orbit.

I want to watch her grow and help guide her life, like Hamsa did for you. You said she'll mostly get your genes, right?"

Jayanthi nodded.

"So as long as we don't tell anyone, no one will know that she's also mine. I don't need the world to acknowledge it. I just want to be part of her life." Zie kissed the tip of her nose. "Did you realize that once you're visibly pregnant, we can stop hiding in here like this? For safety reasons, you'll have to stay on the planet until you've had the baby. This—us—Kaliyu won't be able to stop the project because of it."

"That's true." She hesitated, then said, "You aren't worried about your friendship if zie finds out?"

It pained Vaha that she would ask. As firmly as zie could, zie said, "Never. Let the entire world know. I care more about you than what anyone else thinks."

She sighed, and the millimeter gaps between them grew smaller. "I'd like to get the data to Hamsa somehow. He deserves to know what's happening, and maybe he can counteract whatever influence Pushkara has over the committee. I was thinking of copying everything we have so far to a spare data cube and sending it via a news courier. Could we do that?"

Vaha couldn't think of a way that wouldn't involve Kaliyu knowing. "It's a physical handoff. I'm not sure I could hide that."

After a pause, she said, "Maybe I don't have to send an entire cube's worth. I can include the essential data in a message to Hamsa."

"Do you want to wait for his approval?"

"I don't think so. We could lose months, and as you said, the sooner it happens, the sooner we have proof that Pushkara can't deny." She let out a long, slow breath. "Okay. I'll start on the hormones to get my body ready. Let's make a baby."

—

They had arrived at a decision, but Jayanthi worried about Vaha's part in it. She didn't mind risking her own health, and she knew what the child would go through if they returned to Earth in terms of sickle cell, but she had no concept of what exile meant for an alloy. She looked up what she could in the local databases around Meru. It was a standard consequence for breaking certain laws. Violating reproductive rules fell under that category.

In general, alloys eschewed punitive measures, favoring gene therapy, corrective counseling, or community service, like the alloys who ended up on Earth. They reserved exile for the most severe offenses, especially acts of violence. By putting someone in exile, they removed that person from society for a period of time. The worse the crime, the longer the absence. The intention was to strip that person from the social connections that had empowered their actions in the first place.

She wished she could talk to Mina. Her friend not only understood the alloy legal system, they would sympathize with Jayanthi's predicament. The one action she could take to mitigate Vaha's involvement was to get pregnant on her own. Zie had consented to the use of zir genes for making the embryos, and if she let the womb recycle those, zie wouldn't have broken any laws. But if zie participated in making an unapproved *child*, zie risked exile, and she couldn't bear that thought. Secrets had a way of getting out. For zir own good, she had to take the final step on her own.

On the optimal day for implanting the embryo, Jayanthi waited until Vaha's attention shifted back to orbit, then hurried to the womb. Inside, she stripped to her underclothes and entered the inner chamber and its blissful warmth. A smaller delivery tray sat within the massive alloy-size one. A type of syringe lay upon it. The womb wasn't authorized to do the implantation, but she was able to have it make the right equipment. Jayanthi stared at the device and wondered how in the Nivid she was going to get it into her uterus by herself.

She loaded an embryo into the syringe, removed her undershorts, and sat on the floor with her knees bent. The surface yielded under her, like a mattress, and felt as warm as skin. The womb's ambulatory construct positioned a scanner over her abdomen. She slow-blinked and linked the image to her vision.

Greatness finds those who work without fear.

She grabbed the long tube at the end of the syringe and slipped it into her vagina. After a few failed attempts at getting it past her cervix, she realized that the overlay was inverted from reality.

"What are you doing?"

Vaha's voice nearly startled her into dropping everything.

Jayanthi wanted to do about ten things at once. She did none of them and froze instead, staring at Vaha with her mouth open. Where did she start? What should she tell zir? She grasped for a lie and came up empty.

Vaha looked as confused as she felt.

"Are you all right?" zie asked. "I saw that you'd entered the womb, so I came back."

Jayanthi took a deep breath and pushed the scanner aside, carefully laying the syringe down on the tray. She felt an absurd urge to cover her naked bottom half. *It's nothing zie hasn't already seen.* As a concession to dignity, she moved to a kneeling position, resting on her heels.

"I'm fine. As for what I'm doing here, it's better that you don't know."

Vaha's eyes narrowed. Zie walked over to the incubator, looked inside, then turned back to Jayanthi. "You're implanting the embryo, aren't you?"

Damn. She couldn't think of a plausible cover story quickly enough. "I'm sorry I didn't get it all done before you found me," she said. "I wanted to protect you. That's why I didn't tell you about it, so you could honestly say that you had nothing to do with this."

"Nothing except my human chromosomes."

"You gave me those for my tarawan experiments. Me running simulations doesn't break the law, and anyway, the genes I used can't be traced back to you. You helping me implant a made embryo, on the other hand, is a legal gray area. I don't want to risk you getting exiled. Just . . . leave and pretend you never found me."

Vaha gave her a withering look. "I know too much to testify that I had nothing to do with this. Short of destroying the embryos and revoking your womb access, nothing I do would absolve me in the eyes of any judicial construct." Zie knelt down and said, more softly, "I've spent too much of my life making decisions out of fear. Fear of disappointing my maker. Fear of injury. Fear of failure. I'm done with that. I'm not going to let it stop me from taking part in making my first child." Zie sat back and glanced at the scanner and syringe. "What can I do?"

"You want to help . . . with the implantation?"

"Yes. I'm supposed to take care of your medical needs, remember?"

With reluctance, Jayanthi swallowed her arguments and nodded. She worried about Vaha's fate, as zie worried about hers, but she had to support zir decisions, just as zie did hers.

She described the procedure to Vaha as best as she could, then waited while zie accessed the necessary anatomical knowledge from the womb's memory. They thought-shared the scanner display. Jayanthi positioned it across her abdomen and traced a line over the path where the tube needed to go.

"Once there, you insert the syringe all the way into it, then activate the plunger," she said.

"I understand."

Jayanthi lay back. As she bent her legs, her ears and cheeks grew hot at the juxtaposition of vulnerable, clinical, and sexual that the position placed her in. The warm silkiness of Vaha's hands against her thighs didn't help.

Zie kissed the side of her knee, then got to business. "Tell me if anything hurts or feels uncomfortable."

"Okay."

She winced a little as the tube missed the entrance to her cervix, jabbing its side instead.

"Sorry," Vaha murmured.

"I'm fine."

She could see the intense concentration on zir face as zie worked, zir eyes closed to see the scanner overlay better.

"There," they said at the same time.

Vaha opened zir eyes and grinned at her before grabbing the syringe-like device. That had a more slender, flexible tube that slid into the guiding device. She felt nothing when zie pushed the plunger.

Vaha sat up and gently extracted the tubes from her body. "All done."

Jayanthi propped herself up on her elbows.

"I suppose we shouldn't . . . be intimate now?" Vaha traced a finger along the skin where her thigh met her hip.

"Probably not, but only with that part of my body." She pulled zir down to the floor and flipped their positions. "Besides, I owe you a favor."

"Oh?"

"For helping me."

"Ah." Zie lay under her, their faces centimeters apart. "Yes, you do."

—विक्रान्त

Vikraantha—Bold

Vaha hated to leave Jayanthi before knowing the outcome of their experiment, but after four days, zie had to spend more time exercising zir true body.

"I'll see you soon," zie said to Jayanthi with a kiss on her forehead.

She'd been more tired since the embryo transfer. A check of her bodym showed yellow flags on the sensors implanted in her lungs. Her heme oxygenase level had dropped to that of an average human's, and the damage from Meru's extra oxygen was starting to show. The project plan called for her to resume the HO treatments, and she had, but it would take some time to regain their benefits.

A look at zir incarn's body showed signs of damage from Meru's extra oxygen, too. Vaha had less concern about that than Jayanthi's health, since zie could have zir womb repair zir incarn, but zie made a note to check again in a few weeks. Time spent on the womb's umbilical meant time away from Jaya, and the less of that, the better.

"It took a month for the lung damage to occur," Jayanthi had said upon seeing her yellow flags. "So I'd guess another month to heal."

"What about . . . your other health?" They hadn't come up with a good euphemism for her possible pregnancy.

"It's fine, Vaha. Don't worry."

But as zie left her lying exhausted on her cot, worn out from a walk that barely covered two kilometers, zie couldn't avoid a sense of helpless concern. Had the pregnancy been a bad idea? The embryo might not have much of Vaha's DNA, but it filled zir with a surprisingly fierce possessiveness. Still, zie wouldn't sacrifice Jayanthi's well-being for it.

Zie woke into zir true body and stretched from the tip of zir tail to zir fingers, spreading zir solar wings and flexing them. Kaliyu floated nearby, phores glowing with amusement.

<Welcome back,> Kaliyu flashed. <How's life in the well?>

<You should know,> Vaha flashed back, coloring zir words with teasing. <Or haven't you been doing your job?>

<It's all too boring most of the time. I don't know how you can handle the tedium of being a weller.>

<I enjoy the company.> Vaha regretted the words right after zie flashed them.

<Your little human paramour?>

Vaha couldn't help going white with surprise and then a glow of guilt. Zie forced zir phores back to skin color.

<Did you think I wouldn't notice?> Kaliyu flashed. <Your incarn's phores gave it away. I don't really care. What you do with your incarn is your business. It's temporary. You want to have some fun with a human, explore your curiosity, go ahead. I think it sounds disgusting, personally. All those bodily fluids and air exchanges.> Kaliyu shuddered. <But I won't try to stop you.>

Vaha was taken aback and relieved. Zie preferred this attitude to the accusatory, combative one that zie had expected. <It's not like that at all, I promise you, and Jayanthi . . . well, she's a wonderful person. Brave and intelligent and fierce.>

Kaliyu flashed indifference. <I was about to practice skimming the atmosphere. You want to join me? Your skin looks entirely too pretty and unmarred lately.>

<Sure. I haven't done that in a while.>

They left their berths and slowed their orbital speed until Meru's gravity drew them downward. Vaha signaled via emtalk for Kaliyu to take the lead.

"Follow me if you can," Kaliyu replied. Zie folded zir wings parallel to zir body and shot forward.

Vaha matched zir friend, movement for movement, speed for speed. Meru's upper atmosphere did its best to slow them down. Zie had improved so much in the two months zie had been at Meru. Having access to a planet with a temperate atmosphere had done more for zir skills than ten years at Nishadas. Kaliyu's protective scales flaked off in a trail of glowing fragments. They surrounded Vaha like a celebration.

"Want to see me fly?" Vaha sent. Without waiting for a reply, zie pushed zir wings straight up, shedding speed even faster.

Kaliyu shot ahead and peered under zir wing. "Show-off. You know I can't do that."

Vaha laughed. "So? Loop back and watch me."

The air was clear of clouds. When Vaha craned zir neck, zie could see Kaliyu coming around far above zir. Vaha pulled zir wings down and out, banking into a spiral. Below, the ocean met outcroppings of land that rose, plateaued, and fragmented. Zie vented and accelerated toward one of the wider canyons. Air rushed past zir, an exhilarating and almost overwhelming sensation against zir exposed skin.

"Come on, do something more interesting," Kaliyu sent. "Try a roll or a flip! Show me those air bladders you keep talking about!"

In the joy of the moment, Vaha shed zir fears. Zie forgot every prior failure and crash. Zie inflated the organs along zir torso and opened them to the atmosphere. Zie dipped to the right, pushing the air through as if zie were venting in space but with a lot more force, then glowed with triumph as zie rolled onto zir back. Zie waved at Kaliyu and thought zie could see an arm waving back, though zir friend was so backlit by Meru's sun that zie wasn't sure.

Then, astounded by zir own daring, Vaha arched back, as if trying to form a circle with the tip of zir tail and the crown of zir head. Zie pulled zir tail up, pointing zirself straight down, then thrust with zir anterior vent and bladders. Zie flipped backward, upside down, then back to level.

"Whoooeee!" Kaliyu sent. "Look at you go! I'm jealous."

"This is amazing," Vaha sent back. Zir lungs worked hard, burning through zir water supply to replenish the sudden expenditure of oxygen as well as the hydrogen in zir vent bladders. Zie looked down and saw a yawning canyon below. Zie dove for it. "Okay, and for my last trick—"

As zie came level with the canyon top, the air below zir gave way. Zie thrust, remembering the column of air from the landing with Jayanthi, but instead of speeding past it, zir body was wrenched sideways. The atmosphere pushed zir left wing down. Zie flew straight into the canyon wall. Pain shot through zir shoulder just before zir head smacked into the rock.

Kaliyu watched in horror as Vaha's body slammed against the land far below. Zie couldn't see much other than an inky spot against the rust colors of Meru, but zie winced as zir imagination filled in the details.

"Vaha, are you all right?" Kaliyu sent.

There was no reply.

Zir blood coursing with adrenaline, Kaliyu thrust back upward, out of Meru's atmosphere, and toward the beacon that marked the location of their observation platform. From there, zie could magnify the ground below. Zie overlaid zir vision with the camera feed and scanned the ground until zie found Vaha's body. A sick feeling filled zir lungs as zie enlarged the view. Vaha's tail bent at an unnatural angle. Zir left wing lay in a limp, mangled mess.

The backup construct assigned to their project was currently in space, on the far side of the planet. They'd take far longer than Kaliyu to reach Vaha.

I'll have to do it on my own first.

Kaliyu couldn't launch from the ground, but in theory, zie could land. Zir wings wouldn't bend straight back like Vaha's, but zie had stronger vents. Zie could use those to control zir descent.

Zie grabbed a small kit of emergency medical supplies from zir pack and tucked it into zir torso belt. At the last minute, zie thought to grab a bladder of water. Even if Vaha couldn't use zir tail, once zie was hydrated, zie could use zir vents. *If it's not too painful to do so.*

Kaliyu descended as fast as zie dared. The patches of exposed skin from their earlier exercise now burned. Zie refused to let the pain distract zir too much, keeping zir attention on the landing path zie had highlighted from orbit. The passing kilas felt like masans, but zie forced zirself to maintain the correct speed. Zie lacked Vaha's aeronautical capabilities. Zie had to keep to a precise trajectory to land close enough to zir friend to help.

At last, zir speed slowed, and zie reached the lower atmosphere. The heat of friction gave way to the cool Meruvin air, easing the pain of surface burns. Kaliyu glided the remainder of the way to Vaha, settling on Meru's ground with only a few running steps with zir hands. Zie slithered over to zir friend, who opened zir eyes.

"I can't move," Vaha sent, the emtalk signal weak and garbled.

"Hush," Kaliyu replied and handed Vaha the water bladder. "Your tail is badly hurt. I'm going to give you some painkillers, then splint it as best I can. I've alerted the construct that we might need help lifting you to orbit, but it will take a while for them to arrive. In the meantime, drink up. It'll take your body a few kilas to electrolyze the water and replenish your hydrogen bladders. If you feel up to it, I'm hoping you can get us off the ground. Once we're high enough, I can lift you to orbit."

Vaha nodded and drank while Kaliyu laid the splints along zir tail, then injected the analgesics. Vaha's phores flashed white with shock and pain a few times, but zie managed to lie still as Kaliyu set zir tail straight. Kaliyu worked as quickly as zie could, wrapping Vaha's tail with high-temperature fabric. The injury looked worse than it had from orbit. If Vaha had sustained internal damage, they would need to get zir off the surface as quickly as possible. The fluid in a pilot's body behaved badly outside of microgravity.

As Kaliyu packed up the medical kit, Vaha grabbed zir arm.

"Did you tell Jayanthi what happened to me?" Vaha sent.

"No. Why would I do that? She can't help us."

"My incarn—I can't access it. It might already be dead. She'll be panicked if she doesn't know what's going on."

"That's what you're worried about right now?" Kaliyu couldn't believe zir friend's attitude. Vaha had taken zir infatuation with the human too far. "Forget about her! Focus on getting yourself safely to orbit. If you lose circulation to your tail, you'll need a full rebirth before you can fly again. Let's get you taken care of first; then you can worry about your precious incarn."

Vaha grimaced. Zie tried to haul zirself up on zir arms, zir face contorted with pain, zir phores glowing so white that they shone in the midday sun.

"Let me help you," Kaliyu said. "Put your arms around my neck." Zie struggled for a hectas with the awkwardness of managing both zir own bulk and Vaha's. "Gravity take this planet and everything on it!"

Once Vaha was securely strapped against zir chest, Kaliyu rolled onto zir back, taking care to keep zir wings off the rocky soil. The bladders along Vaha's flanks ballooned outward.

"Do you think you can do this?" Kaliyu sent.

Vaha nodded, face set in a determined grimace. Air blew against Kaliyu's tail in a forceful jet. A massive cloud of dust rose around them, and Kaliyu sent a silent apology to the planet for the damage they were causing. As they lifted clear of the canyon, Kaliyu pushed as much hydrogen into zir internal bladders as zie could. Vents would do little with such dense atmosphere around them, but as soon as the air thinned, zie could take over.

Meru's surface dropped away from them. They arced up into the violet sky, higher and higher, toward the base of the clouds.

Vaha went limp, slumping into Kaliyu's arms. They began to plummet.

"Vaha, wake up!"

Zie tried shaking zir friend's body to no avail. Kaliyu spread zir wings, hoping to stall their free fall. If zie expended gas, it would be a waste. Zie would run out of hydrogen and water long before they reached escape velocity. *Gravity take this thrice-made planet and the womb that birthed it! Think fast, Kaliyu—what can you do?*

Nishadas! Quickly, Kaliyu tried the bodym access codes that Vaha had given zir before zir final test. They worked! Zie flexed Vaha's muscles until zie found the air bladders, and then zie squeezed. It was enough to slow their fall, enough to buy Kaliyu time to understand these new organs and how to work them. Zie flew by intuition, venting down and back, letting the bladders suck in Meru's atmosphere and thrust it out behind them.

As their speed increased, zie oriented them so Vaha was once more on top. Their bodies lifted up toward the clouds again. Zie hoped that Vaha wouldn't wake. If they had to fight for control, they might fall again.

They continued their upward trajectory. Kaliyu breathed hard, willing zir body to process water faster. The sky deepened into rich purple, and Vaha's air jets began to falter. They had reached an altitude where Kaliyu's vents could function again.

Zie didn't give in to relief. *Not yet, not until I have us safely in orbit.* Kaliyu thrust hard with zir vents, rotating so that Vaha's body was toward the planet and putting them on course to their platform. Their surroundings darkened to indigo, then black. The release from Meru's well was as liberating as escaping a tight berth. Zie let go of Vaha's bodym and closed zir vents to rest for a few hectas.

At last, Kaliyu could see their packs and the observation array. Zie adjusted their velocity to match and then carefully guided Vaha's body into zir berth. Zie placed a hose over zir friend's mouth and attached a container of medical microconstructs to the other end.

They confirmed zir suspicions: in addition to a concussion, Vaha had sustained serious injuries to zir tail and wing. Zie would need a pilot-size womb to heal zir—larger than the child-size version on the planet—and Meru's system had none. They had to return to Sol.

Kaliyu could tow Vaha to the RT point. Zie wasn't sure if zir friend had the mental strength to perform the transit, but if the medical kit had something to make Vaha unconscious, Kaliyu could pull them both through. They would have to abandon the observation post, leaving that human alone on the planet doing the Nivid only knew what.

Or . . . perhaps this is it, the opportunity I've been watching and waiting for. The chance to fulfill zir promise to Pushkara. Zie could use this as an excuse to end the surface mission well before the human's health was proven.

Kaliyu would have to make another landing to pick her up or send the construct to do so if they could wait that long. Zie had a human-support chamber. Zie could load the human into it, though it hadn't been tested or equipped like Vaha's. Once in orbit, if necessary, zie could use Vaha's bodym again, open zir friend's mouth, and let the human travel back to Sol inside Vaha. If zie released the contaminant, then by the time someone returned the human to Meru, they would discover the breach of protocol. Hamsa's project would be doomed.

Kaliyu switched zir emtalk channel to the human shelter on Meru's surface. The system prompted zir to choose a voice. *Audio. How quaint.* Kaliyu picked one at random and greeted the human.

After a small eternity, she answered. "Hello? Who's speaking?"

"This is Kaliyu, your observer."

"Kaliyu . . . Is something wrong? Where's Vaha?"

She could reason, at least.

"I'm afraid we have a serious situation. Vaha did some aerobatics and ended up with a badly injured tail and wing as well as a concussion."

"What! How? When?"

Kaliyu ignored her questions. "Zie needs medical attention that we can only get at Sol. I have to tow zir to the transit point, which means that you can't stay on Meru. The project states that you must remain under observation by an alloy at all times. I'm coming to pick you up." Zie did a quick estimation. "Be ready in ten kilas. Pack any essentials in the meantime." By then, the construct would be available to help zir launch.

"Wait! What about Vaha—I mean, zir incarn? And the womb? We can't leave them here."

Kaliyu glanced at zir friend. Zie should retrieve the incarn, for Vaha's sake. "The womb will have to stay. I can't tow it and carry Vaha at the same time. The incarn, though . . . can you bring it with you? If you do, we can transfer it into Vaha's body so they're together."

"I—I'll figure out a way. For Vaha's sake. Can I talk to zir?"

"Zie is unconscious, probably from the pain. You have only ten kilas. Be ready!"

"Wait—"

Kaliyu closed the channel. Zie had nothing more to say, and zie needed to make zir own preparations. Zie started a final backup of the planet-side data, then studied their gear. The two packs were large. Zie wouldn't be able to carry both and Vaha while navigating thamity gradients. Zie filled the extra space in zir pack with the bhojya and water stores from Vaha's. That way zie could wear the pack on zir back as usual and carry Vaha in front as zie had before.

The backup done, Kaliyu removed the data cube and tucked it into zir belt along with all the others. Zie pulled out the contaminant device from Pushkara. Curtailing the project might be enough, but Kaliyu didn't want to take any chances. Zie activated it, programmed it to land between the human shelter and Vaha's womb, and let it go. The passive device would arrive well after zie had picked up the human. The orbital platform's cameras would witness its arrival, but without a fresh data cube, they wouldn't store more than a kilas's worth of data. By the time anyone returned to the site, the device would have dissolved into biowaste, the recorded evidence overwritten.

Kaliyu took a few deep breaths of water and waited for all zir bladders to refill. Zie had expended a lot of hydrogen on the way up. Zie would need more to control zir descent.

Just then, Vaha's phores broke into a riot of colors.

<You're safe,> Kaliyu flashed, echoing the words via emtalk in case Vaha couldn't process phoric. <We made it up to orbit, but you're injured. Don't try to move.>

<Jayanthi—>

<She's fine. I'll retrieve her and your incarn soon.>

<What? Why?>

<We have to return to Sol. Your mission is over.>

<No—>

<I'm afraid so. You need serious medical attention, the kind we can't get here, and we can't leave the human unattended on the surface. Save your strength for transit. I'll help you get there.>

<Leave-her-planet-important.> Vaha's phores flickered with random words.

<You're not making any sense,> Kaliyu flashed. <Dim yourself. Rest. I have to pick up the human and wait for the construct to launch me. I'll see you soon.>

Kaliyu vented from zir shoulders, slowing zir orbital speed and dropping belly-first toward Meru's upper atmosphere. Clouds had started to accumulate between zir position and the landing site. Zie overlaid zir vision with radar and tried to understand what zie was seeing.

Something jolted into Kaliyu from behind. Two blue-black arms appeared around zir hips and arrested zir downward trajectory.

"Vaha? What are you doing?" Kaliyu sent via emtalk.

"I won't let you disrupt this project!"

"Let me go! You're not thinking straight! You had a concussion. You shouldn't exert yourself like this."

They tumbled for a few seconds, then, with a flash of white phores, Vaha launched upward, dragging Kaliyu with zir.

"Stop!" Kaliyu sent. "Don't hurt yourself over the human!"

"I love her, Kaliyu, and I won't let you take this from her."

"You've lost your Nivid-loving mind!"

They emerged from Meru's well. The sky went dark. Stars sprang to life, blurring and streaking as they wrestled. Kaliyu thrashed zir tail, trying to shake Vaha loose without injuring zir friend further. Why was it always the alloys who got hurt by trying to help humans? Vaha didn't deserve this, just as Kaliyu's maker hadn't deserved zir fate—*no, zie is still alive!*—but if zir friend didn't stop behaving like a sunstruck newborn, Vaha would force Kaliyu to take stronger action.

Then Kaliyu had a better idea. Zie activated Vaha's bodym code again. Zie got one good blast from Vaha's vents before zir friend realized what was going on. They fought for control over Vaha's body, flying farther and farther from Meru. Pain tore through Kaliyu's left wing as Vaha wrenched it away from zir back.

"You mudha!" Kaliyu sent, phores blazing.

"I won't let you pick Jayanthi up."

Fine, if Vaha were going to play dirty, so would zie. Kaliyu twisted, reached down, and ripped the splint from Vaha's tail. Vaha's phores flashed white, and zie sent a blast of gas from zir vents, thrusting them in opposite directions. A few seconds later, Kaliyu slowed zir tumble and oriented zirself. Vaha was a receding blot against the stars, speeding away from Meru. Kaliyu moved in a tangential direction, closer to the planet but not directly toward it. Zie could no longer access zir friend's bodym.

"Vaha, you thrice-made fool! Come back! I can't land anymore. You've made sure of that."

"Can't. Muscles are shredded. Bladders are empty."

Kaliyu thrust toward zir friend, wincing as it aggravated zir torn wing joint.

"Stay away!" Vaha sent. "I'll fight you again if you touch me!"

Kaliyu couldn't see Vaha anymore. Zie was another speck in a field of black and silver. Why did every alloy Kaliyu cared about turn into a human-loving idiot? What spell did those little creatures cast, first upon zir maker and then upon zir best friend?

Fine, drift away, then, you sunstruck mudha! Now we both need medical attention. I'm going back to Sol, with or without you.

Kaliyu made zir way back to the platform, taking care not to aggravate zir injury. Every part of zir felt bruised and beaten, but Vaha's words hurt more than anything. Kaliyu grabbed zir pack. If Vaha thought leaving the human alone on the planet would be good for her or the project, zie was sorely mistaken. Kaliyu canceled the lift request to the construct. Let the human try to survive on her own. Zie had neither the ability nor the mandate to carry her back to Sol. That was Vaha's job. Kaliyu powered down the observation platform. The human wouldn't survive long without data support.

Zie pulled on zir pack, wincing as the strap pressed into zir torn wing. With one last glance in Vaha's direction, zie vented away from the thrice-made planet and started the journey back to Sol.

—त्यक्तव्य

Thyakthavya—Abandoned

Jayanthi paced outside the tent. Ten kilas, Kaliyu had said. That translated to 150 minutes. Her timepiece said nearly three hours had elapsed since their conversation. What was taking so long? Had Vaha's condition worsened? She'd packed in a rush, shoving her underclothes and toiletry items into her travel bag, not bothering with food or medicine. Vaha's pack in orbit would have plenty of both. She'd also wrestled Vaha's incarn into the vestibule and somehow managed to get zir into an enviro-suit. Dressing a comatose person was no easy task. She kept glancing at the sky, expecting to see Kaliyu descend. She couldn't recall what zie looked like, but zir body couldn't be that different from Vaha's.

Clouds had gathered all afternoon and now obscured the sun. A major storm was brewing. It wouldn't peak for another Meruvin day, but light rain was expected anytime, and the temperature had begun to fall. Would Kaliyu have trouble flying in that? Was that why zie hadn't arrived?

After another five minutes of wandering in circles, she gave up and went inside. Vaha's incarn lay unmoving in the vestibule, zir violet eyes hidden behind closed lids. She stripped off her enviro-suit and passed into the main tent.

"Hello? Kaliyu? Vaha? Are you there?" Any of the tent's microphones would pick up and transmit her voice.

No one responded.

She slow-blinked and thought-retrieved the status of the campsite's communications. The antenna reported good power and medium signal strength. Was there a problem in space? Had a solar storm damaged their equipment? Had Vaha's situation deteriorated? The conversation with Kaliyu had been frustrating, and zie had cut her off before she finished asking all her questions. Zir voice lacked Vaha's tonality, much like Vaha's had when zie first started speaking to her, but to her ears Kaliyu's words had held no sympathy, no trace of friendliness. She supposed that was to be expected from an alloy. Or she could be interpreting zir speech wrong. After all, zie was Vaha's best friend. *Who doesn't like humans,* she reminded herself.

Whatever the reason, she could do nothing but wait. The alloys were in charge of this mission. She was only a test subject. After her night atop the cliffs, she had promised Vaha that she wouldn't do anything reckless, which meant waiting for Kaliyu to land or contact her with further instructions.

She turned the heat back on inside the tent. With the sun hidden behind clouds, the shelter had cooled off quickly. Then she went to bring Vaha's incarn in. Zir body would get cold in the unheated vestibule, especially as night fell and the outside temperature dropped.

With a sigh, she unzipped Vaha's enviro-suit. Zir skin was cool to the touch as she scooped zir torso out of the upper half. As she laid zir gently back down, she realized she couldn't see zir chest move. She held her finger near zir nose. Nothing.

Dread crept into her stomach and settled there like a rock.

"Vaha," she said, shaking zir shoulder, her instincts lagging the part of her brain that knew the truth. "Vaha! Wake up!"

She placed an ear on zir chest, over zir heart.

Silence.

The trembling began in her arms and spread to her entire body. *This can't be happening. Zie can't be dead. Zie can't!* She clamped a hand over her mouth to hold in the scream that threatened to escape and stumbled backward into the main room of the tent.

"Kaliyu, please answer me! What's happening? Vaha's incarn—I think zie's dead. Is Vaha dead? Kaliyu!"

No response.

She heard a strange keening noise and realized it was coming from her own throat. Pain shot through her legs. She slumped into a sling chair and curled into a ball.

Calm down! It's just zir incarn. Vaha could still be okay. Zie said this would happen if zie lost a link to zir incarn for too long. Maybe zie got knocked out of geosynchronous orbit, or maybe something damaged zir emchannel organs. She had to believe that Vaha, the true Vaha, could still be alive, otherwise she might never move again.

She pressed herself up and crawled to the medical cabinet. Her limbs burned as she grabbed an analgesic ampoule, ripped off the cover, and slapped it against her arm. For a few minutes, she could do nothing but lie on the floor and breathe.

When at last the drug brought relief, she stumbled to the vestibule. Vaha's incarn body lay where she'd abandoned it, and she forced herself to look at it. At zir. *Deep breaths. You can do this.* She wrestled zir body back into the enviro-suit. Vaha had told her the womb could preserve life as well as support it. She had to get zir incarn into the womb for safekeeping and, she hoped, rebirth when zir true body was ready.

Vaha was heavier than she expected, and she had to drag zir down the stairs by the armpits, then across the rough terrain of Meru, thankful that the enviro-suit was sturdy enough not to tear from the abrasion. *Please be alive, Vaha. Please let this be a temporary problem.*

Inside the womb, she stripped the suit off Vaha, then the clothes, and hauled zir into the main chamber.

She activated her emchannel and spoke to the womb's constructed mind. "I need you to take this body and preserve it as best as you can until given different instructions."

"I can do that. Please stand back."

The ambulatory extension rolled toward them. Jayanthi backed away and watched as it lifted Vaha, supporting the incarn's body with several arms, and retreated through the delivery sphincter. Several minutes passed, and nothing more happened; then it emerged and parked itself again.

She stood in the middle of the chamber, her mind stuck in a cascade of what-ifs, until her gaze fell on the lab equipment. *The embryo.* She had an additional responsibility.

"I'd like a hydration push," she said.

The construct came to life once more. She sat cradled by its arms as fluids diluted the sickled cells in her blood. On the floor, Vaha's suit lay in a crumpled heap.

Jayanthi opened her eyes to a dark room in the middle of the night. She couldn't see the arm of the sling chair beneath her. When had she fallen asleep? A vague sense of hunger gnawed at her stomach, but she had no energy to get up. What had disturbed her? Had someone spoken? The question woke her more thoroughly, and she sat up and listened.

Silence from above. Silence inside. Only the occasional creak from the tent as the wind buffeted it to prove that anything existed.

Had it really been only four days since her night with Vaha in the womb?

The first raindrops spattered against the clear roof panel.

How terribly cliché. It's raining.

She closed her eyes.

When she opened them again, dim gray light suffused the room. A steady downpour drenched the outside. It sent rivulets along every outer surface and filled Jayanthi's ears with white noise, broken only by the spatter of wind. Meru's surface gleamed with unfair beauty. Water transformed the boulders into garnets and decorated the ground with silver pools. Under better circumstances, she could appreciate the landscape, but at that moment, it affronted her sense of despair.

She slow-blinked and checked the communications. It showed no incoming traffic, no messages. *No data.* She couldn't access the orbital platform's spool or any of Meru's knowledge bases. Something must have damaged or destroyed the observation deck. Something that also affected Vaha and Kaliyu. They were dead. They had to be or one of them would've contacted her.

She dragged herself to the kitchen corner and took a few sips of bhojya. Her stomach had tied itself in knots and didn't appreciate the liquid. She tucked the tube back into the wall hook.

Nothing to do, nowhere to go.

She ought to check on her lungs. She ought to see if she were pregnant. She ought to do some exercise. Or eat. Or drink. But she did none of those things. Why bother when none of it mattered? The project was doomed. Whether she lived or died made no difference anymore. Who cared what happened to some random human, stuck on a distant planet, far from the only home where she belonged? The two alloys in charge of her well-being had vanished. Whatever had happened to them in orbit, it didn't change her circumstances.

And really, didn't she deserve her fate? She'd come to Meru. Made a hybrid. Fallen in love with an alloy. She'd had delusions of grandeur that she had no right to entertain. *You're just a sad little human, and this is punishment for your hubris.*

The next morning, Jayanthi had a pounding headache and a parched throat. She wanted nothing to do with food or drink, but her body compelled her to consume some of both in great gulps. She was too tired to fight its will to live. She'd spent the whole night shedding tears—for Vaha, for herself, for their dreams. She wanted badly to see her parents' faces one more time. And Mina's. Any human. She was sick of rocks and dust and sand.

And alloys.

Sick of their bigotry. Their arrogance. Their rules. Because of them, she wasn't free to travel the universe. She'd never get licensed as a tarawan. She had to second-guess every dream and desire.

A wave of hot energy passed through her. She wanted to rip the tent to shreds, to destroy everything it represented: her glaring failure to prove her worth. She was supposed to be better than other humans. She'd been raised by alloys, taught by a tarawan, sent to an alien planet, and given opportunities that no other human had. All of it, trashed. Ruined by the very two people who were supposed to be helping her.

What did you do, Vaha? How did you get yourself killed? How could you leave me here like this, at the mercy of your so-called friend? Where is zie? Why is no one answering me?

The rain had stopped. Clouds still scudded across the violet sky, but sunlight hit the muddy ground and made the pools of water steam.

She needed to get outside.

She stepped into the vestibule and stared at the enviro-suit. *Maybe I should leave it and go out there bare-skinned, contaminate this vent-spawned planet. What does it matter?*

But she couldn't bring herself to do it. No amount of grief and rage could overcome a lifetime of conditioning. *Do the least amount of harm to every form of consciousness, alive or not.* A planet might not think and feel, but it had a place in the universe. It deserved respect and kindness, especially from a puny thing like her, whose survival depended upon it.

She pulled on the suit and helmet and stepped outside. The air smelled of ozone and iron. In the west, silvery waterfalls glittered as they poured down the cliffs. Meru continued, even if Vaha did not.

Jayanthi walked laps around the womb. Mist from the puddles surrounded her like wisps, spirits from another world. She stepped between them, leaving boot prints in the muddy silt. Her mission was defunct, but that didn't mean she had to stay idle, waiting to die like Vaha's incarn. She had no idea what had caused Vaha's and Kaliyu's radio silence. What if a solar flare or an asteroid had damaged the communications equipment on their end? What if they weren't dead but only injured, unable to land with no way to tell her so? Vaha would be worried sick. If she could contact another alloy or construct, maybe she could find out.

I might be human, but I'm not helpless. If the alloys can't save me, maybe I can save them.

She'd already lost two days to moping around feeling sorry for herself. She needed a plan of action. Step one: find someone she could talk to. Somewhere atop the cliffs, deep into the plateau, a megaconstruct worked on ground-based research. A megaconstruct that must have the ability to communicate to orbital stations. And to get themself off-planet. Worst case, they would refuse to help her, and she'd have to turn around and come back. Best case, she could find out what happened to Vaha and Kaliyu and figure out what she should do next.

That led to step two: pack for an expedition with the chance of not returning. If the megaconstruct could get her to orbit, and if Vaha needed to get back to Sol as Kaliyu had indicated, she had to be ready to leave with zir. That meant following through the camp shutdown procedures. Kaliyu's original timeline hadn't allowed for that, but she didn't need to rush anymore. She couldn't pack away the entire thing without the help of an alloy, but she could power down all the systems, reduce the chances of their supplies causing any kind of contamination to the planet.

She stopped pacing and went inside. She took the spare enviro-suit, which she had cast aside in an untidy pile, and hung it beside hers for disinfection. They served as outer-space protection, too, with connections for external air supplies. If the megaconstruct took her to orbit to reach Vaha or Kaliyu, she might need air, but the tanks meant significant extra weight while walking and climbing the cliffs. She decided to hedge her bets and bring one. It would let her survive in vacuum for thirty hours, which was better than nothing.

She repacked the bag that she'd readied for Kaliyu's pickup. Out came the spare clothing and all the toiletries but soap. In went packets of bhojya, extra suit batteries, and a spare water bladder. Bhojya alone wouldn't sustain her, so the dehydrated food stayed, along with the small med kit. She threw in a few sealable storage bags as well, to store used diapers. Finding the megaconstruct would take at least one day, possibly more, and the enviro-suits were designed for shorter excursions. It would mean exposing Meru to her body, which would violate the project parameters, but she had no choice. By staying on the planet without alloy supervision, she had already contravened the instructions. She had to break some rules, given the emergency situation. She could only attempt to minimize the damage. Surely the MEC would understand and forgive her?

She made sure the local storage in the tent had a record of her scans, in case she didn't return, then decided to back up all the other test results, too. She copied her bodym and related data to a cube and stowed it in her pack. What if something had happened to corrupt the orbital data? What if no one ever returned to the campsite? If someone discovered her dead body, having the cube on her person could sway the settlement vote in Hamsa's—and humanity's—favor.

She went to the greenhouse. The seeds had turned into bushy young plants in Meru's soil with the addition of some bacteria and organic nutrients. It boded well for feeding a future human population on the planet. Everywhere they'd looked, they had found the surface free of life other than the ocean-borne cyanobacteria. Even the nearby lake harbored only silt. Humans could live comfortably on Meru as long as they had sickled cells or some other way to reduce their oxygen uptake. If the embryo she made proved viable, future generations wouldn't need to supplement with heme oxygenase as long as they expressed the modified HMOX-1 gene.

With a heavy heart, Jayanthi dumped the plants, soil, and containers into the storage boxes that had housed them during transit and sealed them away. If she returned, she'd have to restart them from seed, but that setback seemed like a good trade for knowing whether Vaha lived. She'd stay alone on Meru, with radio silence if necessary, as long as she knew zie was all right. Next she sealed away all the extra food. In the morning, she would shut down the power systems before she left.

With all that done, Jayanthi settled in for a solid meal. Based on the last extended forecast she'd seen, the rain would continue to clear and stay that way for another Meruvin week. She had no desire to scale the cliffs after a storm again, especially while carrying a bulky pack. Her body had weakened from three days of not eating or sleeping well. Her joints ached, and her muscles tingled with a faint telltale burn. She needed rest and energy before she could search for the construct.

She forced herself to swallow the rehydrated rice and vegetable protein, though it held zero appeal, then washed up one last time. When she went outside to close the plumbing valves and disconnect the hoses, she noticed something gleaming on the ground nearby. She investigated and discovered an object the size of her head. Liquid seeped from its base.

Jayanthi picked it up and looked around. Where had it come from? When she examined the ground, there were no signs of tracks. She peered up at the sky. Nothing indicated that the campsite was the intended destination. Could it have fallen all the way from orbit by accident? It was the only logical explanation she could think of.

Not knowing what the object contained, she decided to put it in the womb for safekeeping. From inside the shelter, she grabbed a spade and two sample bags, one for the object, the other for the contaminated soil. The latter went straight into their shelter's biowaste bin. The former she took to the womb, which could safely handle and store harsh chemicals and biohazards. The CM informed her that the outer material was water soluble. If Jayanthi wished, the womb could analyze the contents and possibly neutralize them. *A mystery to solve when—if—I return.* She almost asked the CM to let her see Vaha's incarn one more time, but she resisted the temptation. It would only rub salt in her wounds.

As she returned to the tent, she gazed around at the familiar surroundings. The site had come to feel like home in its own way. The idea of human settlement on the planet no longer filled her with trepidation. They could regulate the number of people who came to live here. Start small, let the population grow slowly. Bring over materials from Earth until they had sustainable resources on Meru. Unlike the checkered past of Mars, they wouldn't have to make any major changes to the ecology. No terraforming disaster loomed. No runaway genetic modifications or alloy-level engineering required. Hamsa was right—this planet would provide an excellent, natural second home.

She wanted to make it hers. She had hoped for a successful pregnancy and delivery to help the project, but she could also see herself living on Meru for the rest of her life, her child by her side, for the sheer joy of the experience. She hadn't scanned to check if the embryo had implanted. With the depression of the preceding days, she couldn't have handled another piece of bad news, but if it had succeeded, she wanted to return to Meru and raise the baby on the planet she was born for. The planet Jayanthi had been born for, too, though she hadn't known it.

She could envision their life: a small home built from Meru's mud. Raised beds full of vegetables and herbs. A laughing face with chubby cheeks. A limber body clambering up fruit trees. The picture needed only one thing to complete it: herself and Vaha, walking hand in hand behind their child.

She didn't dare to hope for that, not with Vaha's incarn lying dead in the womb, not even if zie lived, but she let the image soothe her like a warm blanket. Getting in contact with orbit would bring her closure, not necessarily good news. She wouldn't allow herself to dwell on all the ways her own excursion could go wrong, too: the construct gone, herself injured, getting lost. She'd stayed put long enough to keep her word to Vaha. If zie were in any position to communicate with her or send someone to pick her up, surely zie would have done so already. She had to go looking for zir, and she'd have to do it alone.

—लगति

Lagathi—Contact

Around midmorning, Jayanthi reached the top of the cliffs. The rains and waterfalls from the previous day had stopped, but the muddy soil plus the pack she carried had turned the climb into a slow, exhausting struggle. Pamir gazed down from a crystal-clear sky as she allowed herself a brief rest.

She pulled the tube from the bhojya pouch, unlocked her helmet visor, and opened it with a stab of guilt. The likelihood of her shedding many bacteria or skin cells in such a short time was low, but she couldn't help the instinctive sense of shame. *The project is defunct now anyway,* she reminded herself. *You can't invalidate it more than you already have.* But of course, it wasn't only about the research. She had her own sense of pride and self-worth, and she'd been so careful. She hated that she was spoiling her record. As humanity's lone representative on Meru, she wanted to be perfect. Instead, she was demonstrating exactly what alloys feared the most: that when faced with self-destruction, humans would always choose to save themselves, regardless of the harm they caused.

The planet's natural air chilled her face right through the skin into the bones. It poured into her lungs like a drink of ice water, and her exhale puffed out in a cloud that wafted away. Home never got cold enough for such sensations. She gazed over the expanse below, the landing site in the distance, the lake a silver spot to its left. When night arrived, she would need shelter from the wind and a place to rest. She couldn't afford to linger so early in her journey. With a breath that started from the bottom of her stomach, Jayanthi exhaled the doubts, fears, and recriminations and flipped down her visor. She chose a direction perpendicular to the edge and started walking.

A few hours later, she reached the end of level ground. The mesa formed a broad, flat expanse behind her. Ahead, the land rose in a succession of broken hills. She aimed for the highest point she could see, hoping to get a good look at the surrounding area. The construct's location wasn't on the map she'd grabbed from the tent's data spool, but it had to be large enough to land and take off, like Vaha's true body. It ought to be visible from a good distance as long as she had line of sight.

It took her several more hours to reach the top of a local peak. The low angle of late-afternoon sunlight cast the rocky terrain into a high-contrast jumble. She reduced the tint on her helmet's visor and shaded her eyes. Almost due north, something caught the light. The glint might have come from a body of water, but it was the only feature that stood out, and if her search continued for more than two days, she'd need to replenish her water bladder anyway. She thought-traced a rough line from where she stood to its location on the map and did her best to follow it.

When the sky faded into deep indigo, Jayanthi decided to stop for the night. She didn't trust herself to manage the terrain safely without daylight. She found a jumble of rocks that provided some shelter from the wind and tried to make herself comfortable with her pack as a cushion. Without clothes inside, it wasn't particularly soft, but it had fewer sharp edges than the rocky ground. Exhaustion overwhelmed her pain as the second moon's crescent rose in the sky.

The next day, Jayanthi found herself irritable and achy with a pall of doom cast over the world. Pamir rose into the violet-hued morning, bright and clear, but clouds obscured her thoughts. What right did she have to be optimistic about anything? She'd come to Meru hoping to accomplish something worthwhile, and barely two months into her stay, she wandered alone, without proper food or shelter, in a desperate search for a way to communicate off-planet. She had no idea what she was doing, and she'd be lucky to get through this alive. Who did she think she was, an alloy? She couldn't dynamically change her gene expression, she wasn't born with any enhancements, and nobody would expect her to survive for long.

Yet she trudged ahead, forcing herself to put one foot in front of the other. Within thirty minutes, she had to stop for an analgesic. Once it took effect, she continued to follow the bright-green line she'd drawn the day before. Not a speck of life in any direction. Just rocks and sand and more rocks. She knew on an intellectual level that all matter had some amount of consciousness, woven with the quantum fabric of reality that humans couldn't sense. Conscious didn't mean alive, though, and her instincts screamed that Meru was dead, dead, dead. Nothing moved of its own accord. No speck of green or blue touched the landscape. Her little Earth-based primate brain knew the inherent hostility of her environment even if she didn't want to admit it.

She made a deal with herself: she'd walk until she reached the shiny thing. If it turned out to be water, she'd refill her bladder and head back to the camp. She couldn't handle days more of wandering like this with no guarantee of finding the construct. What if it had left the planet? What if it had been affected by the same thing that had incapacitated Vaha and Kaliyu? She could search until she died of exposure and never find it. *Maybe you should have thought of that before striking out. Maybe you're too much of a human to handle anything on your own.*

She passed a mound of giant boulders and saw the glint again. Now she could also make out smaller reflections sprinkled around a large central one. *Puddles? Some shiny metal sensors in the rocks?*

The land sloped downward from where she stood. Boulders dotted the ground, thrusting up from the surface like the fingers of a tawny giant. Based on the scale of the ones around her, her target couldn't be more than half of Vaha's size. *That would be a very small body of water.* She picked her way through narrow, sandy pathways that threaded between the iron-laced formations. Every so often, she'd scramble up a slab of rock and reorient herself. With each view, her steps gained strength and speed. The object in question was definitely not made of water.

—

She encountered a small six-legged construct first. The little one came up to her waist, its multisegmented body sprouting a variety of sensors. It danced away from her, then beckoned with one leg in a very human *follow me* gesture. She obeyed. It led her to a megaconstruct, one with a squat, rectilinear body on eight cylindrical legs that stood two meters off the ground. It stretched about eighty meters from end to end, its underside punctuated by three doors. The sides and upper surface resembled the small construct, built of sturdy metal and bristling with equipment.

Jayanthi opened a public emtalk channel and sent, "Hello? Are you getting this?"

She had no idea whether all constructs had emtalk capabilities the way alloys did. Back on Earth, many of them used speakers to communicate, since that was all the humans could understand.

Something swiveled atop the megaconstruct. "I'm receiving you." The voice sounded low and feminine to Jayanthi's mind.

"Oh, thank the Nivid. My name is Jayanthi. I'm a human working on some experiments near the coast to the east, collaborating with Vaha and Kaliyu."

"I inferred as much. My name is Varshaneya. Why are you here? I haven't received a request to assist with your objectives."

"I need help." Jayanthi took a deep breath and explained her situation. "Do you have a way to communicate with those in orbit?" she concluded. "Or deliver me to someone there who can house a human?"

"I will begin with the former and inquire about Vaha's and Kaliyu's status."

When Varshaneya sent nothing for several minutes, Jayanthi found a nearby boulder and sank against it. Her shoulders and back felt a million kilos lighter with the pack off. She drank some bhojya as she waited and rested. The construct witnessed her breach of the enviro-suit, but she was too relieved to care. The first sip of the slurry tasted better than anything in her life. After she drank her fill, she leaned her head back and closed her eyes.

She woke with a start as Varshaneya spoke.

"One being in orbit witnessed two alloys departing Meru several kaals ago," the construct sent. "They did not travel along the same vector. No one has arrived or departed since then."

"That's . . . that's all? No solar flare? No widespread loss of communications? No message for me?"

"They mentioned no evidence of those."

Jayanthi sat back down. Both Vaha and Kaliyu gone, and not together? What did that mean? Kaliyu had said that Vaha was badly injured and needed medical attention at Sol. Had Vaha recovered enough to return to the Solar System by zirself? But then what happened to Kaliyu? For someone so suspicious of humans, zie wouldn't have left her unattended on the planet.

One other explanation presented itself to her. One that she did not like. "Varshaneya, what happens to alloys when they die?"

"They cease to function as living beings."

"I mean, what happens to their bodies? What do they do with their dead?"

"I don't know."

Suppose Vaha had died. Suppose Kaliyu had sent zir true body toward Meru's star for a fiery end. That didn't explain why Kaliyu had abandoned her with no word, though. *I need more information!*

"Varshaneya, is there any being in orbit around Meru who can transport me?"

"There is currently one construct in the vicinity whose registration indicates life support for human beings."

"Can you ask them to pick me up?"

"He is not equipped to land. What is your purpose?"

What indeed? What did she think she could do alone, friendless, hundreds of light-years from Earth? Whether they were dead or alive, neither Vaha nor Kaliyu could help her. She could stay and continue the project and hope that the Meru Exploration Committee dispatched a human-capable pilot to pick her up. Surely they would send someone to investigate when she and Vaha didn't return to Sol as scheduled? But she would need periodic food deliveries from Vaha's pack to survive that long. And tools to repair their shelter and equipment. There was also the matter of the potential baby. Every piece of the project depended on another, like a tower of cards, and the alloys formed the base. She was useless without them.

She had to leave. *I should go home. If I'm pregnant, I'll need help, especially for the delivery.* The thought of sitting in her house with her parents and Mina crashed over her like a stormy wave. She shut her eyes against the sting of tears and surge of longing. To feel safe again, comfortable, unworried. Why had she believed that she could do any of this?

Because of hubris. You thought you were so special, the child of alloys. You thought the rules wouldn't apply to you, that you could do more than the average human.

Vaha had helped fuel that belief, too. Zie had inspired the confidence that she could be zir equal. If zie could accept her, respect her, love her, then perhaps other alloys would, too. *Why did you leave me like this? Where are you?*

She hugged herself and took a deep breath. Varshaneya didn't appear to have noticed or cared about her long silence.

What is my purpose?

Megaconstructs were conscious, sentient intelligences who didn't think like living beings. They might lack empathy and have different goals than an alloy or a human, but that didn't mean this one wouldn't help her.

At last, feeling heartsick, she sent, "I'd like to return to Sol. I need someone to transport me there who has a human-habitable chamber. My air supply is limited to thirty hours—Earth hours. If you can get me to the construct in orbit, perhaps he can take me back to Sol or transfer me to an alloy pilot who can."

"No such pilot exists in the vicinity of Meru," Varshaneya replied immediately. "However, I will be launching into orbit in 1.2 Meruvin rotations. You can ride in my cargo chamber and transfer to Manib, the construct I mentioned earlier, if he's willing. He's a sovereign being, not contracted to any registered exploratory projects. He has no obligation to assist you. If he declines, you will return to Meru with me. Do you find this acceptable?"

"Thank you. Yes, I accept."

She hugged her knees. What her future held beyond the next two days, she had no idea. Everything she'd read about free-agent constructs indicated that their interests rarely aligned with anyone else's. Some of them had vastly developed intelligences, far beyond that of any human or alloy, and many of them had little to do with the day-to-day affairs of living beings. At least Varshaneya had a contract with the MEC and would therefore act in a responsible manner. What Manib would do with her, she couldn't guess, but if he had a chamber for her, perhaps he had a soft spot for humans. Regardless, she had no other option if she wanted to get off Meru and get home. She had to rely on herself from now on. She was done putting her life in the hands of alloys.

—नष्ट

Nashta—Lost

Vaha drifted. Through space, through time, through consciousness. The pain from zir injured tail and wing pulled zir back to reality once in a while, but zie couldn't attach zir mind to anything in zir surroundings. After the third day adrift, dehydration kicked in, and zie lost track of what day it was. The patterns of stars looked different from what zie was used to. The Sun's spectrum didn't quite match, either. There weren't enough planets, or padhrans, or people. *Not the Sun. Pamir. Meru's star.*

Zir state of mind reminded zir of the days zie had spent in the womb, healing from zir childhood injuries. How many times had zie gone through that? Enough that zir maker had made the uncomfortable decision to own one.

Ever a failure. I couldn't even come up with a new way to hurt myself. Gravity and atmosphere caught me again. At least I saved Jayanthi and the project. She can handle living on the surface alone. She'll be fine. She doesn't need me.

Nobody would care if zie lived or died. Some other pilot would bring Jayanthi home. Some other pilot would get credit for helping to prove that humans could adapt to Meru's environment. Some other pilot, who had better coordination and strength and didn't hurt zirself while doing stupid tricks.

In more lucid moments, Vaha could feel the resistance of Kaliyu's wing tendons under zir hand as zie yanked them. What a terrible thing to have done to a friend. *I'm sorry, but you tried to cancel the project. You could've left me in orbit. I wasn't going to die once my true body was back in microgravity. I never asked you to take me back to Sol.*

Now zie went in the direction that the universe took zir. Vaha could sense thamity fields all around, but zie couldn't get the organelles in zir tail to activate. It left zir mental map of gradients incomplete and partly obscured. If zie didn't traverse the gradients properly, zie could end up getting stuck in a dark well instead of sliding around it. Venting was impossible. Zie had run out of water, and anything zie drew in from zir body would dehydrate zir further. With one functioning wing, zie barely had enough energy to think, much less broadcast a request for help. If only zie had zir pack. It contained emergency supplies, including a distress beacon, but it was tucked safely in the berth back at Meru. The odds of someone finding zir in a highly populated system like Sol's were already small. In one like this, zie didn't have a chance.

And now zie headed . . . zie didn't know where. Some eccentric orbit around Pamir, most likely. Zir maker would be so disappointed. Or perhaps not. Veera had predicted that Vaha would end up in stasis with no contributions to the Nivid. Now zie had proved zir maker more than right—zie would be lost forever, drifting until death. Zie only hoped that zir actions had helped Jayanthi and would ensure the success of the project. Having known only one human, it wasn't fair to generalize, but she seemed exceptional. If others on Earth were even half as determined and intelligent and creative as she was, they deserved Meru. They deserved the stars.

Zie thought of the first tickle of her hand against zir inner chamber valve. Of her arms around zir incarn body. Her laugh at zir bumbling attempts to be human. Her dark eyes reflecting zir phores, trapping zir soul with their depth. Her fierce expression in the womb, half-naked, holding her precious embryo.

An alert pinged from zir extended memory: a reminder to take shelter. A large coronal mass ejection from Pamir had erupted the day before zir fight with Kaliyu, and it was expected to reach Meru shortly. Zie should take cover in a berth or deploy a shield. *Isn't that just stellar?* The shield was also in zir pack.

Technically, Kaliyu had been within zir rights to terminate the project, but zie should have given Vaha the choice of staying behind with Jayanthi. The injuries to zir tail and wing weren't life-threatening. Zie didn't have to return to Sol for medical attention. It felt like a cheap excuse, one that Kaliyu seemed glad to have. Had it tied into whatever zie and Pushkara had planned? Vaha wondered for the hundredth time if zie should have allowed Kaliyu to drag zir back instead of letting zirself drift away, but it had seemed like the only way to guarantee Jayanthi's continued presence on Meru.

Zie already faced the likelihood of drifting to death. Depending on the strength and direction of the CME's shock wave, it might speed up the process. Either way, zie would find out soon enough. As zie waited, Vaha replayed clips of Jayanthi from zir extended memory. If zie did get hit by Pamir's solar wind, those areas would take more damage than the organic parts of zir body. Zie wanted to remember her face.

The radiation began as a gradual sensation of warmth on Vaha's skin. Zie shut every lid over zir eyes as it built into a feverish heat. The conduits from zir wings to zir extremities blazed with uncontrolled current. Vaha shuddered. Perhaps this would be the death of zir, alone and ignominious.

Jayanthi's face filled zir thoughts with its beloved contours. It was a fitting image to zir end.

But no, as her smile cradled zir, zie felt the solar wind abate. The absolute cold of space gave some relief to zir skin. The fire withdrew from zir conduits. Zie . . . zie couldn't remember zir name.

Who am I, and where am I?

Zir eyes snapped open. Somewhere in space . . . That was briefly comforting, but the stars held no helpful information. Zie stretched out zir arms. Blue-black skin covered in angry pale patches gazed back at zir. *Burn marks.* Zie twisted and caught a glimpse of two wings, one that looked quite broken, which zie confirmed with a slow, painful shrug. Something had gone wrong with zir tail, too. What had happened to zir body? Had something impacted zir? Whatever it was must have given zir amnesia as well.

Zie tried to vent, to turn around, and found zir lungs empty. Zie began to draw water in from zir body but stopped almost immediately. Zir flesh was like a husk. Zie could feel it in the tightness of zir muscles and the rawness at the back of zir throat. Zie had just enough water to live. To draw out more was to risk zir life. Zie felt behind zirself for a pack, for something that might help, and found nothing but zir body.

Zie probed zir memory delicately, as gently as zie had with the injured wing. The extended portions were gone, like dark clouds against a starry sky. *How do I know about clouds?* In zir organic recall, zie could vividly picture the retreating body of an alloy with similar coloring and markings to zirself. *That's . . . my maker!* The name had vanished, but zie knew that zir maker had left to explore the galaxy.

A twist of loss accompanied the realization, which triggered another recollection: zirself leaving a blue-gray alloy, another pilot . . . a friend! Zie could remember the relationship, but not the name to go with it. As frustration washed through zir, a face popped into zir mind, as clear as a picture received by emchannel. The face belonged to a human, and it filled zir with a sense of protectiveness. *Why?* No other details came forth.

What is wrong with me? Stuck in space with no idea where zie was headed or why. Adrift without water or sustenance. A broken wing. Radiation burns. All evidence pointed to something terrible, and zie could do exactly nothing to figure out what, when, or how it had happened.

I should call myself Nakis. The word meant "nobody" in an ancient language whose name zie couldn't recall even though zie knew for certain that zie understood it. With a sense of fatalism settling around zir like a cloud of vapor, zie tried to accept that as another mystery about zirself. Whatever had happened, zie had some momentum, and zie could only hope that it led to someone or something that would explain zir situation.

Nakis drifted for an unknown amount of time, zir body working hard to repair itself with what little nutrients it had, until zie received a signal. A cry for help . . . from a construct. *What can I do to help someone else?* Zir wing had given zir a trickle of power, and zie expended a good amount of it to triangulate the source and chart the being's course. They would almost intersect in four kaals, passing each other within less than two kilometers.

Zie would have to use zir vents to get closer to the construct. That meant diverting some of zir body's water back to zir lungs, as dangerous as it was. The reverse osmosis process would expend more of zir precious power, as would the subsequent electrolysis to make hydrogen for zir bladders, but between that and the extra oxygen, zie would have enough gas to alter zir heading such that they would meet. If the construct had water or bhojya, it could save Nakis's life. Perhaps they could help each other.

After making the adjustment and confirming zir new direction, zie transmitted a short message via emtalk: "I'm coming."

With the sun's light behind zir, Nakis spotted the construct, a shiny blur against the stars. That indicated an old being. No one in recent history would build a reflective outer coating. As they approached each other, its form resolved into a long, sinuous coil, with an obvious kink toward its back quarter. Every segment of the rings was covered in golden sun-gathering scales.

Zie almost couldn't believe zir eyes. This was the legendary Karkothaka, the only construct to ever have this design. Why could zie remember that? Ah yes, zir maker had told zir stories about him—how he had taken humanity past the Solar System with the help of an ancient propulsion system, the first of its kind, that could sense thamity fields and use them for energy. Unlike alloys or other construct designs, Karkothaka didn't need any other fuel, only photons and thamitons.

"It's an honor to meet you," Nakis sent via emtalk. Zie contorted zirself to match zir speed and heading with the construct's, until they flew side by side. "What kind of help do you need?"

"I was struck by a micro-asteroid and took some damage. I need a tow to the local heliopause."

At twice zir size, giving Karkothaka a tow should have been no trouble. Nakis's phores glowed with bitter amusement. "I'm afraid I'm injured and adrift, as well. I have almost no water left. I'm sorry."

"Come around to my front side so I can scan you."

Nakis obliged with the last of zir hydrogen.

"Your arms and hands show signs of heat or radiation burns," Karkothaka sent. "Can you use them?"

"Yes, but I'm badly dehydrated. I can't maneuver much. Do you have any water or bhojya?"

"I'm afraid not, but if you would be so kind as to repair my damaged segments, I can tow you somewhere."

Nakis agreed to the ancient construct's offer. What alternative did zie have? Zie hoped zie had the energy to take care of Karkothaka's needs.

"I'll give you the spare parts," the construct sent, "and then talk you through the procedure."

Karkothaka didn't have a face, but a door swung open from the flat surface of his forward end. Nakis caught the pieces that tumbled out. They were small enough to fit in one hand. With Karkothaka's permission, zie grabbed on to the construct's rings and pulled zirself to the correct spot. The repair wasn't too complicated, but zir hands shook from pain and exhaustion, and zir brain was dizzy from dehydration and hunger. It took zir thirty-seven kilas to complete the repairs. Zie had to repeat some of the steps multiple times because zie was so uncoordinated, but in the end, zie succeeded.

Karkothaka demonstrated with a test push.

"Thank you," the construct sent. "Now I can continue exploring this new system. Where were you headed? Perhaps I can take you there."

"I . . . don't know where I am or where I should be going. In addition to the burns, I have a broken wing and tail and some loss of memory."

"Were you adrift two kaals ago?"

"Maybe?"

"You do not appear to be carrying anything with you. There was a fairly strong solar ejection. Perhaps it affected you."

"That might explain the burns and memory loss, but not the injuries."

"I agree with your assessment," Karkothaka sent. "Let's find you some help. We are in the Pamir System, a relatively new discovery, and there's considerable activity here, but it's mostly around Meru, the inner planet. Constructs like myself are likely to be going outward to explore new regions. I'm on a course that will bring us near Kumuda, one of the system's gas giants. There is a registered alloy pilot in orbit who should have bhojya and water, possibly medical supplies as well. With your consent, I can tow you there in less than one kaal. Do you wish me to do this?"

"Please," Nakis sent, too fuzzy-headed to think through alternatives.

“You will need to secure yourself to my body,” the construct sent. “You may attach a tether to the third ring segment from my front. You will find several hooks along it. I recommend you use at least two of them for redundant safety.”

Nakis’s hands shook as zie looped the tether through the U-shaped anchors on Karkothaka’s body. Zie pulled them tight until only two meters separated them. The construct didn’t object to their closeness. Zie took comfort in having someone nearby, even if that someone was an ancient conscious machine.

“Based on my visual examination, the damage to your tail and wing requires time in a medical facility,” Karkothaka sent. “I doubt you’ll find one in this system. I can fabricate an exoskeleton for your tail that interfaces to your vents. That will allow you to direct your motion again, albeit with less finesse. I cannot do anything for your wing, however. I will assemble the necessary components before we reach Kumuda.”

Nakis heard all of Karkothaka’s words, but the meanings didn’t stick. Zie sensed a shift in zir body, of systems shutting down, processes switching into self-preservation mode. Zir vision blurred. The stars blended into a glowing mass beyond the construct’s golden rings. *I’m going into hibernation.*

The word bubbled up from deep in zir organic memory. It was a final recourse for any alloy lost in space, a desperate attempt to stay alive. Zie tried to fight it off by flooding zirself with stress hormones, but zir body refused to respond. The autonomous systems that knew best had taken over. They would pause all but the critical systems for life. Many of zir cells would die. Over time, zir reality transit organelles would break down, along with the healthy thamity organelles. Zir lungs would stop electrolyzing water, and zir blood would cease to circulate oxygen. Zir eyes would not see. Zir skin would not feel. Zir heart would beat once every hour or two. Only the parts that could survive on pure photovoltaic energy would function . . . and only as long as zie remained close enough to a star.

Radiation had already decimated many of zir bodily functions. A long stay in hibernation would take care of the rest. Relief bubbled up from deep within Nakis's mind. Some part of zir had already accepted that this could be the end of zir life, the end of . . . pain? Disappointment? Zie found a wellspring of sorrow, regret, and resignation, and when zie probed past that, an angular human face filled zir thoughts until zie had room for nothing else. Dark, wide eyes bored into zir consciousness. Long curls floated in a dark corona around . . . her? Yes, that felt right. But what was her name? She loomed as large as a pilot, holding out her arms, pulling zir into her embrace. Zie relaxed into its warmth and released all zir burdens.

—मण्डल

Mandala—Circular

When Meru's gravity released Varshaneya from its grip, Jayanthi felt the world drop out from under her, literally and metaphorically. She had already burned through several hours of air. Her suit had a full charge and could keep her warm and breathing, but unlike the comfort and safety of Vaha's belly, the journey inside Varshaneya took place in a cold, cramped hold full of constructs with sharp edges.

The harsh environment that awaited beyond the megaconstruct's walls sent a shiver through her. Had she made a terrible mistake? At least on Meru, she'd had a chance of survival. Out there, she was as maladapted as Vaha's true body had been on the surface. *All genetics have value; beings are only poorly suited to their environment, not poorly designed*—it was a lovely principle for a tarawan, but the fact remained that a bad environmental fit could be fatal.

Her mind raced ahead several steps. How could she convince Manib to take her back to Sol? If she were pregnant, how would the two-month journey affect the developing fetus? Did Manib have as good a human-compatible chamber as Vaha? Would she ever find out what had happened to Vaha?

She had no answers to any of those questions, but her cursed human brain insisted on wanting them. *Stability, predictability, security.* That's what a warm-blooded mammal like her had evolved to crave. *If only I could tune my gene expression like an alloy, I could repress those needs. I could rise above them and embrace risk and the unknown.*

"We have arrived alongside Manib," Varshaneya sent via emtalk. "You may exit through the door in which you entered."

The hatch swung open. Jayanthi floated toward it. Across a void, another entrance yawned, outlined by a ring of lights.

"Isn't there some kind of connecting tube or guide wire?" she sent.

"I do not have either of those. Neither does Manib. Any suit rated for hard vacuum should have control jets. Do you lack those?"

"No, I have them." But she'd never used them. *Because I was supposed to be with Vaha at all times.* And now she'd have to maneuver across open space without any practice. The stellar depths yawned in her mind, but across from the door was another opening, set in a large spacefaring body that blocked all view of the stars. She shuddered at the thought of jetting herself in some random and wrong direction, then pushed the fear aside. *Think of Vaha and think of home. You owe it to both of them to make this leap.* "Thank you for your help."

"Good luck on your homeward journey."

Jayanthi imagined she was diving and that Manib's entrance was the pool. She pushed off the sides of the door, reached out her arms, and—heart pounding—floated into the other construct, crashing helmet-first into an interior airlock door. Beneath her feet, the exterior door closed. After a minute, the hiss of air filled the chamber.

"Welcome, Jayanthi," said a pleasant masculine voice through her helmet speakers. "I am Manib."

"Hello. Thank you for letting me stay with you."

"You may enter the primary chamber now."

She passed through the inner airlock, into a dimly lit chamber the size of her bedroom, and came face-to-face with another human. She gasped in surprise, and her heart tried to leap from her chest. A light-skinned person with brown hair and matching eyes floated in front of her. She unlocked her helmet and tried to smile, if only from relief. Not only had she made it across from Varshaneya, she wasn't alone.

"I'm sorry, I didn't expect someone else to be here. I'm Jayanthi."

"I know," they said, arms and legs crossed. "Manib already told me. Said you wanted a ride back to Sol."

"That's right. Back to Earth, if possible." Her cheer faltered at the cold reception. "I was on Meru for a scientific project, but my partner alloys disappeared. I'm not sure what happened to them. If you could help me find out, that would be wonderful. Without them, I have no way home."

"We're not going to Sol, and even if we were, we would definitely not go to Earth."

Jayanthi wasn't sure how to respond to that.

"Saunika is another passenger." The voice of the construct emanated into the chamber from a speaker to Jayanthi's left. "He has equal authority to yours. I am changing course for transit to Sol. I will deposit Jayanthi at a padhran before we continue on."

"No, Manib. I've told you a hundred times, you can't trust humans! We need to dump this one before we leave Meru."

"I have made my decision."

"I won't cause any trouble," Jayanthi said quickly. The last thing she wanted was to antagonize her shipmate. "You don't have to help me investigate about the alloys. I just want to get home."

Saunika sneered. "You already have caused trouble. We had to slow down to pick you up, and now you're redirecting my construct to Sol."

He moved backward toward another opening. Beyond it, Jayanthi could see a passageway running perpendicular to the chamber.

"You stay in this room." Saunika twirled a finger in a circle. "The rest of this place is mine. You got that?"

Jayanthi nodded.

On the far side of the chamber, something flew past the opening.

"What was that?" Jayanthi asked. "Is someone else here?"

"Small constructs for maintenance and the like," Saunika replied. "I'm the only human passenger." He pointed to an area on their left. "Here's where you can get bhojya and water. That tube is the toilet and shower. They're standard format. You know how to use them?"

The devices looked similar to Vaha's, so Jayanthi nodded.

"Good."

Saunika exited the room, and Jayanthi let out a breath. The walls around her were made of some kind of rigid, synthetic material, the proportions clearly intended for humans. She wondered if her own kind had built it. If so, it must have been a long time ago. Humans didn't design megaconstructs anymore.

Aloud, she said, "Manib, how old are you?"

"I gained consciousness in the year 359 Alloy Era."

That made the construct 362 years old, well after the time of the compact.

"Did humans build you?"

"My construction was a joint effort between humans and alloys. My original purpose was to allow humans to explore beyond the Solar System."

Saunika stuck his head into her room. "Stop talking to my ship! I won't have you corrupting his mind with any Earther nonsense." He pointed at a button on the wall. "That's the intercom. You have questions, you ask me."

Jayanthi raised her hands in silent surrender. Everything she did seemed to antagonize Saunika. She had to live with him, so she would follow whatever arbitrary rules he imposed as long as it got her home. After he left, she kept quiet as she secured her pack and then, with infinite relief, washed herself and her underclothes. She had nothing else to wear, so she left the damp pieces to dry and dressed in her enviro-suit for modesty's sake. The chamber had no separation from the rest of the ship, and Saunika had proven that he could intrude at any time.

With a clean body and a full belly, she snugged herself into some webbing. Exhaustion had wrung out her body like a wet rag, but sleep eluded her. Varshaneya had made almost a full orbit around Meru before matching course with Manib. They'd passed the observation rig where Kaliyu and Vaha should have been, but they'd found it empty and unpowered. No one had left a message for Jayanthi. Nothing indicated when or why the two alloys had abandoned their post.

She touched her abdomen and hoped with every cell in her body that the embryo had taken root. Two weeks had passed since she and Vaha had implanted it. She hadn't bled, but she felt no different from usual. Had her wild idea worked? A pregnancy would give her a link to Vaha, one that she would protect at all costs. Would she ever find out what had happened to zir? Would she see Meru again? If she had the baby on Earth, how would she know whether her genetic design had succeeded?

At least she had managed to achieve a measure of safety. *And a way back home.* She'd done it on her own, without the help of any alloys. If she could accomplish that, then she'd find a way to answer all the other questions, too.

When Jayanthi awoke, she discovered two things. One, Manib had begun to accelerate, which meant that she'd effectively slept with her head lower than her feet. Two, Saunika was in the room. He was seated on what had become the floor, and he stared at her like someone examining a fascinating insect. She tried to get up and tangled herself in the webbing, then released herself awkwardly, landing butt-first on the ground.

Saunika watched implacably. "Why did they put you on Meru?"

"What do you mean?" Sleep still chased the edges of her thoughts, and she tried to orient herself to reality.

"Humans aren't allowed on other planets, but you said you were conducting experiments on Meru. Are you lying?"

"What? No. I received permission from the exploratory committee to see if I could survive on the planet. We thought my genes might allow me to remain healthy in spite of Meru's high oxygen levels."

"Does that mean you're in Amritsavar's camp? You think humans should spread into the universe beyond Earth?"

Jayanthi rubbed at her eyes and yawned. She couldn't think fast so soon after waking. "Do you mean the politician? I'm not a follower, but after the time I've spent on Meru, I'm inclined to agree with her. The planet is barren, but we could live there with minimal interference if my case is any indication. I was only there for a couple of months, though."

"So you're special, too." Saunika shook his head. "You know humans would ruin the planet. You'd change its natural state. What you're doing, trying to help Amritsavar—it's wrong."

"Are you . . . special? Is that how you ended up here?"

Saunika nodded. "They chose me for my genetics, too. Thought I might have a way to survive long-term exposure to radiation during space travel. They put me with Manib here. We spent ten varshas roaming the known star systems. Turns out my body can repair DNA damage better than the average human, but I became sterile in the process. Not good for taking multigenerational voyages through space. Amritsavar and her party backed the whole thing, though it was alloys who approved it. They gave up after they found my flaw." Saunika smiled. "We're all flawed, you know? They keep trying to find a way for humans to live anywhere but Earth, and they will keep failing. Had you stayed on Meru, I'm sure you would've discovered a problem, too."

Jayanthi sipped on bhojya and did a mental conversion. "So you've been here twenty-eight years, all alone?"

"Oh no, I've been here almost twice that long, and I'm never alone." He patted the floor. "I have Manib. They said our time together was over, but I told them I didn't want to go back to Earth. We've explored so much, just the two of us. We go where we want. He likes to fly, and I enjoy the views. We have the perfect relationship . . . had, until now. You're the first person I've seen since our original commission ended."

Jayanthi tried to imagine living alone with a constructed mind for that long, nearly three times her entire life. How could anyone have allowed it? One of the arguments against Hamsa's proposal for Meru had been the loneliness factor. Human mental health didn't respond well to extended isolation.

"Did they send you here?" he said.

"They?" Jayanthi couldn't keep up with the abrupt conversational shifts.

"Amritsavar and her crew."

"No, I came at Hamsa's request."

"Who's that?"

"An alloy who's trying to get the compact changed so humans can settle on Meru."

"You can't have Manib, so don't try."

"What? No, I—I won't."

"Good. Because he's mine. All of this"—Saunika spread his arms wide—"is mine. They tried to take me away, back to Earth, but Manib said I could stay. He helped me to stay."

Jayanthi nodded, shrinking from Saunika's fierce expression. After he stalked away, she breathed a sigh of relief. That might have been the strangest conversation of her life. Sixty years of living alone clearly had had quite an impact on Saunika's personality. Even the twenty-eight required by the original mission struck her as cruel. She could believe that politicians on Earth might treat him with such callousness, but an alloy committee had approved it. That shook her. Was that all she meant to them, too? An experimental subject, someone to test their theories on? Had they taken advantage of her? Of him?

Not Hamsa. He's always been so good to me. And certainly not Vaha. But Hamsa had discouraged her tarawan dreams. Her parents, who loved and cared for her, hadn't bothered to educate her about much of alloy life. And Vaha—Vaha had abandoned her.

What had zie done to zirself? What had led to zir injury? Why had zie left her stranded on Meru without a word? Maybe zir feelings for her had all been an artifact of the incarn and its human hormones. Maybe the true Vaha cared nothing for her at all.

Or maybe zie was dead. She hadn't wanted to admit the thought while dealing with getting off Meru, but she could no longer hide from the possibility. If zie had loved her, and zie was dead . . . she wouldn't know what to do with herself. *And if I have zir baby, what do I tell everyone?* Would anyone believe that Vaha had chosen to have a child with a human? Did it matter? She'd have the memories of their time on Meru for the rest of her life, and she'd raise their child with stories about her alloy parent, but the thought of doing it all without Vaha made her sick to her stomach. The heartbreak would've happened when their project ended, but she would've had time to prepare for that. She wasn't ready for her first real relationship to end, not so abruptly and with such finality.

I want to go home.

"Manib, how long will it take you to reach Sol?"

"Twenty-two days of acceleration, followed by transit, then twenty-two days of deceleration."

A month and a half of this. Grief pulled at her like an undertow. *I can't allow it to drown me.*

"Where will you go after you drop me off?" she asked.

"I will decide when the time comes," he replied.

"Doesn't Saunika get to choose?"

"Only if I request it. I am a free agent."

Interesting. She had known several constructs back on Earth, though Laghu was the only megaconstruct. They all had conscious, independent thought, but they also served under contract for specific purposes. She'd never interacted with one who was free to do as they pleased. What would an entity like Manib want? Perhaps he truly cared for Saunika. Did Manib resent her presence as much as his other passenger seemed to? If so, he hadn't indicated it.

She was getting ahead of herself again. "Can you increase the light level in here?"

The room brightened until it felt more like daytime. Unlike Vaha's chamber, this one had no windows. Saunika had mentioned admiring the view, so there must be somewhere that she could see outside. She debated asking him about it and decided it could wait.

A strangled scream bounced through the hallway into the room. Saunika spanned the entryway and glared at Jayanthi.

"I told you not to talk to Manib!" he said.

"Sorry," she muttered. "I forgot."

"Jayanthi may speak to me if she wishes," Manib said. "You have no authority to forbid it."

Saunika's tone turned wheedling. "But she's a stranger, and she'll try to poison your mind." He turned and narrowed his eyes at her. "She'll try to turn you against me."

"No, no, I promise, n-nothing like that," she stammered. "I'm so grateful for your help. Truly. I'll try to remember not to speak to Manib again."

Saunika glared at her for a few more seconds, then spun and stalked away. Jayanthi shook her head. She needed to find some distractions, something that wouldn't tempt her into asking Manib questions. She slow-blinked and discovered that the megaconstruct had an older interface, one that she remembered from her childhood. The selection of entertainment was equally out of date, but at least she had something to choose from. With only Saunika for company, she had little to occupy her time. She found one of Vaha's favorite older comedies and settled in to watch.

Jayanthi had gone two days without speaking to Saunika or Manib. She'd blazed through a dozen episodes, letting it fill the void left by Vaha's absence. So far, Manib had maintained a constant acceleration close to one gee. Unlike Vaha, he didn't need rest breaks. She had to admit that it made for a more comfortable travel experience.

She was doing some exercises when she felt arms grab her from behind. She froze. Saunika's breath was warm against her ear.

"I know she sent you to lure me back to Earth. They want to take me away. I won't let them!"

Jayanthi shook her head. "You're—"

"Shut up!"

He shook her hard enough to rattle her teeth.

"It's all lies! That's all human beings know, to lie to each other."

"Let go of me!"

She tried to wrench her way free of his grasp. He wrapped his arms around her chest and squeezed, forcing the breath from her lungs. He picked her up and shuffled toward the airlock door.

"What . . . are you . . . doing?" she gasped.

"Freeing Manib from your devious plan. I told you, we're not going back to Earth!"

The door swung open. Saunika flung her body into the airlock and slammed it closed. Jayanthi landed on her hands and knees. Air hissed. She whirled and slow-blinked, scanning for any way to stop Saunika from venting her.

She banged on the solid metal door. "Saunika! Please! I swear by the Nivid, I'm not here to get you away from Manib!"

The hissing stopped. Then resumed.

"Please!" she yelled.

A muffled scream sounded on the other side. The door swung open. Four small, multilegged constructs had grabbed each of Saunika's limbs. His face was red with fury.

"What are you doing, Manib?" he bellowed. "Call them off!"

A fifth construct entered the airlock, picked Jayanthi up before she could act, and carried her back inside. The others took her place, a sobbing, screaming Saunika between them.

"What's happening?" she whispered. Her heart pounded. "What are you doing to him?"

Manib's voice came clearly through the speakers. "Saunika has violated Code Twenty-Four, Section B, attempted murder of another passenger. I have zero tolerance for violence. As a sovereign entity, I have full jurisdiction over my passengers. He will be evacuated."

"But he'll die!"

"I have made my decision."

"I thought you cared for him! Wait—can't you confine him somewhere instead?"

"I have considered my options and made my decision."

Jayanthi felt sick to her stomach. Saunika had gone quiet, his body crumpled on the floor of the airlock. The constructs came inside, closed the door behind them, and walked past her, their many legs tapping along the floor. She knelt on the ground with her face in her hands. What kind of monster was this construct? What had she gotten herself into?

As her breath hitched, her skin went hot, then cold. Pain throbbed down her neck and into her back. She knew the feeling too well—the start of every sickle cell crisis. *Calm down! Deep breaths!* She didn't need this, not now of all times and not in this place. She closed her eyes and exhaled to a count of five, but the pain continued to spread and build.

She couldn't keep her breath smooth. She forced herself up and stumbled to her pack, keeping her gaze well away from the airlock door. With trembling hands, she dug out the medical kit. She found an analgesic. The last one. She jabbed it into her shoulder and curled up in her webbing, waiting for relief.

—

After a few hours, the pain ebbed. Jayanthi could open her eyes and stand without wanting to die. She gulped down water—dehydration could tip her body further into crisis—and followed it with bhojya. She avoided the dread that lurked at the edge of her thoughts. Part of her wanted to wrap herself in her sleeping web and never leave. Another part felt guilt-ridden relief that Saunika was gone. She didn't wish him dead, but he had almost killed her.

She glanced at the airlock door and shuddered. What if she broke some unspoken rule and Manib decided that she deserved the same fate? *Ridiculous! Saunika lived here safely for decades.* But she couldn't put the fear away. She slipped her enviro-suit over her clothes and placed the helmet on. She'd be safest somewhere away from the damn door.

"Manib, can I move around? Leave this room?"

"Yes."

The construct wasn't much of a conversationalist. How had Saunika survived for so many years like this?

The corridor beyond the room curved in a circle, built of the same utilitarian materials as her chamber. Storage units covered most of the surfaces, but she found a few closed doors in the inner wall. Two ladders bisected it. She climbed one and found another round hallway. How many such ringed segments did Manib have? She thought-searched for a map and discovered a full schematic.

On the third level up, a window wrapped the entire circumference of the outer wall. Jayanthi wandered in circles for a while, taking in the dazzling tapestry of stars on one side and the bright light of Pamir,

Meru's star, on the other. The planet and its moons had receded enough to become three brighter spots in the overall star field.

Manib's voice startled her as it blared from overhead speakers. "I have decided not to return to Sol. I will transfer you in 1.5 Meruvin days."

"What? Why? Transfer me where?"

"I wish to pursue a new opportunity in an unexplored region beyond this system. You will have conveyance."

Jayanthi blinked up at the ceiling. "To Earth?"

"I cannot guarantee that."

"But . . . where, then?"

"I cannot answer that."

"What kind of conveyance? Is it a pilot? Another megaconstruct? Can they support a human?"

"Yes."

Jayanthi closed her eyes against the ambiguity of Manib's response. *Think! How can you get home?* "There are so many alloys working around Meru. Can I talk to one of them through you, explain my situation? Maybe they would know more about what's going on, find a way—"

"They have declined."

What did that mean? Declined to speak to her? To Manib? Declined to carry her back to Earth? She used to assume that alloys would want nothing to do with humans, but Vaha had turned that opinion on its head. Was zie that unusual? Zie had implied that most alloys didn't think much about human beings, but not because they were uncaring. Shouldn't someone in Meru's system have the heart to help her get home? Didn't they owe her at least that?

She cast about for someone to blame—Vaha or Kaliyu or any alloy in the vicinity—but in her heart, she knew the truth. The fault lay within herself. Ratnam's adage came back to haunt her, the words taking on a new meaning: *Ambition and materialism lead to greed and exploitation.* She had been hungry for fame, for knowledge, for an experience granted to no other human being. And that had left her vulnerable to exploitation by the very alloys she'd looked up to all her life.

She thought of the embryo and made a promise: *If you grow and thrive, I won't abandon you. I'll keep you with me, no matter what.*

The stars that had seemed so peaceful a moment before now appeared harsh and unforgiving. She was at the mercy of any being, alive or not, who could give her shelter. Life would have been so much better if she'd been born an alloy. She had been so naive back on Earth, thinking that this would be a grand adventure, that as long as she was in the hands of an alloy, everything would be fine. Even Hamsa, for all his wisdom, hadn't anticipated something like this. Neither had her parents. They'd never left the Solar System. She had, and now she was stranded, hundreds of impossible light-years from her home, with no guarantee of return.

Jayanthi strapped on her pack, sealed her helmet, and checked her air. She floated into the airlock. A small construct followed and closed the door behind her. Manib hadn't given her any more information about her next ride. She had to trust the megaconstruct and hope that whoever took her in was willing and able to get her back to Sol.

She glanced at the small construct. Was it going to assist her across? That would be a relief. The outer door swung open. Her companion reached out with two of its six legs and grabbed her by the waist. It tilted her, head toward the door. Jayanthi looked forward and stretched her arms up, as she had before, to aim for her destination . . . which was a field of stars.

"Manib?" she sent, twisting her head from side to side. "There's nothing out here."

"You will wait," the construct replied.

"What do you mean? Is someone approaching?"

She tried to grab the doorframe, but the small construct had a surprising amount of strength. It pushed her through and let her go. Jayanthi twisted ineffectually, trying to turn back.

"Manib, please! I don't understand!"

The enormous, cylindrical construct moved past with no response. Jayanthi drifted, alone with her racing heart and the absolute finality of hard vacuum, her breath the only sound.

Calm. You must stay calm. With pain lingering from the previous day's crisis, she couldn't let stress get the better of her body. She closed her eyes and pictured herself lying in a hammock behind her house. She breathed until her pulse slowed, then opened her eyes. Nothing in her view had changed except that the hulking shape of Manib receded farther. He'd told her to wait, but for what? She didn't see anyone approaching. The thought of using her jets terrified her. What if she moved herself into a different trajectory, and her next ride couldn't find her? If she'd been an alloy, this would have been no different from being dropped off in a strange location. She could've traveled to find help. But she was human. Even if she could figure out how to maneuver herself, she had no idea where to go. Could she make it back to Meru before her air ran out? She tried a tremulous "hello?" via an open emchannel, but someone had to be nearby in order to pick up her broadcast. With no alternative, she settled in to wait and hoped her ride would turn up soon.

At first, she checked her timepiece every few minutes. She remembered to drink water and bhojya. As the hours ticked by, she found her thoughts traveling the same circles: Vaha, Meru, the embryo, Saunika, Manib. Every terrifying unknown that didn't include her life itself. She'd had twenty-seven hours of air when Manib ejected her. No one knew where she was. Even if someone was looking for her, they had no hope of finding one tiny human in all the vastness of Meru's system. And the only one who might care enough to bother was Vaha.

How could you leave me like this? Where are you? Are you alive? Please be alive!

And so her thoughts went: back to Meru, to the embryo, to Saunika. On and on until fourteen hours had passed. At hour fifteen, she ran out of water. Two hours after that, bhojya. She hadn't thought to refill the packs. Why would she if she were getting "transferred," as Manib had claimed? How much longer would she have to wait? At least the battery had started with a full charge, and luckily Pamir's distance kept the suit at a comfortable temperature without too much power consumption.

She slept in fits and starts, her body not yet acclimated to the lack of gravity. At hour twenty-five, the suit automatically switched to oxygen conservation mode. A dull throbbing started in her head shortly after.

Over the next thirty minutes, the pain spread down through her neck, across her back, and into her arms and legs. With rising dread, she knew: her body was going into crisis mode, and this time, she couldn't stop it. Low oxygen was a well-established trigger. Her blood vessels had started to constrict. Her sickled cells would clump together and clog her blood supply. Let it go long enough and she'd need an exchange. Longer than that and her organs would fail. Her air would run out first, though, and give her a quieter end.

A million needles traveled through her veins, stabbing her from the inside out. She closed her eyes and swallowed as her stomach heaved. Her skull pounded as if her brain were forcing its way out. She hadn't experienced this level of agony in years. A part of her detached and analyzed her situation with clinical precision: one way or another, this would be over soon, and she'd be out of her misery.

She had flaunted her ambitions, and the universe had punished her. Like Saunika, she'd convinced herself that she was special. Because of her alloy parents. Because Hamsa had let her train as a tarawan. Because Vaha had loved her, at least for a little while, at least in zir incarn form. She'd proven how full of hubris she was, like every other human. Callow and fragile, she'd failed everyone. She would die alone, where no one would ever find her.

—ऋतु

Rithu—Season

"You may waken."

The message arrived like a faint glow in zir consciousness.

Who speaks? Who thinks? Who am I?

No one.

Ah, yes, I am Nakis.

"You've been exposed and in hibernation, but you're safe now. Are you receiving this?"

I am.

You need to send that reply the way it came, via . . . emtalk.

Like the Sun emerging from behind a planet, awareness resumed. One by one, Nakis brought zir body's systems online. The intense sensations of heat/cold, prickling/itching, and aching/stabbing took zir by surprise. Had zie come out of hibernation before? Why hadn't zie expected that it would feel so terrible?

Zie shifted and felt the gentle tug of an umbilical against zir belly. Life itself flowed through it into zir body. Zie took a deep breath and felt zir lungs swell with water. Zir heart beat at its usual rate. Zir flesh had lost its parched, stretched state.

A local network nudged zir mind, and zie thought-accepted its offer to connect. It held some basic information about zir location as well as a spool of news and a standard knowledge pedia. *Where am I?* had a straightforward answer: in orbit around a gas giant named Kumuda in the Pamir System, about two hundred light-years from the Solar System.

"I'm awake," zie sent.

Nakis looked up the meaning of *hibernation*. As the words flashed into sight, zie remembered: zie had met an ancient construct named Karkothaka. They had helped each other, and then zir body had begun to shut down. There was a face . . . beautiful but strange . . . human. A woman who held zir as zie entered the long sleep.

That didn't make any sense. Humans couldn't live in space, and they were tiny. Zie blamed zir confusion on the hibernation until zie saw the status reports from zir bodym: extensive radiation burns on zir skin; corruption of massive sections of zir extended memory; damage to zir power conduits; physical injury to zir tail, left wing, and organic brain. *By the Nivid!* What part of zir body hadn't suffered? What had zie done to zirself?

No wonder zie couldn't remember anything about zir circumstances. That explained why zie had gone into hibernation—zie had gotten injured, as zie had so many times before. Had it happened at Luna? No . . . zie had a recollection of leaving the moon for . . . somewhere else. Then it came back to zir: a school for pilots! But what was it called? And what had happened there that led zir to this system that zie had never heard of?

The local network alerted zir to another message, a recording from Karkothaka. The construct said that he'd built an exoskeletal brace for zir broken tail that might allow zir to vent from zir lower body again. That seemed promising. The previous message, the one asking zir to wake, came from an unknown sender. Perhaps that stranger knew more about zir circumstances.

Zir sight and phores resumed last. Zie opened zir lids and resolved the view in front of zir: the familiar contours of an orbital berth frame, and behind it a pale-blue planet swirling with gaseous clouds. Zie turned zir head. The golden coils of Karkothaka were nowhere to be seen. Instead, a pair of dark-brown hands guided a tube into Nakis's mouth. Zie sucked in and tasted a spiced bhojya with flavors of cinnamon, cumin, and fennel. As zie drank, zie felt the hands rotate zir body. Zie came face-to-face with a strange alloy, a pilot—*like myself. I am a pilot!*—judging by their size and shape.

They had a square-jawed face with a wide, flat nose and long, dark eyes. Deep-purple streaks along their torso and tail cut through gray-brown skin. Phores dotted their cheeks, neck, and arms, and teardrop-shaped wings covered in golden cells flanked their body. Nakis had a flash of memory: zir friend telling zir about the greatest microgravity racing pilot of their time, an alloy with purple stripes and gold wings. People had nicknamed him The Royal because of the combination. Surely there had to be plenty of pilots with that coloring?

Zie slow-blinked to see their identifying information. Along with the usual items—name, gender identities, genetic lineage, areas of expertise—there was a list of accomplishments: competitive microgravity flier, twelve-time winner of the Jupiter Grand Prix, Solar System Heliosphere Circuit record holder. So it was him!

<I'm Rithu,> he flashed, not realizing that Nakis had connected to the local network already. <Nod if you can see and understand me.>

Nakis nodded.

<Your phores may not function correctly for a while until your body has replenished its water and nutrient supplies. I only have a small emergency womb, and I hooked you up to the umbilical two kaals ago.>

So zie had hibernated for at least that long.

<Drink slowly. Karkothaka said you may have organ damage from some radiation exposure. You'll be weak from your time in hibernation. Fuzzy-headed for a while, too. I once spent more than a masan in

hibernation before someone found me. It's not an easy recovery.> He indicated the planet. <Do you know where you are?>

Nakis nodded. "I looked it up," zie sent, not trying zir phores just yet.

<Good. That means your emchannel functions are back. Do you know why you're here or what happened to you in transit? Karkothaka told me that you didn't have shelter during the solar storm a few kaals back, but it looks like you've injured your tail and wing, as well.>

Zie shook zir head in the negative. "My memory is spotty. Extended memories are gone."

Rithu glowed in sympathy. <Do you recall anything? Someone I can find who might know your circumstances?>

Zie shook zir head again. "What I remember . . . it happened long ago, and I can't think of any names, not even my own."

Rithu frowned. <Looks like you took some damage to your organic mind, too. If the radiation went that deep, I'd expect you to be dead, so maybe it's from another cause. Some kind of amnesia. You had head trauma in addition to the tail and wing.> His expression cleared. <Well, you're here now, and safer than you were. You're welcome to stay as long as you need to. I'm collecting samples to study the atmospheric composition of Kumuda, so I won't be going anywhere for a while, and I'm well stocked. I did a supply run to Meru not that long ago. I'll have to return a little sooner with two of us here, but that's not a problem. And now I'll stop bothering you and let you rest. Call if you need me.>

Rithu moved aside to his own berth and pulled up the barrier between them. He must have lowered it in order to tend to Nakis. Someone else had shared a berth with zir like that at . . . at . . . but the thought wouldn't complete. The phores on zir arms flashed with frustration. Zie could distinctly recall zir friend telling zir about The Royal, zir friend who . . . also wanted to be a racer! Zie could picture zir: blue-gray skin, hazel-green eyes, silver-black wings, but why couldn't zie remember zir name? By the Nivid, zie had so many holes in zir memory!

Nakis pinched off the bhojya tube with more force than necessary and attached it to the frame. Their orbital platform was spacious enough for a larger group. Consisting mostly of metal scaffolding, it held observational equipment as well as six comfortable-looking berths, though all but zirs and Rithu's were unoccupied. A solid area in the center had several storage compartments, and antennae jutted from the platform's corners. Beyond their output, zie saw nothing but Pamir's glare and Kumuda's bright azure reflection. Not a single dark speck to indicate the presence of a padhran or any other people in their vicinity.

Zie extended zir arms and tried to flash <hello,> but zir phores produced no light. Coming out of hibernation was almost like a rebirth. Going by Karkothaka's message and what Rithu had told zir, zie must have drifted for quite a while. *I was always destined to be a failure.* The thought appeared in zir mind and fit like a well-tailored pack. Zie could recall spending time in a womb, more than once, in zir childhood. Someone . . . zir maker? Yes, zie had told Nakis of this terrible destiny. Zie had wanted . . . wanted Nakis to make history as a multimodal pilot, but when Nakis had failed, zir maker left. The image of zir back receding into the distance—that Nakis could recall with perfect clarity.

Zie had a chance to make a fresh start at Kumuda, at least until zir past caught up with zir. Perhaps it never would. Perhaps zie had finished whatever zie came to this system for. Or . . . another thought arrived, one that had terrible implications. What if zie had done this to zirself? What if zie had wanted to die?

Nakis shuddered and pushed the idea away. *If that's what happened, then I'm glad I've forgotten who I was. I'm not that person anymore.* Judging by the state of zir body, zie would never fulfill zir maker's design anyway. Zie might as well invent a new identity for zirself until someone informed zir otherwise.

Zie created a new public record, filled in zir pronouns, and set zir name to Nakis. Zie left the lineage and expertise portions blank. In zir current state, zie couldn't call zirself a pilot, and zie couldn't think of any other useful skills zie possessed.

Zie sent the information to Rithu. "If I think of my real name—or anything else useful—I'll let you know."

"Welcome to my humble abode, Nakis," the pilot replied. "I have to leave shortly to do some work, but I'll be back in half a kaal. Don't go anywhere." Amusement colored his final words.

"Thank you for all your help," Nakis replied with sincere gratitude. Zie watched as the other alloy gracefully tucked his golden wings along his body and dove toward Kumuda. Trace amounts of water vented along with hydrogen, creating a trail of tiny, sparkling crystals in his wake. The blue light from the planet enhanced the purple streaks on his body.

Why would a microgravity racer like The Royal be sampling atmosphere on the outskirts of the known universe? That was a job almost any pilot could do. Then again, given how little Nakis knew of zirself, who was zie to question someone else's choices? Now that zir body had some energy, zie reviewed zir extended memory and cross-referenced it with the local knowledge base. Most of it had gotten corrupted by the solar CME event, but zie found a few items intact, including two spoken human languages—Precompact Japanese and Modern Sanskrit—as well as an episode of a show called *Across the Orbit*. There were some images from a trip to the Sun where zie looked quite young and floated beside zir maker. Zie had several recordings labeled as lectures on reality transits and microgravity maneuvers. And zie had a recording marked *J_emotions*. Zie replayed it.

A human stood in a pilot's chamber—zir own?—and contorted her face, labeling each with an emotional state. Zie recognized her! This was the person who had held zir as zie dropped off into hibernation. Except this looked real, and she had a proper human size. Had zie ferried her somewhere? Had someone commissioned zir to carry humans through space? That was an infrequent and low-prestige task, so it stood to reason that zie had done it, but zie couldn't find any record of a contract.

Zie checked zir bodym and confirmed the presence of a human-compatible organ. It functioned and had taken minimal radiation damage. A few weeks on the umbilical and zir body would repair it, but that didn't give zir much information about zir past. So zie had carried a human at some point. Zie could get back to Earth and try to find her, but what would she possibly know about zir if she was just a passenger? Like the other fragments of zir memory, both extended and organic, this one was of little use in understanding zir present circumstances.

As Rithu's majestic body disappeared into the clouds of Kumuda, Nakis shut down zir vision. Every part of zir body ached, including zir eyes. The bhojya filled zir stomach like a dense asteroid. That zie could feel exhausted after being in hibernation for so long was mystifying and undeniable. *Stay as long as you need to,* Rithu had said. Zie set aside the questions crowding zir thoughts and let zirself rest.

—यान

Yaana—Vessel

Jayanthi gazed up at green leaves and sunlight against a perfect blue sky. *I'm dead,* she thought, but her body didn't feel dead. It hurt. She glanced down and saw that she lay on a cot with clean white sheets. A diagnostic strip wrapped her arm. A hydration line snaked between it and a squat machine nearby. *That doesn't fit with a heavenly afterlife.* The dead wouldn't need medical attention. As her awareness increased, she noticed other things: her scratchy throat and dry eyes, the sticky residue of unbrushed teeth, the gentle whir of a motor, the distant sound of human voices.

She could turn her head. Her cot lay in a small clearing surrounded by lush trees with tapered, three-pointed leaves. An empty chair leaned against one of the tree trunks. Someone had dressed her in a button-front shirt and loose pants the color of ripe mango, both made of whisper-soft fabric.

She eased herself upright. Blood rushed from her head.

"Oh, no, don't get up!" A human emerged from the trees, their generous form draped by teal and red, with a face beautiful enough to thaw the coldest ice. Wide, dark gray eyes were set in light-brown skin. Rosebud lips formed a kind smile.

Jayanthi slow-blinked and was relieved to see identifying information appear. Their name was Sunanda, and they were only a few years older than her.

"Where am I?" Jayanthi asked, taking their advice and dropping back onto her pillow.

Sunanda pulled the chair closer and sat. "You're in a megaconstruct named Chedi, passing through the Pamir System. She—Chedi, that is—got a message from someone to pick you up. You were unconscious and in pretty bad shape, so we put you in our hospital and treated you. We had to give you an emergency blood transfusion. You're on some strong pain relievers, but Chedi thinks you'll be okay."

"Thank you." So Manib hadn't left her to die. It would have helped if he'd told her what to expect. "And who are you? I mean, not your name. I saw that. Why are you here?" She couldn't help but feel a little afraid and suspicious after what had happened with Saunika, though Sunanda seemed like the exact opposite.

Sunanda grinned. "I live here! When you feel up to it, I'll bring you to the others and show you around. Chedi is enormous and can host up to fifteen hundred human beings, though right now, she's only carrying about seventy of us. We all ended up here in different ways, usually something like yours—dumped by some inscrutable constructed mind or overstaying an invitation from an alloy—and we all love space travel. Chedi is our mother hen. She likes to pick up stray humans and give them a home."

"And she's taking us back to Earth?"

"Oh, no! We pass through Sol to restock our supplies, but we avoid it as much as possible." They leaned in conspiratorially. "Technically, it's not against the law to be here, but since we didn't travel via legal methods, the people who got us here could get in trouble. We all love to explore, as does Chedi, so she covers for us when we're around Earth or an alloy padhran. We vote on where to go, though Chedi always gets the final say, and then we spend as long as we can traveling. Right now, we're exploring the Pamir System, obviously. We're headed to the outer planet, Kumuda. That's how we crossed paths with your construct."

"I see." Jayanthi decided to wait before disclosing her full history. Let the people here assume she was like them for now.

"I can keep talking all day, but I should get you some food and drink. You stay here and rest, okay? You don't have to. You're one of us now, not a prisoner, and here's the button to release the medical sleeve, but that's what Chedi suggests because you were so unwell."

As Sunanda disappeared, Jayanthi spotted a discreet closet among the trees with its door ajar. She disengaged her arm and took her time getting up. Inside the closet, she found a clean, softly lit bathroom, including a set of towels and soap that she used to wash her face. That minimal activity set her heart racing. On unsteady legs, she returned to her cot, propped the pillow against the headboard, and stretched out her legs. The only thing missing from the idyllic surroundings was birdsong. Now that she looked more closely, she could tell that the "sunlight" shone a little too evenly to be natural. She slow-blinked and marveled at what she could access. The menu showed a full library of information, entertainment, and education. There was even a local copy of the Nivid, though it was several years out of date.

She thought-searched for a schematic, as she had with Manib, and found one. Unlike his tower architecture, Chedi had a nested-cylinder design. A massive block of ice formed her outermost layer, then came the level Jayanthi was on, and finally, above her at Chedi's core, an artificial sky and light source. The entire construct rotated to maintain a perfect 9.8 m/s^2. Someone had clearly built Chedi to carry humans through space.

She's marvelous. How had Jayanthi not known such a megaconstruct existed? Mina would have loved to live in a place like this. Precompact spacecraft were made more like Manib—utilitarian and rigid and obviously vehicular. Chedi was younger and felt like a living biome.

"Who built you?" Jaya murmured aloud.

"Some kind alloys who wanted to give humans more freedom," Sunanda answered. They carried a laden tray, which they set across Jayanthi's lap.

Jayanthi lifted the first lid and inhaled the steamy aroma of coriander, ginger, turmeric, and roasted red chiles. Her stomach growled audibly, and they both laughed.

"I haven't eaten anything but bhojya in days," Jayanthi admitted. She shoveled a spoonful of the seasoned rice into her mouth and sighed with pleasure as she swallowed. "Delicious! Please thank the cook."

"That would be Chedi. Some of us cook when we want to, but her ambulatory constructs do most of it."

"Can she hear us speaking?"

Sunanda shook their head. "She likes to give us privacy and independence, so she keeps all the hidden microphones and cameras disabled unless there's an emergency. You have to go to the flight room to speak with her. She likes to see us every day, though—that whole mother hen thing, you know? I promised I'd bring you to visit once you're strong enough."

"A bellyful of this, and I'll be ready to go."

Sunanda beamed at her, their smile rivaling the faux sunshine. "You are *so nice*. You'll fit right in. Not everybody does. We leave those people at the first safe place we can, but I can tell you're not like that."

Jayanthi finished her food, drank deeply and gratefully of the hot tea, and found herself overwhelmed by drowsiness. Her curiosity battered against it, but the exhaustion won. Sunanda removed the tray and tucked her under the sheets. Jayanthi found herself enjoying the pampering, but something nagged at her thoughts. She ought to ask about . . . someone . . . *Vaha.* But her lids were so heavy and her tongue so clumsy, she couldn't form a coherent thought except for one: *I'm safe here.*

When Jayanthi woke again, the light around her was suffused with a warm orange glow. A check of ship time showed early morning, not evening.

Had she really slept for seventeen hours straight? She stretched and found her limbs less achy than before. The rest must have done her some good.

She slow-blinked to search for where she might find Sunanda, but before she could, they appeared like magic, once again bearing a tray of food.

"How are you feeling this morning?" Sunanda asked, radiating concern.

"Much better, thank you."

Their face had a candor that Jayanthi couldn't help trusting. "I'm so glad! If you're feeling strong enough, I'll take you around later today." They placed the tray, this time laden with bread, jam, nuts, and coffee, across Jayanthi's lap.

"This is amazing," Jayanthi said around a mouthful. "Do you grow all this here?"

"We do. We believe in being as self-sustaining as possible, though we do take on supplies from Earth." They waved a hand at their surroundings. "We have enough room for growing all kinds of plants, and we use synthetic dairy and eggs. We don't keep any animals here. It didn't feel right, since they can't protect themselves if Chedi has to stop spinning or if there's some kind of accident."

After breakfast, Jayanthi declared herself well enough for a tour. She followed Sunanda along a path through the trees. They passed by other clearings where she could see people moving about and starting their day. No one lived in any kind of housing.

"Does it never rain?" she asked.

"It does, but it's scheduled. We make sure we're under shelter if we don't want to get wet. Chedi always warms the air first, though. It makes the water feel refreshing."

The path opened into a broad avenue with colorful gardens on either side. At the end stood a two-story pavilion. Pillars carved with intricate geometric designs held up a swooping tiled roof. Sofas and tables and sling chairs sat underneath, arranged in intimate circles. A half-played game of chess sat in one corner, a stack of books in another.

"This is the grahin," Sunanda said. "Our social space."

Beyond the pavilion, the avenue continued, then broke into several smaller pathways that meandered in inviting curves. In the distance, square fields of green and gold curved up Chedi's immense body. The sight took Jayanthi's breath away, and she stopped walking to stare.

Sunanda grinned at her. "Isn't it incredible?"

Jayanthi nodded.

"Chedi's the size of a small moon."

Here and there, the metal bodies of laboring constructs glinted in the morning light. The only artificial structures in view were the occasional metal tower or low building. Where the fields ended, terraced rice paddies rose in graceful arcs. On the other side, groves of trees marched in orchard lines or clustered in natural beauty. Bright-blue pools dotted the spaces between them. Beyond all that, the land fell into shadow.

"It's as beautiful as anything on Earth," Jayanthi murmured. "I could stare at it forever."

"You do get used to it after a while, I promise."

She tore her gaze back to Sunanda. They walked in the opposite direction from the fields, toward a cluster of small buildings.

"These are the basic facilities—bathing rooms, kitchens, workshops, and here is the flight room." They stopped in front of a pale-blue door with a silhouette of a dancer midleap. "Ready to meet Chedi?"

"Very."

They entered a room with three sling chairs, a low table, and a blank viewing wall. A screen was inset into the wall, flanked by two speakers. Jayanthi could see no other sign of electronic life. Sunanda gestured for her to sit, then left the room.

A face appeared on the screen—human-looking, somewhat androgynous, with medium-brown skin and dark eyes topped by a short crop of dark, wavy hair. The lips were generous, and they curved into a smile that reached the eyes.

"Hello, Jayanthi. I'm Chedi, and I'm delighted to have you here."

"Please, call me Jaya. I can't thank you enough for what you've done—the rescue, the medical treatments, everything else. I'm so grateful."

"Well, I didn't consider it a rescue. Was Manib a poor host?"

Jayanthi hesitated.

Chedi's expression turned serious. "Did he mistreat you?"

"Not . . . exactly," Jayanthi said.

"You can tell me. I'll keep anything you say in confidence."

The construct's tone was so different from Manib or the one on Meru, so much more human and sympathetic, that Jayanthi found herself telling Chedi everything. About Saunika and Manib's laconic explanations, her sickle cell disease and the crisis that ensued. The construct nodded along, encouraging but not interrupting, until Jayanthi reached the point where she had lost consciousness.

"Can you show me what happened after that?" Jayanthi pleaded.

"Of course."

The screen went blank, then images appeared: Jayanthi's body retrieved by a multilegged construct, similar to the one that had pushed her out of Manib. Sunanda and others crowding around her, removing her suit, placing her on a trolley. Her body cradled by a surgical construct, tubes going between it and herself. Sunanda sitting by her side, face anxious. Another trolley wheeling her to the cot in the trees, Sunanda walking alongside, staring at her sleeping form, their expression alight with curiosity.

"Your treatment and recovery took almost three days," Chedi said as the last image faded. "You received a full blood transfusion, as there was a significant amount of sickling. I couldn't culture enough of your red blood cells in such a short time, so in a few weeks, we'll do an exchange and use the exact match. I'm concerned for your immune system in the meanwhile. It's important that you rest and don't stress yourself."

Jayanthi took that in as the construct's face reappeared across from her. She'd been Chedi's guest for nearly four days. She tallied up the time since she'd last seen Vaha: two weeks. Slightly less than that since she'd taken her last dose to increase her heme oxygenase levels.

"I had good luck supplementing with a medication that reduced sickling via HMOX-1 up-regulation. Do you have something to help me with that?"

"Unfortunately not, but I might be able to fabricate it. I'll have to see what I can put together from available plant matter. If it's not possible, I can request it as part of my supplies when we next pass through the Solar System."

"And when will that be?"

"A little more than ten Earth months from now."

Jayanthi tried to hide her dismay. Everyone would think she'd died on Meru, somewhere invisible to the people observing the planet. Hamsa would lose his vote to free humans from Earth. Her parents would be devastated. And Vaha . . . would anyone think to look for zir? Zie had no family, no one waiting for zir return.

"You look distressed. Is there something I can do for you?"

"You've done so much already. I don't want to seem ungrateful."

"It's all right. I've decided that my purpose is to enjoy the company of humans and take care of them. That's what I was built for, and while I am a free agent, I find this work quite fulfilling. I'm happy to help you however I can."

Jayanthi explained her mission to Meru, the help from Vaha and zir incarn, then the mysterious disappearance of zir and Kaliyu. She stressed the importance of her survival for humanity's future and for Hamsa's faction. She explained how she'd sought out Varshaneya's help to get to orbit so she could discover what had happened to Vaha.

"You care a lot about zir." Chedi didn't phrase it as a question.

"I do," Jayanthi said. "I'm worried about zir. Kaliyu said zie couldn't fly, and I don't know what happened to either of them. I'm scared that Vaha's adrift somewhere in this system, unless Kaliyu was able to take zir back to Sol. But then why would they leave me on the planet with no word?"

Chedi nodded. "I can't change course without a vote of approval from the other residents, but in the meantime, I'll send out some of my probes to see if I can find any sign of Vaha. Perhaps other alloys or constructs saw what happened to zir. I will also transmit a message back to Meru. A courier there can get word to Hamsa and Earth so that your loved ones will know you're safe."

A rush of tears took Jayanthi by surprise. She wiped her eyes as she said, "Thank you for understanding. Thank you so much."

"You're very welcome," Chedi said gently. "I don't want you to worry about anything, but I also know humans. If you need to talk, you can come here anytime that someone else isn't here."

A weight that she didn't realize she'd been carrying lifted away from Jayanthi. She'd done all she could. She'd survived, left Meru, and begun her search for Vaha. She just had to convince the others to cut their journey short and get her back to Earth. If they were half as kind as Chedi and Sunanda, they would.

—

At lunch, Sunanda brought Jayanthi to meet the rest of the passengers, who sat scattered around in the grahin. They ranged from eighty years old down to—

"A baby," Jayanthi said in surprise.

"Oh, yes," Sunanda said. "Chedi's had several families raise their children here, though they sometimes leave during crucial school years. Raya arrived when she was pregnant, like you, and gave birth here. It's perfectly safe. Chedi's ice shell protects us from radiation, and she maintains gravity, so gestation is fine. We don't have a womb, though. We have to do everything the old way."

Jayanthi lost half of Sunanda's words as her brain processed their central statement: *She was pregnant, like you.* She touched Sunanda's arm to get their attention and pulled them a few steps away from the pavilion.

"Did you say that I'm pregnant?" Jayanthi asked in a low voice.

"Yes." Sunanda's lovely gray eyes went wide. "You didn't know?" They clapped a hand over their mouth, then placed it on Jayanthi's shoulder. "I'm so sorry. I assumed you knew. It was in your medical report. You really had no idea?"

Jayanthi shook her head as her heart raced. *So the embryo stuck!* She was going to have a baby. The enormity of that took her breath away. Somehow it hadn't felt real until she knew for certain. She had to raise a child. She had to—

"Is it . . . not good news?" Sunanda asked anxiously.

Jayanthi forced herself to meet their gaze. "It's wonderful news. I'm just surprised." She smiled. "It's the first good news I've had in a while."

Sunanda beamed. "Then I'm not sorry I told you, although my timing could have been better. Congratulations!"

Jayanthi laughed and touched a hand to her abdomen. *My baby . . . and Vaha's.* She thought of zir incarn lying alone in the womb on Meru and shivered. Was zie dead? Would zie never meet zir child? But no, she refused to believe that, not without some proof. Alloys could die—it was a fundamental axiom of the definition of life—but they didn't do so quickly or easily. *I will find out what happened to you, somehow, I swear.*

She pushed the anxiety over Vaha's fate to the back of her mind and followed her guide into the grahin. She tried to focus on her surroundings rather than the internal chant her brain had begun: *I'm going to be a parent. I'm going to be a parent. I'm going to . . .* Sunanda started her introductions with Raya, Jesan, and baby Hui, a ten-month-old darling with wide dark-blue eyes and ink-black curls. They had been visiting an Earth orbital station and snuck on board Chedi during her supply stop.

In less than nine months, I'll have an infant like this in my arms.

The floor that was reality tilted as Jayanthi considered her body growing an actual human being. She ought to feel elated, but a million *what-ifs* popped into her head, followed by *what have I done* and *can I really handle this?*

Sunanda led her over to the construct's oldest resident, Guhaka, who had a shock of thick white hair atop his light-skinned face. They continued to circulate through the grahin until Jayanthi had greeted everyone and her exhaustion began to show. With one hand protectively against Jayanthi's lower back, Sunanda guided her to a seat at an empty table.

"I hope that wasn't too overwhelming," they said, taking a position opposite her.

"It's all right. I haven't been around a group of people in several months. It feels good, and everyone here seems so happy."

Sunanda inclined their head. "Anyone who isn't happy gets let go as soon as it's safe. We self-select to keep the peace."

As they ate, Jayanthi asked awkwardly, "Are you always the one orienting new people? Is that your job?"

"No one here has a job," they said with a twinkle in their eye. "I happened to be the first to see you upon arrival. I often assist Chedi with medical matters, and I enjoy helping others feel at ease here. Plus, I fell for your looks." They grinned. "Luckily, you have an equally lovely personality. If you're particularly lonely some night, you're welcome to come find me."

Jayanthi felt heat rise into her cheeks. She couldn't deny that Sunanda's voluptuous figure tempted her, but she'd given her heart to Vaha, and until she had some closure as to zir fate, she wouldn't get involved with anyone else.

Some of her thoughts must have shown on her face because Sunanda's expression turned serious. "I've made you uncomfortable. I apologize for flirting. Sometimes my exuberance gets the better of me, so please forget I said anything."

Jayanthi forced a smile and nodded. Sunanda reverted to their sunny chatter for the remainder of their meal, sparing either of them further awkwardness. Jayanthi couldn't help being in awe at their grace. She'd never had that much ease when dealing with other human beings.

She followed along with the conversation, but half her mind kept circling back to her pregnancy.

It lent more urgency to her return to Sol. Chedi might be capable of delivering the baby, but the thought of going through pregnancy and childbirth with a group of strangers scared Jayanthi. Add in sickle cell and all its attendant difficulties, and she wanted *home*, with the comforting presence of her parents, the sooner the better. They might not have experience with pregnancy, but at least they had managed her health and upbringing. They could help her with the baby. But once she left the Pamir System, she'd lose any chance of finding Vaha. Would she ever be able to return? Her carefully constructed plan to position herself for phase two of the project had fallen apart. What would the MEC say when it discovered her pregnancy? She and this nascent child would thrive on Meru, but with everything that had already gone wrong, how would she convince the alloys that she could safely go back? And how would she face life on the surface without Vaha at her side?

Varshaneya had said that Vaha and Kaliyu went in separate directions. More than two weeks had passed since she'd lost contact with them. With zir injuries, she doubted that Vaha could have reached heliopause, which meant that zie had to be adrift somewhere in the system. Or zie could have returned to Meru. What if zie was looking for her there? If only she had an alloy's body, she could search for zir by herself!

She laid a hand over her abdomen. Now she had her own passenger to think of and protect. What did she owe to Vaha compared to their nascent child? Should she prioritize searching for the person she loved or taking care of herself and her pregnancy? She had no one to turn to for advice. In spite of sitting among dozens of people, a wave of loneliness washed over her. The one person she could talk to honestly had gone missing, and she didn't know if she would ever find zir again.

—पिपर्ति

Piparthi—Refresh

After three weeks with the umbilical pumping zir full of nutrients and anti-radiation drugs, Nakis was well enough to detach it for a few hours at a time. Zie felt that zie had the strength to try the exoskeleton Karkothaka had made for zir tail. Rithu had tethered it to their platform, idle and unusable until Nakis's muscles had rejuvenated. Built of a dark, rigid material, it looked almost like a miniature berth frame, mostly hollow and oblong in shape. Flexible suction collars extended from its cross braces to align with zir vents.

Nakis used zir upper body to vent out of the berth and pulled the brace on. The muscles in the lower half of zir body had atrophied, and zir tail floated, limp and distorted, within the harness. Judging by the angle of zir fins, zie hadn't healed correctly. The collars along the front and sides aligned perfectly with zir vents. Karkothaka had tailored it with precision to zir body. Zie peered under zir wings at the back side, then tried to fasten the dorsal suction by feel.

<May I help you put it on?> Rithu flashed.

<I don't think I have a choice but to accept,> Nakis replied. <I can't reach the vents back there.>

As he adjusted the collars, Rithu's hands brushed Nakis's sphincter muscles and sent an involuntary shiver through zir body.

<Sorry,> zie flashed in embarrassed blue.

Rithu's phores glowed with reassuring hues as he continued working. His hands had the deft efficiency of a nurse, and his phores showed none of the awkwardness that Nakis felt.

Zir body continued to betray zir with every touch from Rithu, so zie told zir bodym to dial back on reproductive hormones. It wouldn't take effect for a few days, but better that than never. The racer had an undeniably attractive body—Nakis had never seen someone with such beautiful patterning. It was a shame that he lived in such isolation, where no one could appreciate it. Several times, zie had been tempted to ask about how Rithu had ended up at Kumuda, but it felt like a rude question, especially coming from someone who couldn't talk about zir own past.

<How does that feel?> Rithu flashed, coming around to face Nakis.

Nakis powered the exoskeleton on and flexed zir hips. The brace responded to zir motions, moving zir tail forward, backward, and side to side. Zie wouldn't have the finesse of working muscles, but zie could probably get around.

<Try venting,> Rithu flashed.

Nakis filled zir frontal bladders and squeezed. The first three times, nothing happened. Then on the fourth attempt, zie moved backward—only a little, but enough to send zir drifting away from Rithu. The racer's phores glowed with pleasure.

<Good!> He matched Nakis's speed and heading. <You're weak but functional. How about the other ones?>

They spent almost an hour like that, Nakis surprising zirself with motion, Rithu keeping up and cheering zir on.

<I've seen plenty of racers with injuries like yours who go on to compete again,> he flashed. <If you can get time in a womb, they can

reconstruct your tail and wing, and if not, I'm sure you'll find a way to keep flying as long as you love doing it.>

When Nakis finally tired, Rithu took zir by the hands and led zir back to the platform. Their bodies were close enough for Nakis to feel the warmth radiating from Rithu's sunward side, and zie missed it as soon as they entered their separate berths. By the Nivid! Had zie always fallen so easily for others? Zie hoped zir vent-spawned hormones would adjust quickly.

<You'll be dipping into Kumuda with me in no time,> Rithu flashed. <I'm happy to share my work with you and split the credit if we discover anything novel.>

<That's generous of you,> Nakis flashed, coloring zir words with gratitude.

<I've had enough respect and admiration to last more than this lifetime.> Rithu rotated until he could meet Nakis's gaze. <You saw who I am, I presume?>

Nakis nodded.

<You're probably too young to know about me,> he flashed.

<I'm twenty Earth years—about six varshas. My . . . friend . . . told me stories about you. I know zie wanted to become a racer. I can remember zir having a picture of your team logo on zir berth, but I can't remember what it's called.>

<The Majestics.> Rithu smiled. <I retired before you were born. I suppose you're wondering what someone like me is doing in a place like this.>

<The thought crossed my mind,> Nakis admitted.

Rithu's phores rippled with amusement. <I'm impressed you restrained your curiosity this long. I'm happy to explain. I don't know if you remember when I mentioned that I spent some time in hibernation. You were barely conscious at the time.>

Nakis shook zir head. Much in those first days with Rithu had turned into a blank, like other portions of zir organic memory.

<I'd taken a dangerous course on a bet and nearly fell into a dark well. The thamity effects shredded a lot of my tissue, enough to breach my skin to vacuum. By the time help reached me, my body had shut down. I never fully recovered my strength after that. When I lost the Jupiter Grand Prix for the first time, I couldn't handle it. I'd won for twelve years straight. My ego was entirely tied up in that race, and I didn't know what to do with myself except try again. But I lost a second time, then a third. I didn't want to accept that I couldn't do it, that younger pilots had better designs—some based on my own—and that I would never dominate the sport again. It's silly, right? Racing doesn't add anything to expand our knowledge of the universe. My name is only in the Nivid for my genome.

<At my peak performance, I had plenty of sponsors who enjoyed watching me race and supported me in doing that and nothing else. Once I stopped winning, though, the admiration dried up. I went into stasis almost out of spite. I had offers to become a coach, but I wanted to spend time with fans, and most of them were in stasis, too. Those years weren't bad, to tell you the truth. I played a lot of games, starred in several racing movies, connected with other retirees like myself.> Rithu smiled, his gaze distant.

<What brought you out?> Nakis prompted.

<One of those retirees had educated themself and told me they were going to return to an active life to study primordial black holes. It made me curious, so I started looking into academics. I didn't find much that interested me, but eventually I discovered a love for planetary science. Odd choice for an alloy, right? I'm no weller, but there's plenty to investigate without landing on a surface.>

Nakis winced at the slur.

<No offense,> Rithu flashed. <Nothing wrong with gravity-bound life, of course.>

<Of course,> Nakis agreed. <I don't know why I reacted that way. I don't think I have any connections to . . . surface dwellers. I ferried at least one somewhere in my past, but that's all.>

<Humans are part of alloy heritage, and I fully respect them. I shouldn't have used such a crude term. It wasn't considered an insult in my youth.> Rithu glowed apologetically. <Around the time that this system was discovered, I finished doing a thesis on ammonia-based atmospheres. I came out of stasis with the express intent of studying Kumuda. Given my former piloting record, I had no trouble winning the contract, though it took me half a varsha to get my body back into shape.>

Nakis glowed with surprise. Zie hadn't realized that stasis caused that much atrophy. It made sense once zie thought about it, especially for someone as athletic as Rithu.

<I guess what I'm getting at, in my long-winded, old-person kind of way, is that you can have more than one life. If this>—he waved at the blue giant beside them—<is where you plan to stay for a while, you might as well take advantage of it.>

Nakis looked at zir tail. <How am I supposed to help you when I'm like this? You might not believe me, but I . . . I can't remember how I got this way or how I ended up with Karkothaka.>

<I believe you.> Rithu's phores glowed gently. <You have no reason to deceive me, and I can see your external injuries for myself. What are your piloting skills?>

<According to my bodym, I'm capable of microgravity, reality transits, atmospheric, and surface.>

<You could do all four?> Rithu glowed with surprise and admiration. <A true multimode, then.>

<My maker hoped for that, but I never succeeded,> Nakis admitted. <That much I distinctly remember. Now I'll probably have only one of the four—transits—but I think I was good at those.>

<Then I'll trade you, skill for skill,> Rithu flashed. <My atmo for your RT. Transits have always been my weak point. I've seen plenty of injured racers handle skimming a planetary well, myself included, so I can teach you how to work with the exoskeleton. We had to stay in competitive shape while healing, and we often used assistive devices.>

<I may never recover from this,> Nakis flashed, unable to keep the depression from zir phores.

<Then we'll figure out a permanent way for you to cruise the atmosphere. If you're determined, I'm sure two top-notch pilots like ourselves can make it happen. If you're not?> He shrugged. <You can live here—you can even enter stasis, though you'd be alone, since I have to remain active. Stay for as long as you like, at least until I'm done with my research. At that point, I can take you back to Sol or drop you off somewhere else. If you get tired of my company before then, I'll give you a ride to Meru.>

Stasis had its allure. Nakis couldn't deny that, but faced with Rithu and his story, zie considered trying a second life. Zie must not have been a complete failure as a pilot if zie had ferried a human. Someone had contracted zir services at least once. Rithu's offer gave Nakis a chance to rehabilitate zirself. Even if zie could never be the multimodal pilot zir maker had designed, zie didn't have to surrender to stasis. Zie could live actively, in a different way, and still contribute to society.

<How much longer will your research take?> Nakis flashed, wondering what zie was signing up for.

<I have four varshas left, though if I discover enough interesting things about Kumuda, I may ask for an extension.>

A long-term commitment. Nakis wondered if zie could recover zir microgravity flight with Rithu's help in that time. Atmospheric flight would help with Rithu's work, but MG would allow Nakis to take on longer-range projects.

<How about this?> Nakis flashed. <I'll help you with your research for no credit and teach you what I know about transits. In exchange, you help me figure out how to use my body for atmo *and* MG flight.>

<Microgravity? I can't make any promises about that. If you've lost too much thamity sense in your tail, it would be dangerous.>

<That's okay. I won't hold you to a specific result, but if anyone knows how to optimally navigate gradients, it's you.>

Rithu smiled. <Then we have a deal.>

—त्याग

Thyaaga—Sacrifice

Jayanthi spent her first week on Chedi recovering her strength and getting to know the other residents. They weren't all quite as friendly as Sunanda, but they were welcoming and kind. Some lived for pure hedonism, swimming in Chedi's pools, playing games, eating delicious meals, catching up on a year's worth of entertainment. Others balanced their pleasure with simple work, as people did on Earth, and a few studied and attempted to master subjects.

She discovered that Chedi's pedia had plenty of literature about human pregnancy, so that became her main occupation for several days. Her body had started to change in noticeable and expected ways. Her bladder acted like it had shrunk to the size of a pea. Her breasts felt sore for the first time she could recall. And her stomach alternated between ravenous and rebellious.

When she read the parts about giving birth and the many risks and complications, she wondered if she'd made a terrible mistake. Humankind—and mammals in general—had produced children for millions of years, but plenty of mothers and infants had died in the process. Science and medicine had helped over time. The development of womb technology had, of course, voided it entirely. Not getting pregnant came with its own set of costs, though, only some of which could be avoided later in life. The topic fascinated her endlessly.

Raya had been thrilled to learn that Jayanthi was pregnant. She'd insisted on Jayanthi holding Hui while she related everything that had happened with her own body. Raya had dealt with some complications, and her descriptions of Chedi's care were wrapped in glowing words.

"Chedi has delivered quite a few babies," Raya had said. "And Sunanda was a gem when it came to assisting me with the labor and the first weeks with Hui. They didn't have any prior experience with it, but they were so calm and supportive. Jesan was too much of a nervous wreck."

Hui had stared at Jayanthi with wide eyes as his mother talked. She'd expected the baby to feel delicate, but he was solid and warm in her arms, and he smelled wonderful. *Will it be the same with my child?* It was so strange to say those two words—*my child*—but the more she did, the easier it got. She wished that Vaha's incarn had been there to experience it all with her.

At every conversation with Chedi, she asked whether there had been any sign of zir. She received the same answer every time: no news. She hadn't mentioned Vaha or Meru to any of the passengers, and none asked, not even Sunanda. They'd acknowledged her desire to return to Earth and agreed to put it to a vote at their next full meeting, which was two weeks away. In some ways, it was a relief to move among them without the weight of responsibility on her, and with Chedi acting as her confidante, she didn't feel guilty about neglecting her obligations to the Meru project. She allowed herself to relax a little for the first time since she'd left home.

Guhaka, the oldest resident, had taken a liking to her, and the three of them had tea together every day in the shade of the grahin.

"So, Jaya, you've been here a full week," Guhaka said one afternoon. "What do you think of the place? Do you like our little floating paradise?"

Jayanthi smiled around the rim of her teacup. "I think it's amazing. I don't know why everyone doesn't live this way."

"Not everyone wants to inhabit a megaconstruct," Sunanda said. "And not everyone is suited for this kind of life. We're a small group with a limited set of activities."

"From what I've seen," Jayanthi said, "you have a great variety of things to do—study, play, relax, create, cultivate. You have everything good about Earth *and* you don't have to live under the rules of the compact. You get to travel the universe. No one cares if you have excess ambition."

"So you think everyone should have access to this kind of life?" Guhaka said.

"Oh, here we go." Sunanda rolled their eyes.

Guhaka feigned innocence. "What? Can't an elder inquire about a young person's philosophy?"

Jayanthi laughed. "I'm not a strict follower of Sahaya Amritsavar, if that's what you're wondering. I don't think human beings need the same rights as alloy beings, but neither am I a conservative like Bantri. For something like life on Chedi, I guess I'd like everyone to have a choice, but I don't know if that's practical. You'd need millions of constructs to carry everyone, and making them would create an enormous environmental impact."

"Most humans don't want this," Sunanda said. "I can almost guarantee you that. We've had so many people leave over the years. They get bored, or they miss their families, or they want to see the real sun and birds and animals. They want to eat meat. They want human tutors for their children. The reasons are endless. And some people just aren't happy in space. That's why we still have humans, right? Otherwise we'd all be alloys."

"I'd give anything to be an alloy," Jayanthi said.

"Then you should stay with us," Sunanda said. "Living with Chedi is as close as it gets."

"For space travel," Jayanthi agreed, "but not for rebirth or baby making or contributing to the Nivid."

Guhaka clasped his hands behind his head and settled back in his chair. His mouth curved in a small smile as he half turned toward Sunanda. They must have had this kind of discussion many times.

"We don't need any of those," Sunanda said. "Most of the alloys don't, either. Think of life in Chedi like being in stasis. Our basic necessities are taken care of—food, health, climate, education, and entertainment. We can spend our days producing or consuming, as we choose. We're only constrained by Chedi's resources. What do we want reputation or respect for, other than the minimal amounts to get along with each other?"

"Ambition, Sunanda," Guhaka said. He pointed his chin at Jayanthi. "I suspect she has it."

"We can accommodate that," Sunanda said. "You can achieve things here. We won't ask you to curb yourself or your pursuits."

"Achievement in a vacuum—pun fully intended—doesn't gain you a legacy," he said. "Most people are content with having others think well of them, but some need more. They want to feel accomplished, like they've pushed at the boundaries of all knowledge and made it yield to their efforts. They want to make a lasting contribution that will carry their name forward into the centuries after they're gone. This is why we have the Nivid."

Jayanthi found herself nodding in agreement. "Did you?" she asked Guhaka. "Want that?"

"In my younger days, yes. That's how I ended up here. I was a Voice of Compassion and traveled as far as the Venusian padhrans. I saw the Primary Nivid once." His eyes went distant. "It is truly a marvel, and beautiful to behold, too. Then I hitched a ride with a retired pilot for a while, and she brought me to Chedi, and I've never looked back. The alloys have a whisper network for humans like us and those who wish to support us. Of course, Hamsa has turned the volume up now. When his proposal inevitably fails, it will reduce the likelihood of getting more constructs like Chedi."

"What do you mean?" Jayanthi asked.

"Hamsa's the one who commissioned Chedi. She's a negative mark on his record. Now he's staked his reputation on opening Meru to human settlement. If he can't get that done, people will start questioning his judgment. They won't vote to expend resources on his future project proposals, especially those that involve human space travel, and they certainly won't vote in favor of his amendment to the compact. Those who attempt similar ventures in the future will have an uphill struggle to show how their ideas are different and why they're more likely to succeed—"

"But," Jayanthi interrupted, "there's nothing wrong with Chedi."

"She's at a fraction of her capacity," Guhaka said. "That's a problem." He popped a cardamom cookie in his mouth and pushed the plate at Jayanthi. "Eat!"

"What Guhaka means," Sunanda said amiably, "is that after they finished making Chedi, they asked for volunteers to populate her. At the start, she had a thousand passengers. We're down to less than a hundred now, between the travel restrictions and the people who keep leaving. Humans think they'd love this life, but more often than not, they hate it. *Beings are maladapted to their environment, not their bodies.* Most people don't feel like they belong here. This great experiment"—they gestured expansively—"demonstrated that humans prefer to live on Earth, where we naturally fit. That's the argument that some alloys use against Hamsa and people like us. They're skeptical that humans would want Meru, no matter what Amritsavar and her faction say."

"Even if the vote to amend the compact goes in Hamsa's direction," Guhaka said, "if he can't find a heritable way to integrate humans into Meru's ecosystem, or if not enough humans decide to relocate, people won't give him a third chance, nor will they look favorably upon anyone who wants to build more Chedis."

Jayanthi looked at the two of them with a growing suspicion. "Do you know who I am?"

Two quizzical expressions faced her.

"Should we?" Sunanda asked.

As Jayanthi debated whether to tell them, Guhaka slapped his knee and leaned forward.

"Really? You? Is that why you're in this system? But what were you doing drifting away from Meru?"

Sunanda looked back and forth at the two of them. Jayanthi watched as realization dawned on their face and their lips formed a pink O of surprise.

"It's a long story," Jayanthi said.

Guhaka leaned back again. "We don't have anything pressing to do."

So she told them the abbreviated version that she'd given Chedi: about her sickle cell gene and Meru's atmosphere, about Vaha and the first weeks on Meru, about Kaliyu's and Vaha's sudden disappearances. By the time she finished, they'd drunk four pots of tea, and their daylight had dimmed. In the opposite corner of the grahin, two people played a long game of chess, but the pavilion was otherwise empty.

"We should get you back to Meru, not Earth," Guhaka said. "Let you continue this grand experiment, since it appears to be working in Hamsa's favor—and therefore ours, too. Then we can return to Sol and tell the Exploration Committee to send you a new pilot."

"Wait a minute," Sunanda said. Their eyes dropped toward Jaya's midsection. "What about . . . ?"

Jayanthi bit her lip. Her pregnancy wouldn't show for many more months, but Chedi, Raya, and Sunanda already knew.

"That's a slightly longer story," she said and then hedged, "one that involves some . . . questionable activities."

Sunanda propped their chin on their hands. "Now I'm intrigued. Do tell."

With a deep breath, Jayanthi confessed how she'd used Vaha's womb to make the embryo. She explained their suspicion about Pushkara and the potential to accelerate stage two of the project. She omitted the details of her relationship with Vaha, and she left out any mention of zir incarn. They didn't need to know the full extent of her foolishness—that she'd fallen in love with an alloy. That she'd taken zir DNA and made a child from it. The sight of Vaha's incarn lying dead in the vestibule was a painful canker on her heart, and she didn't want anyone prodding it.

Sunanda let out a low whistle. "Aren't you a sly one. I'm inclined to agree with Guhaka—"

"That's a first." He chuckled.

"Don't get used to it." They elbowed him in the ribs. "I don't know that leaving a pregnant person alone on a planet is the best decision, but taking you back to Sol has risks, too. If the alloys figure out what you've done, you'll never leave Earth again. I think . . . the best course of action is for you to stay here, deliver the baby, then go back to Meru. At that point, the deed will be done."

"That's months away," Jayanthi protested. "By then, the MEC will have canceled the project. For all I know, they already have because of whatever happened to Vaha and Kaliyu. I won't be able to provide the evidence that supports Hamsa's proposal."

"You're still thinking that the general vote matters," Sunanda said.

"Doesn't it?"

"The amendment will never pass," they said, "no matter what the data show about you. Don't you see? The alloys don't really care about what happened on Mars or what happens to Meru. They use those as excuses to keep us under the thumb of the compact. As long as they have humans on Earth to take care of, they continue to have unlimited access to Earth's resources. If we leave—if Hamsa's amendment passes—the population on Earth will shrink. Fewer alloy services will be needed, and unless they amend the compact further, they'll have to proportionally reduce what they extract from the planet."

"Do you really believe that?" Jayanthi turned to Guhaka. "Both of you?"

The elder shrugged. "I'm afraid I'm as cynical as Sunanda. Decades of roaming the galaxy have shown me two things: one is that Earth is truly a special place for our species; the other is that nobody willingly gives up power."

Jayanthi thought about Vaha, about Hamsa, and shook her head. At least some alloys respected humans and wanted more for them.

Sunanda reached out and patted Jayanthi's hand. Their brow crinkled in sympathy in the waning light. "I'm sorry, love. Alloys might be more capable than us, but that doesn't make them better people."

Every alloy I've known has been good to me, she wanted to say. But the words died before they reached her lips. Her parents had never taken her off-planet. Hamsa had indulged her tarawan studies, but not her ambitions. They only let her go to Meru because it was an easy way to advance Hamsa's agenda. Vaha and Kaliyu had abandoned her on a barren planet. Had she spent twenty-two years believing a lie? Had the alloys in her life acted only from self-interest? Had Vaha's love for her been a chemically induced aberration because of zir human incarn? Had zie intentionally left her on Meru?

No, zie loved me. My parents love me. That's real! But that didn't preclude them from having other motives. The universe was vast and complicated. Her travels had shown her that all too well. Of course alloys would act in ways that benefited them and their goals. Of course some of them were selfish and greedy and broke laws. She had deluded herself into thinking she knew and understood them because of her parents, but she couldn't extrapolate from a sample size of two to all of civilization. *Maybe Sunanda and Guhaka are right. Maybe alloys are just as selfish and flawed as humans. Maybe I don't owe my life to anyone else.* On Chedi, Jayanthi would have access to information and technology. She could design her own children, explore the galaxy. She could stay and live on her own terms.

"Today, you get to experience the best part of living here," Sunanda said to Jayanthi.

Along with everyone else, she rode on constructs that traversed the length of Chedi. They headed toward one end of the massive cylinder, passing through farmland, orchards, and forests along the way. Working constructs dotted the fields. Tiny insect versions buzzed around the flowering plants. Jayanthi could almost pretend she was on Earth.

"We call it the playroom," Sunanda continued. "The children especially love it for the zero gravity. The adults do, too, though we mostly go there for the view." They grinned at Jayanthi. "Wait until you see it!"

They hadn't pressed Jayanthi about the pregnancy, baby, or her return to Sol since the conversation with Guhaka. In another week, the group would have their monthly meeting, where they could vote on whether to redirect Chedi's path. Jayanthi had to decide what she wanted before then. Staying on Chedi would mean a place to raise her child while giving them both the opportunity to see the universe. The environment was at least as idyllic as Earth. Jayanthi could see to her child's education, allow her to be as ambitious as she desired, but they would both struggle with the effects of sickle cell disease. Chedi's air composition matched that of Earth's, and although they'd get good medical treatment, pain crises and lung complications would be a part of their lives in a way that they could avoid on Meru.

Was it fair to bring another child like herself into the world? *I designed you for a planet where you could thrive.* A planet that had represented only the potential for a better life, not a guarantee. Jayanthi could elect to get gene therapy, to end the expression of her sickle cell disease, and her child could eventually do the same once she reached the age of consent. But whether that happened on Earth or Chedi, it would mean abandoning all her efforts toward Meru and Hamsa's amendment. And in the meantime, she'd have to watch her child suffer through pain, exhaustion, and illness. Didn't she owe her child a better life than that?

The construct beneath her swayed, and she swallowed against a wave of nausea.

Sunanda chattered on, oblivious to Jayanthi's discomfort. "Kumuda is ten times the mass of Meru! As stormy as Jupiter but blue like Neptune, with a mix of water vapor and methane in the atmosphere."

They moved from the constructs into lifts that traveled to Chedi's central axis. Gravity fell away as they rose, and Jayanthi had to grab a sickness bag. Sunanda waited until she finished emptying the contents of her stomach. They floated into a corridor and out through an oblong cutout. A giant bubble surrounded a dark, cavernous space. Guide wires crisscrossed the room, lit from within by dim red. Sunanda grabbed Jayanthi by the sleeve and gently tugged her to a clear viewing spot.

A pale-blue orb swirling with lighter and darker patches hung in front of them. A smaller, brownish-gray moon was off to the upper right. Stars filled the backdrop like ground crystals. Jayanthi held on to a guide wire with one hand and drank in the sight. To spend a lifetime this way, something every alloy could do, struck her as pure bliss. She touched her abdomen with her free hand. If she returned to the Solar System, her child might never see anything like this.

How dare the alloys deny these sights to humankind? Yes, they had done terrible things in centuries past. Yes, their physiology made them dependent on a vessel. Not every human being would want to experience this, but they should have that choice. They should have room to grow and change and explore. If only she could make that happen.

What if she didn't run straight home to Earth? What if she sought Hamsa out, offered herself as evidence of the Meru project gone right? Would her pregnancy convince the MEC to send her back to the planet, to finish the research they started? Could the child be enough to sway the general vote in favor of his amendment? A way to drop a stone into still waters and create ripple effects that reached every being in the CDS, living and non-, and overcome their cynicism?

She'd always considered herself outside of the rules that applied to people on Earth, even if she weren't truly exempt from them. Could she leverage her alloy connections to help others? While growing up, she'd often resented humanity, but between her pregnancy and the tableau before her, her heart swelled for her kind.

"What do you think?" Sunanda asked softly.

"It's magnificent," Jayanthi replied. "And terribly unfair."

"Unfair?"

"That we're the only human beings who will see this in person. I know tourism led to all kinds of problems in the past, but Chedi is a solution to that. We can travel the stars safely and without disturbing the environment."

"Someone still has to bear the expenses. Chedi requires supplies and maintenance. She can sustain a city's worth of people, but her construction and repairs mean materials taken from Earth. Then there's the recruitment effort. Medical risks if Chedi is injured. The psychological stability of megaconstruct minds. Alloys have made these arguments time and again. That's why Chedi is independent and no longer contracted to the CDS. She relies on the charity of previous residents and sympathetic alloys to keep herself going."

"If they'd let us do research—discover knowledge worthy of the Nivid—we could make the effort and resources worthwhile."

"You want to go back to Sol." Their starlit profile was sad but not disapproving.

"I have to try. I have to know if I can make a difference to the course of history."

"Even if it means never leaving Earth again?"

Jayanthi gazed at the azure glow of Kumuda. Could she spend the rest of her life like this? Forget her parents, Hamsa, Vaha . . . just drift through the amazing galaxy and raise her child? By the Nivid, it was a tempting vision of her future! But she thought of Mina. And her other friends in SHWA, the ones who craved more than their Earthbound lives offered. And Vaha, should zie be out there somewhere, looking for her as she did the same.

"Yes, I need to take that risk. If I stay here until she's born, the MEC will assume I'm dead and cancel the project. If I go back to Meru and live without alloy oversight, I violate the research parameters, and Pushkara gets his opening. I need to convince the committee—and maybe all of the CDS—that they should allow the Meru project to continue. That we're fit enough to settle another planet, to justify Hamsa's amendment, and to change the compact. I want my child to go to the stars, but I don't want to be selfish about it. I want the chance for every human child to experience this at least once in their life."

—

Jayanthi sat on the sofa facing Chedi. "Ninety-six days?"

"Approximately, yes," the construct confirmed.

"That's over three months! You can't go any faster?"

"No. I'm not like a pilot. I have to avoid accelerating faster than one-tenth of Earth's gravity in order to maintain structural stability. As a biome, that's important for the internal ecosystem."

The group had agreed to cut their exploration of Meru short and get Jayanthi back to Sol. Sunanda had supported her decision. They'd even made an impassioned speech on Jayanthi's behalf, lending weight to the possibility of increasing humanity's options, in spite of believing that most humans would choose to stay on Earth.

"And you've still had no sign of Vaha?" The answer was always negative, but Jayanthi couldn't help asking.

"None. However, I did come across another pilot who said that a courier has entered the system."

Jayanthi sat straighter. "Is it Kaliyu?"

"No, someone else. They're on a quick turnaround to deliver news. They'll reach Sol months ahead of us. Would you like to send a message to someone there?"

"We should get word to Hamsa that I'm coming straight to him. I'd like to send a brief message to my parents as well, to let them know where I'm going."

"Send me your recordings by sunset today and I'll dispatch one of my constructs to Meru."

Jayanthi nodded and started to rise.

"One more thing. The pilot had a copy of the latest news spool from Sol. I found an item in there that Kaliyu reached the Solar System. Zie is with the heliopausal medical construct."

"What about Vaha? Did it say anything about zir?"

"There was no mention of Vaha, nothing to indicate that zie has gone missing from Meru's orbit, nor of you or your status."

Jayanthi frowned. "Why would Kaliyu leave that out? Unless . . . could zie be worried that zie will get in trouble for leaving me alone on the planet?"

"Perhaps," Chedi said. "But only if zie is aware of Vaha's absence. What if Vaha departed after Kaliyu?"

"Varshaneya said they left Meru around the same time, but I suppose it's possible. Why would Vaha leave after Kaliyu, though?"

"Zie might have lost interest in the contract or decided to get help for zir injuries."

"If Vaha could travel like that on zir own, why wouldn't zie have told me before leaving?" *Because zie doesn't really love you.* Despite everything that had happened between them, despite knowing that Jayanthi might be pregnant with their child, maybe Vaha had intentionally abandoned her. *Alloys and humans can't have an equal relationship.* She'd been so naive.

No! That's your hormones talking nonsense. You know in your heart that zie felt the same about you as you did about zir. But did she really, or was that what she wanted to believe?

Chedi made a sympathetic face. "There is another possibility, though it would imply an unfortunate outcome for Vaha."

"What do you mean?"

"Zie could be adrift."

Jayanthi froze. "You mean like what they do to exiled alloys?"

"Yes. It can happen by accident. Alloys have gone adrift within the Solar System when they're too far from the Sun and run out of energy. If their bodies enter a protective state of hibernation, they can survive for many years as they continue whatever trajectory they're on."

"We might never find zir if that's the case. The Pamir System is practically empty." *But it would mean zie didn't leave you.*

"Not in your lifetime, perhaps. As long as Vaha was trapped by Pamir's gravity, zie would eventually return. If zie were still alive, zie could be brought out of hibernation. Zie would need a rebirth to correct for extended radiation burns, and zie would have lost most of zir memories, but zie would live."

"You sent out your satellite constructs, and they found no sign of zir, right?"

"That's correct. However, the likelihood of someone spotting a drifting alloy, even one of Vaha's size, is vanishingly small. I'm sorry. I wish I had better news for you."

Jayanthi couldn't decide which alternative was worse: that Vaha had abandoned her or that zie had gone adrift. Either way, zie was lost to her. She'd never hold Vaha in her arms or be held by zir. She'd never see the stars through zir true body's belly. No alloy would want her like Vaha had, assuming zie had truly cared about her at all. The fragile hope of reunion that she'd held now lay in fragments.

She thanked Chedi and left the room with her legs on autopilot. She took a roundabout path back to her clearing, avoiding the grahin, and stumbled out from the trees and onto her cot with a sob that wrenched its way from the bottom of her lungs. Her entire body shuddered with the force of it. She was a thrice-made fool! And now she was on her way back to Hamsa, another alloy. For what? So they could trap her on Earth for the rest of her life? By leaving Chedi, was she compounding one mistake with another?

A pair of strong, warm arms wrapped her up and drew her in. She leaned her head into Sunanda and wet their tunic with her shattered dreams.

—परीवर्त

PAREEVARTHA—TURNAROUND

Kaliyu flexed zir wings. The shoulder joint still twinged, but zie had almost fully healed from the fight with Vaha. The hardest part of the return to Sol had been the reality transit. Zie had trouble quieting zir mind at the best of times. Doing that while under immense pain, compounded by the memory of Vaha drifting away, had proved nearly impossible. Only zir desperation had allowed zir to push through.

Zie had spent eight kaals at the medical platform near the RT point in Sol. Zir arrival at the facility had triggered a notice to the Meru Exploration Committee. Upon hearing zir brief report, they scheduled a meeting to discuss the project and told Kaliyu to report to Pushkara, zir project manager, when zie could travel. The sling for zir wing had come off two kaals earlier. It felt good to be able to move both shoulders again, though the injured joint ached in a constant reminder of zir best friend's final betrayal.

During zir stay, Kaliyu had tracked down Pushkara's schedule. As before, the old politician insisted on meeting in person to keep their conversation private. It took Kaliyu seventeen kaals to reach the inner orbit padhran, between Venus and Mercury, where zie could finally tell Pushkara what had happened at Meru.

The padhran had more people than Kaliyu had expected. Thousands of alloys of various sizes swarmed around a massive central frame made of ceramic. A nascent megaconstruct rested inside, their shell half-complete—the kind that, if it was willing, would RT as far as possible through known space, then take a long, cold voyage to an unexplored destination. It wouldn't house any passengers, so it had a blocky, efficient body pockmarked by thrust vents. The early stages of the struts that would support its solar sails formed an exoskeleton.

Nearby, a smaller group worked on manufacturing the materials for the interstellar voyager's assembly. A string of constructs and alloys moved to and from the padhran like shadow pearls along a necklace, ferrying raw material in and waste products out. One of those broke away and headed toward Kaliyu. Zie had no idea what Pushkara was doing there, but it didn't matter to zir task. Fifty kaals had passed since zie left Meru. Zir news may have lost its sense of urgency, but it hadn't lost its significance.

Kaliyu cupped the small alloy in zir hands and flew away until the crowded twin padhrans dwindled to a dark spot against the star field.

<I've done what you asked,> Kaliyu flashed. <Vaha sabotaged the mission zirself by getting injured during a practice flight and then getting angry with me over it. Zie fought me, tore my shoulder and wing so that neither of us could land on the planet. I was forced to abandon the human.>

<And what of your friend?>

<After zie hurt me, zie shot off into space, away from Meru. I don't know what got into zir, but I suspect zie is now adrift. Zie was injured pretty badly. I had intended to help zir get back for medical care until zie refused to come.>

Kaliyu left out the finer details. None of them mattered, especially now that Vaha was gone. Kaliyu's rage had burned white as a neutron star in the first kaals after zir friend's actions, but it had faded, leaving Kaliyu with a sense of despair over Vaha's fate. Zie had wondered a thousand times whether zie had made the right choice in letting Vaha go. Zie hoped that, against all odds, zir friend had found a way to safety.

<Do you think Jayanthi still lives? How was her condition?> Pushkara asked.

Kaliyu passed Pushkara the cubes with all the data zie had backed up from the observation platform. <When I left, she was healthy but suffering some lung damage. She'd stopped taking whatever had helped her avoid that in the first weeks. It's possible she's alive, but I doubt it, and even if she is, her presence on the surface violated the project parameters as soon as Vaha and I left orbit. That should be enough, right?>

<Perhaps.> Pushkara glowed with concern. <Given the injuries to you and Vaha, however, they might grant Hamsa a waiver—if she lives. Why did Vaha attack you?>

<Zir injuries were bad enough that I would have had to carry zir back to Sol. I reminded zir that we couldn't leave the human alone, and zie realized that meant the end of the project. Zie tried to prevent me from lifting the human off Meru by tearing my wing. I could've had the local construct retrieve her, but my chamber wasn't prepared to carry her back to Sol.>

<Do you have proof? Any recordings in your extended memory?>

<It all happened too fast.>

Pushkara patted a spot on Kaliyu's wrist with his small hand. <I understand. It must have been very distressing. For now, let's hope that zie stays lost, at least until the MEC makes a decision about the situation. Since Vaha has no immediate family, I doubt anyone will look for zir. The only loose end is the human.>

<I did drop the . . . special package before I left.>

Pushkara's phores brightened to violet. <That should settle the matter, then. I don't have to worry about sending one of my people as the follow-up pilot. I can let Hamsa contract with whomever he wants. It's better that way. No one can accuse us of a biased report.>

<Will you be able to stop the project?>

<I won't have to. Once the contaminant is discovered, the MEC will do it, and they'll censure Hamsa in the process. He will lose the vote and his credibility on this matter. Thank you, Kaliyu. You've done well.>

<And my maker?>

<I'll write a recommendation to release Nidra immediately from zir term of service on Earth. If zie wishes a chance at serving as a pilot again, I will urge the Earth Ground-Based Service Committee to allow it, and I'll offer a simple mission as an initial task. You can carry my words to the committee yourself.>

Kaliyu had lost a friend, but at least zie would regain zir maker. To see Nidra again, to have zir free of Earth's hellish well, that would make everything that had happened at Meru worthwhile.

<Thank you,> Kaliyu flashed.

<The gratitude is all mine. I'll also submit your data on a fast track for review at the Nivid. One last thing before we part ways: I want you to know what a great service you have done for the future of Meru, and alloys, and even for humanity. It's easy to vilify them, but human beings are our kin. It's our duty to take care of them, and sometimes that means making hard choices, ones they don't like. Unfortunately, that can hurt people who are our friends. I'm sure you feel Vaha's loss, and I am sorry that had to happen, but I want you to remember why it happened. What we've done is in the best interests of all beings. When too much time passes, people forget why laws were instituted. Hamsa and the humans who support him come from that misguided place. We haven't trapped humans on Earth as a punishment. We've made them a safe, comfortable home there as the best environment for them. Do you understand?>

Kaliyu nodded. That home came at the expense of alloy lives like zir maker's. People who maintained the Earth's environment, ate human garbage, built their constructs, tended their forests and wild animals. The compact allowed alloys to take natural resources from Earth in exchange for their services, but it didn't specify which alloys would provide those services. Over time, that labor had ended up being a judicial consequence, with incarns made to work on Earth as compensation for wrongdoing or overuse of resources. Kaliyu didn't have the power to end that practice for all alloys, but at least zie could liberate zir own maker from it.

—

Kaliyu pushed hard over the next two kaals, resting for only half a kaal along the way to Earth. Zie took the steepest thamity gradients zie could find, accelerating for half the time and decelerating for the other half. Zie hadn't seen zir maker since zie was two varshas old. Zie knew Nidra's face only from extended memory images that zir grandmaker had provided. Any organic memories had faded during zir childhood.

Nidra would have even less recollection of Kaliyu. *Rebirth, especially a full one, is often accompanied by memory loss,* Pushkara had said when they first met. Would zir maker be happy to see Kaliyu? Nidra would be glad to end zir weller service early, of course, but how would zie react to a child who hadn't visited or sent a single message over the span of four and a half varshas? Did zie think that Kaliyu blamed zir for zir failures?

In truth, it was Hamsa's fault first. He'd bungled the designs that were supposed to transform Nidra into an organic vessel for human spaceflight. People valued Hamsa's tarawan skills and past successes enough that he was able to deflect his failures and rebuild his reputation. Had anyone spoken up for Nidra? Had the humans zie was supposed to serve tried to get zir service time reduced?

Kaliyu could probably dig through the records at the Primary Nivid and find out, but perhaps it didn't matter anymore. Between the passage of varshas in between and the endorsement Kaliyu held from Pushkara, Nidra would be freed at last. Kaliyu imagined Nidra's joy at being rescued from the well of Earth, and zir heart swelled with pride that zir actions had saved zir maker.

Zie slowed as zie approached Earth for the first time in zir life. So many people had sung the praises of the planet, in art and literature, in games and immersives, but Kaliyu saw only superficial beauty. Zie preferred the white heat of Venus or the dark gray of Mercury. Earth was a chaotic mess of greens and blues and whites—a honey trap, much like Meru, and zie refused to get stuck.

At the first station that zie could approach, zie transferred Pushkara's recommendation to the alloys who managed it. They would get it to the ground-based committee. True bodies studded berths in long rows, sustained by bhojya and sunlight, their eyes closed, their limbs slack. Kaliyu shuddered at the sight. *Wellers. Let that never be my fate.*

Zie settled into a berth to wait for a response and caught up on a backlog of messages, including some from the Majestics, the racing team that had offered zir a position. They had heard of Kaliyu's return from Meru and invited zir to join them anytime. Perhaps zie could bring Nidra along. Zir maker would have no memory of seeing Kaliyu fly, and to watch zir child race would surely make Nidra happy.

Kaliyu also scanned the news spool for any word of Vaha's fate. There was disappointingly little information from Meru. Most people in Sol had their attention on a different upcoming vote, a proposal to relocate all padhrans from beyond the asteroid belt so the astronomers out there could have unobstructed views. Most exiles orbited that far out, if not farther, and debate raged on whether they deserved to be moved inward as well.

An emtalk request came in from the station manager. Kaliyu accepted it.

"You have a message from your maker," the manager sent. "Nidra would like your presence at a geosynchronous location for better communication. Here are the coordinates."

Kaliyu was puzzled but did as the manager instructed. Zie found zirself feeling nervous and a little guilty. Zir absence wasn't zir fault, but zie felt a tremendous pressure to open with an apology to Nidra. Somehow, Kaliyu should have known the truth, as if a cosmic connection should have revealed it to zir. So many great works of fiction said that a heart knows when someone it loves is alive. Kaliyu's heart had failed zir.

Zie couldn't use thamity to travel while this close to a planet, so it took several kilas to get zirself into the right location. Zie didn't mind the extra travel time. It gave zir a chance to rehearse zir words, to think of ways that the conversation with Nidra might go. Zie would have preferred to meet in orbit for the first time, but zie supposed that getting committee approval and then getting zir maker's true body out of stasis would take more than a kaal or two.

After zie settled into a berth at the right orbital location, zie opened an emchannel to Nidra.

"Kaliyu, thank you so much for coming to visit me," Nidra sent. Zir words glowed with polite affection.

"Hello, Ma—Maker," zie replied, unsure if zie should use the term of address. Zie forged ahead with zir prepared speech. "I'm sorry it took so many varshas for me to come visit you. I didn't know that you were alive. Grandmaker said that you hadn't survived your weller rebirth—"

"Don't use that word," Nidra cut in. "I prefer *surface alloy.*"

The admonishment caught Kaliyu off guard. Zie hadn't imagined it in any of zir rehearsed scenarios. Zie blanked on what zie had intended to say next.

"I read about what my maker did to you," Nidra sent. "Pushkara included a private letter to me along with his recommendation to release me from service. I'm so sorry I left you in the care of your grandmaker. She isn't the role model I would choose today."

"There was no one else," Kaliyu sent. "You left me to work with Hamsa." The words shone accusingly in zir thoughts.

"Yes, I should have designated him as your guardian after my first death. It was my mistake."

"Hamsa?" Kaliyu glowed incredulously. "Wait—you remember all of that? You remember what happened to you?"

"Not organically. I've reconstructed it from various recordings and with the help of Hamsa and others."

"Then why didn't you reach out to me?" Kaliyu couldn't keep the pain from seeping into zir question. Other than the greeting, no part of this conversation was going as planned.

Hues of regret and uncertainty bled into the emchannel from Nidra's side. "While she was alive, your grandmaker refused to let me. She had full custody, you were a minor, and because of my status on Earth's surface, I couldn't overrule her wishes. After she died . . . I thought it best to wait for you to contact me. Perhaps I was wrong, but I didn't know how you felt about me. I didn't want to intrude. When the years passed and I saw nothing, I thought you must hate me. I could understand and forgive that. I never imagined that my maker had lied to you like this. I'm sorry. It doesn't make up for what's happened, but I want you to know that I regret the time we've lost."

Kaliyu latched on to those words like a lifeline. "Yes, so do I! I'm sorry, too, but now we can be together. We can put all of this behind us and be a family again. I have a position on a racing—"

"No, my child, not yet. I'm not coming up until I finish my original term of service."

"I don't understand. Did the committee say you couldn't? I thought they'd respect Pushkara's wishes in this matter."

"They do, and they've offered to let me off the planet, but I'm going to stay."

"But . . . why? They never should have sent you here in the first place. What happened to you was because of the humans and their greed! And Hamsa's poor designs! He should be the weller, not you."

Seconds ticked by with no reply.

"Maker?"

"Kaliyu, why do you think I'm here on the surface?"

"Because you burned through too many resources with your rebirths for Hamsa's human transportation project. You had to serve . . ." Kaliyu let the words fade. That's what zir grandmaker had told zir. Was that a lie, too?

"I think you might have the wrong idea about my situation." Nidra's words shone with the softest colors. "And based on Pushkara's letter, he didn't look deeply enough to understand it, either. Kaliyu, I volunteered to come to Earth, to take on this form and support the planet and the people who live here. When I couldn't serve as their vessel for space travel, I decided to help them in this capacity instead." A pause, then: "I left myself an extensive recording before my final rebirth explaining my reasoning and my goals. I knew my mind. No one forced me into service. I wanted to do something that improved the lives of human beings, and this was the only way I could. I made a commitment when I signed my contract to be here. I have no desire to end it early."

Reality fractured at Nidra's words. Kaliyu tried to piece it back together and failed. Zir maker had *chosen* to live like this? Grandmaker had warned zir that Nidra had an unhealthy love of human beings, but Kaliyu had never entertained the thought that anyone—especially zir own maker—would voluntarily condemn themselves to a weller's life.

"I didn't discuss this with you when I made the decision because you were too young," Nidra continued. "I had designed you to follow in my footsteps. I hoped that you'd grow up to be my partner, that we'd work in tandem one day to carry humanity to the stars. I thought that you'd rebel against my maker's antihuman stance like I did. I'm gathering from your reaction that I was wrong."

"By the Nivid! You have no idea how wrong," Kaliyu sent. "So you're still a human lover, even after all this time eating their garbage? After losing your organic memories? You have no regrets about your life?"

"None. It's not as bad as you make it sound."

"What about me?" Bitter rage suffused Kaliyu from head to tail. "Do you regret what you've done to me? I lost my best friend to help you. I went to Meru to make sure that humans would never leave Earth, to guarantee that alloys weren't complicit in corrupting another planet's natural state. I let my friend *drift away* so that I could return to Sol and save you from this wretched planet. You've turned all of that into a waste, just like the trash you consume!"

"I didn't force you to take this path." Nidra's words were carefully neutral. "If you had asked me, I would have told you to preserve your integrity and save your friend. I am disappointed in your antihuman sentiment, ashamed even. That *my child* would align with Pushkara—you can take his tainted recommendation and go! I'd choose being a garbage-eating *weller* over abandoning a friend any day."

Kaliyu trembled so hard, zie thought zir wings would snap off. Zir vision of a happy reunion had turned into a corrosive mess. How had living on Earth increased zir maker's affinity for humans? Kaliyu wanted family. Zie wanted a bond with zir maker, but if zie couldn't convince Nidra to leave this thrice-made planet, what hope did they have for a future relationship? Zie had wasted more than a masan away from the racing team for this.

Worst of all was what zie had done to Vaha.

"Fine. I'll go. Don't expect me to return."

Zie cut off the emchannel and vented in circles to calm zirself, dispersing zir rage into a cold fury. After sending a notification to the station of zir departure, zie thrashed zir way out of Earth's grip, uncaring of which direction zie flew as long as it was somewhere far from that cursed place.

—गवेषण

Gaveshana—Seeking

The farther Kaliyu went from Earth, the more zir anger evaporated until nothing was left but exhaustion. The future zie had constructed for zirself over the past masan sloughed away like atmo-burned skin, taking Vaha and zir maker with it. Each of them had betrayed zir in their own way. At least zie could still join the Majestics. Zie could do what zie loved best. Nothing created exhilaration like finding a perfect path through a complex thamity field.

Zie would have to forget Nidra, forget Meru, and focus on zir original path: to become the premier racing pilot in the Solar System. It would be harder to forget Vaha, but zir friend was an adult. Vaha had made zir own choices, and Kaliyu couldn't hold zirself responsible for them. It didn't matter if zir heart had broken as zie left the Pamir System. It didn't matter if Vaha drifted somewhere in the universe, alive and well and hating Kaliyu. Zie had to put all those feelings aside before they consumed zir.

Kaliyu allowed zirself to take a rest after zie'd gone halfway to Mars. Between the rapid journey to Earth and the violent escape from it, zie had exhausted zir energy reserves. The double rejections, first from

Vaha, then from zir own maker, hurt more than zie wanted to admit. Zie needed to be alone for a while with zir misery.

Nidra's final words surrounded zir like a ring of debris: *I'd choose being a garbage-eating* weller *over abandoning a friend any day.*

Zie refused to acknowledge any truth in zir maker's accusation. *Vaha left me first, and Nidra loves humans more than me. I owe them nothing!*

So why did zir victory at Meru taste like stale bhojya?

After some rest, Kaliyu continued on toward Mars, with the Majestics' location as zir destination. Races happened out past Jupiter to avoid the more populated inner orbits, and teams established their padhrans near the courses for practice. As Kaliyu flew by the angry little red planet, zie felt the ping of a personal message from one of the orbital data stations. Zie spooled it along with the latest news.

The message was from Pushkara, and it was as brief as it was cryptic: *Are you fit for a return to Meru? I think your reputation will make you an ideal candidate, and the committee supports it.* Kaliyu couldn't fathom why Pushkara would ask this of zir. Zie checked the news spool and discovered that the MEC's hearing on the human trial had finished. That would probably supplement whatever Pushkara had omitted from his message.

Kaliyu slowed enough to spool the entire recording into zir extended memory before accelerating past Mars. Zie had no desire to be within sight of other people, not yet. Zie fell into orbit a bit past the planet's pull and took a rest. As zie drank bhojya, zie replayed the meeting, hoping that it would explain why the committee wanted zir back at Meru. Zie skimmed past the first several kilas of procedural business until the committee arrived at the topic of the Human Habitation Project.

The MEC members had convened at the Primary Nivid, with Hamsa and Pushkara present as well. Time lags across the Solar System were too great for a back-and-forth meeting. Six of the nine committee members had fully space-adapted bodies, though not so large as a pilot's. The other three trended humanoid, like Pushkara. Kaliyu was surprised at Hamsa's more modern form and a little envious of his elegant, almost translucent tail. Hamsa's chromatophores swirled in patterns reminiscent of wispy clouds. He had a reputation for making subtle alterations to his superficial phenotypes during each partial rebirth. Kaliyu could see why people had such respect for his tarawan abilities. He was a floating advertisement of his skills.

<Pushkara, please present your data,> the committee chair, Nadapar, flashed. She had inky-black eyes in a blue-gray face, her skin pale enough that she must spend the majority of her time at the Primary Nivid, sheltered from the Sun. <You have five hectas.>

<Thank you, Nadapar. I've copied everything from the final courier drop into the Nivid Vestibule for consideration. The data bundle includes visual recordings that show Vaha—the pilot assigned to this project—getting badly injured and the observer, Kaliyu, helping zir off the surface of Meru. The observer determined that the pilot required medical assistance from Sol and intended to follow the project parameters, which state that the test subject cannot be left unattended on the surface. While we don't have a recording of what ensued, the observer returned to Sol alone and stated that the pilot violently prevented zir attempt to retrieve the human. The pilot also refused to return to Sol, thereby stranding the human on the planet.

<I believe the evidence speaks for itself. The heliopausal medical facility treated the observer's injuries, and I'm sure the next pilot to make a round trip to Meru will confirm the presence of the human on the planet. I propose that the project be canceled in light of this violation of regulations. In addition, I request that any results obtained subsequent to the observer's departure be disallowed from entry into the Nivid due to lack of alloy corroboration.>

The committee members took another five kilas each to respond to Pushkara's proposal and ask questions. Four of them seemed to support Pushkara, while two others were opposed. The chair and remaining members kept their phores neutral and didn't ask any follow-up questions before yielding to Hamsa.

Kaliyu almost skipped past the human-loving alloy's statement, but zir curiosity overruled zir distaste.

<I appreciate my colleague's position,> Hamsa began, zir phores colored with graciousness. <However, I must respectfully disagree that the project should be scrapped. I will support the omission of any data gathered while Jayanthi, the human subject, is alone on Meru.>

That was a surprise.

<At this time, I think it makes the most sense to send someone back to Meru who can function as pilot and courier and who can retrieve Jayanthi and the supplies, including the womb, at the end of the original project timeline. I see no reason to terminate the study early. Any data collected upon resumption of legal observation should be allowed entry into the Nivid. To do otherwise is to waste all of the resources that we've invested into this project.>

Of course Hamsa wouldn't let it go so easily. Kaliyu could see how the tarawan's argument might persuade some people, and zie wondered how Pushkara would counter it. Then zie noticed that the chairperson's phores had gone bright pink with displeasure.

<Hamsa, did I understand you correctly that a womb is on the planet's surface?>

<Yes, that's what I saw in the visual data for the ground-based site. The womb belongs to Vaha, the pilot. I'm not sure why zie landed with it; however, it has a metal exterior that would have been sterilized during atmospheric entry. Its presence on the surface shouldn't have created any contamination.>

<Perhaps, but this is rather irregular. The womb should have remained in orbit for emergency use only.>

The gazes of all nine committee members went distant as they conferred via a private emtalk channel. Pushkara and Hamsa exchanged a look, but Kaliyu couldn't tell whether they also had a parallel conversation going on.

<Based on what we know,> the chair flashed, <we're inclined to agree with Pushkara. This project was high-risk to begin with. With a pilot in breach of contract, an observer who barely made it home, an abandoned human who could be dead by now, and a potentially contaminated surface, the cost of this endeavor is already too high. We agree to send a pilot who can retrieve all related items from the surface, including the test subject. The observer who recently returned has done a commendable job so far. Zie seems like a good choice, as long as zir injuries are sufficiently healed for the journey, and assuming zie is willing to take on the task.>

Pushkara glowed with satisfaction. Hamsa's phores stayed neutral, though he must have been disappointed.

<The data deposit in the Vestibule will be reviewed for novel information without prejudice,> the chair concluded. <We'll now move to item seven on the agenda.>

So they had done Hamsa a small favor. It might help him salvage some of his reputation, but nothing in the existing data could validate the long-term viability of humans on Meru. The test subject had completed only a portion of the required trials. The project would never advance to its later stages, and Hamsa had little to justify the amendment to the compact.

Kaliyu read the message from Pushkara again: *Are you fit for a return to Meru? I think your reputation will make you an ideal candidate, and the committee supports it.*

It made more sense now. Reputation would come into play when Kaliyu "discovered" the contaminant that zie had released onto the surface. Zie didn't relish the thought of returning to the site of zir fight with Vaha, nor of ferrying the human, assuming she lived. If zie were lucky, she would be a corpse like Vaha's incarn and not someone zie would have to interact with. Vaha, on the other hand . . . if zir friend were alive and adrift, perhaps Kaliyu could find zir. The return contract would give Kaliyu a legitimate reason to be in the Pamir System, and if zie spent a few kaals wandering the vicinity of Meru, no one would care. All zie wanted was the peace of knowing zir friend was all right.

Zie could still see Nidra's words flashing before zir eyes, glowing with contempt: *I would have told you to preserve your integrity and save your friend.* If Kaliyu accepted the MEC's offer, zie could redeem zirself by looking for Vaha. Zie shouldn't care what zir human-loving maker thought of zir, but zie couldn't help it. Maybe zie needed to adjust some hormones, or maybe zie couldn't let go of the hope that zie could convince Nidra to leave Earth.

If nothing else, by completing the MEC's tasks, zie would remain in Pushkara's good graces. There were worse allies to have. And best case, zie would find Vaha, clean up the mess on Meru, and return a hero. Then zir maker would have to retract zir harsh words. A quick turnaround trip wouldn't cost much time, and it was a small price to show Nidra that zie wasn't a monster.

Kaliyu composed a reply to Pushkara: *I am nearly healed already. By the time I reach heliopause, I should be fine. I will have to stop to get my human chamber prepared for a passenger, in case the test subject is alive. Thank you for trusting me with this opportunity.* Then zie turned around and headed back to Mars to send it.

The journey to Meru took thirty kaals, and Kaliyu spent far too much of it brooding. Zie had given Pushkara what he wanted to the point that thousands of Pushkara's supporters had sent zir congratulatory messages while zie'd traveled toward Solar heliopause. Why couldn't zie be happy and enjoy zir success? Why couldn't zie let go of the hope of finding Vaha alive, of saving zir maker from zirself? Was zie doomed to a life of chasing after impossible things?

Zie stopped first in Meru's orbit, at the observation rig, which had lost some altitude while it had been powered down. Kaliyu towed it back to the correct location and turned it back on. No one answered when zie tried to communicate with the human's living site. That was promising. Zie had left three-quarters of a masan earlier. That was a long time for a lone human to survive on an uninhabited planet. Kaliyu waited another two kaals, watching for the human to show up on one of the cameras, but she never did. Zie didn't think she could spend that much time in the womb or the washroom, the only two places with total privacy.

With a sense of relief, Kaliyu landed, but the sentiment was short-lived. The bare surface of Meru surrounded Kaliyu in all its reddish-brown glory. As zie examined the ground around the tent, zie saw no sign of activity. No footprints, and no contaminant, either. When zie lifted the tent and peered inside, zie found more nothing. Where could the human and Vaha's incarn be? The womb wouldn't open for zir, but if the human was inside, surely she'd have exited upon feeling the impact of Kaliyu's landing. Had Vaha returned and taken her? It seemed impossible given the injuries zir friend had sustained. Plus zie wouldn't have left the womb.

Kaliyu scanned the horizon in all directions. Perhaps the human had wandered off somewhere and died, but zie hadn't seen any indication of organic matter from the observation platform. Had she drowned in the ocean? Zie felt a spark of pity for the little human, left to her own devices with no way to communicate to anyone, as betrayed by Vaha's abandonment as Kaliyu had been.

Zie shook away the sudden empathy. Packing up the shelter involved an extensive and specific procedure to avoid breakage or contamination. As the final step, zie coiled up the waterline that had drawn from the nearby lake and stuffed it into a sack. Once zie had that done, Kaliyu sent a message to the nearby construct, Varshaneya, who would help launch zir into the upper atmosphere, saying that zie was ready for a pickup.

As zie waited for the megaconstruct, zie examined the area again. Slithering around in gravity was beyond awkward, but zie needed to find proof of contamination. That was the final piece to secure the end of the project as well as guarantee that Hamsa's amendment would lose the general vote. Zie grew increasingly frustrated as zie found nothing, and zie wondered if the scanner from orbit didn't work. Could the container have gone off course? That could prove catastrophic, especially if it had ended up in the ocean or some other large body of water, but if that had happened, surely one of the other orbital observers would have noticed? Zie would have to move the platform to some other orbits and look for zirself.

Varshaneya flew in and landed more gracefully than Kaliyu had. Zie strapped Vaha's womb to zir body and clambered onto the construct's back. With the help of Varshaneya's eight powerful legs, they thrust upward.

As they flew, Kaliyu sent a query via their emchannel. "Have you seen any sign of a human around here?"

"Seventy-eight kaals ago, I carried a human named Jayanthi to space, where I left her with another megaconstruct."

That was not the answer Kaliyu had expected. "Why? Was she returning to Sol?"

"She stated that as her goal."

"And the construct took her there?"

"The construct was a free agent passing through the system and willing to give her passage. I'm not sure what his destination was or where they might be today."

"And you don't know anything more, like why she decided to leave?"

"She inquired about your whereabouts and expressed concern that she could not communicate with you."

By the Nivid! The human had gone rogue, running off with a strange megaconstruct. She could be anywhere, or she could be floating in space, as cold and dead as an asteroid. Kaliyu wanted to spin in frustration. Zie didn't want to return to Sol empty-handed, but it appeared that zie had no choice.

Zie thanked Varshaneya as they reached an altitude where zie could safely detach, then engaged zir ventral sphincters and squeezed, pushing zirself higher and safely into orbit. Zie would have to split zir remaining kaals between looking for the contaminant and for Vaha. If zie didn't find at least one of the two, the excursion to Meru would end up a disappointing waste of time.

Kaliyu had searched in a conical spiral from Meru outward, in the rough direction that zie recalled as Vaha's final trajectory. Zie had expended extra power to listen for the faintest hint of emchannel activity, but after nearly ten kaals, zie had encountered nothing but the steady silence of the galaxy. Zie hadn't dared to transmit a message. If Vaha felt as angry at Kaliyu as zie had during their fight, a message from Kaliyu might chase zir farther away.

The stars glared at zir with recriminations galore. What kind of friend was zie to allow Vaha to drift away? So what if zie had threatened to fight Kaliyu? If Kaliyu had been a better person, zie would have found a way to overpower Vaha and drag zir back to Sol and safety.

A kaal into zir exploration, zie had remembered the solar weather that had blazed from Pamir through the system. Vaha would have been caught in that with no shelter. Had zie managed to survive it? Perhaps zie had tried to course-correct with a flare-addled mind and ended up drifting along a different vector. If that had happened, Vaha could be anywhere in the system, and Kaliyu could search for the rest of zir life without finding zir friend. Or perhaps a megaconstruct had picked Vaha up, as it had the human, and zie had chosen to run away.

Kaliyu had failed to find any sign of the contaminant on Meru's surface, land or sea, and now zie had failed to discover the fate of zir best friend. Frustration infused zir phores with a deep-apricot glow. No one could see zir, so it didn't matter. Zir shame was entirely zirs to bear. With a flick of zir tail and an unlit apology to Vaha, zie engaged zir thamity senses and found the steepest gradient toward Pamir's heliopause. The faster zie could get back to Sol, the sooner zie could put all this behind zir.

I'm sorry I failed you again, my friend.

Coming back to Meru had been a mistake. Zie had let the MEC's request feed zir ego. Zie thought zie could achieve the miraculous, and instead, zie would have to report to Pushkara the lack of evidence of contamination. The fruitless search for Vaha wouldn't win zir any points with zir maker.

Kaliyu had acted like a thrice-made mudha once again. Zie resolved that after zie completed this task, zie would do nothing but race. At least there, zie knew zie could excel. Gravity could take the MEC and Pushkara and Hamsa. It could take the humans and zir maker, too. Zie wanted nothing more to do with any of them.

—सुरक्षा

Surakshaa—Recovery

Nakis rotated zir body off-axis as zie flexed zir tail up and vented zirself down. The icy upper atmosphere of Kumuda stung the exposed skin where the exoskeleton had rubbed away the outer layer. High as zie was, the air currents didn't disturb zir flight. Zie had a tendency to panic when they did, which zie attributed to the deep-seated feeling of incompetence that zie had yet to shake loose. Rithu claimed he didn't mind coming to Nakis's aid as needed. He could scoop zir body up and lift zir back to their platform with minimal effort, or so he said. For all that he called himself old, Rithu still had the well-toned muscles of a racer. Nakis could feel them flex and extend under the pilot's skin whenever he carried zir.

Zie had made the right decision by staying with Rithu. News spooled in regularly from courier drops at Meru, and Nakis always looked through it for headlines regarding Pamir, Meru, or Kumuda. Once, while Rithu was out collecting samples, zie had found an item about the Meru Exploration Committee regarding a human survivability experiment. The article mentioned that a pilot named Vaha, who had flown the human to Meru and was supposed to remain at the planet, had departed early in breach of contract. Vaha had attacked and injured another pilot named Kaliyu and was presumed adrift. The text had concluded by stating that Kaliyu would return to Meru to shut down the project and carry the human back to Sol.

Vaha. Nakis had rolled it around in zir mind, trying to see if it fit anywhere or knocked loose more memories, but nothing had happened. Zie had never shown any violent tendencies during zir stay with Rithu, but perhaps zir personality had changed. The story fit—zie *had* carried a human somewhere. Zie *had* ended up adrift until Karkothaka had picked zir up. Zie must have had a reason to come to the Pamir System. But zie could recall none of it.

Meru might hold some answers to zir past, but what if they confirmed yet another failure to add to zir childhood record? And a violent one, at that. *I wouldn't have ended up injured and in emergency hibernation because I did something right.* Maybe it was enough to know as much as the news item had divulged. If Vaha's assignment had been to ferry the human, Nakis might as well ignore it. With zir injured tail, zie couldn't transport anyone anywhere. The other pilot, Kaliyu, would finish the work that Vaha had abandoned.

Zie had decided to delete the article from their news spool. Zie didn't want Rithu to judge zir by Vaha's actions—assuming they were in fact the same person—and zie saw no need to involve Rithu in zir speculations. Vaha no longer had obligations to the MEC, not if everyone presumed zir adrift or dead. Nakis was free to start a new life at Kumuda—free of zir maker and the haze of failure that lingered in zir organic memories—so that's what zie had done.

In the half masan since, zie had anxiously scanned every incoming spool, but no further news had arrived about the situation. Zie put all zir energy into regaining zir flight skills, though zie progressed at a frustratingly slow pace. Zir wing had healed at an awkward angle. Zie had lost the full range of motion at zir shoulder. The torn solar skin had scarred over, leaving the wing with 30 percent of its original power production. Nakis had learned to work with what zie had, including how to balance zir body during flight in a gravity well. Thrusting and turning with the exoskeletal brace had become second nature, at least in orbit. Fine adjustments were the easiest. Zie could skim the atmosphere without Rithu's help as long as zie didn't go too deep.

Zie had also recovered more of zir organic memories, especially those from childhood. At first, they had made it harder to keep pushing. Every failure cemented the notion that zie didn't deserve to call zirself a pilot. Zie would have given up and lost zirself to stasis except for Rithu's persistence. Unlike Nakis's maker, Rithu gave encouragement after saving zir from further injury. He wouldn't let Nakis give up from despair.

Zir spirits had lifted once zie could help Rithu with his scientific work, even if zie had to limit where zie flew. They had divided up the sampling tasks after Nakis had gained enough confidence. Rithu handled the stratosphere; Nakis stayed with the outer layers, the exosphere and thermosphere. They worked in parallel so that they could spend their leisure time together, gaming or watching shows. Rithu had amassed a varied collection over the years, and he had a surprising fondness for human-made entertainment. Nakis enjoyed those, too, and zie shared with Rithu the fragmented recording of zir passenger. They laughed at her exaggerated facial expressions and admired her features, which were well proportioned for a human.

They spent every other kaal on meditation. Nakis knew different techniques from Rithu's, newer methods as well as tricks that zir maker had discovered on zir own during zir interstellar voyages. Nakis also had some recorded lectures on transits that had survived in zir extended memory. They couldn't RT from inside Pamir's heliosphere, but they could practice getting close to the right state of mind. Younger pilots like zirself had better biological capacity in their shashtam to perceive the fabric of reality. Rithu had to enhance that organ with drugs, but the end result was nearly the same. Thankfully, Nakis's quantum sensing organelles hadn't taken damage from the solar storm.

"You have to let go of every other sense until your entire consciousness is submerged in shashtam," one of the lectures said. "The breath in your lungs is a starting point. Controlling your breath also helps infuse your blood with oxygen, which energizes the shashtam. You can't let it distract you forever, though. It's easy to remain subsumed in breath, as our ancestors did. Dissociative drugs can help you block out your physical senses, including your thamity sense, but they can only do so much. Transit depends on your ability to focus your consciousness down to the nebulous state of the quantum universe. You must see beyond the illusion of matter to its true nature, which is fluid. Space doesn't exist. Time doesn't exist. You have to sift through all probable states of energy and find the one that puts you where you want to be."

They couldn't complete the final step because Kumuda, Meru, and Pamir exerted too strong an influence. The nonliving but massively conscious bodies dominated local reality, but Nakis could tell during practice that zie would get it right at heliopause. Zie had a vague recollection of the first time zie had mastered the technique, and it made zir glow with joy. The feeling of zir body dissolving away as a solid mass, the vast *connectedness* of everything in the universe, the shifting realities like a dreamscape of infinite probabilities, where if you concentrated enough—but not too hard—you could emerge in a place you'd never been before: nothing came close to the experience. Words certainly couldn't do it justice.

Zie scooped one last air sample and thrust forward, letting Kumuda's gravity give zir some speed before pushing up and around, back to the observation platform. Zie found Rithu already in his berth, a water tube in his mouth. As zie deposited the samples in the analysis tool, Rithu made a surfing motion with his hand and raised his brows in a wordless question. Nakis knew the sign—Rithu wanted to practice microgravity flight.

<Let me take a half-kaal break first,> zie flashed.

Watching Rithu traverse thamity gradients was like watching an artist at work. Pleasure radiated off the racer in almost visible waves. Nakis could understand how "The Royal" had become a fan favorite. Zie felt like an infant venting their first puffs compared to him, especially in zir current state. Rithu had been the model of patience, but Nakis's microgravity flight hadn't made the same kind of recovery as zir atmospheric and reality maneuvering. Zie couldn't sense thamity at all with the lower half of zir body, and steering a gradient with only zir upper half proved more challenging than zie had anticipated.

Despite that, Rithu was willing to work with zir. If Nakis couldn't learn adaptive MG techniques from an expert like Rithu, zie had little chance of ever figuring it out. The only person zie knew who approached Rithu's grace was zir friend back at school, the one whose name zie could still not recall. Zir friend also had an intuition for MG traversal and had always beaten the other students when it came to speed.

With a pall of frustration surrounding zir like a nebula, Nakis pulled out of the berth.

Rithu must have sensed zir mood. He flashed, <Shake it loose, Nakis. I know you haven't progressed as much as you want, but you are improving. A masan ago, you slipped down the shallowest gradients, and now you can ride your momentum up small slopes. You're young. You don't have to rush this.>

Nakis nodded. Zie opened zir thamity sense and found the shape of the local gradient. The field stretched wide across the Pamir System, operating at longer scales than gravity. The gentle slopes were enough to build up plenty of speed, though, especially near the dark wells that peppered the universe.

With a deep lungful of water, Nakis launched "down" a slope—a helpful illusion for zir thamity organelles as they flowed from a higher-energy state to a lower one—and kept zir body mostly parallel to the gradient. Zir tail dragged behind zir. As long as zie kept it in line with zir upper body, zie remained stable. Zie pointed zirself back upslope and slowed.

"Good," Rithu sent via emtalk. He was not far from Nakis, as always, in case zie needed help. "Now try going a little faster, and remember to use the brace to keep your tail extended."

Nakis found it hard to concentrate on manipulating the exoskeleton at the same time as sensing thamity, but zie tried. Zie let zirself point farther downslope, gaining more speed, until it felt as good as MG flight used to.

"Excellent!" Rithu cheered. "Now follow that curve to the right and slow down."

Nakis did as asked. Zie twisted zir upper body to cut across the field. For a second, zie had it. Then zir forgotten tail whipped around in the opposite direction, wrenching the muscles at its base. Zir phores flashed white with pain, and zie tumbled through the field like an out-of-control asteroid.

Rithu came up behind zir and pulled Nakis's body against his, wrapping zir in his arms and steadying their course.

<It's the thrice-made brace!> Nakis let a few more choice curses fly. <It takes too much concentration.>

As Rithu stabilized them, Nakis leaned zir head back against his shoulder. The racer's body wasn't as long as zirs, but he was broader, bulky with thamity-laced musculature. The warmth radiated from him into Nakis's wings and back. Nakis couldn't help the instinctive heat around zir groin. Alloys didn't need to mate like their human cousins, but they'd kept the ability because it felt so vent-spawning good. Sexual intimacy was the one time they generated significant body heat. Zie kept having to fight zir instinctive attraction to Rithu, and after a while, zie had stopped trying.

Whether zie was lonely or zir feelings for Rithu went deeper, Nakis still wasn't sure, but something held zir back from giving in to zir desires. Based on Rithu's physical reactions, Nakis had no doubt that the other pilot reciprocated, but he had kept their relationship respectful and didn't allow his vents to open or his hands to stray. That hadn't helped with Nakis's uncertainty.

The gaps in zir memory made zir wonder: Was there someone else in zir life? What if zie had partnered during or after school? The student zie could picture so clearly in zir mind—they'd been more than friends. Romantic, physical, sharing a berth at times. Had that evolved into something more?

For all the months that they had spent together, Rithu hadn't quizzed Nakis about zir past even once. Zie couldn't fathom the depths of the other alloy's patience. Zie had expressed zir own curiosity several times, and Rithu had spoken about his life with the practiced ease of a celebrity. Nakis had considered offering what zie remembered, but to what purpose? Like telling someone the fragments of a dream, it would make no sense to Rithu. It barely made sense to zirself.

<Let's try something a little different,> Rithu flashed. <Not every method works for every person.> He moved his hands lower, to Nakis's hips and then to the exoskeleton. <What if I turn this off, and you try MG flight without it?>

<No!> Nakis grabbed Rithu's hands and pulled them away. <How would I maneuver?>

<I'm thinking it might be easier for your mind to map a passive tail than an active one that fights your thamity sense. You don't need your vents for microgravity, and you can switch the brace back on when you do.>

Nakis's phores pulsed with panic, but then zie thought, *Rithu is here. He will stop me from going adrift.*

<All right. Let's try,> zie flashed.

With the brace unpowered, pinpricks flooded zir senses whenever zie moved zir tail. The muscles and nerve endings had atrophied to the point that they were barely usable. Nakis let zir lower half float behind zir, like a dangling pack attached to zir hips, and once again opened zir upper body to thamity.

The same gradient from before spread ahead of zir. With another deep breath of water, zie traversed along the shallow slope. Zie tried a tentative turn, remembered the brace too late, shifted zir hips to compensate, and realized zie had already succeeded. Emboldened, Nakis oriented zirself more aggressively. As zie picked up speed, zie saw Rithu shadowing zir in zir periphery. *Focus on yourself!*

Nakis chose a deceleration line and shifted zirself to align with it. As zir upper body moved, zie kept zir hips relaxed. Zir lower body swung passively around to follow zir, and zie cruised to a stop.

Rithu's phores lit in a celebratory sparkle. <That looked great!>

<It felt great!> Nakis flashed. Zie glowed with pleasure. <You were right. That was a lot easier.>

Rithu thumped zir on the shoulder. <I knew you'd figure it out eventually.>

Nakis looked at him in a daze. Zir maker had never said those words to zir, at least not that zie could recall. Zir phores dimmed.

<What's wrong?> Rithu flashed.

<My maker used to wonder aloud where zie could have gone wrong in my design. Zie only had faith in zirself, never in me, and zie didn't hesitate to let me know. I can't help but wonder what my childhood would have been like if someone like you had raised me instead.>

Rithu shook his head. <I've known some coaches who think that way—that negative feedback will motivate their students more than encouragement. It never worked for me, and I certainly don't think that way about you.>

<I'm happy and grateful for that, and to have you here in my life.>

Nakis took Rithu's hands in zirs and gave them a squeeze. The other pilot drifted closer and cupped Nakis's face gently.

<What I'm doing is nothing special, and a maker who treated you like that was being abusive.>

Their faces floated a few meters apart. Their phores glowed with matched desires, and Nakis's heart beat faster.

<May I?> Rithu flashed.

The human passenger's face popped into Nakis's mind, and zie flinched at the intrusion. Rithu drifted back.

<No, you're okay,> Nakis flashed, trying to correct Rithu's misapprehension.

But his phores blended into a neutral skin tone. <I'm sorry.>

<I didn't mean—>

<No, don't apologize. I shouldn't impress myself on someone as young as you, especially when you have so many gaps in your memory. When we get back to Sol, after we've solved the mystery of how you came here, then we'll have plenty of time to be together in that way . . . assuming you still want to.> Rithu patted zir shoulder. <It's all right. I'm not upset.>

Somehow this made Nakis feel even worse, like zie was a child who had to be soothed. Zie flicked on the exoskeleton and puffed back toward their platform. Rithu followed without saying a word. Nakis felt the sting of vestigial tears. Why couldn't zie get something this simple right? Why had zir stupid brain thought of a human passenger at that particular moment? Would zie never escape zir past?

As zie pulled into zir berth, Nakis resolved to make zir way back to Sol as soon as zie could navigate thamity gradients on zir own. Zie would have to fly at a child's pace, but slow was better than stalled. If zie could make it to heliopause, zie could transit. If nothing else, the Genetic Review Board could match zir DNA to zir true identity, and if zie was indeed this failed pilot named Vaha, zie could officially shed the identity—along with the stigma and any romantic attachments—and return to Kumuda and Rithu with a clear conscience. Then they would be free to spend the rest of their lives together.

—स्कम्भ

Skambha—Fulcrum

Jayanthi had lived on Chedi for nearly four months by the time they reached Pamir's heliopause. Eighty-three days since her realization that Vaha was probably lost to her forever, many of those spent taking solace in Sunanda's friendship. They shared Jayanthi's love for biology and medicine and stargazing. They anchored her as she dealt with the compound stresses of her pregnancy, her distance from Earth, and Vaha's loss.

At nineteen weeks pregnant, Jayanthi had mostly passed through the perpetually nauseated stage. Her hips had widened enough that she had to ask for new pants. Her belly had started to protrude along with a mirrored ache in her lower back. Her appetite had returned with a vengeance, and she slept every afternoon in spite of an early bedtime. Chedi made her a special pillow to help with the discomfort that often spread through her whole body. She could no longer take the pain medications she relied on, and the ones that were safe for fetal development had almost no effect. Had she been on Meru, she would have been more comfortable, though she wouldn't have had the benefit of Raya's company and experience.

"You're in the good part," Raya kept saying. "Wait until the third trimester."

In addition to her physical problems, Jayanthi's mind wouldn't stop worrying about the future. Unlike a baby born from a womb, hers would have environmental and epigenetic factors that couldn't be controlled. Would the baby express the genes that Jayanthi had so carefully selected? What if, after all this effort, after risking her own life, the child was unsuitable for Meru? Unsuitable even for Earth? The child would have the option of gene therapy, of course, but until she reached maturity, she might suffer. *My parents had to watch me go through that. If they could do it, so can I.*

Raya did her best to reassure Jayanthi that most parents had similar concerns. That didn't help Jayanthi's brain stay quiet, nor did it help with sleep, which she needed increasingly more of. On the positive side, she'd begun to feel motion, a bubbling sensation in her lower abdomen. When she placed her hand over the fetus, tiny flutters pushed against it.

"May I?" Sunanda had asked after hearing about it.

Jayanthi had nodded and guided their hand to the right place.

"It's so marvelous," they'd said, their eyes shining. "I remember when Raya was further along. I could see the baby pushing against her belly."

As the primary medical assistant to Chedi, Sunanda helped Jayanthi with every check of fetal health. They would place the sensor net over her bare belly, hold her hand as she waited, and coo with her over the results. As grateful as she was for their companionship, she couldn't help but imagine how those moments would've happened on Meru. She could picture herself in a sling chair with Vaha's cheek resting against her abdomen. Sometimes she missed zir so much, she couldn't breathe.

Sunanda helped her manage her stress levels, too. Jayanthi had resumed taking the heme oxygenase booster as soon as Chedi had it ready, but pregnancy introduced other complications with her sickle cell disease that medications couldn't address. She had regular hydration infusions, but they could only do so much. She spent a lot of time lying in her cot.

In Jayanthi's better moments, she had hope of returning to Meru, of convincing the MEC and the general public that it would give her and her child a better life. At her last private session with Chedi prior to reality transit, she asked about Vaha and received the same answer as always: no sign of zir; no word about zir.

"I've had my constructs travel at top speeds," Chedi said. "I've scanned as much of this system as I could for signals, but space is vast, and it's possible that I missed zir. You shouldn't lose all hope. You might find zir again one day."

That didn't console Jayanthi much. If she found Vaha decades hence, it would do nothing for her current heartbreak. Their child would grow up knowing nothing about her alloy parent. Word had come back from Hamsa that they'd had no sign of Vaha at Sol, either. He'd expressed joy at knowing she was well, though, and agreed to see her: "Come straight to the Primary Nivid. I'll meet you there."

Guhaka had clapped with delight when she told him of her destination. "It's rare for a human to get the opportunity," he'd said. "The Primary is the greatest marvel of architecture and engineering that I have ever seen, in person or virtually, and its beauty rivals that of many planets."

The entire group had gathered in the grahin for the transit back to Sol. Jayanthi lay on a mat between Guhaka and Sunanda. She might never see Pamir or Meru again. Sunanda reached out and gave Jayanthi's hand a gentle squeeze.

"Make ready for transit." Chedi's voice sounded through the speakers in the ceiling.

The sedative began to take effect. Constructs had the same issues as alloys when it came to transporting other beings across reality. Highly complex or large quantities of consciousness would interfere with the process, so they all had to quiet their minds. Chedi's passengers turned it into an event with all of them gathered under the pavilion.

"Sweet dreams," Sunanda whispered.

Jayanthi nodded and let her heavy eyelids fall shut.

When she reopened them, nothing had changed. The worn patches on the underside of the ceiling looked exactly the same. The view of the stars through Vaha's belly had made transiting more exciting. She missed the quiet intimacy of travel with zir. She'd be alone again soon, though. The travel time to the Primary Nivid would take months at Chedi's minimal acceleration, so the construct had offered to send her on a small shuttle instead. That would get her to the Nivid in four weeks.

Others stirred as Jayanthi sat up. Expressions ranged from grins to resignation. Not everyone had chosen to return to the Solar System, though the majority wanted to support Jayanthi's and Hamsa's efforts. Chedi had set a course for Earth, about eighteen billion kilometers away, to pick up supplies. Jayanthi would leave on the shuttle the next day, and the group had decided to give her a festive send-off. Since Chedi was restocking early, they could use up their rarer food items.

They went as a group to the pond, and everyone stripped and jumped in. The air temperature was a pleasantly warm twenty-eight Celsius, perfect for relaxing in water. Jayanthi lounged in a tubular float, feet dangling and a refreshing fermented fruit punch in one hand. Sunanda occupied a similar doughnut. Younger children shrieked as they jumped off their parents' shoulders. The teenagers splashed and teased and flirted along the sandy bank. Jayanthi gazed at the scene and wondered again if her departure was a mistake.

"None of that," Sunanda scolded, wagging a finger at Jayanthi. "You are not allowed to frown today."

Jayanthi caught their hand and pulled them closer. "Can I talk about how much I'll miss being here and how much I'll miss you?"

"No," they said with a mock scowl. "You know the rule. Unhappiness is not allowed for more than five minutes on Chedi, especially during a party!"

"You're starting to turn red. Maybe we should move under the shade."

"Just because you have lovely dark skin doesn't mean you have to rub it in my face."

"Be careful. I might take you literally."

"If you put it that way," they said with a grin, "I might not mind so much."

Jayanthi laughed. Sunanda loved to flirt, but they'd never pushed beyond words. Jayanthi hadn't told them about her feelings for Vaha, though she had confessed that her heart belonged to someone else. Some nights as she lay in her cot alone, the memories of her pilot would pierce her like a thorn through a dewdrop, sharp and clear, overwhelming the daily aches and pains. She'd muffle her tears with her pillow so no one would hear.

As their daylight waned, they dried off and dressed in festive colors. Strings of lanterns came on all around the grahin. People set up platters of roasted and fried vegetables, beds of fluffy quinoa and delicate amaranth, tureens of creamy dal, and bowls of fresh fruit. The true indulgence was the pile of fresh-baked bread with heaps of butters and cheeses, items that could only come from Earth.

Working on her third portion, Jayanthi said, "Why is wheat and dairy such a magical combination?"

"I presume that's a rhetorical question," Guhaka said.

She laughed. "Yes, I suppose sugar, salt, and fat is the simple answer." She sighed. "Too bad that alloys have lost the ability to appreciate solid food."

"I'm sure the omnivores on Earth would feel the same way about us and our lack of meat," he replied. "So what's your plan when you get to the Nivid?"

"I'll give them the data I brought from Meru to show them that the planet improved my condition and then hope that my pregnancy convinces them to send me back there and accelerate to stage two." She placed a hand over her abdomen. "A healthy child could change minds about what's possible for Meru's future—and ours."

Chedi had sent a message to Hamsa upon their arrival at Sol. It would take thirty-three hours to get a response, and by then Jayanthi would be on her way, but she didn't intend to say much to Hamsa until they could talk in person. She didn't trust the security of their communications, and she didn't want anyone learning about her pregnancy until she was safely at the Primary Nivid.

The news spool at heliopause had informed them that the Meru Exploration Committee had halted the Human Habitation Project. They'd sent Kaliyu to retrieve her. It would have been only a matter of weeks before the pilot had returned to the planet. What had zie made of the situation there? Had zie figured out that Vaha's incarn was in the womb? Not that it would do zir any good unless zie knew something more about Vaha's fate.

"I'm glad to see that your time on Chedi hasn't dulled your ambitions," Guhaka said, "but I will admit out of pure selfishness that I'd prefer to keep your company. I wish you could stay."

Sunanda, who'd been unusually quiet through their dinner, stood up and walked away. Jayanthi pushed her chair back, intending to follow them, but Guhaka placed his hand on her arm.

"Give them a few moments," he said softly. "They might not show it, but they will miss you most of all. I've lived here a long time, and I've never seen Sunanda get as close to someone as they have with you."

Jayanthi gave his hand a grateful squeeze. "I will forever treasure my stay here, and I will miss you both tremendously, too."

After a few minutes, she pushed her plate away. Her appetite fled as her stomach roiled. She mustered a faltering smile as others came by the table to say their farewells. Most would still be asleep when she departed on the next local morning. Raya gave her a long hug, and Jayanthi saw a glint of tears before Raya turned away. The older residents said good night to each other as well, and the younger ones began to play music and dance.

Sunanda hadn't returned to the grahin, and after a few dances, Jayanthi pled exhaustion and slipped away. She wandered through the trees, following the bioluminescent edging of the path. Honeysuckle and angel's-trumpets scented the air. She inhaled and tried to memorize all of it—the sounds of the music and distant revelry, the twinkling of artificial lights high above, the low-level rumble of Chedi's rotating body. She wouldn't experience any of it again.

At last, she arrived at Sunanda's clearing. With no great surprise, she found her friend awake and pacing. They stopped as they caught sight of Jayanthi and held out their hand, cupped, with something small gleaming against their palm.

"This is for you," Sunanda said. "Something to remember me by."

Jayanthi picked up the object, a gold ring with a glittering opal set in the center.

"It belonged to my father," Sunanda said. "I had Chedi size it for you."

Jayanthi slipped it onto her middle finger. "It's perfect. Thank you."

Sunanda smiled. In the dim light, Jayanthi could see the sadness on her friend's face.

"Jaya . . . I won't see you off tomorrow, if that's okay?" They took her hands in theirs. "In the past few months, I've grown closer to you than I had any right to. I think—I didn't want to admit it to myself, but I can't deny it any longer. You're my best friend here, the nearest to my heart. I wish you all the luck in getting what you want, and I'll come to the hub if you really want me to, but it will be hard for me."

"I understand, and you're my dearest friend here, too. I'll miss you. I'll miss Chedi and Guhaka and Raya and everyone else. If there's any way I can come back one day, I will."

Jayanthi gave their hand a squeeze and returned to her cot alone. She had a monumental task ahead of her, a purpose: to deliver her data to Hamsa, to help open Meru to other human beings. She had to put aside her selfish desires to explore space. Leaving Chedi would be as painful as leaving Meru—maybe more so, knowing that here she could choose to stay forever—but the future prospects of her child might rest on her actions. She could not waver in her resolve.

Kaliyu slipped out of zir berth at the Primary Nivid and vented away. Pushkara rode in zir cupped hands. When they were far enough for privacy, Kaliyu lifted the old alloy to face level.

<It's good to see you again,> Pushkara began. <You're looking healthier than the last time we met.>

Kaliyu shrugged zir wings and nodded. <The injury has healed completely. I'm ready to race.>

<Then let's not linger. What did you find at Meru?>

<Not much,> Kaliyu admitted. <The shelter was empty. I packed it all up and turned it in to the MEC. I saw no sign of the human or Vaha's incarn. The construct who lifted me into orbit said that the human had asked for a ride as well and that she'd then gone with a megaconstruct. I couldn't find out anything more than that. She could be anywhere.>

To Kaliyu's surprise, Pushkara smiled. <Not to worry. She has found her way back to Sol via a bohemian megaconstruct, and she's currently in transit to the Primary. Hamsa received word from her. He's hoping that she's well enough to convince the MEC to restart the project, but I know we can thwart that.> Pushkara glowed with satisfaction. <With proof of contamination, nothing they can say or do will sway the committee.>

<About that . . . I didn't find any sign of contamination.>

Pushkara lit with surprise. <I thought you deployed it?>

<I did. I looked all around the site from the ground and then again from the orbital platform. I even spent a few days scanning other possible locations in case it had gone off course, but nothing turned up on the scans.>

<That is disappointing.>

<I'm sorry. I can't imagine what happened to it, but if I couldn't find it, perhaps it burned up in the atmosphere?>

<That would be the best-case scenario. However, it means that we have nothing to hold against Hamsa and Jayanthi.> Pushkara shrugged. <We did our best. I may try again with another courier if the project gets resurrected. You should go enjoy your time with Nidra and get started on your promising racing career. You've done enough for me.>

Kaliyu controlled zir phores as Pushkara's words sank in. The old alloy didn't know what had transpired between zir and zir maker, and it left a bitter taste in zir throat. In the end, neither of them had gotten what they wanted. At least zie had wasted only a couple of masans of zir life on the endeavor.

<I'll drop you back at the Primary,> Kaliyu said.

<One last thing. I'm afraid I won't be able to cover for you if someone does find the contaminant on Meru.>

<Cover? But it was your idea.>

<Yes, but your execution. I can't be responsible for your negligence, nor can I endanger my work. Voters follow me out of respect for my achievements in planetary protections. I can't allow that trust to be broken. If the blame falls on you, it won't matter. You'll suffer some minor consequence, I'm sure, but it won't impact your career.> The old alloy patted Kaliyu's thumb. <Don't worry yourself about it. Meru is a large planet. The likelihood of anyone finding something in the near future is slim.>

Kaliyu nodded, but zie felt cold inside as they flew back to the Primary. Pushkara's reassurances had done the opposite. Zie didn't want sole responsibility for harming Meru, especially when zie had done it at Pushkara's behest.

They parted ways without further communication, and zie returned to zir berth in a daze. Vaha's womb, attached by a tether, floated in silent disapproval. Was this how Pushkara treated all his collaborators, or had he taken advantage of Kaliyu's youth and inexperience? Either way, zie resented the implication that zir ambitions were worth less than Pushkara's. He'd had hundreds of varshas to accomplish his goals. If anything, he ought to take more care with a younger alloy who was just starting out.

Zie felt the sting of betrayal a third time. Vaha had been first, Nidra second, and now Pushkara. Could zie trust no one who claimed to be zir friend? Did Pushkara think zie would stay neutral while the MEC falsely accused zir of a crime? No, zie would defend zirself. Gravity could take the old alloy's political maneuvers.

With a thought-search, Kaliyu found the schedule and agenda for the next committee meeting. They were waiting until the human's arrival so they could interrogate her in person. Zie had to stay until then, in case they needed to ask zir any questions, and in case zie had to explain zir actions. If Pushkara thought Kaliyu would go peacefully as he flung zir at a black hole, he had chosen the wrong pilot to do his dirty work.

—प्रत्यागति

Prathyaagathi—The Way Home

Chedi's shuttle held a fragment of the megaconstruct's consciousness, enough to keep Jayanthi from feeling completely alone during her monthlong journey. The projection on the viewing wall looked exactly like the Chedi she was used to. The whole experience reminded her of being in Vaha, though the environment was drastically different.

The shuttle was roomier, for one. The toroidal craft had ten sleeping cubbies with a shared living space and a washroom at the center. An outer ring of clear material wrapped the craft and provided a 360-degree view as well as a place to run or walk. The entire journey was under one gee of acceleration, half toward the Primary Nivid, then half in the opposite direction. Unlike Vaha, the shuttle didn't need to take breaks.

By the second day, loneliness had thrust its way in, and she found herself near tears almost every hour. She tried to tell herself it was the pregnancy hormones, but that didn't help. Eventually, she thought to ask shuttle-Chedi whether she could communicate with people on Earth.

"Yes, it's possible," Chedi had replied, "with a one-way delay of approximately sixteen hours and forty minutes."

A little under one and a half days of roundtrip lag still meant that she could exchange quite a few messages during her journey. She wrote to her parents first, telling them that she was fine and had arrived in the Solar System. She let them know that she'd arranged to meet with Hamsa at the Primary Nivid before returning home.

Her second message was to Mina, of course. She repeated much of the same information, but she added bits about Meru and Chedi and space travel—all the wonderful things they'd dreamed of while growing up—and asked Mina to pass it on to the SHWAs. She left out details about Vaha and the womb and her pregnancy. The messages were aimed at Earth with no protection. Anyone with an antenna could pick them up, and she didn't want the public learning about the pregnancy before Hamsa and the MEC. She'd rehearsed what she would say to them, but she wanted to deliver her words in person so that she could respond to their concerns before they made any decisions.

According to her bodym's metrics, the baby continued to develop in a healthy fashion. Regular gymnastics in Jayanthi's uterus made sure she never forgot about being pregnant. She continued to walk several times a day to help with pain and keep her legs strong, but the baby crowded her lungs enough that she'd had to slow her pace. Her abdomen had firmed up, too. She wondered how much longer the enviro-suit would fit. The material had some elasticity to accommodate weight gain, but amniotic fluid didn't yield like fat and muscle.

Her parents' first reply brought tears to her eyes—what didn't?—and Mina's made her laugh. Ekene, Jean, and Li Feng sent shorter messages. Seeing all of them in immersives rather than flat videos cheered her up. After those, they all settled into their typical conversation patterns, though they were in a one-sided fashion. Jayanthi kept shifting the topics Earthward. She couldn't talk about the pregnancy—the only interesting thing happening on the shuttle—and she was curious to catch up on everything in the many months that she'd been away.

Polls on Earth showed less support for human settlement of Meru than Jayanthi would have liked. Only 53 percent were in favor. She recalled what Sunanda and Guhaka had said about Chedi, how the construct had never filled her capacity of residents. It seemed like many earthbound humans didn't care about a new planet, either. Perhaps they supported Hamsa's amendment to the compact more on principle than out of desire. She could understand why humanity would give up on small-craft travel, like her journey in the shuttle, which had grown tedious after the first few days, but how could they lose their curiosity and passion for the stars? Had centuries of directed evolution deprived humankind of all sense of adventure?

The natural state of Earth had improved since the dawn of the alloy era. Air and water quality were better. Wild flora and fauna had reclaimed more than half the planet. Alloys and constructs had made life comfortable in the temperate belts with planetary climate control and labor provisions.

All that had come with a price, a massive change in lifestyle from the days of Jayanthi's ancestors. A significant reduction in consumable goods. The end of mass transportation. Very little travel, except for academic or familial necessity. The sociopolitical fallout from the Anthropocene extinction followed by the Directed Mutation Catastrophe and the ruination of Mars had led to the fall of consumerist thinking. The goal to end scarcity on Earth was replaced by post-necessity austerity in space. Driven by socially focused philosophies, with a sizable topping of guilt and desperation, alloys and humans had engendered a seismic shift across cultures and laws. Perhaps the unforeseen consequence of that was that humankind had lost their curiosity.

How ironic that would be, she thought, *if after all this effort, the alloys vote to allow human beings on Meru but no one wants to go.* She could feel her heart breaking at the idea. It must have pained Hamsa so much to see Chedi go to waste. How had he bounced back enough to push to amend the compact? She had to find a similar strength, to convince others on Earth to rediscover the joy of adventure, or at the very least to open the door for a new generation to do so.

All thoughts of politics fled as the shuttle approached the Primary Nivid. One of the only permanent structures in space allowed by alloy law, it was almost as massive as a moon, but its shape—from their approach—resembled that of a jellyfish floating on its side. A giant hemispherical structure anchored one end and housed the archive of all knowledge. It gleamed as it soaked in sunlight from its golden solar surface, like a miniature of the star it reflected. From its underside, hundreds of "tentacles" jutted out in a tangle, not one of them in a straight line.

As they neared, she could resolve more detail: berthed pilots with their tails pointed outward, tiny exterior lights aglow with bioluminescence, millions of windows and segments on the tentacles. And then the Nivid itself, bejeweled with a dazzling array of panels in gold and silver. The reflection from the Sun grew almost unbearable as they approached, until they swung around behind it. She could understand why all the living quarters pointed away, hidden in shadow with a view of the stars.

She had thought Vaha enormous when she'd first glimpsed zir. Next to the Nivid, the pilots in their berths looked no bigger than an airplane in a Human Era megacity. Had Vaha ever visited this place? She should have ridden here in zir belly, with their baby in her own. *Why did you leave me? Where are you now? Are you alive?* Would she ever know what had happened to zir?

"I've been assigned a berth in the oldest limb, the only one that can house human beings," shuttle-Chedi announced. "You should strap in while I dock."

Jayanthi obliged. She sat in the living space, which had clear panes on its apparent floor and ceiling. She usually kept the floor side closed. Walking on it while open induced terrible vertigo. Once she buckled in, though, she uncovered it and watched as Chedi navigated through the maze of limbs, which grew in size until each one looked to be about thirteen meters tall, about three times as high as the shuttle, though the diameter of her craft extended a couple of meters beyond in either direction.

"We have successfully docked," Chedi announced. "Hamsa sent a message that a person named Devasu will meet you at the airlock in four kilas, or approximately one hour. She will take you to your living quarters. Do you need more time to get ready?"

"No, I'm all packed up. Thank you, Chedi."

"It's my pleasure. You might like to know that Kaliyu arrived here fifteen days ago. If I recall correctly, you wished to meet with zir and ask questions about Vaha. According to the logs, zie is still here, pending the next meeting of the Meru Exploration Committee."

"When is that?"

"In about a kaal, a little over one day."

"Thank you. I'll ask Hamsa if I can talk to Kaliyu or if he has done that already."

"Good luck, Jayanthi."

Gravity had disappeared the day before as Chedi matched speed with the Primary Nivid. Jayanthi's arms and legs floated free, and reality gnawed at her stomach. She'd spent the approach to the Nivid sightseeing, too awed by the structure to think about what would come next. The little being growing inside her made herself known, too, with a burst of activity as Jayanthi's organs rearranged for zero-g. She put a hand over her belly. *I have to deliver some very important information here, little one. If I get it right, you and I will spend our lives on a new planet.*

Devasu greeted Jayanthi with folded hands as Jayanthi emerged from the airlock into the Primary Nivid. Aquamarine bioluminescence shone in rings around them. As with Vaha's womb, the light level was dim enough to see the stars outside, and Jayanthi's pupils took a minute to adjust from the shuttle's bright interior. Glowing arrows indicated an up-down orientation, and her alloy guide floated in midair with her head toward the labeled ceiling.

Devasu was small for an alloy—about one and a half times Jayanthi's height—but the resemblance ended there. She had an almost childlike appearance with wide, round alloy eyes—amber colored and multi-lidded—and a heart-shaped face that tapered to a small chin. Her blue-black skin was a shade lighter than Vaha's and created a striking contrast with her fringed tail fins, which matched her eyes. The tips of two gold wings peeked above her shoulders, but they lay furled against her back. Her phores branched along her arms and torso in fractal curves. Vents the size of a belly button puckered various parts of her body. She resembled a mermaid, minus the hair, nose, and ears. Like most younger alloys, she had slits in place of those organs, though she kept them unsealed in the protective atmosphere inside the hallway. On her head, she wore a white turban with gold fringe that formed an undulating halo, almost like hair.

"Welcome to the Primary," Devasu said with perfect speech.

"You can talk!" Jayanthi blurted in surprise. "Sorry, I didn't mean to be rude."

Devasu's laugh sounded like wind chimes. "That's partly how I got this job—I still have organs for speech. I've practiced for the past three varshas to speak to a human, but you're the first one I've met. I'm so glad you can understand me."

"Perfectly. Your voice is lovely."

Devasu smiled as her phores glowed with pleasure. "Please follow me."

With a flick and twist of her body, Devasu floated down the corridor. Jayanthi adjusted her pack and used well-placed handholds to push herself forward. They moved from the airlock receiving room into a long corridor that Jayanthi guessed ran the entire length of this limb. It was small, maybe four meters in diameter, enough for humans to pass by in opposite directions. They turned right. Based on Chedi's berth location, that meant they headed closer to the Nivid.

Jayanthi wasn't sure what the pale walls were made of, but she could see minute cracks in the surface and patches of discoloration. Devasu's tail and head tassels gleamed in the gentle ambient light, their beauty in sharp contrast to the careworn surroundings. The lack of upkeep made sense—how many humans had visited this place? Perhaps enough to fill it in the early years when the Primary was first built, but now?

"When was the last time a human being came here?" she asked her guide.

"Hmm," Devasu said. Then, a few seconds later: "It's been more than fifteen varshas since we've had a human visitor."

Jayanthi converted that in her head: *fifty years.*

"We always make sure to have at least one speaking guide available, though, and a group of constructs assigned to maintain the facilities. I asked for the role. I love human culture! I'm so eager to learn more about it from you." Her tone shifted to one of apology. "The Primary says it isn't suitable for long-term stays by humans because of the radiation exposure and lack of gravity, so we won't have as much time together as I'd like."

"That's too bad," Jayanthi said. She couldn't help but enjoy Devasu's bubbly enthusiasm. "I wish I could stay longer, too, but I only expect to be here a few days—kaals."

The alloy twisted to face Jayanthi and moved neatly backward. "Oh no! I hope you'll get much more than that—at least one masan. I want to know all about your life on Earth. I watch lots of shows, but it's not the same as being around an actual human. Oh!" She stopped and caught Jayanthi, then pointed straight up at another passageway. "That's the way to your rooms."

Devasu led them to a door, which led into a bubble-shaped chamber with another, smaller space on the far side from the entry. A clear window occupied one quarter of the big room's wall, showing the activity around the Primary Nivid.

"May I help you with this?" Devasu indicated Jayanthi's pack.

Jayanthi nodded, and the alloy removed it and secured it.

"The Primary's CM—constructed mind—will listen for your requests and pass them on to me if necessary," Devasu said. "We have a fully open network that you can connect to and, of course, all the knowledge of civilization at your fingertips." Devasu smiled, her lips curving but closed, alloy-style.

Jayanthi matched her expression. "When can I see Hamsa?"

"Svah. For adhia, we want to get you settled in and do your medical."

"My what?"

"A medical exam. Before you can enter the other parts of the Primary, we have to make sure you're healthy. It's standard for every visitor. People come here from all over the place, and we want to ensure that they're free of harmful microbes or chemical contamination. Would you like some time to rest or drink first?"

"No, I'm fine. Will anyone besides the CM see the results of the exam?"

"Not without your authorization."

Greatness finds those who work without fear. "I'd like to authorize Hamsa and the members of the Meru Exploration Committee to get it."

"Certainly. The CM can send it to them."

The alloy excused herself for a few minutes, then returned with a container in tow. It wasn't large—maybe thirty centimeters to a side and roughly cube-shaped.

"You'll need to give the Primary construct access to your bodym," Devasu said. Then, after a moment of hesitation: "As a human, you're required to do that for your entire stay." Her tone sounded apologetic.

Jayanthi felt certain the given reason would be, *For your own good,* but considering that the rule didn't apply to alloys, the truth was more likely for their benefit. It fit with alloys treating humans like children. Parents had bodym access to minors, after all. Clearly they didn't trust human beings to take care of themselves while at the Primary.

With a mental shrug, Jayanthi slow-blinked and opened an emchannel with the Primary's CM, then sent it the access codes to her bodym.

"Open your mouth, please," Devasu said, extracting a squeeze bulb from the container. "I'm going to spray these microconstructs into you to do the scan."

Jayanthi obliged.

"It will take several kilas to complete the process," Devasu explained. "I'll be back once they're done. You can do anything you like in here while you wait." She indicated some now-familiar tubes attached to the wall. "Bhojya and water. We have all kinds of flavors. You can browse a menu and make any request you like. I'm afraid we don't have any solid food. Sorry."

"That's fine—I packed some of my own. Thank you."

While she waited, Jayanthi thought-searched and found the interface to the Nivid. A beautiful double-helix logo spun in her mind. It represented the twin aspects of the archive—data and knowledge—and reflected the fundamental encoding of life. The great artist Ayonika had designed it.

Jayanthi started by looking up entries about Meru, figuring that would make for a manageable amount of information. She thought-retrieved the most recent results. It took her ten minutes to get through 1 percent of the resulting titles. Each of those led to texts that began with a summary of knowledge gained and links to all the supporting evidence, with names for who was credited with what.

Giving up on that, she tried a query for Vaha. There were quite a few alloys with that name, but only one was a twenty-year-old pilot with a maker named Veera. For that Vaha, the Nivid had only one entry, which was zir genome. Out of curiosity, Jayanthi searched for her own name. It turned up in an entry credited to Hamsa that included all his tarawan work. She was one of the few living humans who he had designed. He had worked on Earth more during his early life. Going by the dates of the entries, his focus had shifted in his hundred and fifties to politics and proxy work, with less time spent on genetic design.

Jayanthi followed her curiosity from one detail to the next, letting that drive her searches. She couldn't fathom how long it would take for someone to read through all the knowledge in the Nivid. Even the multiple centuries of an alloy lifetime wouldn't be enough. She got so lost in it all that she failed to notice the hours passing. The door chime pulled her from her reading.

"Open the door," she said aloud.

Devasu swam in, her sunny demeanor gone. "I think something might be wrong with the scan. It claims you have a baby growing in your body. I've tried everything to see if it made a mistake, but the medical CM says that multiple factors about you confirm this, including indications from your bodym. I don't understand it. You're supposedly 1.4 masans into gestation—sorry, five months—but you've been away from Earth for eight months. It's not possible!"

Jayanthi didn't know what her face was doing, but Devasu stopped chattering and stared at her.

"You're not surprised," Devasu said. "You already knew this."

Jayanthi's heart hammered in her chest. She'd become so distracted by her reading that she had failed to rehearse a good response.

"But how? Aren't you sterile?" Devasu's phores colored with embarrassment. "And wouldn't you need . . . another human?"

"I had access to a womb," Jayanthi explained. "And I have some tarawan knowledge. It's all part of the second stage for testing human fitness on Meru."

"You're growing a child of your own design?" Devasu's phores went white with surprise, then returned to neutral. "You know what? None of this matters to me. I apologize for my intrusive questions. The fact is, you cannot remain here for more than ten kaals without risking developmental issues for the fetus. Hamsa told me he hoped to let you stay for a while, but that won't be safe." Her face broke into a smile again. "A pregnant human! My friends will be so jealous. I never would have imagined I'd get this lucky in a million varsha!"

The fetus under discussion reacted to all the excitement by doing backflips.

"Would you like to feel the baby move?"

Devasu's amber eyes went wide. "Oh yes, please," she breathed.

Jayanthi placed Devasu's hand on her belly.

"There! I felt it!" Devasu cried, her phores like amethysts on fire.

Jayanthi did her best to return the enthusiasm as her stomach churned. Would the MEC accept her reasons for making this child? Would they allow her to return to Meru where she and her child belonged? The meeting was the next day. She wouldn't have to wait long to learn her fate.

—

Not long after Devasu left, Hamsa arrived. For a second, she didn't recognize him. Hamsa's true body was the polar opposite of his feathery-white incarn. Here, he was covered in jet-black, scaly skin, with black wings in a birdlike shape. Phores outlined his body in streaks that ran from his temples down to his fluttering tail fins. Jayanthi had seen images of him in this form, but in her mind, she'd scaled them to her size. His true length was almost twice her height, and his embrace left her feeling like a child in comparison.

"Do you have any idea how glad I am to see you?" he sent via emtalk. "What in the name of the Nivid have you done to yourself?"

"I'm very glad to see you, too," she sent. All her carefully rehearsed words fled as her heart raced. On the one hand, she had accelerated his plan and brought data to support human settlement on Meru. But on the other, she had acted in the capacity of a tarawan without any kind of license. How would he react?

He took her hands in his. "Tell me everything that's happened."

With a deep breath, Jayanthi plunged in. She worked backward, first talking about Chedi, then her departure from Meru, and finally her good health on the planet as long as she'd used the HO treatment. She told him about Kaliyu's suspicious statement, about the idea to jump to the second stage of the project, and then, with her heart pounding, she confessed the source of her pregnancy. "Vaha left zir womb on Meru's surface. I had access to it for medical treatments, so I used it to create an embryo, a child who can thrive naturally on the planet, who has sickle cell disease as well as naturally elevated heme oxygenase. The womb couldn't develop it past a few weeks, so I implanted it into myself."

A riot of colors cycled across Hamsa's phores. "I thought perhaps Vaha had incarnated in a human body, but this . . . Why didn't you send me any of this by courier? We should have discussed it first! The risk to your body—"

"I couldn't talk it over with you. I was afraid of what Pushkara might do if he found out. Besides, at some point, humans *will* get pregnant if they live on Meru, and they'll have sickle cell genes like mine. All I did was skip a couple of steps ahead. Now that I'm pregnant with a healthy fetus, no one—including Pushkara—can deny that this child and I have viable genomes for Meru."

"He doesn't have to deny anything. Vaha abandoned zir post. That was enough for the committee to shut down the project."

"What do you mean, abandoned? Kaliyu told me that Vaha was injured and so zie would pick me up, but zie never did. What happened after that? Do you know?"

"Thought-share with me, and I'll show you."

Jayanthi watched as Pushkara told the committee what Kaliyu had claimed: that Vaha attacked Kaliyu, then refused help and let zirself drift away. Her stomach turned to lead as the implications sank in.

"Zie's gone, then," she sent. "I don't understand. Why would zie do that? Why attack Kaliyu? Why fly away?"

If Hamsa wondered at the unshed tears in her eyes, he didn't ask.

"I think zie did it for you," Hamsa sent. "Zie prevented Kaliyu from taking you off the planet and thereby ending our project. We all expected Kaliyu to find you there when zie returned to Meru. Instead, zie arrived here five days ago with the news that zie couldn't find you at all. If you hadn't sent that courier message via Chedi, you would've been presumed dead."

The constricted sensation in Jayanthi's stomach spread into her chest, making it hard to breathe. The baby's incessant kicking didn't help. "Vaha sacrificed zirself for the project, for me? And I . . . I did everything I could to leave the planet." She had nearly killed herself trying to find out what had happened to Vaha. Her vision grew blurred, and she blotted at the tears. "By the Nivid! Why didn't Kaliyu tell me all this from orbit?" Grief fled in the face of anger. "Zie just left me there! I understand why zie didn't come pick me up, but zie could have said something. Vaha said zie didn't like humans much. Did zie leave me in ignorance on purpose?"

Hamsa's phores glowed teal. "That I don't know. Kaliyu is here in a berth. You can ask zir yourself, if you're willing, or I can talk to zir on your behalf."

"No, I'll do it. I want to hear what zie has to say." She took a deep breath. "What about the project? Will they let me go back to Meru? Can we at least get my data into the Nivid?"

"Your data?"

"I brought a cube with all of the information we gathered while there." She unzipped a pocket and handed the cube to Hamsa.

At last, a tinge of violet appeared in Hamsa's phores. "Kaliyu claimed that the site had been shut down when zie arrived. Zie said there was no data except for visuals from the observation deck. So you had it all along! Good. I'll take a look at it and prepare my remarks for tomorrow. You should get some rest. Think about what you want to say, because the committee is likely to ask you for a statement."

Jayanthi nodded. "How do you think they'll react to all this?"

"They've invested quite a bit in this project, so I'm hoping that with the evidence you've brought, we can convince them to resume the work. They won't be happy about the pregnancy. Let's hope that doesn't bias them—and the world at large—against the whole endeavor, but just in case, I'll apply to the general elections committee for a postponement of the vote on the amendment."

After Hamsa left, Jayanthi stared through her window and tried to quiet her mind. So Vaha had tried to save the project. Zie hadn't abandoned her, not in the way she had feared, not because zie didn't love her. She had to believe, then, that zie was still adrift somewhere in the Pamir System. That someone might find zir. That someday, they could meet again. And with that as a possibility, she had to do everything in her power to make sure zir sacrifice didn't go to waste.

—न्यास

Nyaasa—Deposit

Jayanthi slept poorly during her first night at the Primary Nivid. She kept dreaming that she was back on Meru, but she was outside without an enviro-suit. Vaha's incarn would yell at her until she woke, sweaty and tangled in her sleep web. She'd spent too much time in gravity since her departure from Meru. Her subconscious had forgotten how to relax in zero-g. The anxiety about the MEC meeting and her now less-secret pregnancy didn't help. What would happen to the baby? Would they force her to return to Earth? Would the child do better or worse than Jayanthi had with sickle cell disorder?

Primary "morning" arrived with a gradual increase in ambient light. The bioluminescence made the room feel like Earth or Meru on a day covered by storm clouds. Alloy eyes had greater dynamic range than hers, and they kept their structures dim so they could see the stars. For Jayanthi, the low light on top of the poor sleep left her tired and drowsy.

She ordered a bhojya spiced with coffee, cinnamon, cardamom, and chocolate with a hint of honey. She had low expectations, but she had to admit that it tasted delicious, with a creamy texture and depth of flavor that implied they used real cacao. It helped wash away the chalky coating of her daily medicine, which Chedi had augmented with pregnancy vitamins.

Devasu met her at the door to her room. They had several hours before the MEC's meeting, so her guide had offered to give Jayanthi a tour of the Nivid, and she'd accepted. It would serve as a distraction, and she might never have another opportunity to see it. Devasu had changed her headdress to a midnight-blue wrap that matched her skin and added a matching sleeveless vest that draped her body to just past the curve of her hips. Both items had gold embroidery worked in a fine diamond pattern. Jayanthi had donned a fresh jumpsuit in light brown from her pack. It made her feel drab next to Devasu, but her spacesuit covered it, making her fashion choice irrelevant.

They coasted through the tunnel to a curved hub, where Jayanthi caught her first glimpse of other residents and visitors. The chamber was so vast that she couldn't see the far side of it. An assortment of alloys, many of them tailed and a few with fused legs, floated from one tunnel to another. Most were larger than Devasu, making Jayanthi feel like an infant in comparison. No wonder they treated human beings like children.

Built for alloys with vents, the hub had no handholds. Devasu hooked her arm through Jayanthi's and towed her to their destination limb. They moved along a much wider tunnel than the one in the human limb, this one at least fifty meters across. Jayanthi held tight to Devasu. She'd had no chance to practice using her jets, and she was surrounded by too many alloys to think of trying. At first, Jayanthi tried not to gawk, but people stared at her as often as she did them. They passed through several more hubs and branches until Jayanthi felt utterly lost. She could track their location in the Primary's map overlay, but the complex three-dimensional structure made it a navigational nightmare for someone used to moving across surfaces.

Finally, they arrived at a vast, disc-shaped space, their entry tunnel terminating at its center. They faced a round glass wall through which

Jayanthi could see three levels of the archive, each as tall as one story of a human house. Stacks upon stacks of data cubes lined the walls. Conduits for power and communication ran along their backs. A few alloys moved among the racks, and in one section, a swarm of constructs performed some kind of maintenance.

Devasu pulled Jayanthi to one of the many "spokes" that radiated away from the space. It was marked VISITOR ENTRANCE. They flew into a rectangular pod, large enough for several alloys to comfortably fit inside. After a few seconds, its doors slid shut, and it began to move. The only light came from aquamarine bioluminescence that traced the pod's corners in elaborate scrollwork.

"Almost there," Devasu said.

"I'm already so full of wonder at what I've seen, I don't know if the Nivid can top it."

Devasu smiled. "I guarantee it will."

The pod slowed, and the guide took Jayanthi's arm once more. Their doors opened to a room so well lit that Jayanthi had to squint. When her eyes adjusted, the sight made her forget to breathe. Before them floated the double helix of Ayonika's design, a three-dimensional sculpture that stretched across fifty meters of a chamber spanning three times that length. One half of the spiral was tipped by a rainbow of spheres, lit from within, to represent the optical storage of data. The other half was made up of models of life-forms, ranging from bacteria to elephants, each one scaled to the size of Jayanthi's hand. Strands of banded metal linked the two helixes. They represented a section of the DNA from the life-form they attached to.

"By the Nivid," Jayanthi whispered as she exhaled. She understood for the first time why people swore by the archive.

On the far side of the sculpture, a bubble-like window with heavy tinting showed that they had arrived at the edge of the great structure. Outside, the solar panels that powered the Nivid glared with the reflected light of the Sun. The tiled array curved away into the distance. On their left was a large set of double doors, which stood open.

They passed through the entry, turned right, and found themselves greeted by a dinosaur skeleton, a cross section of rock, and a suspended blob of what appeared to be molten lava.

Devasu gave Jayanthi's arm a gentle squeeze. "The visitors' section is organized chronologically, like a museum. Every item has links to entries in the Nivid via your emchannel interface."

Here, too, electric lighting created a brighter ambiance than the rest of the Primary. Devasu had dropped two of her eyelids to compensate.

"This segment is all early Earth history, before the Anthropocene," Devasu explained. "We've collected some artifacts from the planet, since most alloys will never get to land there. Let me know if you want a closer look at anything."

The alloy guided Jayanthi around the rectangular chamber until she'd had a quick look at all the displays. Jayanthi slow-blinked and found that each item pointed to two sections in the Nivid—information about the subject and the data and evidence in support of that knowledge. The next room was more like an immense tube formed by a series of connected rings.

"Each of these segments is one hundred meters wide and two hundred and fifty meters in diameter," Devasu said, "and there are a total of twenty. They represent different eras of history. We try to ensure that every item here has an analogue back on Earth. Unique items are usually left there, where they originated, with only images or models shown here."

Jayanthi paused to take a closer look at one of the first examples of writing and, later, printing. With travel on Earth limited by necessity, she'd never had the chance to see these artifacts in person, though with her parents being anthropologists, she'd witnessed more history than most humans.

They moved through the rings that ushered in the modern eras—feudalism, capitalism, expansionism. The last few rings covered the periods that Jayanthi knew better.

"These are models from the directed mutation age." Devasu pointed at various attempts at chimeras, most of which had failed to thrive, before they moved to more successful examples. "Here are the human phenotypes that were popular in the second century HE, and these are the precursors to modern alloys."

The display showed people who measured two meters in height with light skin, eyes, and hair. Alongside them were beings with metal and plastic bodies. The next ring showed the devastations of Mars and Earth. Jayanthi's home planet looked almost as brown and barren as its distant cousin, nothing like the verdant landmasses that she was familiar with. A chart plotted the catastrophic years, showing the rapid drop in human population due to the narrowing range of genetics and an increasingly hostile environment. In parallel, android beings—the first fully artificial replications of humankind—came into existence and grew in number.

At the end of that segment, they came upon a plaque with the words of Ratnam inscribed in glowing letters: *Ambition and materialism lead to greed and exploitation.*

"We have a copy of every draft of her treatise in the Nivid," Devasu said. "It's one of the most well-maintained and protected data cubes in storage." She pulled Jayanthi around to see the other side of the plaque. "And here are the names of the fifty-four people credited with the discovery of thamity. Their first paper and all their research notes are equally well cared for."

Jayanthi nodded. It made sense to highlight both of those. Ratnam's words had begun the movement from post-scarcity to post-necessity, and she had laid out the necessary social structures and values to make that transition. Thamity had revolutionized space travel and allowed people to travel beyond the Solar System. The marker divided the

Human Era from the Alloy Era in the ring sections, mirroring the effects of the ideas on actual history.

The first thing Jayanthi saw in the next section was an image of the earliest tri-chromosome people, Tertius and Mixturia. They had dark skin and webbed feet but otherwise resembled human beings. Features changed as alloys adapted better to life in space. With each passing section, the knowledge on display became more familiar to Jayanthi. The famous names transitioned from New Latin words to Archaic Chinese to Classical Sanskrit. Body characteristics became more about fashion than function.

"And here's the discovery of Meru," Devasu said.

They paused in front of an image of the planet with the name of an alloy pilot next to it: Jiangnu. Meru was the fourth planet she had discovered over several centuries and multiple rebirths. She had died not long after returning to Sol for the last time.

As they approached the exit, Jayanthi twisted and looked back. She had gone through a fraction of the knowledge encompassed by the Nivid, but at least she'd seen it, the first human visitor in half a century. *The bulk of our history belongs to humankind. Getting us into space and on Meru is only a start. We need to participate in the expansion of knowledge once again.*

The MEC meeting took place in a spacious conical chamber with the entrance at the broader end. At the tip, ten webs were arranged in a circle. Rounded cubbies of various sizes dented the walls of the room, which were made of dark-gray stone. Patches of bioluminescence lit the space with a gentle yellow glow.

Jayanthi and Hamsa floated in a cubby and watched as the chamber filled up. Alloys flew into the room and tucked themselves into the empty spaces. Most were of similar size to Hamsa or slightly larger.

Some had tails. Others had fused legs. A few were wingless. All had vacuum-adapted features—large eyes with gelatinous lids gathered above, flaps that could seal over their ears and nostrils, phores that blinked too fast for Jayanthi to interpret. About half of them wore wraps over their torsos and heads, like Devasu had. Gems glittered from neck- and armbands, the first jewelry that Jayanthi had seen anyone wear.

"Who are all these other people?" she sent to Hamsa.

"Some have agenda items to discuss with the committee. Some are reporters, and many are probably here to look at you. You might be the first and only human being they see in person. The MEC usually holds its meetings in a smaller chamber. They had an exceptional number of people request to attend today."

That didn't help settle her nerves. With every new cubby that filled, Jayanthi felt more out of place. *The only human they've ever seen—and I'm here to be judged.* Would they find her wanting?

When the nine members of the Meru Exploration Committee took their spots at the apex of the cone, all heads turned toward them, and all phores went dark.

"Ask the CM to give you an emtalk translation," Hamsa sent.

Jayanthi slow-blinked to interface, then made the thought-request.

"Are you visually impaired?" came the response.

"Yes, I'm human," she sent with a twinge of irritation.

"Do you wish to receive text or audio for translation?"

"Audio," she replied.

The option was a pleasant surprise as speech came through her suit speakers, with full tonal cues. The committee began with formalities, then presented the latest information regarding Jayanthi's arrival at the Primary Nivid and the results of her medical exam. They called on Hamsa as the project lead to propose the next course of action. He moved to float at the center of the committee.

<I have reviewed the data from Meru,> he flashed. <The initial results of the experiment show that Jayanthi suffered no detrimental

effects to her lungs or other organs from the high oxygen atmosphere on Meru, except when she discontinued use of the HMOX-1 up-regulation treatment, as required by the test protocol. In an abundance of optimism, she advanced to stage two of the project, and her latest medical exam shows that the fetus is in good health. In addition, the observer, Kaliyu, found no indication of contamination or violation of project parameters at the habitation site. Jayanthi left the surface on her own and found passage here, which indicates her compliance with the rules the committee put in place. My recommendation, given the state of her pregnancy and her overall health, is to allow Jayanthi to return to Meru and to allow me to deposit her Meruvin data, which she has brought with her, into the Nivid.>

A ripple passed across the audience's phores.

<Rather than waste the efforts made so far,> Hamsa flashed. <We should complete the remainder of the project as planned so that people can make an informed decision on allowing humans to live on Meru. I have already requested to postpone the general vote that requires this data until we can complete a full project cycle.>

<Thank you, Hamsa,> the committee chair, Nadapar, flashed. <Next, we'll hear from Pushkara, who has requested to comment.>

Jayanthi watched as a very humanlike alloy moved to the apex of the room while Hamsa returned to her side. *So that's Pushkara.* Except for his eyes and webbed feet, he could have passed for human. She thought-retrieved his information from the Nivid. He was older than the compact! She had thought Hamsa old, but he was young compared to Pushkara, who was descended from one of the earliest and wealthiest alloy families, back when those things mattered. Pushkara had built a reputation for planetary stewardship, and he'd gone through multiple full rebirths, most of which had been requested out of a general vote so that he could continue his work. *He's the enemy, but he looks more like the grandfather I never had.*

Pushkara's phores were simple spots along his arms and cheeks, like Vaha's incarn. She felt a pang at the thought of her beloved pilot floating somewhere in the Pamir System, all alone, in hibernation or perhaps dead. *I am so sorry I doubted you. You fought for me, and I wasted your sacrifice. If only I'd known!*

<Given Jayanthi's pregnancy, I must disagree with Hamsa's benign assessment,> Pushkara flashed, his phores neutral. <This project continues to violate its parameters. First the unauthorized womb on the surface, then the pilot who absconded, and now an unexpected gestation of a made child! How much more of this will we tolerate? As I've said from the start, this is the danger of involving human beings in any of our endeavors. If we cannot trust even one of them to respect the limitations of a *preliminary* project, what do you think will happen when we broaden the scope of this exercise? What do you think they'll do if they're allowed to settle on Meru?>

Jayanthi held her arms across her chest, almost hugging herself. Pushkara's anger wasn't directed at her, but her decisions lay at the center of his accusations.

<You're probably too young to remember,> Pushkara continued, <but I witnessed the travesties of Mars and precompact Earth. I saw firsthand the damage humankind will do if left to unfettered consumption. The endless, corrosive Martian storms we have today resulted from the rush to *terraform* that planet. Yes, I used the word. Back then, it was lauded, not cursed. The mass extinction of billions of Earth species, both flora and fauna, can be laid at humanity's feet. When I was a child, the seas had only a few hundred types of fish. Farmland and cities covered eighty percent of the landmass.

<We have expended so much effort to provide human beings a good life on Earth, a balanced one that respects the planet. On Meru, we will have accidents. People will suffer. They will die. That will lead to demands. Living beings have a built-in drive to stay alive and reproduce, and when those beings are citizens of the Constructed Democracy

of Sol, we will have to prioritize their needs over the planet's. Ancient indigenous humans understood the value of nature better than our more recent ancestors. They may have attributed its behavior to gods rather than physics, but the result is the same: they treated all things with respect.>

Nadapar's phores flashed. <While I'm sure the audience is appreciative of your commentary, Pushkara, the committee has many items on today's agenda. You have two hectas to conclude your statement.>

A few flickers of amusement shone among those watching. Jayanthi couldn't help a bit of shock at Nadapar's boldness. She wouldn't have thought that the committee had more power than Pushkara.

<I will conclude with this,> Pushkara flashed. <I propose that we cancel this dangerous endeavor and protect the rights of Meru. In addition, I propose that any data presented by the human, Jayanthi, be voided given her unethical actions. Thank you for your time.>

"Can they do that?" she sent Hamsa.

He nodded.

Her heart sank, but before she could dwell on it, she heard her name. It was her turn to give a statement.

"It's all right," Hamsa sent. "Hold my hand. I'll guide you there."

With Hamsa at her side, she floated to the center of the group and faced the person who had called her up. Nadapar's phores flashed, and her words echoed in Jayanthi's helmet.

<We would like to hear more about your pregnancy. How did it happen, why has it happened, and what do you propose to do with the child once they're born?>

Jayanthi stuck to the same story she'd told everyone—that she designed the embryos on her own and made them using Vaha's womb without zir knowledge. That she had intended her pregnancy to be a test case for Meru, a genetic blueprint for future generations, and she had planned to deliver the child on the planet to demonstrate the effectiveness of her design and its fitness for Meru's environment.

"The fetus is healthy, as am I," she said. She took a deep breath and lifted her chin, meeting Nadapar's gaze. She had to convince the committee to accept Hamsa's proposal, otherwise everything—her voyage to Meru, her violation of tarawan ethics, the piercing loss of Vaha—would have been a colossal waste. "The Second Principle states that all forms of consciousness have equal value in the universe. My *alloy* parents showed me what that truly means. I believe that denying my data entry into the Nivid would be a form of discrimination against humankind. Ending the human trial on Meru with an incomplete experiment would be another form of discrimination. We humans deserve to live anywhere we choose."

Nadapar's phores flashed. <You have the right to believe whatever you like; however, I would disagree. I will point out that your own actions have jeopardized the data you brought from Meru, not our biases, real or imagined. How are we to verify the accuracy of the information you brought? Your current health and that of the fetus are not in question; however, your fitness for Meru very much is. You've carried that data cube across the universe, allowing it into the hands of sovereign megaconstructs. It should have remained with the pilot under contract to the project. Worse, you *made* a child. You—a human!—with no supervision from a tarawan, no approval from a genetic review board, and no permission to use a womb in this capacity. Frankly, I am appalled at your behavior. Thank you for your statement.>

Jayanthi opened her mouth to respond, but she felt Hamsa's hand on her arm and stopped.

"They're conferring by emtalk," he sent to her. "I don't know what they're saying, but the signals among them are dense."

After a few minutes, Nadapar flashed again. <The committee has arrived at its decisions on these matters. First, the data from Jayanthi will remain in the Nivid's vestibule until its integrity can be corroborated by the project pilot, Vaha, or whenever additional data are procured that support its conclusions. Until then, we recommend against any further human trials on the planet Meru. Second, the test subject,

Jayanthi, will be returned to her home on Earth as soon as safe passage can be arranged. We strongly suggest that she consider treatment for Aspiration and Avarice Disorder after the birth of her child.>

Phores flashed around the room at this statement.

<Third,> Nadapar continued, ignoring the audience, <since the project is defunct for the time being, we believe the general vote can be preponed to fifty-eight kaals from today rather than delayed as Hamsa suggested. In the next five kaals, we will create a report summarizing the results from the abbreviated experiment on Meru based on the data brought by the observer. After that, couriers can deliver the report to all systems populated by alloys, give those alloys ten kaals to consider their decision, and then return with votes or proxy designations. We will submit our recommendation to the general elections committee. Any comments or concerns regarding our decision can be filed with us in the next five kaals. Thank you, Hamsa, Pushkara, and Jayanthi, for being here today. We'll now proceed to the second item on our agenda for this meeting.>

Hamsa guided Jayanthi through the chamber toward the exit. Jayanthi felt as if every pair of eyes in the room tracked their path. Phores flashed in a riot of colors, too quickly for her to parse a single word and without any consensus emotion. Then they were outside in the empty passageway.

"You're going to ask them for an appeal, right?" Jayanthi sent. "You've known me my whole life. Can't you vouch for the integrity of my data? Or can't Kaliyu? There must be a way that doesn't involve Vaha!"

Hamsa closed his eyes for a few seconds. When he opened them, she saw anger there for the first time in her life. His phores glowed deep orange, almost red. Jayanthi recalled what Guhaka had said—this was Hamsa's last chance to salvage his efforts to get humans off Earth.

He turned away and towed her through the tunnel. "I did my best to put a positive spin on your actions, but you can't blame the committee for mistrusting you when you behaved in such a human manner. You took advantage of a legal gray area. What did you think would happen? That they'd commend you for your genetic engineering and give you a plaque in the Nivid?" He nodded at her uncomfortable silence. "Yes, I know you well, and that's all the more reason I'm disappointed in you. If only you'd reached out to me before making this child—I know, you didn't trust Pushkara, and neither do I, but we have no proof that he was going to sabotage the project. Without that, your actions look very bad."

"I hadn't intended to carry the damn cube and this baby all over the universe," Jayanthi sent. "I was going to ask Vaha to send the data early, get the approval for stage two, and then reveal the pregnancy." She took a sharp breath as pain shot through her neck and back. "Yes, I wanted to use my design skills, but I became pregnant for *your* amendment. I want it to pass. I did all of this so I would have a chance to spend my life on Meru with my child and so that others would have the same opportunity."

"And I share that desire. Do you have any idea what I have staked on this venture?" Hamsa sent, his phores shifting to peach and yellow.

Jayanthi swallowed hard. She hadn't known, not before meeting Chedi and her residents, but she did now. Would that knowledge have changed her behavior on Meru? Would she have held back on making the embryos if she'd known the risks to Hamsa? Perhaps. But the hypothetical didn't matter now.

"I'm sorry," she sent, wishing a primordial black hole would appear and swallow her up.

Hamsa said nothing more until they reached her door. After the crowds in the meeting room and other passageways, the empty human-habitable limb felt hostile.

"You haven't made it easy for me, but I'll do my best to salvage the situation," Hamsa sent. "Stay put for the rest of today. Do you have some food? Bhojya won't be enough to sustain you while you're pregnant."

"I have some in the pack from Chedi."

"Good. Best that we get you home as soon as possible. I've asked the Primary to send over a medical construct to assist you in the meantime." His glow shifted to sage-colored resignation. "At least the committee agreed to share some of the data with voters. I'll have to look through it and make a case for stage two. If by some miracle the vote goes in favor of the amendment, we might have a chance to salvage this endeavor. I'll find you a ride back to Earth, too."

"I can do that," she offered. "I'll ask Devasu to help me."

Hamsa nodded, his gaze inward and distant. "Thank you. Give my regards to your parents when you see them."

He left her after a brief embrace.

Jayanthi pulled herself up the tunnel and into her room. She held herself near the window and curled into a ball of pain. Over and over, all she could think was: *It's not fair.* She shouldn't have indulged her ambitions at Meru, but at the time and with what she and Vaha had known, it had seemed like the right decision. If Vaha hadn't fought Kaliyu, or if zie had sent her one last message, she would never have left Meru, and the committee wouldn't have been able to question her data.

Her heart ached in concert with her body. With each passing day, the odds of anyone finding Vaha alive diminished. If she could find zir—*alive*—then zie could corroborate the information she'd brought to the Nivid. They could save Hamsa's reputation and the outcome of the vote—the vote that might now take place in just sixty days. Chedi had spent four months looking for Vaha and failed. What chance did Jayanthi have of success in half that time with no pilot at her side, no idea where to look, and everyone bent on sending her back to Earth? It was impossible, just like the dream she and Vaha had shared on Meru.

Little limbs nudged her from the inside of her belly, and she placed a hand over her abdomen. *You're angry, too, aren't you? You deserve a chance to live on the planet where you were conceived, and not only you but others as well. You deserve to roam through space and make discoveries, to bond with constructs, to fall in love with alloys.*

—निराशा

Niraashaa—Hopeless

As local night dimmed the light in her room, Jayanthi received two messages from Earth. Enough time had passed for the meeting to spool there and for the people on her home planet to watch it. She played the one from her parents first.

"Jayanthi, why didn't you tell us you were pregnant?" her mother began. "All those messages on your way to the Primary, and you didn't think we should know?"

"Kundhina," her father murmured, stemming the flow of her mother's words. "It's all right, Jaya. Come home safely. That's the most important thing now. Come back before you get sick or something happens with the fetus. With your sickle cell disease, you've taken such a risk with yourself. We thought we might have lost you once already on Meru. Find a good pilot to bring you here. We can help with that, if you need us to. Just tell us."

"We love you," Kundhina added.

They made no mention of her return to Meru. Did they care so little for Hamsa's amendment, for the future of humankind? *They are alloys after all.* It was an uncharitable thought, but Jayanthi was exhausted, and she couldn't fight her own family as well as the MEC.

The other message came from Mina. *Please don't tell me to return home with my tail between my legs. Not you, too.*

Her beloved friend's face projected itself into her vision.

Mina mimed applause. "So not only did you convince Vaha to let you use zir womb's simulator, you went and got *pregnant* with your own design? I have no idea what you were thinking, but I'm impressed." Their expression turned more serious. "The MEC is so damn transparent. Moving up the vote's date like that—they're obviously in Pushkara's pocket. Sahaya Amritsavar is going to lose her mind over this. Do what you need to, Jaya. Keep trying to change their minds! You're not stuck on Earth yet. We can commiserate in person once you're back, but reply anyway."

Before Jayanthi could formulate a response to either of them, another message arrived, a document from the Tarawan Ethics and Standards Council. They had charged her with the unlicensed use of a womb and the unauthorized making of a child, even though she wasn't an alloy. She would stand trial at an Earth orbital station in one and a half masans, three months after her due date. If found guilty on all counts, they could send her to the Out of Bounds, away from the alloy-supported regions of Earth. In addition, the Child Welfare Committee on Earth had charged her with negligent pregnancy due to illegal space travel. The consequences ranged from mandatory counseling to a live-in monitor to removing the child from her custody. She hadn't expected the CDS to treat her case like that of an alloy's. Exile and living in the Out of Bounds weren't equivalent, but it seemed like the judiciary thought of them as analogous.

The reality of her situation dove down her gullet and churned the bile in her stomach. If she couldn't clear the charges, they might take away her child. As if in response, the nascent being nudged her from inside. The baby was Jayanthi's last and only connection with Vaha.

Jayanthi buried her face in her hands. *Damn you, Vaha! Why didn't you tell me what you were doing? You should've saved yourself! What am I supposed to do now, all alone, a human in this world of alloys? What can I possibly accomplish?*

She leaned her head against the cold window. A pilot hauling a pack three times their size threaded their way through the limbs. She would never see such things again—not the Primary, not Meru or Kumuda, Venus or the vast tapestry of the galaxy.

A pilot.

There was one person who might have a clue about Vaha's fate. Who had witnessed zir departure firsthand. Who owed her some answers.

She slow-blinked and found Devasu's address on the local network. She recorded a message to her guide: "I need to meet with Kaliyu, preferably in person. Can you arrange for me to do that?"

As she sent it, Hamsa requested an emtalk with her. She accepted.

"You've seen the accusations from TESC and the others?" Hamsa asked without preamble.

"Yes."

"Good. First of all, don't panic. The odds of the inquiry finding you guilty as charged are high, but removal of a child from a parent is unusual except in cases of gross negligence or abuse. Some might argue that your space travel counts as such, but I think we can make a case in your favor, especially if you don't leave Earth again. We wait until your child is an adult, and—assuming she doesn't elect to undergo corrective gene therapy—we propose a new project to test her fitness on Meru."

"That's years—decades—away, and in the meantime, we could lose the vote to amend the compact."

"Then we try that again as well, later in your lifetime or your child's. I've been in touch with some of my supporters, and we've come up with a backup strategy if the vote doesn't go our way. Don't fall prey to short-term thinking. It's a trap for humankind. Instead, be grateful that we continue to have alloys on our side."

She pulled away from the glass. "On your side, you mean. Who's taking my side in this? The rules against human ambition are outdated, and I want alloys to acknowledge that. If you can support having us on Meru, why can't you also see that we should get to design and make children? The Directed Mutation Catastrophe is centuries in the past. So is Mars. If I'd been a licensed tarawan, I could have allowed the womb to gestate the child. Instead, I'm going to be trapped on Earth, as is this baby, and made to suffer when there's a far better place for us to live." She stared through the window. "Look at the Primary! Humankind is inherently denied all of this. Why can't we have a little more freedom in our lives?"

"Exactly because of your reaction," he sent. "You're illustrating the reason—impatience, anger, desire, ambition. Alloys struggle with these qualities, too, but we have ways to regulate ourselves. This is why most of us spend our lives in stasis and put very little burden on the universe. Humans aren't capable of that. By your biological nature, you need to consume material goods to survive, and you have a deep-seated instinct for accrual. We've worked hard to help you overcome that. How would we control this additional freedom granted to you? Yes, I trust that you, Jayanthi, would make ethically correct and healthy choices as a tarawan, but if we opened the field to all humans? Not a chance. We cannot legally remake you the way we do with failed alloy designs. What about the suffering of human children? It's too great a risk to allow."

"Then change the laws! Rewrite the damn compact. It's hundreds of years old. Maybe that doesn't matter when you measure a lifetime in centuries, but it does for humans, and we're citizens of the CDS, too."

"What do you think I'm trying to do?" he sent. "Change takes time, and I'm sorry, but one human life span might not be enough. Think of your child, and her children, and their children. You've done a lot for them already. We've planted the seeds of opportunity on Meru. The first batch might not sprout, but others will lie dormant in the soil, and if we continue to nurture them, one day they will grow."

Hamsa's words reminded Jayanthi of her own thoughts back on the planet. That her design could form the foundations of a new society of hybrids. That this child was the first of many stepping-stones, each lasting an entire generation. No one had taken a close look at her design yet, but if this baby emerged into the universe with working chromatophores, they would, and if Hamsa was right, that dream could still come to fruition.

She took a deep breath and sent, "All right. I'll play the long game."

"As for your immediate future, I've found a pilot who runs a shuttle service who can take you home. They haven't carried a human passenger in a while, but they're in Earth orbit now and will get a thorough checkup before coming here. It should take less than a week for them to arrive. In the meantime, get some rest and take care of your health."

"Thank you," she said and tried to mean it.

She wished she could pace around her room. Flinging herself from one handhold to the next did not have the same effect. How had her life gone up and down so much in less than a year? From all the promise she'd felt after meeting Vaha and their time together on Meru to facing a lifetime stuck on Earth. She had to make sure that she didn't lose custody of her child, too.

She placed a hand over her gently rounded abdomen. *I hope you're well in there and that after you come out, you grow up and shatter the barriers that alloys and our ancestors have built.* She tried to take solace in the idea that she'd leave behind a legacy, but then she thought of Chedi, the wonders she'd seen on her journey through the Pamir System. It pained her that she'd never have experiences like that again.

Jayanthi played with Sunanda's ring. She could go rogue like Raya, be free of alloys and their constraints. She could have her baby in the megaconstruct's world, raise her there, and return her to Earth after she became an adult. That way, Hamsa could still follow through with his backup plan.

It was a tempting idea.

But it would mean giving up on her parents, her friends, and all the human beings on her home planet. She'd have to live as a fugitive. No, she couldn't bring herself to do that, not yet, not until she'd exhausted every other option. Not until she knew for certain that Vaha was gone forever.

The room construct woke Jayanthi from a deep sleep. "Devasu is at the door. May I let her in?"

"Yes."

The alloy floated in with an apologetic smile. "I hope it's not too late for you, but Kaliyu said zie plans to leave soon. Zie can meet you anytime in the next fifteen kilas. Would you still like to go? I decided to come in person in case you said yes."

Jayanthi blinked and tried to shake the sleep from her head. "I would like to meet zir."

She held out a hand for Devasu to lead her. The alloy didn't take it.

"I'm afraid you'll have to wear your spacesuit and helmet. There's no air where Kaliyu is berthed."

"Right, sorry. I forgot about that."

A few minutes later, they were on their way. At the first hub, they took a different direction than before.

"We're heading away from the Nivid's housing this time," Devasu sent via emtalk, "into an older section of the Primary. These limbs mostly serve material interests—shipping and receiving of the goods we need to live here, as well as parts that we need to maintain the knowledge and data archives."

Devasu pointed out various features as they moved through passageways of increasing size. Less humanoid alloys floated by, often towing containers or construction materials. These people reminded her of the alloys serving on Earth. They didn't have legs. Many had rounded bodies like manatees or hippos, built for strength. Some had protective carapaces around their torsos in whorls, like giant snail shells.

Finally, they turned down one of the massive limbs, and shortly after, they ducked into a side tunnel and stopped near a round door. It spanned a diameter four times that of Jayanthi's height. Adjacent to the door was a transparent cupola that jutted outward. Devasu drew them into the space so that they could see outside. A blue-gray alloy with rectangular solar wings floated in the scaffolding that extended from the door. Vaha had different coloring, but this person was equally massive and unmistakably a pilot.

None of this would be happening if Vaha hadn't disappeared. *Where are you? Are you out there somewhere, alive and adrift? Will I ever see you again?*

As Devasu's and Kaliyu's phores flashed in silent conversation, Jayanthi spotted Vaha's womb tethered to the berth. It gave her an idea. A completely absurd, audacious idea. And the one person who could help her carry it out was right in front of her.

—वैधुर्य

Vaidhurya—Desperation

Kaliyu didn't know how the universe had so conspired against zir, but somehow it brought Vaha's human to zir at the worst possible moment. Zie had watched the MEC meeting with trepidation and hadn't relaxed until after the human settlement agenda item. No one brought forth evidence of the contaminant on the surface, and Pushkara made his arguments against Hamsa's latest proposal without involving Kaliyu's name. Relief had offset fear and left behind only bitterness, like the aftertaste of an overheated bhojya.

Zie had been so wrong about everyone in zir life. Zir maker wasn't a victim of human interference. Zir best friend was probably dead. And the politician who'd hired zir in the name of planetary ethics had set zir up to violate those very principles. Kaliyu had prepared to leave the Nivid and head out to meet zir racing team. Zie wanted nothing more than to put all thoughts of Meru behind zir. Instead, zie faced Vaha's little human.

She stood next to the door of zir berth, her face obscured by the reflective surface of her helmet. She had one tiny hand pressed against the glass and the other gripping an attractive young alloy who floated beside her.

The human greeted zir via emtalk. "Thank you for seeing me, Kaliyu. I know you must be wondering why I'm here. I heard what

Pushkara told the MEC about the events at Meru. Is that the truth? Vaha attacked you? I only knew zir for a few months, but zie had never once acted violently. What happened? Why did you leave without telling me? Is there some way we can speak privately?"

The alloy beside her flashed a question at Kaliyu. <Can you bring Jayanthi aboard into your human chamber? Is it functional?>

The thought of allowing a human inside of zirself filled Kaliyu with disgust. She was the reason Vaha had lost zir vent-spawned mind at Meru, and she was the reason Kaliyu had implicated zirself in a potential crime. Yet Vaha had cared for her. As unfathomable as it was, zir friend had claimed to love this creature. Kaliyu owed her nothing, but after Pushkara's betrayal, zie felt zie might owe Vaha an apology. It was Kaliyu's insistence on ending the Meru project that had led to their fight. Zir best friend and zir maker both loved human beings. What if they knew something zie didn't?

<She can come in,> Kaliyu replied in phoric. <I'm not sure if the air supply is still good, but she can rely on her suit if necessary.>

Zie took an empty tube hanging in the berth and fitted one end over zir mouth and the other across the door. It swung open, and zie unsealed zir lips to allow the human inside. Zie hadn't carried a passenger—alloy or human—since basic training at Nishadas, and her presence tickled zir mouth.

Kaliyu activated zir internal bioluminescence to guide the human to the chamber and breathed air into it. Zie felt the human settle against one interior wall.

"Try setting your suit to external air," zie instructed. "Is it good?"

After a hectas, she replied. "It's good. Thank you. Now, tell me what happened at Meru, please."

"Everything I told Pushkara was true," Kaliyu sent. "But there's a little more to the story." Zie could tell this human the whole truth. No one would believe her, and even if they did, it wouldn't matter. None of it mattered anymore.

Zie described the events at Meru: how zie and Vaha were flying together, Vaha showing off, the terrible accident, the splint, and then, after they'd returned to orbit and Vaha had regained consciousness, the fight. With clenched vents, Kaliyu confessed the moment when zie ripped off Vaha's splint and then the worst part: "Vaha told me zir bladders were empty and then threatened to fight me off if I tried to bring zir back, but zie was in more pain than I was. I could have overpowered zir, flown zir back . . . Instead, I let zir go. I was angry. And hurt. And I let zir drift away."

The confession, even to a human, relieved a pressure that Kaliyu hadn't realized zie'd held. The human sent nothing for a long time.

"I should have gone after zir," Kaliyu sent. "When I returned to pack up your site, after I realized you were gone, I tried to search for Vaha, but I found no sign of zir."

"I believe you," she sent. "I asked Chedi—the construct who brought me here—to look for Vaha. She couldn't find zir, either."

Kaliyu's vents relaxed a little. Zie hadn't been the only one to search for Vaha and fail. But where had zir friend disappeared to so thoroughly? *Zie must be dead, perhaps crashed into an asteroid or one of the moons.*

"Do you have a way of knowing Vaha's exact trajectory?" the human asked. "Then we could trace zir path and find zir, especially if zie had no way to change course."

"That's what I thought, too." The little human was clever. Zie recalled thinking that back at Meru. "I flew as fast as I could in that direction for kaals, spiraling around in case zie redirected, but I found no sign of zir. Zir speed wasn't that high relative to Meru's. I can't imagine zie could have gone far, but if zie had drawn water in from zir cells, zie could have vented and changed course."

"Maybe a construct picked zir up, like they did with me?"

"Not many constructs can carry a pilot, though I suppose they could tow one. Where would they have taken zir? And why not return to Meru?"

"I don't know." There was a pause, and then: "I have an idea for something we can try."

<Is everything all right?> flashed Devasu from inside the Primary.

<Fine, I think,> Kaliyu replied. <We're still talking.>

The human still hadn't sent anything, so Kaliyu prompted her. "What's your idea?"

"Here's what I'm thinking. If we can go back to Meru, you can put a message in the general spool, an announcement that I'm ready to head back to Earth. Add that I need a pilot who can host a human. Maybe we can even say that we're looking for Vaha specifically. If someone is carrying zir, perhaps they'll hear our message and bring zir back."

Kaliyu's phores flickered in disbelieving amusement. "Do you have any idea how many layers of trouble we'd cause by doing something like that? I have no authorization to carry you back to Meru."

"I'm in plenty of trouble already," she sent. Zie could almost feel her indifference. "What's a little more if it means we can save Vaha? Also . . ." She hesitated again.

"There's more?"

"That's Vaha's womb you have, right?"

"Yes."

"Good. Zie authorized me to operate it, so I put Vaha's incarn on life support in there. We should bring it with us, in case we do get Vaha back."

Clever indeed. Maybe zir maker had been right. Maybe alloys had spent too long looking down on humans, not giving enough credit to their ability to change. Or maybe Vaha had it right, and this one was special.

If zie followed through with the human's plan, Kaliyu would lose the respect zie had earned from Pushkara and his supporters. Zie could see zir maker's words as if they flashed in front of zir. *That* my child *would align with Pushkara—you can take his tainted recommendation and go! I'd choose being a garbage-eating* weller *over abandoning a friend any day.*

What did zie have to lose, really? The racing team wouldn't care if zie took another round trip to Meru.

"If your plan works," zie sent, "and we find Vaha and restore zir incarn to zir body, then your findings from Meru will pass into the Nivid. Is that your real motive? I gave you my truth. What's yours?"

Sweat trickled down Jayanthi's back in spite of the enviro-suit's fans. Her heart hadn't stopped pounding since she'd entered Kaliyu's body, and the fetal inhabitant in her own belly kept doing backflips. Trickles of fire ran from her neck to her limbs.

Just confess your stupidity to Kaliyu, she told herself. *If the truth helps to save Vaha, then you can't spare yourself.*

"I love zir," she answered. "Is that enough of a truth? I know it sounds ridiculous. After our time together on Meru, we would have had separate lives, but I love Vaha—and not just zir incarn, all of zir. Yes, getting zir back would let us push my data into the Nivid, but more importantly, it would help Vaha. Zie would have zir name in the Nivid, and zie could face zir maker proudly, though I don't know why zie still wants to please Veera."

"I told Vaha so many times to forget zir maker," Kaliyu sent. "Veera was a real mudha. What kind of person leaves zir child behind and tells zir it's because zie's a disappointment?"

"A terrible one," Jayanthi agreed, happy to find some common ground with Kaliyu. Kaliyu didn't hate Vaha, as far as she could tell. Zie seemed to want to find and rescue zir friend as much as she did.

There was a long pause. "I think Vaha loved you, too, as strange as that sounds."

She wasn't sure whether to feel happy or insulted. "So, will you help me?"

Jayanthi held her breath as she waited for Kaliyu's answer. She had no idea how much worse her punishment would be for running from the Primary back to Meru, but she had passed the point of caring. In the world of space travel, the alloys had the advantage, and the only way she could help Vaha and her fellow human beings was with a pilot on her side. She knew none except Kaliyu. If zie rejected her, she'd have nowhere to go but Earth.

Her hands clenched. *Please, please say yes.*

"All right," Kaliyu said.

She exhaled.

"I'm ready to go, but I imagine you'll need some time to prepare?"

"I don't have much with me," she said. "I can be back here quickly."

"I brought Vaha's packs from Meru, too. Do you need anything from them?"

"Yes! There's food and medicine in there that I'll need. Is there any way I can access the womb while we travel? I might need medical attention along the way."

Four months of travel time. Chedi had given Jayanthi her last blood exchange, and she would need another, as well as hydration and nutrition. By the Nivid! She'd have to deliver the baby during their voyage. Where would she give birth? On Meru? In space? If they found Vaha, zir incarn could help her. If not . . . well, she wouldn't be the first human to give birth alone. She couldn't help but shudder at the thought.

Greatness finds those who work without fear. She'd already endured so much more than she'd ever imagined. She would find a way to survive the rest.

"It's unorthodox, but the womb might be safer than my chamber," Kaliyu sent. "I can bring a transit tube along in case you need to move back and forth. Go get your things. I'll collect the womb and the packs as we're leaving. If I do it any sooner, it will attract attention."

Jayanthi hauled herself along Kaliyu's gullet with ease, boosting her speed with alternating handholds, almost like swimming. She could understand why her alloy cousins opted for tails and vents.

Devasu smiled as Jayanthi emerged into the Primary.

"Did you have a good conversation?" her guide asked.

"Very much so," Jayanthi replied.

It occurred to her that she would need Devasu's help to return to Kaliyu and to keep their departure secret long enough for them to get a good head start. She didn't know how fast Kaliyu could travel, but once Hamsa, Pushkara, and others realized where she'd gone, they could send someone to retrieve her.

The activity in the tunnels had already slowed, with local time on the Primary shifting toward rest. They moved swiftly back to the human-habitable limb.

"Devasu, you're fond of humans, right?"

"Generally speaking, yes, and of you in particular, definitely. Why?"

They floated toward the side tunnel to Jayanthi's room. She recognized it by the specific worn patches of paint where the walls bent.

"I need your help. I have to get back to Kaliyu in a few kilas."

"Sure, that's what I'm here for," Devasu said.

"You can't tell anyone about it, though."

The alloy's phores glowed with excitement. "A secret meeting? Like in the latest chapter of *Charana and Jaiva*, only I suppose you wouldn't have a romantic tryst with Kaliyu."

"No, of course not." Jayanthi forced a smile. *Alloys and humans can't be lovers, right?*

Devasu cocked her head in a birdlike fashion and examined Jayanthi's face. "You're not telling me something."

"I'll explain more when we're on our way back to Kaliyu," Jayanthi promised. "Meet me here in three kilas?"

Devasu agreed and left, her expression more curious than suspicious. Jayanthi entered her room and gathered the few items she'd unpacked. She left instructions with the Primary construct to deliver a text message to Hamsa when he next arrived at her room: "I'm sorry to do this, but I can't see a better choice. I'm going to look for Vaha and bring zir back if I can. You asked me to wait patiently on Earth until my child is grown, but I am only human. I have one life to live, and I will not spend the next two decades doing nothing."

She scheduled a similar message to her parents, to be delivered after Hamsa retrieved his. To Mina, she wrote: "My dearest friend, you'll have to wait a little longer before I can tell you all about my adventures in person. I hope you'll forgive me. I can't risk disclosing any of the details, but trust me that I'm doing this for the right reasons, for ones that Amritsavar would approve of. Give my regards to the other SHWAs. Their support and yours have lent me the strength to do what I must."

And if her plan failed, if Vaha didn't return to Meru after Kaliyu broadcast her message, she'd ask Kaliyu to take her to Chedi. After hearing the MEC's verdict, Jayanthi had little faith that the general alloy population would pass Hamsa's amendment. She would rather abandon her friends and family than confine her child to Earth.

—

An hour later, Jayanthi once again flew with Devasu's help to Kaliyu's berth. This time she had her pack slung on her back, her suit fully charged, and her emergency air tanks filled. Her alloy guide had raised her hairless brows at Jayanthi's pack, but she was circumspect enough to wait until Jayanthi explained.

"I don't know how much you like humans," Jayanthi told her, "but if you want to help us, the best thing you can do right now is tell no one what's about to happen."

The bioluminescent rings in the corridors glowed with a fraction of the light they had emitted during local daytime. They passed only a few people as they moved through the first hub.

"And what exactly is about to happen?" Devasu said.

"You mentioned that scene in *Charana and Jaiva*."

The alloy nodded.

"Remember when Charana had to sneak away on her construct so she could meet Jaiva under the bodhi tree?"

Understanding grew on Devasu's face, then dissolved into confusion. "You and Kaliyu are like—"

"No, no," Jayanthi interjected. *Though I am like that with Vaha.* "Let's say Kaliyu is more like my construct in this case. I need to go somewhere that's not Earth, and zie is willing to take me there in secret."

"This is so exciting! Won't you tell me where? Are you meeting a rogue human somewhere nearby? Oh! Are you returning to Chedi? I promise I won't give you away."

Jayanthi shook her head. "The less I tell you, the better. I won't ask you to lie for me, just stall for time, please. When Hamsa asks, tell him the truth—that you dropped me off with Kaliyu and that's all you know."

"Oh, well, I suppose it's for the best, but I wish you could tell me more!"

"If I succeed—and probably even if I don't—you'll find out."

Outside the door to Kaliyu's berth, Jayanthi pressed her palms together in front of her heart and bowed her head. "Thank you for all your help."

Devasu flicked her tail and mirrored Jayanthi's gesture. "Thank you for giving me your company. I hope we meet again."

With that, Jayanthi made her exit, this time into Vaha's womb. At the sight of the familiar interior, her stomach clenched. *Don't cry!* But she couldn't stop the tears from springing to her eyes. She removed her helmet and suit, then used her sleeve to blot them away. On the other side of the delivery valve lay Vaha's incarn. *Please be somewhere in the Pamir System. Please come back to me . . . to us.*

She stowed her pack and strapped into the webbing, then opened an emtalk channel to Kaliyu. "I'm ready. Do you think they'll send someone after us when they know I've gone with you?"

"They might try, but I'm faster and stronger than most pilots when it comes to microgravity flight. I doubt there are other racing types here. The womb will make things a little more awkward than usual, but I can sustain two gees for most of the way to heliopause if you can. We were told in school that humans could handle that kind of acceleration for an entire masan if necessary."

"I'm not sure because of the baby," she said. "I'll check with the Nivid while I can access it."

A quick search of the knowledge archive didn't add much to Kaliyu's assessment. In the precompact days, around the second century HE, people had done more extensive testing of human physiology, and it continued until the compact was signed three hundred years later, in 100 AE. After that, humans had rapidly disengaged from space travel. No one had the motivation or opportunity to continue that kind of research, which meant they knew little about what their bodies could tolerate with present-day capabilities.

She worried about the health of the fetus growing inside her, but according to some really old information, the baby was cushioned by so much fluid, she would tolerate the acceleration better than Jayanthi.

"How long will you accelerate at two gees?" she asked Kaliyu.

Her body pressed into the side of the womb as they began to move.

"Twelve and a half kaals to heliopause here, and a similar number in the Pamir System. I'll take very short breaks along the way to nap."

She did the arithmetic in her head. That was half the time Vaha had taken. If they stayed at Meru for a week, the round trip back to the Primary would take about nine weeks. She'd be into the start of her third trimester of pregnancy. No need to fret about giving birth on her own.

Would a week at Meru be enough? Their message would have to get carried through the system. Would Vaha receive it? If someone had picked zir up, they could have carried zir anywhere. A megaconstruct like Chedi could reality transit while holding a pilot of Vaha's size inside themself. Had she set herself on a fool's errand? *But Kaliyu wouldn't agree if zie thought we had no chance. This is my last attempt,* she promised herself. *If this fails, I'll focus on my child and her future.*

"We're clear of the Primary," Kaliyu said. "Are you secure?"

Jayanthi pressed a protective hand to her abdomen and felt a little push in return.

"Yes," she said. "Let's go."

—सत्य

Sathya—Truth

One and a half masans had passed since Nakis arrived at Kumuda. Zir MG flight skills hadn't progressed much after that day with the brace powered down. Zie could follow the shallower thamity gradients and stay on course, but zir maneuverability hadn't improved beyond that. If zie wanted to travel across a system at more than a crawl, zie would need the help of another pilot or a megaconstruct. Returning to Sol on zir own had turned into a dream rather than a goal, so zie had set it aside and thrown zir energy into helping Rithu with his work. Nakis had adjusted zir hormones, and after the awkwardness between them faded, zie had spent less and less effort trying to improve zir flight skills.

They passed their leisure time with entertainment, especially a show called *Across the Orbit*, which they both loved. The character Avarya was Nakis's favorite. Zie related to her feelings of inadequacy as a tarawan. Being a comedy, the show didn't take it seriously when she made mistakes, and Nakis tried to internalize the attitude about zir own circumstances. Avarya had a different disability than zir own, but no one in the real alloy world would hold that against her. Nakis was being unfairly hard on zirself, as Rithu frequently reminded zir.

Between the regular courier drops and Rithu's supply runs, they always had several spools' worth of news, games, and fictions. Nakis skimmed the headlines, but zie never found anything of interest. The items mostly focused on projects that had concluded or were starting up in the Pamir System, as well as brief notes about Nivid deposits, politics, and exploration. Rithu had tried talking to zir about the upcoming vote for human settlement on Meru, but Nakis didn't find the topic particularly compelling.

At some point, Nakis had settled into this new life and found zirself quite comfortable at Kumuda. Rithu made an excellent and supportive coach, much better than zir maker had been. They had interesting work with Nivid potential, and after Rithu's contract ended, they could return to the Solar System together. Nakis had to wait only another four varshas or so—not much time really, especially when zie had such a satisfying way to spend it.

They had just returned from a particularly fruitful experiment with Kumuda's thermals when they found that a fresh data drop had spooled into their platform's receiver. It included an urgent system-wide message.

Rithu thought-shared the playback with Nakis. It began with a still image of a familiar human face, followed by text: "My name is Jayanthi, and I'm the human subject of an experiment on Meru. I was brought here by a pilot named Vaha who went missing approximately one and a half masans ago, and I need zir to carry me back to Earth. If you know of Vaha's whereabouts, or if you are a pilot with a working human-habitable chamber, please contact the following Meruvin orbital platform."

At the end was an address and another still image: zir own face with the name Vaha attached to it.

Out of the corner of zir eye, zie caught Rithu's glow of surprise.

<That's you!> he flashed. <Your original name is Vaha.>

<I . . . I guess it is. It doesn't mean anything to me.>

<Do you remember this Jayanthi person?>

<I recognize her face from the clip in my extended memories, the one I played for you a while back. I guess I brought her here, to Meru.>

Rithu's gaze bored into Nakis's. <You can't fly her back to Sol. If you're curious and want to meet her anyway, I'll help you get to Meru, but you can choose not to respond. What would you like to do?>

After that, he said nothing. Rithu would wait patiently for an answer, just as he had waited all these months for Nakis to share anything about zir memories. He had given Nakis the same rationale for ignoring the message that zie had told zirself. It would be so easy to say that zie wanted to stay at Kumuda, to leave the past where it belonged and continue moving forward as Nakis.

But every time zie heard the name *Jayanthi*, it elicited a strong reaction from zir body. Her face kept intruding into zir thoughts, sometimes in zir dreams. She had been important to zir, and yet zie couldn't figure it out. Why had a human left such a strong impression? Zie had no guarantee that she would have an answer to that question. Zie had fled Meru—had *injured* another pilot. Going back there, talking to her, might confirm zir worst suspicions about zirself, but it might also free zir of whatever guilt zir subconscious carried. Perhaps then zir body wouldn't war with itself over its attraction to Rithu.

Vaha.

Jayanthi.

The thought of seeing her again unlocked inexplicable feelings. Zie wanted to shelter her, protect her. With that came a sense of comfort. She belonged with zir, and zie with her. *Why?*

The only way to find out was to have courage, to face zir insecurities head-on and push through them. Zie had developed more than scars during zir stay with Rithu. Zie had calluses. Thanks to Rithu's unwavering acceptance of Nakis's limitations, and his faith in zir eventual competence, Nakis had learned to believe that zir life had value. If zie went to Meru, no matter what zie learned about zirself, zie had to remember that. Zie couldn't repay Rithu by abandoning him.

<I think I want to go,> Nakis flashed, <and then return here with you. I'd like to get more answers about my identity, and I'm hoping to find them at Meru. Is that okay?>

Rithu glowed with gentle amusement. <Of course. I'm surprised you had to think about it for that long. You have people looking for you and a human in need of your services. Both of them must hold some keys to your past. I didn't expect that you would stay.> Sadness tinted his phores. <I admit that out of pure selfishness, I don't want to lose your company, but in case you decide to come back, I'll tow you there.>

<I'm tired from today's sample run. Let's leave after some sleep.> Nakis reached a hand through zir berth's framework and gave Rithu's shoulder a gentle squeeze. <Don't worry. Even if I am still under some kind of contract, they can't hold me to it, not with the condition of my tail. I'm useless as a microgravity pilot now. We'll go to Meru and get some closure, that's all. I can't think of anything a human could say that would keep me from you and Kumuda.>

After about seven hours of sleep, Nakis tethered zirself to Rithu, and they left. Rithu proved his worth as a racer. He rested for about a third of their travel time, but otherwise he averaged an acceleration of nearly two and a half gees. Nakis used every bit of concentration, strength, and thamity sense to hold on and remain stable while Rithu towed zir. Zie marveled at how quickly Rithu could choose the right path to traverse the gradients around them. He carefully picked lines that wouldn't challenge Nakis too much in spite of their steepness, and yet he made it look effortless.

In four and a half days, they covered all six hundred and fifty million kilometers from Kumuda to Meru. The sight of the planet tickled something in Nakis's memory. Here and there, small padhrans of alloys reflected Pamir's light as they orbited the blue-and-ochre globe. The contours of the landmasses felt familiar but unrecognizable, like an itch zie couldn't reach.

Zie hooked into the local network around Meru, which was much more extensive than the one at Kumuda, and found the location from the message.

"I'm going to untether myself," zie sent to Rithu via emtalk.

Zir friend spooled the harness against his waist pouch and waited for Nakis to come alongside him. They vented toward and around the planet. Nakis spotted black and silver wings with a familiar contour—zir friend from school! Zir friend was next to an observation station that pinged in Nakis's organic memory as soon as zie laid eyes on it. Tethered to it was an oblong womb—*that's mine!* How had zie forgotten about that?

Forcing a glow of pleasure, Nakis approached zir friend with a tentative smile. <Forgive me,> zie flashed, <but I've forgotten your name.>

The pilot's eyes went wide, and zir phores paled. <Vaha—you came! You got our message!> Zie glowed chartreuse with concern. <My name—it's Kaliyu. Are you all right? Did you undergo a rebirth? What else have you forgotten?>

<Give zir a chance to answer,> Rithu flashed, glowing faintly with irritation as zie floated next to Nakis.

Kaliyu! That was the name of the person Nakis had attacked at Meru, according to that old news item. But if Kaliyu were here and looking for Vaha, then zie couldn't be upset about the fight. Had there been some extenuating circumstance?

Nakis rested a hand on Rithu's arm. Zie had so many questions for Kaliyu, but zie had to give zir own answers first. Where to begin? <I'm not sure what happened to me, but I haven't had a rebirth that I'm aware of. I do have a bad tail and wing. We suspect that I was exposed to a large coronal mass ejection about one and a half masans ago.>

<The storm!> Kaliyu flashed. <I was afraid of that. You had no pack and no shelter. By the Nivid! I'm glad you're alive.>

<I lost most of my memories at that time. Karkothaka, the ancient construct, gave me a tow to Kumuda, where I've been ever since. I remember some of my childhood and bits and pieces of my later life, but I've forgotten a lot of names. I recognize you, though. We went to school together.>

<Yes, at Nishadas. And who is—> Kaliyu stopped and stared at Rithu. <Gravity take me! Are you—is it really you? The Royal?>

The racer smiled. <Yes. You must be Nak—Vaha's friend from piloting school.>

<I'm going to join your old team, The Majestics. I'm honored to meet you,> Kaliyu flashed, pressing zir palms together in front of zir heart.

<Any friend of—Vaha's is a friend of mine,> Rithu flashed. He returned the greeting, but his phores stayed neutral.

Nakis suspected that in spite of zir assurances, Rithu was still worried that zie wouldn't come back to Kumuda with him. *Only one way to put that to rest.*

<I need your help, Kaliyu,> Nakis began. <I can't sense thamity with my lower half anymore, so I'm no good as an MG pilot. I saw the emergency broadcast. I can't fly Jayanthi back to Sol. I'm trying to figure out what my situation was and whether I'm free to stay here. Until we received her message, I had no idea why I was in this system. Do you know anything about what I did to myself? Will I need to go back to Sol to close out a contract? Is anyone there looking for me?>

Kaliyu glowed with a mix of bitterness and amusement. <I know some of it, yes. I witnessed your departure from Meru firsthand. You . . . you left Meru with your wing and tail broken from a bad landing on the planet. Your bladders were empty, and you were badly dehydrated from the effort it took us to get you back into orbit. And then . . . we fought over the fate of the project—the human-settlement trial that Jayanthi was here for. You pushed me away and wouldn't let me bring you back. Does any of that flash a light on your memories?>

Pamir moved behind the planet and plunged them into shadow. Nakis opened zir inner lids and tried to absorb Kaliyu's words. Why had zir friend hesitated in the telling? What had they fought about? Zie could recall Kaliyu having a hot temper at Nishadas, but they'd never stayed angry with each other for long. No matter how hard Nakis tried to remember zir departure from Meru, zie couldn't. Zie shook zir head.

<Nothing. Sorry,> zie flashed.

<Do you remember your incarn?> Kaliyu flashed.

Nakis let the surprise show in zir phores. <Not at all!>

<Your womb has it in a state of suspension. Perhaps you should revive it and reintegrate yourself.>

Did zie want to know? Zie glanced at Rithu. The old racer looked expectantly at Nakis as if to indicate that the choice was obvious. They needed the truth before they could move into the future together.

<Yes,> Nakis flashed. <That's a good idea.>

Nakis followed the tether to the womb, which hung against the star-bright background like an oval black hole. Rithu's and Kaliyu's eyes tracked zir every move. Zie placed a finger on the lock, then opened an emchannel to the womb's constructed mind. It confirmed the presence of zir incarn and advised that it would take five kilas to bring it back to functional consciousness.

Nakis turned back to zir friends. <May I borrow one of the transfer tubes from the platform?>

<Of course,> Kaliyu flashed. <Take anything you need.>

Nakis extracted one and held it as zie waited for the womb to ready zir incarn. How could zie have no recollection of making it? What would the integrated memories reveal about zir past? Rithu's phores stayed carefully neutral. The racer must have been as nervous as zie was about what they would discover next, but zie had all the courage zie'd gained from the months at Kumuda. Whatever came next, zie could face it as long as Rithu was at zir side.

Jayanthi had spent most of the journey to Meru in the womb. She'd needed its abilities. Between the rapid growth of the baby and the high acceleration, her sickled cells had caused her frequent pain. The womb's construct had spent most of the journey at her side. It had kept her hydrated and massaged her limbs. At one point, her body had decided to go into labor—terrifyingly early—and the womb had given her medication to prevent it from progressing. After they'd settled into orbit, Kaliyu had detached the womb from zirself and then asked her to move back into zir body. The pilot had felt that she was safer there in case of structural emergency.

She was reading about the differences between womb delivery and human birth when she got a request from Kaliyu to thought-share zir vision.

"Vaha is here," zie sent via emtalk.

Her heart instantly picked up its pace. She closed the text and watched through Kaliyu's eyes as Vaha's glorious blue-black form floated before them. Zie was so thin! One wing hung at an awkward-looking angle, and a metal brace enclosed zir tail. *What happened to you?* She wanted to reach out and hold zir, as impossible as that would be. *Everything will be okay now.* She blotted at the bubble of tears that accumulated over her eyes. This time, she didn't blame the hormones. They had found Vaha! Her plan had worked! A knot that she'd carried in her chest ever since she left Meru finally loosened itself. Now all they needed was to get back to the Solar System and the Primary Nivid.

Another alloy floated beside Vaha. The three of them conversed in phoric, too fast and complex for her limited understanding. She tried to open an emtalk with Vaha, but their previous emchannel was marked invalid, and zir current access was set to private.

In frustration, she sent to Kaliyu instead. "What's happening?"

"Please wait," zie replied.

She did, though every fiber of her thrummed with impatience. She hugged herself and was rewarded with a swift kick to her arm. Her bones had shifted and spread to accommodate her growing passenger. Microgravity had brought some relief to her aching back and hips.

Your other parent is here now, little one. You'll get to meet zir after you're born . . . someday.

Motion caught her attention, and she watched as Vaha made zir way to the womb.

"I can't hold two conversations at the same time," Kaliyu sent. "Vaha says that zie has lost most of zir extended memories and suffers from severe amnesia as well. Zie remembers nothing about what happened at Meru."

"Nothing? Is it permanent?" she asked, aghast.

"I don't know. Both zir extended and organic memories were compromised while zie was adrift. This other alloy sheltered zir and has been helping zir since zie was found. Now Vaha's trying to resurrect zir incarn. We're hoping the incarn's memories are intact and that they can reintegrate, though they've been apart for so long. I have no idea if it'll work."

The mental whiplash stunned her into silence. If Vaha didn't remember anything, then she had lost zir all over again. Not only would zie be unable to corroborate the data from Meru, but zie would have also forgotten everything about her. About the baby.

She wanted to cry. She did cry. Again.

Of all the possible scenarios, she had never imagined that finding Vaha wouldn't be enough.

"Jayanthi?"

"I'm here," she sent. She took several long, deep breaths until she stopped shaking. "Can I—can I talk to Vaha? Can you ask zir to open an emchannel with me, or if zie's willing, I can enter zir?"

"I'll ask."

What would she say to Vaha if zie agreed to have her? *Please remember me? I'm carrying your baby? I love you?* None of that would matter if zie had no recollection of who she was or what they meant to each other.

Jayanthi didn't allow herself to hope a second time. How long had Vaha's incarn lain in the vestibule as a corpse before she took it to the womb? She didn't know exactly when the incarn had lost its connection to Vaha's true body, but it must have been hours before she realized it. How much would the brain have degraded in that time? A reckless despair seized her, and she didn't care how Vaha responded. She had to be with zir, even if it was only to say goodbye.

"Jayanthi?"

"Yes?"

"We may need your help getting the incarn safely into Vaha. Zie will have to connect it to zir internal umbilical to integrate with it. That means transferring it from the womb. We're not sure if the incarn will be ambulatory. If you're willing—"

"Of course!"

"Then I suggest you eat and drink and make sure your suit is charged up. I'll transfer you to the womb in three kilas."

Forty-five minutes. Plenty of time to do as Kaliyu recommended. She didn't think she could eat, but she forced herself to drink some salty bhojya, the only thing her tongue and stomach would tolerate.

In the month since they'd left the Primary, the little fetus growing in her own womb had decided that a drink meant it was time to wake up and play. She danced inside Jayanthi as if anticipating their impending departure. Jayanthi rested a hand against her abdomen and took comfort in the activity inside. If only she could share the joy with Vaha.

No—she couldn't allow herself to go down that path. This was not her Vaha, not yet, perhaps not ever again. Whatever they'd had between them before was dead. She had to remember that. All the tears she had shed for zir while she was on Chedi had meaning after all. She didn't need to let her heart break a second time.

It did anyway.

—संयोजन

Samyojana—Integration

Vaha opened zir eyes to Jayanthi's face hovering over zirs. The gentle pink glow of the womb surrounded them. Zie turned zir head and realized that zir body floated—they were in microgravity. Recollection trickled in: leaving Jayanthi so zie could exercise zir true body. The atmo maneuvers with Kaliyu . . . aerobatics . . . and then nothing. Zie tried to turn and discovered that zir limbs didn't want to move.

"What happened?" Zir voice sounded hoarse in zir own ears. "Why am I in here? Why are we in space?"

"Do you know who I am?"

Zie stared at her until zie realized she meant the question seriously. "Of course. You're Jayanthi. Did I hit my head? I don't remember falling."

To zir astonishment, Jayanthi began to cry. Water pooled around her eyes and clung to her lashes and cheeks. With effort, Vaha extended a trembling hand and touched her face.

"What—"

"Hush," she interrupted. She kissed zir fingertips and pressed zir hand back to zir side. Then she placed a tube between zir lips. "Drink."

Vaha did as asked, though zir curiosity burned for answers. Jayanthi caught her breath and blotted her cheeks and eyes with her sleeve.

"I don't know where to begin," she said with a mirthless laugh. "Maybe you should integrate with your true body. That might explain the situation faster than I could."

"Why would I need to . . ." Before zie could finish the question, zie realized that zie had no link to zir true body. Zie trembled and caught at Jayanthi's sleeve. "Tell me the short version first."

"I don't know everything that's happened, but here's what I've pieced together."

Vaha listened with building horror as she relayed a story of zir true body getting badly injured—some kind of fight with Kaliyu—then going adrift and being exposed to a solar flare without any shelter. Zir true body had taken organic and extended memory loss. Then she told zir about leaving Meru on her own, nearly dying, and being rescued by a benevolent construct.

"We looked all over this system for you, and we couldn't find you. I suspect now that when we were at Kumuda, you were there, too, but the local network had you listed under the wrong name—"

"How long," Vaha interjected, "since we were last together?"

"Two hundred days."

"By the Nivid!" Zir hands clenched involuntarily.

Then she told zir about visiting the Primary and the discovery of her pregnancy.

"The fetus—is it all right?" zie said, interrupting her again.

Jayanthi smiled. "Judging by the activity, yes."

Vaha turned so zie could see her belly. It swelled like a viewing bubble. She placed zir hand upon it. Something firm moved against zir palm and then pushed against it. Vaha's phores glowed with wonder at this ancient version of the womb that surrounded them. Zie could move zir body more now, and zie rotated to plant a kiss atop their growing child.

"Incredible," zie murmured. Zie kept zir arms around Jayanthi's waist and smiled up at her.

She reflected it with a toothy human one.

"Who else knows about this?"

"Everyone." At zir expression, she quickly added, "About me being pregnant, not about how it happened. You're safe."

"I'm more concerned about your safety than mine! What will they do with—"

She pressed a finger against zir lips. "We'll talk about all that later. I could spend the next year in here with you, and it wouldn't be enough, but there are people back home waiting for us." She rushed her next words. "The MEC said that if you corroborate my data from the surface, they'll allow it into the Nivid. We need to get back to the Primary as quickly as possible, before the vote for the amendment. I think your . . . other self doesn't want to go. Oh, Vaha, zie doesn't know me at all! I don't know what to do."

Her eyes brimmed with tears again. Vaha rotated and pulled Jayanthi against zirself.

"My true body will know you again and will love you. All of me will, I promise." Zie cupped her face in zir hands and pressed zir lips to hers, tasting salt and softness. "But first, I need you to help me get back to myself."

Nakis watched as Jayanthi towed zir incarn from the womb into zir mouth via a flexible sealed tube. Zir incarn looked as human as she did. A piece of zirself had been missing all these months, and zie hadn't known it. Now that zie did, zir mind groped for the connection they should have had and found only a painful emptiness, like the ache of dry lungs.

Jayanthi floated into zir mouth and pulled the incarn with her into the human chamber. Nakis discovered that zie had cameras, microphones, and speakers in that organ of zir body. Zie enabled all three as she secured zir incarn into a web and attached the umbilical. As soon as it connected, zie established a link.

The human tucked herself beside zir incarn and placed her arm possessively around zir chest. Their closeness made Nakis uncomfortable, but before zie could protest, her eyes closed. To Nakis's surprise, zir incarn had access to her bodym in zir memories. Jayanthi's regular heart rate and breathing indicated that she had fallen asleep.

<I'm going to integrate myself,> Nakis flashed to Rithu and Kaliyu.

Zie tucked zirself into a berth at the observation deck. They followed suit, and zie let zir lids fall shut. Nakis muted the input from zir physical senses and waited for the missing parts of zir memories to fill themselves in.

Zir experiences pieced themselves together in fragments, not always in chronological order. There were glimpses of wide, rocky vistas. A muddy lake. Deep-purple skies studded with orange clouds. Jayanthi. Helping zir walk for the first time. Laughing as she tried to learn phoric. Tending to seedlings. To her own health. *To me. I am Vaha!*

Identity fractured, churned, and blended like the heart of a star. *Nakis* folded into a chapter of zir life, one part of the whole, but the entire self was most definitely Vaha. And *Vaha* had fallen in love with a human.

Zie recalled hours spent inside the womb, bodies entwined, hands in tender places, lips and tongues gifting each other with explosive pleasure. Jayanthi had *made a child* with zir, the same one that she carried in her body, with the dangers that entailed. And then, zie had left her without a word and forgotten all of it.

Vaha realized that zie could never reabsorb zir incarn. Zie needed that extension of zirself to hold Jayanthi, to kiss her at least once more—if she could find it in her heart to forgive zir.

Zie reengaged zir outward senses and discovered that Rithu was also awake. Their gazes locked, and in that moment, Rithu saw what lay in Vaha's thoughts.

"You're not coming back," Rithu sent via emtalk, his phores invisible against his skin.

What could zie tell zir friend? That zie was in love with a human? That zie had been a colossal mudha to leave her once, and zie could never do it again? That she had grown their child by herself, inside herself, and all the while zie had orbited Kumuda in blissful ignorance.

"I'm sorry," Vaha sent. The two most inadequate words in all of language. "I'm in love with someone else."

Rithu nodded. "Some part of you knew that all along, the whole time you were at Kumuda. You always held back, just a little. I suspected . . . I shouldn't have allowed myself to hope."

"There's more. I have to go back to Sol and get Jayanthi's data into the Nivid. The MEC said that they would allow it if I could corroborate it, and my incarn remembered everything that happened while Jaya was on the surface. I can make a difference to the outcome of the vote on human settlement."

Rithu's phores glowed with a mix of resignment and tenderness. "That's a worthy cause indeed."

Vaha threaded a hand through the frames of their berths and squeezed Rithu's. "I'll be forever grateful for your love and your kindness. You gave me something no other alloy has: confidence in myself. I can't thank you enough for that."

"At least come and visit once in a while, or let me know where I can find you when I'm done here."

"I'll do that."

"Then it's time for me to go." Rithu disengaged Vaha's hand and pushed himself out of his berth.

"So soon?"

"I'm rested and nourished. I don't think you need me anymore, Nakis—Vaha. I hope we meet again one day."

And with that, Rithu waved and flew away. Vaha watched him recede into the black, as zie had with zir maker, but this time instead of a sick disappointment, zie was filled with a profound sense of gratitude.

Jayanthi awoke with no Vaha beside her. She twisted around to look for zir and struggled in the sleeping web like a trapped fly.

"I'm here—don't worry." Vaha's incarn floated in the lower part of the chamber next to the transparent window flesh of zir true body.

"Is it all done? Are you—?"

"Yes, I've reintegrated. You slept for nearly ten hours. This whole journey must have exhausted you." Vaha pushed off and floated toward her, catching the web in zir arms. "I'm so sorry, Jaya. This is all my fault. I left you alone on Meru thinking that you'd have no choice but to stay and continue the project. I made such a terrible mistake." Zir arms tightened around her. "Will you forgive me?"

"Of course," she said, weak with relief. She'd feared that the integration might go the other way, that Vaha's true body would dominate as zie absorbed zir incarn's memories. She tucked her head against zir neck. "I forgave you long ago. I wouldn't have come all this way to look for you if I hadn't."

"I still don't remember everything that happened that day, after I returned to my true body at Meru. There's a gap from then until when I arrived at Kumuda—and I still can't remember much from before I had this incarn body—but I had one video of you in my extended memory that, thank the Nivid, didn't get corrupted. I didn't know what it meant, only that it was important. *You* were important. I don't ever want to leave you again."

Jayanthi's heart shattered like a comet gone too close to a star.

"You'll have to," she said, choking on the words. "When we return to the Primary Nivid, they're going to send me to Earth and forbid me from traveling in space again."

"Then let's stay here."

"What?"

"I'll keep my true body in orbit, like before, and we'll live on Meru. We'll stay long enough to have the baby, and then we'll flee. Maybe to Kumuda or some other system entirely. You can be a rogue human, like the ones you told me about."

She shook her head. "That's impossible on so many levels. I'll need supplies, solid food, medicines. The great human weakness, right? I can't survive in space without consuming significant resources. There's our child to consider, too. But above all that, there's Hamsa's ballot proposition. My time on Chedi opened my eyes, Vaha. Human beings are capable of so much, but we've been confined for too long, our natural curiosity and ambition repressed. You and I hold the key to unlock humanity's potential. If we don't return to the Primary, if you don't get my data into the Nivid, no one can move forward with the work we've done here. The clock on the human settlement project will either get reset or nullified, depending on which way the next vote goes."

She drew zir to the window so they could gaze upon Meru together. "I spent all my time on Earth wanting freedom, to live like an alloy, to work like a tarawan, to have the respect of spacefaring society. These last few months have taught me to look beyond that. Alloys are fallible. Constructs, too. You're not better than humans; you're just better suited to living with less. There are other human beings who want what I want. I know at least a few—my friends on Earth, Sahaya Amritsavar, Sunanda and the others on Chedi. If we run away, then I'm abandoning them all. I—I can't be that selfish. Not even for us. I'm sorry."

Vaha looked as if zie could cry, but for once, Jayanthi had shed all her tears. Resolve settled inside her, as firm and alive as the fetus in her womb.

After a long silence, Vaha nodded. "I understand, though I can't help but wish that we could be selfish. The thought of losing you so soon after finding you again—it's too painful." Zie let out a strangled groan. "I could stay in orbit around Earth. Maybe the CDS would grant me an exception, like they did with your parents, and let my incarn live on the surface. I can't be apart from you again. I won't! I'm nothing without you, Jaya."

"That's not true. Look at how much you've done! You can't waste your life watching me live mine. You have your friend at Kumuda. You can go back there after we're done at the Primary and visit me once in a while at Earth. They let alloys come down-well for short-term stays. Hamsa does it regularly. Maybe they'll allow you to do that, too."

"Are you sure this is what you want?" Vaha said, zir face a picture of despondency.

She gripped zir hand. "*You* are what I really want, but I'm willing to sacrifice my happiness for the good of my people. I know it's not fair to ask you to do the same, but I'm asking anyway. Will you help me?"

Vaha pressed zir lips to hers, then pulled back and met her gaze, zir expression resolved. "I will."

"Thank you," she whispered.

Zie pulled her close and spoke softly against her ear. "But I want one day with you like this before we go. I'll need all my attention on my true body while I'm flying."

Jayanthi nodded. They could afford the small delay, and she couldn't have resisted the offer even if she had wanted to.

—सख्य

Sakhya—Alliance

Vaha held tight to the womb. It was strapped to zir chest, but with Jayanthi and zir incarn inside, it was truly the most precious thing zie had. Zir body, in turn, was held by Kaliyu in a similar fashion. Zir friend flew across the local thamity gradients at two gees, almost as fast as Rithu had, but they had to sustain the pace until they reached heliopause for Meru's star.

"Don't worry," Kaliyu sent via emtalk. "I did it on the way here. I have enough energy and strength to make it even while towing you."

The arrangement made their traversal more precarious. It took most of Vaha's focus to maintain the balance between zirself and zir friend, but zie kept up a slow conversation with Kaliyu as well, a sentence or two every kilas.

"Tell me more about what happened at Meru," Vaha sent. "Why did we fight?"

"When I came to Meru, I had so much hatred for humans. I didn't tell you then, but my hope was to sabotage your efforts, and when you injured yourself, I saw it as an opportunity to end the project early. I was within my rights to pull Jayanthi off the planet, but . . . I didn't have to do it. You suspected my true motive, I think. So we fought, and you nearly ripped my wing out of its socket so that I wouldn't be able to land."

From Vaha's perspective, those actions belonged to a stranger. That zie had inflicted such violence—and on zir friend, no less—zie found it hard to fathom. But when zie thought of Jayanthi, of someone laying waste to everything she had accomplished on Meru, then zie could feel the anger ready to coalesce like a newborn star. Zie would have thought zirself incapable of such an act, but zie wasn't the same person zie had been before.

"I'm sorry," Vaha sent. "I wish I hadn't hurt you like that."

"It's all right. I deserved it. In my pain and rage, I left Meru without telling Jayanthi anything. That's why she got herself off-planet."

"That was a mistake on my part, too," Vaha sent. "I should've tried to reach her. I guess I didn't expect someone in her position to take so much initiative or such desperate action."

"Humans are full of surprises."

"So why did you help her? Why are you helping us?"

"Two reasons. The first is because of my maker. I don't know if you remember, but the whole time we were at Nishadas, I thought zie was dead. It turns out that my grandmaker lied to me. My maker is on Earth, a—a surface alloy who's serving humans there."

"I don't remember any of that," Vaha confessed.

"It doesn't matter. The point is, I discovered that everything I had thought about human beings and what they'd done to my maker was wrong. Instead of blaming them, I should've looked to my grandmaker. Learning the truth was hard, but it forced me to reconsider what happened between us at Meru. I . . . I want to make it up to you. To Jayanthi, too. My maker was horrified when I told zir what I'd done to you. I was angry at first and then confused. I started to wonder if zie was right about me."

After a long pause, Vaha prompted, "And the second reason?"

"Because of you," Kaliyu sent. "Because of our friendship. I had been so convinced that you were wrong about humans that I threw away the dearest person in my life. I regretted it, but I couldn't admit it to myself, not until I came back to Meru alone and couldn't find you anywhere. I followed my best estimate of your trajectory for several kaals. I asked everyone in orbit around Meru. No one had seen you. I figured you were either dead or hiding."

"A bit of both, in a way."

"I've missed you, Vaha. I dreaded the thought of you in self-imposed exile or adrift in some long, eccentric orbit. When Jayanthi asked if I would help her look for you, I didn't have much hope, but I couldn't refuse one last attempt. I'm so glad I said yes."

Vaha composed zir reply with care. "I forgive you, and I ask your forgiveness in turn. I acted out of anger and fear, too, and I hurt you. I'm sorry."

"I suppose that's fair. Let's say we're even, then?"

Vaha reached back with one arm and gave Kaliyu's hand an affirmative squeeze.

"So what's next?" Kaliyu sent. "After we get back to the Primary, you'll corroborate Jayanthi's data, but what if the MEC doesn't let you both go back to Meru? If you end up with Rithu, I'm going to be terribly jealous."

Vaha colored zir words with bitter amusement. "I'm not in a position to take advantage of him as a racing coach. It's ironic. At Meru, I finally became what my maker wanted. I was a multimodal pilot. Now I can barely traverse a thamity gradient." Zie shook zir head. "I don't want to go back to Kumuda. I want to be with Jayanthi. She's convinced that the CDS will confine her to Earth."

"She *made* a baby, Vaha. Justice will not let that go."

"I know."

Vaha didn't want to admit that Kaliyu was right, but with Jayanthi saying the same thing, zie knew that the verdict would likely go against her. Zie had seen the document to her from TESC and the potential consequences they could enact. If the CDS took their child away, or if they sent Jayanthi to live in the Out of Bounds on Earth, zie would have no future with her as a family.

"I considered putting myself in stasis around Earth to watch her live her life," Vaha confessed, "and I've been thinking, even if I can't have my incarn on Earth, I could volunteer for service. I like the idea of being close to her." *And to my child.*

"At least you have some idea of what you want to do. I'm scrambled."

"Aren't you going back to the Majestics?"

"After all that's happened, the idea doesn't bring me the same joy it used to. I don't know what else I'd do, and stasis still sounds unappealing."

With zir heart aching, Vaha sent, "You could go to Kumuda in my place. Rithu is doing good research work, and he's happy to share the credit. He's also lonely. He wouldn't say so to anyone who asked, but I could tell. I think he would welcome you as my friend, and you could train with him until his project cycle is over."

They had moved past the orbit of Venus with the Primary Nivid in sight before Kaliyu responded. "I suppose the Majestics might wait a few varshas if I spend the time with The Royal. Getting away from the Solar System might do me some good. Thank you for the idea. We shouldn't get too ahead of ourselves, though. The CDS could still dump me into stasis for the illegal transport of a human. If they don't, I'll consider Kumuda."

Vaha hadn't visited the Primary since zie was a child, before Veera left zir, but the scale of it felt just as enormous as it had then. Zie had requested and received a berth assignment at the human-habitable limb. As zie maneuvered around the other branches, Vaha realized how instinctive zir use of the tail brace had become. The only time it gave zir any problems was when zie moved in and out of tight berths. And microgravity flight, of course. That dream had evaporated for good. Zir imagined happy reunion with zir maker would never happen. Vaha hadn't felt the loss acutely until the reintegration with zir incarn. Knowing that zie'd had zir destiny in zir grasp, that zie had thrown it away to show off—but zie had the peace from Kumuda to mitigate the pain. And zie had Jayanthi and the child to think about, which brought its own set of joys and frustrations.

"We're almost here," Vaha told Jayanthi.

"Can you come inside with me?"

"No, they only gave me permission to have my incarn on the surface of Meru. Technically, I shouldn't have kept zir separate after I reintegrated with zir memories. I'll stay in touch with you through emtalk, though."

She kissed zir incarn's forehead and whispered, "I love you," before slipping into her suit.

It took every ton of willpower that Vaha had not to pull Jayanthi into zir incarn's embrace. Instead, zie attached the transfer tube to the womb. Jayanthi's tiny figure floated through and into the airlock. She had taken all her belongings. "In case they don't allow me back," she'd said. Vaha hoped it wouldn't come to that. Zie wondered if someone had met her inside, if they would try to restrain her from leaving again. After detaching the tube, zie tethered the womb to float behind the berth and wriggled zir way in. The docks at the outdated limb were built for mechanical shuttles, not pilots, and zir tail exoskeleton made it impossible to vent without hitting something.

Two struts from either side of zir berth extended outward and clamped around the base of zir tail, just above the top of the exoskeleton.

Zie opened an emchannel to the Primary's central constructed mind. "What is happening to my berth?"

"The CDS has charged you with assaulting the pilot known as Kaliyu, as well as breach of contract with Hamsa and the Meru Exploration Committee. You must remain here until your case is presented to Mithva, the presiding judicial construct at the Primary Nivid. You are considered a flight risk and are therefore restrained."

The phores on Vaha's arms went white. With an effort, zie brought them back to neutral, then sent a message to Kaliyu. "You seemed so friendly and helpful on the way here. Was it all an act again? A ruse to trap me and Jaya at the Primary?"

"What are you saying? What's happened?" Kaliyu responded.

"The CDS has accused me of assaulting you."

"I didn't ask them to—I swear by the Nivid!"

Their next messages arrived at the same instant: "Pushkara!"

"He must have received notice when we arrived at the RT point," Kaliyu sent. "Gravity take him! I'll file a request to speak on your behalf. They can't hold you to the charge if I refuse to support it, right?"

"I have no idea," Vaha admitted. "I don't know anything about legal matters."

"What's the worst they can do? Temporary forced stasis?"

"They're also charging me with breach of contract, probably for leaving Meru like I did."

"Gravity take them all!"

Neither of them sent anything for a while after that. Vaha decided not to tell Jayanthi. She had enough concerns of her own. She'd had frequent medical treatments during their return journey, and though she didn't complain, zie could tell she was often in pain. Her belly had swollen visibly with their child, an item to add to both of their worries. At least the Primary hadn't blocked zir network access. Zie couldn't see inside Jaya's room, but a quick, "Are you okay?" had met with an equally prompt, "I'm fine, just tired. Going to take a nap."

Zie accessed the general knowledge base and thought-searched on legal proceedings. Every padhran had a central constructed mind that handled its affairs, including the dispensation of justice. The Primary had several CMs, since it was a permanent structure with a vast population. One by the name of Mithva presided over all legal matters. Since they were nonliving beings, constructs didn't have the potential conflicts of interest that living beings would. Mithva could adjudicate many cases in parallel, but they still had limited resources. The backlog meant that Vaha's trial would be held the next kaal. There was no need to delay it further because zie could appeal the outcome at any time, anywhere, in stasis or not. The only exception was for those who were exiled, the worst of all consequences.

I nearly did that to myself, Vaha thought with a shudder. Zie had almost thrown away zir life in one impulsive move. *If they sentence Jayanthi to be Earthbound, I will join her, even if it means getting reborn into service as a surface alloy. No matter how long it takes, if I have to wait out a few varshas in stasis, I'll find a way to live with her.* She could protest all she wanted to, but the decision belonged to zir. Vaha had let others rule the direction of zir life for too long. Rithu had given zir a taste of true independence, and zie was not about to let anyone—not even Jayanthi—take that away.

"Hamsa is at the door and requests entry," the CM announced to Jayanthi.

Upon her second arrival at the Primary Nivid, the central constructed mind had directed her back to the same room. Jayanthi hadn't seen Devasu at all, and she hoped the young alloy hadn't gotten in trouble for her clandestine actions. She assumed that Vaha or the Primary had notified Hamsa of their arrival, but out of politeness, she'd sent him a message as well.

"Let him in, please," she said aloud.

To her surprise, he smiled when he entered.

"My dear child, whatever will you do next?" he sent via emtalk. He floated forward and took her hands in his. "So you found Vaha. I'm sure your first words will be to demand that your Meruvin data get considered for the Nivid."

At least he wasn't angry with her anymore. "Yes, that's right."

"This won't absolve you of breaking the laws with the womb, though." He looked pointedly at her visibly swollen belly. "And you're nearly at eight months pregnant. We need to get you to Earth quickly. You could deliver any day now."

She put a hand protectively over herself. "I spent the journey in Vaha's womb. There were some complications, but the fetus is healthy, and the pregnancy is stable."

"That's good, but the Primary construct has no experience with a human delivery in microgravity. Neither do I. Frankly, the only knowledge we have in that regard is theoretical. I've already found a pilot to take you home. We can have you back there in a few days, but since you're already here, you'll stand trial tomorrow."

"I thought that wasn't for another five months!" To go on trial before the delivery meant she'd have no healthy baby to hold up as mitigation for her transgressions. Had she gone through all the risk of pregnancy for nothing? *No, of course not!* The child would exist, a hope for the future of humanity on Meru. Jayanthi stretched and flexed her hands and feet. The lack of gravity had shifted her swelling from her muscles to her joints, and no position was comfortable.

"They changed their minds when you left with Kaliyu," Hamsa sent. "Because you're a flight risk, they want to make sure no alloy can transport you without the explicit permission of the government. Mithva, the local justice, has sent for a human Voice of Compassion to be present at your sentencing, should you be found guilty on any count. Vaha will meet with Mithva as well."

"Vaha? But zie had nothing to do with my pregnancy." That was a lie, but no one knew the truth except for Vaha. She glanced through the window, where she had an oblique view of zir berth. Had zie confessed without telling her?

"They're trying Vaha separately for assault and breach of contract. It has nothing to do with what you're accused of."

Relief warred with outrage. "Zie tried to protect me!"

Hamsa followed her gaze and floated to the window. "That might help mitigate zir sentence, but it doesn't excuse zir actions."

"What about the data and the Nivid? Will they still allow zir to authenticate it?"

"Vaha gave zir statement to the committee earlier today."

"So it's done? They've accepted it?"

Hamsa nodded. "The data will go through a review process, but assuming they find no irregularities, any novel information will get entered into the archive."

At least one thing had gone right. No, two things: she had found Vaha, and she had validated the work they'd done on Meru. No matter what happened with the trial the next day, she had done everything she could to help Hamsa's proposed amendment.

"Do you think it's enough to sway the vote in our favor?" she asked. "The test results clearly show that my genetic makeup combined with elevated heme oxygenase would make a natural fit for Meru's environment."

"I know, and that information was made available to all soon after you left, though it was marked preliminary. We'll find out the day after tomorrow whether it has changed any minds."

She, Vaha, and Kaliyu had arrived three days before the vote. *Barely in time.* "How fast will they decide my case? Could I stay here until we have the results of the vote, too?"

Hamsa's phores shone with pale spring green. "What good does it do you, my dear? You can appeal the verdict from anywhere."

They locked eyes as they arrived at the same conclusion. Jayanthi sent the words anyway. "If it goes in favor of humans on Meru, I'd rather be confined there than on Earth."

“Think it through,” Hamsa cautioned. “You’d have to leave behind your friends and family. You’d have little to no help on the planet until we could find enough candidates to settle there. It would be a lonely life, and dangerous, as you now understand.”

“That’s all I’ve thought about since I left the Primary. I want to have my child on Meru, where we belong, and I’d have Vaha with me.”

“Vaha? Zie isn’t fit to travel that distance. We’d have to find you a different pilot to accompany you.”

She couldn’t tell Hamsa the truth, that she and Vaha loved each other, that they dreamed of raising their child together on Meru.

“I trust zir,” she sent. “And I think zie would want to come.”

“Then let’s ask Vaha directly.”

Hamsa invited Vaha to join their emchannel, and then posed the question.

“Yes,” zie replied. “I would very much like to help Jayanthi on Meru again, if that’s allowed.”

“Vaha, I told the committee that I don’t want to press charges for breach of contract,” Hamsa sent. “As cosigners, they still have the right to sue and, unfortunately, they’re going ahead with that. I’m sorry. I have, however, secured permission for you to get a rebirth regardless of the outcome of your trial. Once that’s complete and assuming you’re free, I can contract with you again for a return trip to Meru. In the meantime, Jayanthi can go to Earth and deliver the baby in safety. By the time you’re ready to travel, she and the child should be as well. After the rebirth, your physical functionality will be fully restored, and your memories—well, you’ve been through a reintegration once. Rebirth isn’t all that different.”

“I’m grateful for your offer—” Vaha sent.

“It’s the least I can do for all the support you’ve given to Jayanthi and me.”

“But I’m going to decline. I’d rather save my rebirths for when I really need them. For now, I’m content with the exoskeleton. I can traverse shallow thamity gradients with it, which is enough to get by in an emergency. As for the wing, it's true that I get tired faster with its current state, but I've learned to manage it. Thanks to Rithu's help at Kumuda, I'm confident that I can navigate atmospheric flight and gravitational landings as I am. I don't plan on doing much microgravity flight anymore. If we need to get back to Meru, we'll get a tow like I did with Kaliyu."

"Vaha—" Jayanthi began.

"It's my decision, Jaya." Zir tone was gentle but firm. "I spent my entire childhood trying to fulfill my maker's goals, to be the pilot zie designed me to be, and when that finally happened, my actions led to the mess we're in today. My dreams were never truly my own. The exoskeleton, the broken wing—they've freed me from those. A rebirth would feel like a step backward, toward my maker's ambitions again. I know what I want for myself, and that's to help you and, one day, all of humankind. If I'm going to put myself through a full rebirth, I'll do it for a form that *I* choose."

Jayanthi swallowed her protest. Her own upbringing had fed her desire to become the first human tarawan on Earth. She'd chased an alloy ideal until Meru and Chedi had opened her eyes to a different path, new possibilities. *Sometimes, it takes losing a dream to figure out what you really want to do with your life.*

She pulled herself to the window and gazed out at Vaha. Zir face turned toward her, an alloy smile curving zir lips. She marveled at the change in zir. When they'd first gotten to know each other, she'd been astonished that zie lacked confidence in zirself. *How could any alloy feel inadequate?* she'd wondered. That diffidence had emboldened her, had allowed her to open her heart. She'd given it freely, and Vaha had responded in kind, in a way that no other alloy had, not even her parents.

She pressed a hand to the cold window. "I understand."

—विवेक

VIVEKA—JUDGMENT

Five minutes before Jayanthi's appointment with Mithva, the judiciary construct, Devasu showed up at her door.

"I thought you might like some physical company during your hearing," the alloy guide said upon entering. As before, she wore an elegant tunic and headpiece, this time with coordinating jewelry around her upper arms and neck.

"Devasu! You're all right!" Jayanthi took the alloy's hands in her own. "I'm so happy to see you."

Devasu's phores glowed with deep amethyst. "The pleasure is equally mine. They didn't give me any trouble for your departure, though Hamsa was irritable for days after." She looked down at Jayanthi's bulging abdomen. "You've grown so much bigger since I last saw you!"

"Yes, I'm about ready to have it over and done with. I can't eat more than a few bites at a time, especially without gravity, and I'm constantly exhausted."

"I can't even begin to imagine what it feels like," Devasu said. "Are you going to allow an immersive recording or just emtalk?"

"I had assumed just text. Why would I want a visual?"

Devasu glowed with surprise. “Everyone is paying attention. Ever since you, Vaha, and Kaliyu came back to the system, you’re all anyone has talked about. The outcome of your case could sway people for tomorrow’s vote, and allowing them to see you might make a difference.”

“All right,” Jayanthi said. She swallowed against the bile that churned in her stomach. She’d thought that getting her data into the Nivid was all she had to do. She hadn’t considered that alloys might care what became of her personally. “I’m glad you came,” she said. “It’ll be good to have a friend with me.” The legal proceedings didn’t require a physical gathering, and having Devasu in her room would make her less nervous.

When Hamsa arrived, unannounced, two minutes later, Jayanthi couldn’t keep the tinge of mania from her laughter. He had come for the same reason, and his phores lit in surprise at the sight of Devasu.

“Thank you both for your support,” Jayanthi sent via a shared emchannel.

With a deep breath, she slow-blinked and turned her attention to the blank viewing wall in her room. Her companions did the same. She thought-shared her projected vision with them, then navigated to her judicial invitation. A single face appeared with an identifier that included the name Mithva along with gender and title. The construct had chosen an older, humanlike face, with a lined forehead and wrinkles at the corners of the eyes. The skin tone and eye color matched Jayanthi’s, and graying hair fell in gentle waves. The image disappeared below the shoulders, which were draped in somber white.

“Greetings, Jayanthi,” the construct said, their voice coming through speakers set into the wall. “Are you ready to conduct our meeting?”

She took a deep breath. “I am.”

“Very well. I will begin by stating the charges against you and presenting any supporting evidence that has been entered into my record. I will give you an opportunity to dispute any or all of these. If we have items of contention, we will reconvene after I can collect additional statements and evidence. After all such disputes are resolved, you will have an opportunity to name any accomplices as well as to present any circumstances that you believe should mitigate the severity of your actions. Do you understand?"

Between her pounding heart and the pressure of the baby against her ribs, she could hardly draw breath. "I do."

"You have been accused by the Tarawan Ethics and Standards Council of the following violations: the making of a child with an unapproved DNA design, unapproved use of a womb, unauthorized genetic engineering by a human, unauthorized human fetal development in microgravity, and unauthorized human fetal exposure to radiation. Have you read and reviewed the full details of these charges?"

When they put it like that, her transgressions sounded severe even to herself. *But I was as careful about it all as I could be, and I had good reasons for everything I did.* "I have." She hugged herself and was rewarded by an answering push.

"You are on record at a meeting of the Meru Exploration Committee as having admitted to all of these activities. Do you dispute this record?"

Jayanthi lifted her chin slightly. "I do not."

"Additionally, I have on record two standard arrival medical examinations at the Primary Nivid, which have confirmed that you are carrying a human fetus via biological pregnancy, and that you've spent more than one masan traveling in space while pregnant. Do you dispute this?"

From her left, Devasu reached out and gently took Jayanthi's hand.

"I do not," she answered. The fetus in question chose that moment to start hiccuping in a distracting fashion.

"Did anyone coerce or entice you to commit these acts?"

"No, I acted alone." She had rehearsed these answers instead of sleeping for much of the previous night.

"Do you have anything to say that might mitigate the circumstances of your illegal activities?"

At last, the question she'd been waiting for. Jayanthi thought-retrieved her notes. She had reviewed them with Hamsa and Vaha after working on them feverishly the day before. Her right hand began to tremble. Hamsa took it in his and gave it a squeeze. Jayanthi let out a calming exhale. If people, alloy or human, might use the outcome of her case to decide how to vote, then this was her best chance to convince them to take her side.

"I have a statement to enter into the record," Jayanthi said, her voice shaky from adrenaline.

"Proceed."

"If we begin from first principles with the axiom that life exists in order to protect and reproduce itself, then society is a natural outgrowth of that. A society exists to safeguard its weakest members, beginning with its young, but later, with greater sophistication, it can expand its custodial sphere to include people with varying abilities, ages, and illnesses. This can eventually grow to encompass the life-form's environment and ecology, including other types of life that coexist with it.

"That is where our civilization arrived at the time of the compact. We realized that alloyed beings were the stronger members of our society and that they were therefore better equipped to care for others, including humans. With the alloys in charge of governance, the Constructed Democracy of Sol was able to restore the ecology of Earth, safeguard the environment, and, consequently, preserve the health of all human beings as well as less-developed forms of consciousness. Like parents and children, alloys and humans have developed a mutually beneficial relationship.

"What the compact and our present society don't allow for, however, is that children can mature, that people with illnesses can get well, or that people with different abilities find ways to adapt to their environments. We have arrived at a time when the dominant guardians of our society have become overbearing—not because they've changed but because the rest of us have. The collective actions of alloys do not exist in a vacuum, just like the actions of an individual do not exist apart from society and environment. We are connected, and over time, we coevolve.

"The notion of individual rights as separate from all others is a fallacy on the order of classical mechanics relative to quantum theory. The reality of the universe is that everything is entangled. We can model macro-level behavior and interaction, but those models will never reflect the underlying truth. At best, they will be an approximation. At worst, they serve to obscure and impede our interaction with our environment."

From the corner of her eye, Hamsa nodded. Devasu's phores glowed with admiration, and Jayanthi gave both of their hands a gentle squeeze. Whether her words would make a difference, she couldn't tell, but speaking each one aloud lifted a weight from her shoulders.

"In the previous millennium," she continued, "humankind committed terrible mistakes. We hurt ourselves; we hurt other forms of life and consciousnesses, including Earth and Mars. At that time, it made sense to hand alloys authority over ourselves and our surroundings. Like children, we needed protection from our own behavior. We needed time to atone. We needed to remain constrained until we learned new values.

"But who decides when we've achieved that state? Who decides when children no longer need constant oversight from their guardians? If our protectors rely on old models that ignore present reality, if they continue to restrain us in the name of misdeeds long past, then like overbearing parents, they are abusing their power. I believe that alloys have fallen into this trap. They insist that the only way for humans to *grow up*, so to speak, is to be like them—in other words, to evolve into alloys. I would argue otherwise.

"Why must our world limit itself to only three forms of higher intelligence? Human ingenuity led to the development of alloys and constructs. Perhaps if released from their fetters, humankind will come up with a fourth alternative. Perhaps we'll do it jointly with the other two. Or perhaps we're fine as we are, with a different mindset that will allow us to roam the galaxy and not commit the same errors that we made as a younger society.

"It's time for alloys to acknowledge the truth, to open their shashtams to the fabric of the universe and to stop treating human beings like truculent children. Let us make our own choices. Let us make new mistakes. Let us live our fullest lives."

And now she came to the most difficult part of her speech: the confession of what she had done, the evidence of her gross ambition and the embodiment of what humans had learned to suppress over centuries of genetic engineering. Could she make the alloys understand and sympathize, or would they end up condemning her? At least she had the support of the ones who floated on either side of her.

She took a deep breath and continued. "In order to support this belief and this plea, I acted on my own to demonstrate two things. First, that human beings are capable of more than they are presently allowed. In my case, this was to work as a tarawan, to make a healthy child with a new set of genes. Second, that human genetic variance will allow us to adapt ourselves to the environment of planets like Meru, which have a sufficiently similar ecosphere to the habitable zones on Earth.

"I ask lenience from the court to continue my work, both in terms of gestation and beyond, by allowing me to raise this child on Meru in order to validate her health and the health of the planet. I've done my best to protect her for nearly eight months." Jayanthi paused to disengage from Devasu's and Hamsa's hands. She placed hers on either side of her abdomen and said softly, "And I love her so very much already. I promise to take equally good care of her for as long as I can. This concludes my statement. Thank you."

"Noted and entered into the record."

With a wavering sigh, Jayanthi relaxed her neck and shoulders. She hadn't realized how much she'd tensed up while talking. Pain bloomed between her shoulder blades and made that clear as awareness of her surroundings returned. *Not now, body. Hold on a little longer, until we safely deliver this baby, and then you can have a crisis.*

"Is there anything else you wish to state for the record?" Mithva asked.

"No," Jayanthi said.

"Then based on my understanding of current laws, I find you guilty without malice on all counts."

Jayanthi closed her eyes. Constructed minds could think much faster than organic ones, but the speed of the decision still took her by surprise. Any lingering hope of special treatment turned to ash, like the remnants of childhood fantasy. Her human brain needed time to process the finality of the situation. *But this isn't the end. There's still the sentencing and tomorrow's vote.*

Mithva continued. "A Voice of Compassion who represents your peer group is en route to the Primary. We apologize for the delay, but it took some time to find a qualified person close to your age and cultural values. Tomorrow we will reconvene with the Voice to determine your sentencing. A complete recording of today's proceedings is being provided to the Voice as they travel. That concludes this session. If you wish to make these proceedings public, you can notify the central constructed mind to do so."

The judicial construct folded their virtual hands in front of their heart and then disappeared from Jaya's visual field. She sent a message to make the recording openly available. Her words hadn't been for herself. She wanted everyone to see, hear, and consider what she'd said. Then she slow-blinked and closed her connection.

"You made an excellent effort," Hamsa sent. He took her chin and gently turned her face toward himself. "Jaya, as I said when you sent me the notes, you made some valid points. Even if you must suffer the consequences of your lawbreaking actions, I think people need to hear your words. It's far better that they came from your impassioned mouth than mine. I fear that the recording of your statement will not spread widely enough to sway tomorrow's vote, but as I've said before, we're playing a very long game. If we can open Meru to human settlement in your lifetime, we should count ourselves lucky. No matter what, you did well. I'm very proud of you, and I hope that you're proud of yourself."

"I think your speech was brilliant," Devasu declared. "Life consumes. The evidence is all around us. Why should alloys have the right to build and take from Earth and believe that we can do it responsibly, but you're denied the same opportunity? Considering the span of your lives, you have passed through so many generations since the catastrophic years that you deserve a second chance. Maybe Meru can be that chance. Hamsa, you have my vote. And, Jayanthi, you deserve to live on Meru with your child for as long as you both desire."

Jayanthi forced a smile in spite of the burning sensation taking over her limbs. "Thank you both." The occupant in her uterus had stopped hiccuping while Jayanthi was talking, which seemed to be her pattern. She must have liked the sound of Jayanthi's voice—at least that's what Jayanthi told herself. She massaged the lower part of her rotund belly. At least she had protected Vaha from being outed as her coconspirator. She would happily keep that secret for the rest of her life.

"Can we watch Vaha's proceedings?" she asked.

"I believe it's happening concurrently," Hamsa sent, "and for privacy reasons, we'd need zir permission to share in the viewing. It's too late to ask for it now. You can review it when it's over, if zie allows."

After they left, Jayanthi settled herself into the ambulatory medical construct. The Primary CM had confiscated Vaha's womb, in part because of her actions and in part because of zirs, and assigned the construct as an alternative. With the demands of late-stage pregnancy, she needed near-constant supervision and treatment to keep her sickle cell at bay. She tried to relax into the construct's padded arms as they cradled her, but her mind refused. What would Vaha's fate be? Until she knew, she couldn't rest.

—अपकर्ष

Apakarsha—Annulment

Vaha met an extension of Mithva in space, where they could communicate in phoric. A paralytic prevented Vaha from venting. A Voice of Compassion, also a pilot, had carried zir to the site, and Kaliyu had come with them as Vaha's witness. The four of them floated within sight of the Primary but far enough away to maintain privacy.

Vaha kept zir back to the dazzling hemisphere that housed the Nivid. It drew zir eyes too easily, and zie didn't want to get distracted. Mithva's ambulatory extension resided in a boxy housing with multiple control jets. Their "face" consisted of a single circle of color-varying light with two optical sensors above it that served as eyes.

The judicial CM went through the formalities of stating the purpose of the meeting and the charges against Vaha, which were originally filed by the CDS's enforcement branch. When it was zir turn to speak, Vaha stated honestly that zie had no memory of the violent encounter with Kaliyu, nor the events that surrounded it.

<I believe Kaliyu to be a more reliable witness for what happened at Meru,> Vaha flashed.

<Kaliyu, you gave a statement about your injury prior to treatment. Have you reviewed it, and would you like to change or add anything to it?>

<Yes to both,> Kaliyu flashed. <I would like to add that I believe Vaha acted in what zie thought was the best interests of the project we were involved with.>

<So you don't think zie acted out of hatred or anger?>

Kaliyu glanced at Vaha before replying, <There may have been some anger, but it was justified. I took a unilateral action without offering explanation or even conversation. I did this because . . .> Kaliyu's phores stopped flashing and glowed in a variety of blues and greens. After a few seconds, zie continued. <Because I had promised Pushkara that during my time observing Vaha and Jayanthi on Meru, I would find a way to guarantee the failure of their efforts. I had a lot of animosity toward humans. Vaha's injury on Meru provided me an excuse to cut short Jayanthi's time on the surface. In addition, I deployed a device that Pushkara gave me in order to contaminate the surface of the planet.>

Vaha forced zir phores to stay neutral. That would explain why Kaliyu had acted so smug at Meru! Zir suspicions had been correct.

<Kaliyu, do you realize,> Mithva flashed, <that by making this statement, you have incriminated yourself?>

<I do,> Kaliyu answered. <I am prepared to accept the consequences of my actions.>

<Are you aware that Pushkara has given me a statement that you might level these exact allegations against him? He claims that you acquired the contaminant and deployed it on your own, with neither his knowledge nor his permission.>

Kaliyu's phores paled so briefly that Vaha almost wasn't sure it happened.

<I was not aware of that.>

<He stated for the record that you harbor resentment toward him because he revealed an unpleasant truth about your maker, Nidra, and because you were unsuccessful at removing her from Earth-based service, in spite of his best efforts to help you both.>

<That's a lie,> Kaliyu flashed.

<Do you have recorded proof of Pushkara giving it to you?> Mithva asked.

By the Nivid, please say yes!

Kaliyu's phores remained neutral, zir posture relaxed. Vaha remembered how well zir friend had played bluffing games back at Nishadas. Kaliyu had to feel an even greater sense of anger and dread than Vaha did at Mithva's words, but zie managed not to show it.

<I do not.>

Gravity take the Nivid and every thrice-made, vent-spawned mudha in the system!

<This is a serious allegation that will require further investigation,> Mithva flashed. <However, it does not have bearing on Vaha's case. Do either of you have anything more to add regarding Vaha's actions at Meru?>

With reluctance, Vaha flashed, <No.> Kaliyu did the same.

<Then, based on both of your statements, I find Vaha guilty of physical assault committed due to anger. Given Vaha's loss of memory and Kaliyu's statement of forgiveness, I would say that the consequences for Vaha's actions may be mitigated. The standard penalty would be ten varshas in stasis. I propose reducing it to five.>

Vaha's lungs turned to ice. Five varshas was more than sixteen Earth years. Zie would miss all of zir baby's childhood.

Mithva rotated to face the Voice. <Do you agree with this, or do you wish to appeal for a different consequence?>

The Voice opened an emtalk channel with Vaha. "My inclination is that it's a fair assessment. You did injure Kaliyu's wing, which is an essential organ for any alloy but especially for a pilot." They gestured at Vaha's body. "Of course you understand that from your own experience of it, hence the mitigation. Five varshas in stasis is only a fraction of your life, and perhaps it will give you time and space to move past your attachment to the Meru project. How do you feel about this?"

Vaha couldn't prevent a faint blue glow from leaking out of zir phores. Some part of zir was still embarrassed to admit to the alloy world that zie loved Jayanthi—the same part that worried what zir maker, Veera, would think. What could zie ask for, though? If they allowed zir to orbit Earth in stasis, zie still wouldn't have the equipment to observe Jayanthi and their child, which was what zir heart desired. Zie could ask to be reborn into service on Earth. Zie would prefer that to stasis, but it wouldn't necessarily keep zir close to Jayanthi. *I want to spend my life with her and our hybrid child. I want to plead for leniency because I fell in love with a human.* Zie couldn't tell these people any of that.

Or could zie?

Zie had spent too many years trying to be someone zie wasn't. Vaha had already freed zirself from the tether of zir maker's expectations. Zie could dare to defy those of other alloys as well.

<I don't want five varshas in stasis,> zie flashed at the Voice. *Let the world see my words.* <I'm in love with Jayanthi. I want to orbit Meru or Earth so that my incarn can be with her.> *And with our child.* <I'm willing to enter into service on Earth's surface as an alternative, and I request that I get assigned somewhere near her location.>

Mithva and the Voice stared at zir, while Kaliyu glowed with a mix of violet and navy that Vaha interpreted as zir friend being proud of zir.

<Do you . . . wish to enter into a committed relationship with this person?> the Voice asked, their phores carefully neutral.

<I do,> Vaha flashed. And with those words, the ice cold in zir chest seemed to melt away, and zie could breathe again. <I wish that very much.>

Emtalk signals emanated from both the Voice and Mithva. They held a private conversation that Vaha couldn't interpret, but zie had no doubt of what they were discussing: How could an alloy and a human have a committed, equitable relationship?

<Are you all right?> Kaliyu flashed.

<Never better,> Vaha replied.

Zir friend glowed with such saturated skepticism that it almost made Vaha's phores ripple with laughter.

<I have a modified recommendation,> the Voice flashed. <What if you still spend five varshas in stasis, but the CDS provides a dedicated channel for two-way communication with Jayanthi on Earth? Would you agree to this?>

The majority of stasis berths orbited the Sun between Venus and Mercury. The round-trip delay would prevent real-time communication, and it would take days to spool high-detail immersives, but at least zie could interact with Jayanthi and their child. *Maybe I should have taken Hamsa up on the offer for a rebirth. If I could fly faster, I could get Jayanthi and leave this gravity-taken place, find some other planet that's not Meru where we could live together.* It was too late for any of that. Rebirth would take months, and by then, Jayanthi would be gone. The baby would be born. Zie would have no way to reach them. And there was nowhere in the known universe that they could safely hide.

<There's no alternative?> Vaha flashed.

<None that satisfy legal requirements, I'm afraid,> the Voice said, their phores a dim yellow. <I'm sorry.>

<She'll wait five varshas for you,> Kaliyu flashed. <I'm sure of it.>

I hope so. The icy sensation had returned to zir lungs. Vaha wanted to blaze *no* from every phore on zir body. Zie wanted to thrash, to strike out. Was zie doomed never to hold on to the people zie loved? With a sense of despair, zie used zir bodym to down-regulate the negative, violent hormones that flooded through zir blood. As zie flashed an acceptance at them, a tiny rebellious phore lit in zir mind. *If there's another way, I'll find it—I swear by the Nivid!*

<Your agreement is noted, Vaha,> Mithva flashed. <You have ten kaals to exit any outstanding contracts and fly yourself to a stasis berth, which will be assigned to you. For the duration of your stasis, you will be provided a healthy supply of bhojya, water, and sunlight. If you need flight assistance to get to your berth, you can inform the central CM, who will get you the help you need. If at any time, you wish to present new facts about your situation or your prior actions, you may send me a

message. Adverse health conditions, in particular, should be something that you raise to our attention. Your berth monitor will also flag these in case you become incapacitated. If you do not arrive at your berth within the specified time, you will be labeled a fugitive, and your presence will be unwelcome at all padhrans. Do you understand?>

<I do.> The muscles around zir vents tightened as zie flashed the words.

I lost and found you once already, Jaya. I won't do it again. I'll spend every waking moment trying to make my way back to you, for as long as it takes, until we arrive at a place where we can live together forever.

Jayanthi moved through the connecting tube from the Primary's limb into Vaha's mouth. Zie had told her what happened during zir meeting with Mithva, about zir disclosure of their relationship, Kaliyu's confession, and zir time in stasis. She floated down the passage to the human-habitable chamber. As soon as she entered it, Vaha's incarn took her in zir arms.

"Send me a message at least once every day," zie murmured. "Record as much as you can. I don't care how many kilas they take to spool. I'll watch them all."

"I will," she promised. "There's something we need to talk about, something to help Kaliyu."

Vaha pulled back and listened as she told zir about finding the contaminated soil and the leaky container.

"One is in your womb; the other was with the waste collected at the site," she said. "If we can get them, we'll have evidence to support Kaliyu's accusation against Pushkara."

"I don't have the womb anymore, and I have no idea what happened to the supplies."

"It's okay. Devasu found out for me. I claimed that I'd left personal items in each—and I really did with the supplies—so the Primary is going to allow me to access them. Don't say anything to anyone—not even Kaliyu—until I get them. I don't trust the Primary or anyone else, not after everything that's happened. If Pushkara anticipated that Kaliyu would confess about the contaminant, who knows what else he's done to stack the situation against us. That's why I didn't say anything to you until now." She leaned in and kissed zir. "Kaliyu's trial begins in a couple of hours. I'll be back as soon as I can."

"Jaya—" Zie caught her arm as she turned to leave. "Be safe."

She nodded. She didn't think Pushkara would resort to violence, but Vaha's words set her heart beating faster. What if the old politician had already searched through the materials Kaliyu brought back from Meru? What if he'd orchestrated the repossession of Vaha's womb?

Devasu met her at the airlock. They nodded at each other and set off through the corridors. After the initial, familiar hub, they took yet another new route. The arms of the Primary that had seemed so wondrous on her first visit now loomed dim and cavernous with menace.

They stopped first at a room lined with a hundred storage cabinets, each more than two meters tall and equally wide. The door of one swung open as they approached and revealed the familiar packing containers from Meru. Jayanthi floated inside. After a few minutes of searching, she found her clothes. She saw no sign of the biohazard waste, and she could think of no reason to ask about its fate. It made little sense for her to need something like that or for the Primary to have kept it.

"Do you have everything?" Devasu sent via emtalk.

"I think so," Jayanthi said reluctantly.

For the womb, they had to backtrack, then head toward the medical arm. As with the Nivid, the lighting in that part of the Primary was brighter and more artificial. Vaha's womb hung by a tether from a narrow exterior limb, alongside several others. They had to exit the Primary into open space to get to it. Jayanthi had learned to use her suit's jets better, but vacuum still disoriented her, and she had to ask Devasu for help. The alloy guided Jayanthi to the womb's opening and then inside. They closed the exterior door and waited for the vestibule to fill with air.

"Welcome, Jayanthi," sent the womb's CM.

"Hello," she replied, relieved that it still recognized her. "I need access to the delivery chamber."

"Please present your biosample for verification."

She put her hand on the panel, her mind flashing back to the first time. Vaha's skin against hers. Their kiss.

The interior door slid open.

"I've never been inside a womb," Devasu said, peering around the large chamber curiously. "Except when I was born, of course, but I barely remember that."

Jayanthi smiled a bit and asked the CM about the container.

"Yes, I still have it," the womb responded.

Her limbs went weak with relief. "Can you deliver it to me?"

It arrived in the same transparent, sealed bag that Jayanthi had placed it in back on Meru. Inside, the device had partially dissolved into a pale sludge. She shuddered and placed it carefully in the sack that held her clothes.

Before they left, she took one last look around. Some of her happiest memories were from the inside of the womb—the spot where she'd been intimate with Vaha, the lab equipment where she'd made the embryo, the ambulatory construct that had taken care of her. In two days, Vaha would leave for stasis, and she would leave for Earth, and she wouldn't see zir again for more than sixteen years. Jayanthi couldn't fathom what that might mean for them. The stasis belt sat between the orbits of Venus and Mercury. Could they sustain their love across that great a distance and time?

We have to, because there is no one else in this universe, human or alloy, who loves me like zie does, who accepts me, faults and all. I'll never give you up, Vaha.

"Thank you for all your help," she sent to the womb's CM.

As soon as they entered the Primary's arm, Jayanthi made contact with Kaliyu. "I need to meet with you. It's urgent."

Zie was berthed next to Vaha and replied with zir usual terseness: "Come." She clung to Devasu's waist like a child, and the alloy sped them back to the human arm.

Kaliyu held out zir hand and watched as the attractive guide alloy—whose name zie had to access to remember—helped Jayanthi onto zir hand. The human held out a small packet with some whitish stuff inside. In zir peripheral vision, Vaha glowed with mauve and lavender.

"The container," Jayanthi sent. "The one Pushkara gave you? This is what's left of it. I found it before I left the site and sealed it away. I scooped up the contaminated soil, too, and put it into biowaste, but I couldn't find that among the supplies."

"Probably destroyed," Kaliyu sent reflexively. "But I'll ask the Primary about it." *Clever human indeed!*

Zie took the packet from her and tried to link with its ownership token. The device responded with the chain-of-possession information.

"Well?" Vaha sent.

Kaliyu opened a group channel for all four of them. "It's intact enough to prove that Pushkara had it in his possession. Jayanthi, thank you!"

She nodded her tiny head. "I hope it's enough to exonerate you. You and I have had a . . . complicated history, but you helped me find and save Vaha, and no amount of thanks will ever be enough for that."

"Zie's my best friend," Kaliyu said, glancing at the berth next to zirs. "I would have done anything to have zir back. Thank you. I'm grateful for this." Zie placed the packet with care into a rigid storage container from zir pouch.

To think that a human had helped zir, and with something so important—*you were right, Maker. One day, perhaps soon, I'll tell you so in person.*

The clamps on zir berth unlocked. Time for the trial. Pushkara would be present, along with their Voices of Compassion. Rage at the older alloy's accusations nestled against zir heart. *I promised I wouldn't go without a fight. Now I have a weapon to make you hurt.*

Zir Voice waited outside the berth and flew along with Kaliyu to the meeting point. Pushkara and his Voice already floated there, along with Mithva's embodied form.

The judicial construct rotated toward Kaliyu and flashed, <Pushkara wishes to make this trial a live public broadcast. Do you give permission to do so?>

The politician's phores were placid, neutral, without a hint of the smug surety that Kaliyu knew he must feel.

"What would you like to do?" Kaliyu's Voice sent privately. "You don't have to agree."

"It's all right," zie replied. *Let the world see Pushkara's reaction to the evidence in real time.* Zie flashed, <I give my permission.>

Mithva began by stating the charge against Kaliyu, that zie had illegally and willfully contaminated the biosphere of Meru. Next, they turned to Pushkara and formalized Kaliyu's declaration that Pushkara had requested and enabled Kaliyu to commit zir crime.

<Pushkara has already stated that he believes Kaliyu's accusations to be in bad faith,> the construct flashed. <Considering that we have no evidence to the contrary—>

<I do have evidence,> Kaliyu flashed. Zie pulled the sealed bag from zir pouch.

Was that a hint of brown in Pushkara's phores?

Mithva extended an arm and took it from Kaliyu.

<This is what's left of the device that Pushkara gave me, and the ownership token is intact. Also, if the Primary hasn't destroyed the waste containers from the human site on Meru, one of those holds the contaminated soil, proving that the planet itself hasn't been permanently harmed. Credit for all of this goes to the quick thinking of Jayanthi, the human test subject, who discovered the device and recognized its danger.>

Kaliyu tried to imagine zirself saying something complimentary about a human a masan earlier, especially in public. To think that zie had abandoned Jayanthi on Meru and, at one point, hoped she would die there—the person who was now instrumental in zir exoneration! And the person who Vaha, zir best friend, was in love with. Even if all humans weren't as clever as her, Kaliyu could no longer believe that the entire species was worthless.

Pushkara's concern leaked through his phores. <Honorable Mithva, isn't it possible that the evidence has been tampered with?>

<One hectas, please,> Mithva flashed. <I've sent a request to the Primary's CM to verify the token's integrity, and I've inquired about the status of the waste container. I'm waiting for a response.>

Kaliyu imagined the chatter at the Primary as people watched and speculated on the results, but zie didn't try to access it. Too much of a distraction. For a moment, zie wondered what the CM would say and whether someone *had* breached the token—to remove Pushkara's part in the device. The politician's gaze remained steady, and he had brought his phores back under control. *The benefit of centuries of experience.*

<I have the results,> Mithva flashed at last. <All waste containers have been dispatched for solar incineration. They are still en route and will be paused until they can be inspected. As for the contaminant, the CM can find no sign of tampering with the ownership token and has discovered cross-links to raw-materials records.>

Kaliyu allowed zir phores to saturate with a brilliant plum color.

<While this mitigates Kaliyu's actions,> Mithva flashed, <it does not fully excuse them, especially zir abandonment of the human subject on Meru. It does, however, prove the culpability of Pushkara in the pollution of Meru. I have sent both of your Voices of Compassion the details of the default consequence, which is one hundred varshas of exile for each of you. You may confer with them as to your preferred courses of action.>

Kaliyu couldn't keep the flash of white from zir phores. Neither could Pushkara. *One hundred varshas!* Zie might as well let a black hole swallow zir.

"Don't panic," zir Voice sent. "We can ask for a reduction in the time. After all, you helped the human and rescued your friend and, most of all, you confessed your crime and have obviously repented of it. I suggest that we ask for ten varshas because of your mitigating actions. What do you think?"

It looked a lot better than a hundred, but zie could forget coming back to a racing career. In ten varshas, zir muscles would atrophy, and zie would lose enough memory that zir skills might erode, too. Somehow that didn't leave zir with the sense of despair that it should have. Kaliyu thought of The Royal, quietly doing research at Kumuda, moving away from decades of racing fame. Zie could see the appeal in that kind of solitude. Time with The Royal, too, if he would have zir. Vaha's suggestion was a sensible one, and Kaliyu could picture zirself making a slow comeback. *Or perhaps exile will change me even more. Perhaps I'll head in an entirely different direction.*

"I can accept that," Kaliyu sent. After all, zie had done terrible things. Zie deserved to suffer for them.

The sentencing proceeded with various private conversations in parallel, between zirself and zir Voice, among the two Voices and Mithva. In the end, Kaliyu received fifteen varshas of exile and Pushkara fifty-four.

<Given your experience and reputation,> Mithva flashed at Pushkara, <you should have known better. You took advantage of Kaliyu's youth.>

<In my defense,> Pushkara flashed, <every action I took was to protect Meru and the compact. I have seen firsthand what comes of letting humans run loose in the universe, and I fear that by the time I come out of exile, I will have to witness those atrocities once more. To the people of the Constructed Democracy of Sol, I leave you with this plea: Do not vote in favor of this amendment! Do not unleash this evil upon Meru or anywhere else!>

And then it was over. Kaliyu's Voice gently took zir by the elbow and steered zir back toward zir berth. They were sending zir some information about the details of exile, but Kaliyu let zir extended memory record it. Pushkara's words circulated in zir mind until zie realized what had tripped in zir subconscious: the amendment! Kaliyu thought-retrieved zir ballot and changed zir vote to *Yes*.

Vaha watched through Jayanthi's window until she fell asleep. The medical construct had a mask over her face and slender tube attached to her arm through which clear fluid flowed. Zie pried zirself from thinking about her precarious health—which zie could do nothing about—and turned zir attention to the impending vote for the fate of Meru. Zir incarn had retained only a passing knowledge of the political situation, and Vaha could grasp the basic ramifications, but amnesia had stripped zir of the emotional connection. Instead, zir focus stayed on Kaliyu's future. Zir feelings on their friendship predated the events at Meru, and while the memories of Nishadas remained nebulous, the affection for Kaliyu shone bright and steady throughout.

Motion at the end of the human-habitable limb caught Vaha's attention. Kaliyu's blue-gray body approached, tail held gracefully back, arms across zir chest. Another pilot hovered nearby until the berth clamped around zir friend's body. Kaliyu turned zir emerald-brown eyes toward Vaha.

<I'm so sorry,> Vaha flashed.

<Don't be. Of all the people involved in this mess, you have the least to apologize for. All you did was try to defend Jayanthi. I should have followed your lead then. I was too much of a mudha, too consumed by misplaced rage over my maker's fate.>

Vaha reached zir left arm through a gap in the berth's open frame. Kaliyu stretched out zir right hand and took Vaha's. All around the Primary, the crosstalk of thousands of emchannels filled Vaha's receivers. Over the next several hours, public condemnation of Pushkara built to the intensity of a white-hot neutron star. The information about his fate ricocheted throughout the Solar System, and alloys from as far as the Kuiper Belt weighed in with their opinions on the situation. A number of people suggested that Kaliyu's consequences were too harsh in light of the judgment against Pushkara.

<Perhaps you should appeal for something else,> Vaha flashed at zir friend. <Maybe they can put you in stasis rather than exile.>

<No, I deserve every varsha they've given me. I was so angry when I accepted Pushkara's offer. I knew it was wrong even then, but I didn't care, not until I watched you drift away from Meru. That's the first time I ever

saw *you* get angry, Vaha, and it shocked me. After I went back and couldn't find you, I realized what a price I'd paid—we'd both paid, as it turned out—for my hatred of humans. I don't want to feel like that, or live like that, again. I'm afraid that if I don't go into exile, I'll fall back into old habits. Honestly, after seeing how rebirth changed my maker, I think some time away might be good for me. Like both of you, I can make a clean start.>

Whatever Vaha had felt at Meru, the suspicions against Kaliyu or the rage that had driven Vaha to hurt zir friend—all of that had vanished from amnesia. Zie couldn't bring it back, and zie didn't want to. The solar flare had saved their friendship. The only trauma zie still carried was that of Veera's departure, and Rithu's mentorship had eased that pain. Perhaps Kaliyu was right about zirself. Exile sounded terrible on the surface, but at its core, it could provide a form of healing.

<I'll miss you,> Vaha flashed. <You're still my best friend.>

<You'll have Jayanthi.>

<That's not the same, plus I'll be in stasis.>

<I'll only be gone for fifteen varshas, you mudha. Stop being so maudlin. When I come back, you'll be in your prime. We'll have plenty of time together.>

With Kaliyu's and Pushkara's fates sealed, and zir own assured, all that remained was Jayanthi's. The vote for Hamsa's amendment loomed, and Jayanthi's human Voice of Compassion approached. Vaha hoped that she would get to keep their child, for both of their sakes. Neither of them had disclosed that she'd combined zir DNA with hers or that zie had helped her with the implantation. She'd kept all that secret to protect Vaha from exile. Had they made the right choice? Had zie unfairly let her shoulder that burden alone? Would anyone care if zie told them the truth, that zie wanted so badly to be part of zir child's life that it left zir vents aching?

—अनुकम्पा

Anukampaa—Compassion

Jayanthi had never seen Hamsa flustered or nervous, but in the hours leading up to the voting results, he showed unmistakable signs of both. He had come to her room in part from solidarity and in part because—or so she suspected—it would look good to his faction to be with an actual human being when the results came in. He couldn't seem to stay still. He puffed this way and that, setting his tail fluttering in a nonexistent breeze.

The previous day's announcement about Pushkara's exile had disrupted the ordinary business of the entire Solar System. If Jayanthi hadn't been worried about her own situation, she would've taken more satisfaction in the ancient alloy's consequence. She had to wait another day for the arrival of her Voice of Compassion, and her mind kept wondering what the outcome of her sentencing would be.

"It could happen," Hamsa sent via emtalk.

He hadn't stopped checking the preliminary tallies since he'd arrived in Jayanthi's room. Early votes had come from other systems, all with far lower population numbers than Sol's.

"The relays at heliopause have been busy over the past day," he sent. "Only a few couriers have come through with revised votes so far, but they've mostly swung in our favor."

"I suppose we should thank Pushkara for that," she sent.

"Hah! That's one way to look at the situation. For all that we held opposite views on human expansion, I had always kept Pushkara in my highest esteem. He did so much good work in his past. I can't believe he would try something as underhanded as planting evidence. It makes me question everything about him, but I hope no pattern emerges and that this is a onetime folly born of old age and desperation. I would hate for this to tarnish his entire record."

"Devasu would like to enter," the central CM announced.

"Let her in, please," Jayanthi said aloud.

Devasu floated in with three bags in her hands and a wide alloy smile on her face. "Whether we get to celebrate or we need to evaporate our sorrow, these will help."

"What's in them?" Jayanthi asked.

"Drinks," she said. Her phores rippled with amusement. "The fun kind. We call it chaytha. This one"—she held up her left hand—"is diluted and should be safe for you, even in your pregnant condition."

"Should?"

Devasu shrugged. "It contains a newer drug, and it's not as if the designer had the opportunity to test it on gestating humans. The medical CM ran a simulation at my request. It came back with ninety-seven-percent confidence that it won't harm you and a ninety-nine-percent chance that it won't pass into the fetus."

Jayanthi glanced at Hamsa for a second opinion, but his gaze was distant. He probably hadn't noticed that she and Devasu were talking.

"Those sound like reasonable odds, especially at this stage." She took the bag from Devasu, uncoiled the sipping tube, and tasted it. The liquid had a milky-sweet flavor with a hint of bitterness and aromas of rose and saffron. It reminded her of bhang, the popular festival drink back home. That provided some "fun" effects on human physiology, too.

"By the Nivid!" Hamsa sent. "It's done!"

His phores had turned seafoam and purple with disbelief and joy. Jayanthi didn't need to look at the results to know the outcome of the vote.

"By the Nivid, indeed," Vaha sent on their group emchannel. "The numbers are overwhelming."

Devasu spun in place.

Jayanthi slow-blinked and thought-retrieved the results. They took a few seconds to appear in her vision, probably because everyone in the local area was trying to access the same information.

"Eighty-seven percent in favor!" she sent.

Breath fled from her lungs. No wonder Hamsa looked so stunned. Polls regarding the Meru habitation project had garnered only 51.4 percent. A considerable number of people in the Solar System, both alloy and human, had rescinded their proxy designations in favor of a direct vote. While many of them were swayed by Pushkara's crimes, a good portion also changed their minds because of sympathy for Vaha and Jayanthi. The majority favored a mixed settlement of Meru, with humans, alloys, and constructs sharing the planet's surface as they did on Earth.

Devasu's face floated into Jayanthi's peripheral vision, pulling her focus back to her surroundings.

"May I embrace you?" asked the alloy, who glowed like an aubergine star.

Jayanthi grinned and opened her arms. As Devasu hugged her close and spun her around, Jayanthi glanced wistfully at the window. If only Vaha's incarn could join them! She wanted to feel zir arms around her, too. They slowed, and Devasu gently disengaged, making sure Jayanthi was steady before letting go. Hamsa enfolded her into his arms next.

"The CDS and MEC will have to forgive you now," Devasu sent as she sipped on chaytha. "At the very least, they'll have to let you keep your baby."

"Do you think so?" Jayanthi sent, her gaze locked with Hamsa's.

He didn't look so certain. "Laws are laws, and people must suffer the consequences of breaking them, even if the public votes to move forward in ways that would exonerate them. Speaking of which—" His bird-black eyes twinkled. "Let me share with you the new proposals I've made now that the amendment has passed."

Jayanthi shifted her focus back to the viewing wall and accepted Hamsa's thought-share. His propositions took her breath away. The first: that humans be allowed to deposit knowledge into the Nivid without alloy corroboration. The second: that humans be allowed to train and practice as licensed tarawans. If they both passed, Jayanthi could apply to have her child's design entered into the Nivid. She could—after completing whatever consequence they demanded of her—resume her studies to become a tarawan.

"Hamsa," she whispered. The nascent person in her womb squirmed and kicked.

He smiled like a human, his toothless gums showing. "I'm pushing the boundaries hard, but I want to capitalize on this wave of pro-human sentiment as much as we can. There are members of my faction who have called for these changes for decades, so I know we have some support, but their numbers are small. Don't get your hopes too high."

She pressed her palms together and bowed her head. "Thank you," she sent.

Her tears took them both by surprise.

"Oh, my dear child," he sent.

She soaked them up with her sleeve and laughed. "It's all so overwhelming. Vaha! Did you see what—"

"He just sent it to me," Vaha replied. "I hope they both pass, for your sake."

Emtalk didn't convey the emotion behind zir words, but they didn't carry the enthusiasm she'd expected. *Of course!* Even if Hamsa's proposals became law, it wouldn't change anything for their personal situation. With Vaha going into stasis and herself stuck on Earth, they wouldn't get to live together as a family, on Meru or anywhere else. They wouldn't benefit at all.

But her child—*their* child—would.

At two hours to local morning, Jayanthi floated in the medical construct's arms and stared through the window. Nothing moved outside, and nothing showed except for a few stars that weren't obstructed by the tangle of the Nivid's limbs. All was dark and still, and by right, she ought to have been sleeping. She couldn't tell if the pregnancy had caused her insomnia or if the stress of everything that had happened was to blame. Perhaps the lack of gravity made her restless. The first day in microgravity had been a relief, especially after living through almost a month of double Earth's gravity on the way back from Meru, but the respite had faded as her body found new ways to torment her. She could understand why people opted to use wombs rather than their own bodies for gestation.

She prodded gently at the firm surface of her abdomen. "Your incessant kicking is not helping." For all the pain, she had to admit that there was something nice about having another person with her at all times. "Just so you know, baby, I'd rather have a pilot's body and a smaller passenger." As if in response, she received a swift kick at her hand.

She gave up after another half an hour of staring at the backs of her eyelids. She disengaged from the construct, cleansed her body, donned a clean jumpsuit, and packed her other clothes. Devasu had brought her a new enviro-suit, one that fit more comfortably around her bulging midsection, and she hung the packed bag next to it. No matter what the outcome of her sentencing, she wouldn't be at the Primary much longer.

When she thought back to her initial project planning, she could see how naive she'd been. She'd grown up idolizing her parents, dreaming of living like an alloy. Yet every time the universe had given her the opportunity to fulfill that dream—first on Meru, then on Chedi, then with Vaha—she had turned away from it. For good reasons, of course, but she had to wonder if she'd made the right choices. Eleven months had passed since she'd left Earth. She'd had a lifetime's worth of experiences since then, but it wasn't enough, and now she might end up back at home, never to roam the stars again.

She rested a hand on her swollen belly. Given that the amendment to the compact had passed, would Mithva relent and let her take the baby back to Meru? She could deliver on Earth and then make the journey after three months or six or whenever the child was strong enough to travel. But leaving the Solar System meant leaving Vaha. They would have no way to communicate on a daily basis. Zie would miss so much of zir child's life. *Can I do that to zir? Can I do that to you, little one? On Earth, at least you'd get messages from your other parent.*

But on Earth, their child would have to struggle with sickle cell disease, as Jayanthi had. She would be subject to the biases against AAD, which Jayanthi hadn't removed from her DNA. On Meru, those struggles might not vanish, but they would be significantly mitigated. *I wish I knew what to do!* She had been so confident when she'd left home. The universe had exposed to her the inherent fragility of life, of connection, and that former self-assurance had come from a place of ignorance, not strength.

"Jayanthi." Vaha's voice interrupted her internal dialogue. "A pilot is pulling into the berth on my right. I'm guessing your Voice has arrived. You might want to meet them at the airlock."

"Thank you, Vaha. I'll do that."

She zipped up her suit and then attached her helmet. The Earth had its share of Voices, but they rarely left the surface of the planet. Sometimes they went to an orbital station to advocate in cases that involved human-alloy conflicts, but she'd never heard of one traveling this far. Why would they when they advocated only for humans? She wondered if this person had volunteered for the work or if they'd arrived full of resentment at the long journey.

From the window next to the airlock, she watched as a figure in a spacesuit struggled out from the pilot's mouth and into the connecting tube. Remembering her own awkwardness the first few times, Jayanthi took pity on them and moved forward to help. They didn't see her coming and almost flew headfirst into her. With a friendly smile, Jayanthi pulled them up so they were face-to-face—and saw that the face inside the other helmet belonged to none other than Mina.

"By the Nivid," Jayanthi swore. "You graduated!"

Mina grinned and then tapped the side of their helmet. Their communications weren't yet linked through the Primary's network. With an impatient shake of her head, Jayanthi grabbed her friend by the elbow and towed them through the airlock. As soon as she shut the door, she removed her helmet and then helped Mina take theirs off.

With cries of mutual delight, they hugged each other.

Mina's eyes went wide. "Your belly—it's so much bigger than I thought it would be!"

Jayanthi grinned. "And it's going to get even bigger. So you're my Voice of Compassion! When did you finish your training?"

"About a month ago," Mina said. "When I heard that you'd need a Voice, I applied, and Mithva said yes. The judiciary likes Voices who are as close to peers as possible, and the others who applied were all super old."

"I can't believe it! I thought I'd end up with some stuffy government official." Jayanthi held on to Mina's shoulders. "You have no idea how happy I am to see you."

"And I, you." They put their hands on their hips. "You're the one who disappeared for months! Do you realize how worried we were? And then to find out that you're pregnant"—they gestured at her midsection—"only to have you run off to Meru again without telling anyone?" Mina shook their head. "When you get home, your parents might never let you out of their sight."

Jayanthi smiled so wide, her jaw muscles ached. "Come, let me show you to my room."

As they made their way through the passage, Mina's expression turned serious. "We're to meet with Mithva in half an hour. You have that much time to tell me what your perfect outcome is and what might help me plead for leniency."

"You heard about Pushkara and the vote this morning?"

"Yes. You saved Meru from contamination. That should work in your favor, but it has no bearing on the pregnancy or space travel. What were you thinking?"

Jayanthi sent a message to Vaha. "Are you awake? I need somewhere private to talk with my Voice."

Zie replied within a minute. "Yes. Come in."

Once they were inside, Vaha said zie would disable the microphones and cameras.

"We have nothing to hide from you," Jayanthi sent. "You can leave them on."

"It's okay. I'd like to go back to sleep."

Mina was staring at Vaha's incarn, who lay securely in a web.

"This child," Jayanthi said, drawing her friend's attention back to herself, "is half mine and half Vaha's. Both in genetics and in spirit. We . . . we love each other."

Mina pointed at the incarn. "But . . . how? Is zie male—and fertile? Were you?"

Heat flushed into Jayanthi's cheeks. "I designed and printed the egg and sperm in the womb that Vaha brought to Meru, as I said to the MEC. That part is all true. I left out my feelings for Vaha because they're nobody's business but ours, and at the time, zie had disappeared. We feared that zie had gone adrift and died somewhere in the Pamir System. Now that zie's back . . . well, I suppose it still doesn't matter, since zie will have to go into stasis for the next sixteen and a half years." She couldn't keep the bitterness from her tone. "But zie ought to have the right to watch zir child grow up. I didn't want to implicate zir in the making of the baby, so I haven't told anyone that I used zir DNA in the design."

"Vaha stated zir love for you during zir hearing," Mina said softly. "Everyone knows that much. That's what got you the dedicated emchannel to each other. If we disclose that the child is also zirs, perhaps we can petition to allow zir incarn to stay in a geosynchronous orbit around Earth, like your parents."

Jayanthi shook her head. "It will be enough if I can keep the child. We'll be patient. We can't tell the alloys that the child is half Vaha's. The consequences for zir would be too severe. The truth is, we did break the law, and we knew it, even if we thought it was unfair. I used to think of myself as exceptional because of my parents—"

"What? You?" Mina's eyes widened in mock surprise.

Jayanthi jabbed them with a finger, sending them both drifting in opposite directions. "I know I'm not special. I don't deserve special treatment."

"No, but considering what all you've done, you mostly acted out of love. You left Meru because you wanted to make sure Vaha was okay. You left the Primary for the same reason. I could even argue that making the child was an act of love—for humankind. You wanted to prove a point." Mina sighed. "If only there was some way to let you and Vaha suffer your consequences together, somewhere with stasis support and gravity and atmosphere—and whatever else you'd need to live—that isn't Meru or Earth. The purpose of the judiciary is to make you contemplate your mistakes and convince you not to commit the same crime again. That's why they're called consequences and not punishments. That means you can't have access to a womb, and it means that Vaha can't do anything productive until zir stasis term expires. But it doesn't have to mean keeping you apart for sixteen and a half years."

Jayanthi grabbed her friend's arm.

"What?"

"Maybe there is a place like that." She held up the ring from Sunanda.

"Jewelry?"

"This represents a place with gravity and atmosphere and everything we'd need to live that's far from alloys and planets."

With a look of suffering patience, Mina waved at the golden object—now on Jayanthi's little finger, thanks to swelling—and said, "Explain."

As quickly as she could, Jayanthi summed up her experiences with Manib and then Chedi. While she talked, she thought-searched for the last known location of the megaconstruct. Chedi hadn't left the Solar System yet.

"How soon can we get this settled?" she asked Mina.

"Today, if Mithva has no concerns. Otherwise, it might take a little longer. Why?"

"Chedi is still here, in the system. Once she leaves, we'll have to send a courier after her, which will make all this much harder. We could frame our stay as a sort of exile for Vaha and me."

"So we wouldn't see you for sixteen years? That's . . . terrible, Jaya. The past eleven months have been hard enough. Think of your parents."

"I've missed you, too."

"Liar. You've clearly been having too many adventures to miss any of us."

Jayanthi couldn't muster the smile that Mina's teasing required.

"I'm sorry," Mina said softly. "I'll make the case that being tied to Chedi is practically equivalent to exile, but I can't promise that the CDS will see it that way. If it were up to me, I'd drag you back to Earth and lock you in your house forever, but I'm here to represent your best interests, not mine." Mina pointed a finger at the incarn and said briskly, "We'd better talk to Vaha and make sure zie is okay with this plan of yours. We don't have much time. You should send a message to this megaconstruct, too. Warn her that you might be returning."

"Let me make sure I understand you, Vaha." The alloy Voice of Compassion's incredulity colored zir words. "You want to go into effective exile with the human, Jayanthi, and attach yourself to a sovereign megaconstruct rather than live comfortably in stasis?"

"That's correct," Vaha sent.

Zie had no idea what it would feel like to leave zir true body attached to Chedi, but if it meant zie could keep zir incarn and be with Jayanthi, zie would manage it.

"It's an unusual appeal, but everything about your case has been unusual so far. I've already filed a request with Mithva, and they've agreed to let us join the ongoing meeting with Jayanthi and her Voice as soon as we're ready. Is there anything else you need to tell me?"

"No."

They opened an emchannel with Mithva and shared it with the Primary's CM, who could translate between emtalk and audible speech. Vaha kept zir gaze fixed on the window into Jayanthi's room. Alongside her was Mina, who had impressed zir almost as much as Jayanthi herself in the brief time that they'd spoken.

After a few minutes of formalities, Mithva stated, "I deem it an equitable trade for Vaha—five varshas in exile while attached to Chedi—however, for Jayanthi, it strikes me as too severe. While I can appreciate the value of keeping her and Vaha together, this consequence seems punitive toward their child, who deserves to grow up among other human children. I will need some time to research historical and medical records for outcomes in similar situations, if such exist.

"In the meantime, I recommend that we do not delay Jayanthi's departure from the Primary Nivid any further. At present, I will allow Vaha to carry Jayanthi and Mina back to Earth with the assistance of a faster pilot. After I complete my investigation into the child's well-being, I will relay my verdict to you all. In parallel, I will obtain consent from Chedi and make sure she understands the terms of your exile in case my findings go in your favor. Is this acceptable to all of you?"

Inside the room, Jayanthi nodded. She had no objections. Zie could think of none, either. This was the best chance they had.

"I accept," Vaha replied.

If nothing else, they would have a few days together as they traveled back to Earth. Vaha hoped with all zir might that those would not be their final days for the next five varshas.

With the meeting concluded, Jayanthi and Mina donned their helmets and grabbed their packs.

"I'll say a quick farewell to Devasu and Hamsa; then we'll come to you," Jayanthi sent via emtalk.

The berth detached the restraints that had held Vaha in place. Zie was free to leave as soon as Jayanthi and Mina returned. Zie threaded zir hand through the framework of Kaliyu's berth and grasped zir shoulder. The same type of restraint now held zir friend.

<I'll be leaving soon,> Vaha flashed.

<What happened with your appeal?>

<Mithva needs to consider it further. I'm taking Jayanthi and her Voice back to Earth. If Mithva allows us to go to the megaconstruct, we'll leave from there.>

Kaliyu gave Vaha's hand a squeeze. <See you in fifteen varshas, my friend. Come back to the Solar System from wherever you are then and find me.>

<I will,> Vaha promised, glowing in a bittersweet mix of cocoa and aquamarine.

Zie resisted the temptation to beg Kaliyu to reconsider and ask for a less severe consequence. They were adults now. Kaliyu had made a hard decision, but it was zirs, just like Vaha's with regard to zir own body.

Zie turned away and gazed at the vast structure of the Primary Nivid, the crown jewel of alloy civilization. Zir name had entered the archive alongside Veera's as the first successful multimodal pilot design. Zie didn't need to accomplish anything more for zir maker.

Vaha had spent so much of zir life in uncertainty. Unsure if zie would become the pilot Veera wanted. Wondering when zie would need another round in a womb. Hesitant to make choices about zir future. At last, zie knew exactly what zie wanted, and it was no one's dream but zir own: to spend the next decades at Jayanthi's side. To support humankind, on or off Earth. And one day, to return to Meru and reveal to the world the truth of their hybrid child.

—अक्षय

Akshaya—Eternal

Half a day out from Earth, Jayanthi received a message from Mithva: they had approved the exile on Chedi. The construct had sent her shuttle to Earth for resupply, and it would wait for them there. Jayanthi would have shouted for joy, but Mina was fast asleep in the adjacent web.

At thirty-four weeks of gestation, her nascent child seemed determined to deprive her of rest, tossing and turning in her womb whenever Jayanthi tried to sleep. She spent half of their local night awake and half of the local day napping from exhaustion.

"Vaha," she sent by emtalk. "Did you see—"

"Yes, I received the news from Mithva," zie replied, zir words drenched in violet.

Jayanthi lumbered out of her sleeping web and took a drink of water. Her heart sang at the thought of spending the rest of her life with Vaha and zir incarn by her side. Getting back to Meru would have been the best outcome, but a life on Chedi as a family felt like a close second.

"But this means we can't stay on Earth for very long," zie sent.

"I know."

She ought to have another six weeks before the baby came, but deliveries happened on schedule only from wombs. They needed to get to the safety of Chedi as soon as they could.

"You're sure, right?" she sent. "About going into exile? It has a different meaning for you than for me, and you've never met Chedi. Plus, you'll be surrounded by human beings."

"I'm sure," zie sent. "It means that I can keep my incarn with you and our child. There's nothing I want more."

The baby kicked—or perhaps punched her fist—as if to agree. Jayanthi groaned softly and massaged her lower back. "Why did I wish for gravity again? All it did was shift the pain from my chest to my back."

"Maybe you should stay and have the baby on Earth," Vaha sent, zir tone pitch-perfect with concern.

How much we've both changed since we left for Meru together. She would have laughed off anyone who'd told her then that an enormous alloy pilot would one day become her life mate.

"Space flight with a newborn isn't recommended," Jayanthi sent. "Never mind the launch forces. It's safer to travel while I'm pregnant. Chedi will take good care of me—don't worry. She has experience delivering babies."

Jayanthi knelt over the clear section of Vaha's skin to gaze at the Earth. *Home, but not for much longer.* Nearly a year had passed since she'd left. She couldn't fathom what another seventeen would hold. She'd be almost twice as old by then! And she wouldn't get a chance to see her house, to say goodbye to Laghu or her walking routes or the banyan tree. Tears sprang to her eyes, as they did so easily now. She wanted to blame her hormones, but these feelings ran deeper, toward something more like grief. Earth had so much green compared to Meru. Would she ever call this planet her home again?

From orbit, the modern cities of humanity blended into their surroundings. Jayanthi couldn't see the people she had tried to help. How many of them cared? How many had voted in favor of the amendment? Hamsa wouldn't stop pushing for change, and if he succeeded, she might have a thriving settlement to join on Meru after their period of exile. She felt a pang of jealousy at missing that but then banished it. She hadn't accomplished everything she'd wanted to do on Meru, but she had done enough: she had paved the way for others to continue her work. Her genetic design would form the foundation from which many generations would grow.

The baby she carried would be a teenager by the time they returned. What kind of person would she be? As if in answer, Jayanthi received a painful kick. *I'm eager to meet you, too.*

—

Vaha swooped into the upper layers of Earth's atmosphere. The phores on zir arms shone in plum tones as zie listened to Jayanthi's and Mina's exclamations from inside zir body. The room cameras showed them watching through the transparent panel on zir underside and holding on to the sides as zie dipped and rolled.

"Could you have done this at Meru?" Jayanthi demanded. "If the answer is yes, and you chose not to let me experience it . . ." She left the threat unfinished.

Vaha laughed. "No, I didn't have this much control then, and there'd be too much heat if I were lower. Rithu taught me how to fly like this, while I was at Kumuda. I thought my broken wing and tail would hold me back, but the brace made it possible for me to perform atmospheric maneuvers and compensate for the skew."

"Can I do this again?" Mina asked. "Are there others in orbit like you, Vaha? I can think of some friends who would love to experience this."

"I don't know," Vaha replied. "Pilots wouldn't have much reason to stay around Earth." Zie rolled sideways, giving them a view of the stars and then back to the twinkling lights of civilization.

"Enjoy it while you can, Mina," Jayanthi said.

"Oh, I am!"

After an hour flying them around the planet, Vaha settled at the orbital station where zie had first picked Jayanthi up. The loss of that memory stung zir like a stray asteroid fragment. What had zie thought at the time? How had zie felt while watching Jayanthi enter zir mouth? The medical construct at the Primary had said zie might still recover zir organic memories, but no one could predict if or when that would happen. Zie had let go any expectation that zir amnesia would clear up. Like zir wing and tail, zie had learned to live with it as a part of zirself.

As Jayanthi entered the station, Vaha wanted to stuff her small figure back inside zirself, where zie could keep her safe, where zie didn't have to worry that zie might never see her again. Her belly had grown to the point that it looked like it might pop. The old records from industrial times indicated that her body would decide when to deliver the baby and that this could happen at any time. It astonished zir that life had sustained itself with such imprecise functions for as long as it had.

She turned at the door and waved her tiny hand before she went inside with Mina. Her parents flashed words of gratitude to Vaha through the station window. They would spend just two days together on the station before Jayanthi and Vaha left for Chedi. The medical construct at the Primary had advised against the stress of having Jayanthi travel from Earth's surface. Even during their journey, Vaha could tell that Jayanthi was in a lot of pain. She did her best not to show it, but zie knew her too well. Zie could see it in the way she held her body. Zie could hear it in the cadence of her speech. Zie wanted nothing more than to have zir incarn hold her and comfort her, but that would have to wait until they reached Chedi.

"Try not to have the baby in there," Vaha sent.

"I'll do my best."

Zie could hear the laughter in her voice, and it warmed zir core. They'd left the Primary with an ambulatory medical construct that acted as a bridge between Vaha's internal umbilical and Jayanthi. It had loaded her with medications to prevent an early birth, but biology was fickle. Zie didn't trust her body the way zie would a womb.

Vaha settled into the berth and tried to distract zirself with the news. Zie watched the recordings of Pushkara's and Kaliyu's exiles, zir heart breaking at the sight. Their wings were bound to their backs, and tubes of bhojya were inserted into their mouths and sealed. Maintenance pilots would replenish their bladders as needed. Other pilots wrapped their two bodies with insulation, for warmth and to block their vents so they didn't accidentally alter their orbits. Those same pilots then tethered themselves to tow Pushkara and Kaliyu away. Vaha viewed the raw camera footage from the Primary Nivid until their shapes dwindled and disappeared.

The most vivid memory from zir childhood was watching zir maker fade into the black the same way. At least zie knew when zie would see Kaliyu again. Zie had entertained a spark of hope that Veera would hear about zir work at Meru and zir Nivid deposit, that zir maker would take some pride in Vaha at last and return from wherever zie had gone.

But Veera had sent no message. Zie made no appearance at heliopause. Vaha shouldn't have expected it—had told zirself to put the idea out of zir mind. Veera had gone into the unknown, flying through unexplored space. Until zir maker arrived at a star, which could take centuries, zie would not reality transit back to a populated system. Veera wouldn't hear about Vaha's accomplishments until zie returned to a place with a padhran, a network, and a news spool. And even then, zie would have to actively search for Vaha's name. They might never see each other again.

The pain of that thought no longer shone with the intensity it had in zir youth. Vaha had a new family now, one that loved zir in spite of zir faults. Zie gazed at the station's hull. The person responsible for zir success was in there, not some vast empty place, and she would not abandon zir.

Jayanthi's mother held her so tight for so long that the nascent being in her womb pushed uncomfortably against her ribs.

"Let me have a turn," Vidhar said with a laugh. He disengaged Kundhina's arms gently and pulled Jayanthi into a briefer but equally firm embrace.

"Look at you!" Kundhina exclaimed as they floated in their private room.

"Tell us everything," her father said.

But first she had to say goodbye to Mina. Her friend was departing for the surface right away.

"Your child will be sixteen years old by the time I see you again," Mina lamented, taking their turn embracing Jayanthi.

"You could run away with us and live in Chedi."

"Don't tempt me."

Mina had found their own calling, and after the high-profile Voice of Compassion work on Jayanthi's case, half of Earth wanted to engage their services.

"Maybe I can come visit you when Chedi's in the system," they said. "Now that the amendment has passed, I can legally travel."

"That would be wonderful."

After Mina left, Jayanthi settled in to recount her many adventures to her parents. They listened for an hour, then made her rest. After the tension of the events at the Primary, Jayanthi's body had entered a permanent state of fatigue. It warred with her desire to maximize the time with her parents. They had cooked all of Jayanthi's favorite foods and brought the dishes up to the station. After weeks of nothing but bhojya and rehydrated packets, each morsel tasted like divine nectar. She couldn't do the meals justice, though, not with her uterine occupant taking up so much of her abdomen. Everyone worried about the baby coming too soon, but as far as Jayanthi was concerned, she couldn't come soon enough—after they reached Chedi.

"You must transmit a full recording of the birth," Vidhar instructed. "And remember to have blood ready for transfusion."

"I will—don't worry. Vaha and Chedi and Sunanda will take good care of me."

"Sunanda?" her mother asked.

Jayanthi showed them the ring and told them about her friend and Raya, baby Hui and the elderly Guhaka.

"So you won't be alone out there," Kundhina said. "I'm so glad! I had this dreadful vision of the three of you rattling around in that enormous space."

By the end of Jayanthi's stay, her parents knew every detail of the past eleven months—except for one. The station wasn't private enough for her to tell them about Vaha's part in their child's DNA. *One day, perhaps when we return to Earth, we can reveal the truth to the world.*

Her parents watched as she entered the transfer tube, just as they had for her previous departure. They couldn't cry, but Jayanthi had known them for her entire life. She could see the sadness on their faces as clearly as the golden glow from their phores. She put on a brave, cheerful expression for them. It wasn't entirely false. Her spirits rose with every meter as she approached Vaha. Unlike her first departure, this time she had no fear entering zir mouth. This time, when she drifted into her chamber, she knew exactly where to place her hands to feel Vaha's warmth, to ensure that zie felt hers in return.

"Are you ready?" zir voice said through the room's speakers.

"Not really," she admitted. "But it's time for us to leave."

Through the clear pane in Vaha's belly, she watched the figures of her parents dwindle into specks. Then she whispered a silent farewell to the planet she'd called home. *See you in seventeen years.*

Jayanthi rested in her cot, her body in a deeper state of exhaustion than she'd ever known. Vaha sat beside her, holding her right hand. To her left, one of Chedi's mobile extensions pumped her body full of well-formed blood cultured from her own cells. Its quiet hum lulled her. Behind Vaha, Sunanda stood near a table carved from wood, their body blocking the view of their actions, but Jayanthi could guess by the thready cries what must be going on. Her arms itched to hold her newborn, but she had to let others do the work of cleaning, weighing, and checking the baby's health.

Three days earlier, they'd left Vaha's true body tucked against Chedi's exterior. The megaconstruct had prepared for their arrival by running bhojya and water lines to a spot near a protruding exterior wall. It wouldn't provide as much shelter as a berth, but they hoped it would be enough to shield Vaha's true body from space debris while exposing zir wings to light.

"At least I'm only unconscious, not in stasis or hibernation," Vaha's incarn had said. "I'll transfer my attention whenever it's nighttime here and make sure I'm all right."

Jayanthi's center of mass had been thrown off by the gigantic being growing inside her, and she had needed Vaha's help navigating their way through open space to Chedi's entrance. She had wondered then how she could possibly expel something so large, and now she knew: with great effort.

Sunanda had assisted Chedi's ambulatory constructs while Vaha watched. Jayanthi had felt an intense sense of accomplishment when they showed her the wailing mess of an infant, still attached to her body by an umbilical cord. It made the whole ordeal worthwhile.

"She's more beautiful than either of you," Sunanda pronounced with a grin. "What are you going to name her?"

Vaha looked at Jayanthi with a stricken expression. "We've had so many other things on our minds that we never talked about it."

Sunanda laughed. "You have plenty of time. She won't care for a good long while. Isn't that right, my little love?"

They moved away from the table with a cloth-wrapped bundle in their arms.

"Here she is, all clean and sleepy as a dove." Sunanda placed the infant into Vaha's arms and turned to Jayanthi. "You have one more hour left on your blood exchange, but your bodym shows good vitals. You did so well. I'm proud of you." They planted a kiss on Jayanthi's forehead. "I'll leave you three alone now. Call me if you need anything."

"Thank you," Jayanthi whispered.

One more hour until she could hold their baby. She stroked the dark, downy curls with her free hand.

"Look at how tiny she is," Vaha said. "And so helpless, not at all like a newborn alloy."

Above them, the artificial sunlight had begun to fade, and fireflies blinked in the shadows of their grove.

"I thought of a name," Jayanthi said.

"Oh?"

"How about Akshaya? It means—"

"Eternal," Vaha finished. "I remember." Zie gazed down into zir arms. "Is that who you are? Will your name endure forever on the lips of our people? Akshaya." Zie looked up and smiled at Jayanthi. "I like it."

Jayanthi closed her eyes. Her lids had grown too heavy to stay open. She contemplated the irony of someone like her—someone who had worshipped alloy culture and wanted so desperately to live among them, someone who was the antithesis of what people like Bantri stood for—to have given birth to a baby. And yet, she hadn't surrendered to her assigned life as a human, either. Akshaya represented a new future and a new frontier, one that embodied the union of alloy and human. In this child, Jayanthi and Vaha had entrusted the fate of Meru and of themselves. One day, as with humankind, she would grow into an adult and find her own dreams.

—

समाप्त

ACKNOWLEDGMENTS

I started the first draft of this novel in the summer of 2020 as an escape from the stress and isolation of the COVID pandemic and shelter-in-place lifestyle. Spending time in a world far removed from the problems of the present was exactly what my brain needed. A couple of weeks after I finished the manuscript, despite my best precautions, I fell sick with COVID. A few months after that, I developed long COVID with symptoms of myalgic encephalomyelitis. By the time I was working on edits for the book, I had much stronger empathy for Jayanthi's physical situation. I always put a piece of myself in my stories—this one turned out to be much bigger than anticipated!

Meru started as a kernel of an idea inspired by a story within the *Mahabharata*, and it grew from there into an epic space opera. Many people helped me along the way—foremost, my agent, Cameron McClure, who didn't blink when I said I was taking a story that was millennia old and setting it a millennium into the future, and Adrienne Procaccini, for loving it enough to give it a home. I also owe a tremendous thanks to Navah Wolfe, who edited the manuscript from a rough cut to a high polish. Thanks to Stacy Abrams and Kellie Osborne for copyedits; Mike Heath, who brought the book to life with the beautiful and cinematic cover; and the rest of the team at 47North for their efforts in delivering this novel to the world.

A huge wave of gratitude goes to Ashley Hall, the sickle cell warrior who gave me critical feedback and encouragement. Thanks also to Anatoly Belilovsky and Kenneth Roy for technical advice, and to Marshall Robin, J.B. Manipal, Owen Landgren, Kathryn Eberle, David Kammerzelt, Sloane Leong, Daniel Whiteson, and Benjamin C. Kinney for their insightful critiques.

In closing, I have to give my love and gratitude to my family, Ryan and Maya, and my parents, Anusha and Shaker, for their support of both my writing and my health. I couldn't have completed this journey without them.